Twice a
TEXAS
Bride

LINDA
BRODAY

S sourcebooks
casablanca

Published by Sourcebooks Casablanca, an imprint of Sourcebooks,
Inc.
P.O. Box 4410, Naperville, Illinois 60567-4410
(630) 961-3900
Fax: (630) 961-2168
www.sourcebooks.com

Printed and bound in the United States of America.
RRD 10 9 8 7 6 5 4 3 2

I'm dedicating this book to a homeless woman named Angela whom I became acquainted with. I love her dearly. Each day she struggles just to take care of her basic needs. Angela lost a well-paying job during the big layoffs six years ago. Now, she's in her late fifties and no one will hire her. She's extremely driven to try to regain all she lost, though not many people will give her a chance. I was struck by her amazing computer skills, but not as much as I was by her will to survive no matter what. She reminds me of my heroine in this story, Callie Quinn. Angela shares the same need to matter to someone, to have all the things she feels she's unworthy of. You are my hero, Angela. May God continue to keep you safe and warm. You are seen. You are loved. You are important to me.

One

UNDER A GRAY SKY, RAND SINCLAIR'S SWEEPING glance took in his newly purchased Last Hope Ranch. The outbuildings, the barn...shoot, even the fences had a permanent lean like drunken sailors after a year at sea. He pulled up the collar of his coat against the biting January wind.

What had he been thinking? What did a former saloon owner know about ranching, anyway?

The only thing he could rightly claim to understand were the drunks he'd served whiskey to at the Lily of the West in Battle Creek, Texas, three miles away. A drunk wanted his whiskey straight from the bottle, his woman warm and willing, and a soft place to lay his head. Rand had no idea how to care for the cows he'd buy come spring. All the beasts seemed to do was eat, drink, and moo.

Come to think of it...maybe cows and drunks were more alike than he thought.

Yet despite his reservations, he wanted this ranch more than anything else in the world.

This was his dream.

His chance to prove to himself that he could be the kind of man Isaac Daffern, the rancher who'd raised him and his brothers, had wanted him to be. He *needed* to prove that he measured up, not only in his brothers' eyes, but in his own.

If he failed, he would lose everything that mattered.

A door banged. He glanced down the ramshackle porch in the direction of the sound. Must be the wind. Every door on the place needed work, refusing to stay fastened. Tall weeds littered the yard, and the sucker rod of the old windmill groaned and complained with each rise and fall, the sound amplifying the stark emptiness around him. He was unprepared for the overwhelming loneliness of this new life he'd chosen.

Maybe diving into work would help. But not today. Making the ranch fit for living would have to wait for a warmer day.

He swung to go back inside by the fire when he caught a flash of blue disappearing into what must've been an old bunkhouse.

What in God's name?

The tall grasses whispered in the stiff breeze and he heard the unmistakable sound of a door closing. The deliberate softness of that sound raised the hair on the back of his neck. Maybe he wasn't so alone out here after all. He reached for his Colt and stole forward. Between the building's slatted wood, he glimpsed movement.

Rand took a deep breath and yanked open the door. "Whoever's in here had best come out."

Soft scurrying provided no clue.

Maybe he was mistaken and it was a small animal after all.

But no animals he ever knew wore blue.

A poacher? A thief? Most likely someone up to no good.

Cautious, he stepped inside. Thick gloom closed around him and the dank air clogged his throat. Spiderwebs hung from the ceiling like torn gossamer fabric from a dance-hall girl's dress.

And then he caught the faint whiff of some sort of scent. Flowers?

"Anybody here?" Eyes were watching him. He renewed his grip on the Colt, readying for anything. "You're trespassing on private property. Come out. I won't hurt you."

Three more steps, then four. As his eyes adjusted to the dimness, he saw two forms huddling in a far corner. When he got closer, a woman leaped to her feet, brandishing a stick that came within a hair of whacking his leg. Surprise rippled through him as he jumped back. He'd never expected a *woman*. She was shivering either from fear or the icy wind.

"Please, I don't mean you any harm, ma'am. My name's Rand Sinclair, and I'm the new owner here." His gaze flicked to the second person, a young boy.

The boy gave a sudden lunge, positioning himself in front of the woman with his arms extended. "Get back, mister. Leave us be. We ain't hurtin' nuthin'."

Rand finally remembered the Colt and slid it back into the holster. "I know, son, but it's dangerous out here. Let's get inside out of this weather. From the looks of you, I reckon you're cold and tired and hungry."

"We don't need you," the slip of a boy flung at him.

"Maybe not. But seeing as this is my land, like it or not, right now you have me. I have a fire going, and food. I'll share it. You don't have to be afraid."

"We always have to be afraid." The woman lowered the stick, though. "It's the only way to stay alive."

That said it all. Clearly, she had trouble trailing her. He knew all too well what that was like.

"Ma'am, *can* we eat?" the boy asked, his teeth chattering. He seemed to be relaxing his guard too.

Rand said softly, "Think of your son if nothing else. He needs a warm fire and food. He'll get sick. You wouldn't want that. I won't hurt you. Please, I just want to help. I think you'd do the same for me if I were in your shoes. Out here we take care of each other."

She took his measure with a hard stare. After several long seconds, she dropped the makeshift weapon and reached for her son's hand. Rand removed his coat and put it around her shoulders. He held the door, then led them toward the two-story frame house.

As they walked, he viewed their condition out of the corner of his eye. The woman's torn, dirty blue dress. The youngster's grimy face and clothes. Yet the mysterious trespasser carried herself straight and tall like someone who was accustomed to a better life and who took pride in herself.

Inside the warm kitchen, he put three sticks of wood into the cookstove and moved the skillet onto the fire. "I take it you've been traveling a ways. Where are you from?"

"That's not important," the woman replied absently, taking off his coat. She stood looking around the room for several minutes, taking everything in.

With his attention split between trying to watch her and cracking eggs, Rand discovered some had missed the bowl entirely and landed on the counter. He scooped them in with the others, then fished out several pieces of broken shell that were swimming amid the whites and yolks.

When he glanced her way again, he found her running her fingers across the faded wallpaper.

The boy sat at the table sniffling, and when he coughed, it came from deep inside. "We didn't steal nuthin', mister."

"No one's saying you did, son. I can see you're not that kind. You have kin around here?" Rand asked the woman.

She didn't answer. She stood lost in thought, staring at two sets of horizontal marks beside the door. Her spine straightened and she sucked in a breath as she touched the penciled-in measurements.

Rand guessed she was remembering something that meant a lot to her. Unexpected memories could certainly jar a person. He wished he could say something to offer comfort, but nothing came to mind.

"I'm not much of a cook," he rambled on. "This is only my second day at it. Surely I'll get better." He gave her an apologetic grin. "How long have you been in that old bunkhouse?"

Her head snapped up. "You're full of questions, mister."

"Sorry. A bad habit. My brothers always say that

I should've been a census taker. I get on their nerves sometimes, especially my oldest brother's."

With a sudden swoosh, flames erupted in the skillet.

Before thinking, he grabbed the handle. The instant his hand came in contact with the heated metal, he pulled back with a yell. Searing pain radiated through his hand, every curse word he knew poised on his tongue, wanting to come out.

Only a day and a half and he was already burning down his house.

Quick as a flash, his mystery woman grabbed a flour sack as a mitt and carried the skillet of burning grease to the door, where she set it on the ground. Then she came and gently took his hand, dipping it into the pail of cold water he'd carried in that morning. The relief was welcome.

"Thank you. Like I said, I'm a stranger to this." He met her stare and saw compassion in its depth, a far cry from the brittle anger that had been there just minutes ago. She wasn't as hard as she wanted him to believe.

Her dark brown hair shot through with strands of scarlet was warm in the lamplight. But her soft amber eyes, the exact color of whiskey, revealed a deep-seated distrust and a whole lot of grit.

"Do you have some salve, by chance?"

"On the shelf above the stove. I never thought I'd need it this quick."

"Sit at the table, and I'll doctor your hand."

"You don't have to do that, but I appreciate your offer." He took a chair next to the boy, who had laid his head on his arms. The lad was clearly ill.

Before she went for the salve, she felt the boy's forehead. Her frown told Rand his suspicions were true.

"It would be best if he lies down," he said quietly. "At least until I get you something to eat. You'll find some quilts in front of the fireplace in the parlor."

A gentle shake roused her son. "Come, Toby."

Rand's gaze followed them to the parlor, which was visible through the doorway. Great love for her son shone in the way she tucked a quilt around him, then kissed his cheek. Rand was glad he'd persuaded them to come inside.

Returning, the mother found the ointment and carefully spread it across the red welt on Rand's palm. He'd never known such a soothing, tender touch. As the owner of a saloon, he'd been touched by lots of women, but this was different. It almost felt like the feathery caress of a whisper. He closed his eyes for a moment, savoring the sensation.

Finally, she put the lid on the salve, then tore a strip off the flour sack and wrapped it around his hand. "There, that should do it."

"I owe you." He gave her a wry smile. "But I'm afraid it'll take me awhile to get you that breakfast I promised."

"You sit here. I'll fix it." She rose and took another skillet from a shelf under the counter.

He watched, amazed at her competence as she put a dollop of butter into the skillet, beat the eggs, cut thick slices of toast, and had it all ready before he knew what was happening. It astounded him how she seemed to know her way around the kitchen. Where he kept the skillets, the butter, the eggs. But he decided that most kitchens were pretty much laid out the same, and women instinctively knew where everything was.

"I don't have milk for the boy. Haven't had time to get a milk cow."

Her amber stare met his. "No need to apologize. I can't let him have it anyway. Fever will curdle milk."

"I believe I might've heard that somewhere. Sorry." His gaze drifted to the mound of scrambled eggs on their plates. They sure looked fluffy and light, just like the café in Battle Creek made them. His mouth began to water even though he'd already eaten.

It became more apparent that she had good breeding a few minutes later. She went to get the boy from the pile of quilts but wouldn't let him eat until they'd both bowed their heads and given thanks.

Toby, she'd called him. The lad's fevered eyes lifted to Rand's. "Thank you, sir."

"You're welcome, son." Rand swallowed a hard lump in his throat. The scrappy child reminded him of himself and his two brothers seventeen years ago. They'd had nothing and no one except for each other, were on the run for their lives, forced to trust strangers for survival.

He poured himself a cup of coffee. "I would've made biscuits, only I don't know how. Me and cooking are like two snarling strangers, and I'm pretty sure I'm not going to win."

She spoke low. "This is fine. It's filling. More than we had outside. You have no woman?"

"No." And that's the way Rand wanted it. He would live alone the rest of his life. "What's your name, ma'am?"

"It's not important. I deeply appreciate your kindness, but we won't be here long enough to socialize, mister."

"Like I told you, I'm Rand Sinclair, not mister. And a name is always important…to someone."

"Not anyone I know." She sighed. "It's Callie. That's all. Just Callie."

"Glad to meet you, Callie."

"I didn't know anyone lived here." She forked a bite of food into her mouth. "I'm not a poacher."

"I guessed that," Rand said quietly. "You're welcome to stay as long as you want. But it's too cold out there. I can't in good conscience let you go back to that bunkhouse."

Callie's chin raised a notch. "Then we'll move on."

He couldn't let this woman and child risk it out there in the unforgiving Texas winter. His conscience would never forgive him. And he suspected he needed them as much as they needed him. This morning had already proved he might well starve if left on his own.

An idea took root. "Wait a minute and hear me out first. I'm looking to hire a cook for me and a few ranch hands when I bring them on in a few months. I'd love for you to fill the job. If you're willing, I'll furnish room and board in exchange. You'd live off this kitchen." He walked to a door and opened it to show her the small bedroom that had not one single stick of furniture in it. "I know it isn't much, but it's warm."

She lifted an eyebrow. "And you? Where would you sleep?"

"Upstairs. You have nothing to fear from me. This kitchen would be your domain. You alone would rule it. I have some furniture ordered that will be here in a week or so. As I told you outside, I recently bought the place. It'll take time to fix it up and get it looking decent. Frankly, I could use the help."

The boy coughed, the sound rattling from deep inside his thin chest. Concern darkened Callie's eyes. She tenderly smoothed back his hair.

"Winter is supposed to be a bad one," Rand pressed.

"I make no promises about how long Toby and I will stay."

"Agreed."

"And no one can know about us being here."

"Can't promise that. I have two brothers, and they'll both be here helping me. The oldest, Cooper Thorne, is now the sheriff in Battle Creek. Brett Liberty is the youngest. I won't lie to them. But I can agree to not tell anyone else."

"You swear?"

"Yes. My word is my bond."

"You're not to ask any questions."

"Understood. Do we have a bargain, Miss Callie?"

The lines in her face relaxed a bit. "Toby and I will stay. Just for a while."

Why it meant so much to help them, Rand couldn't say. Maybe he simply wanted to pay forward Daffern's kindness to him. Yet when he and Callie struck the deal, it seemed to lift the dreariness of the gray gloom that had closed around him.

What had seemed overwhelming before now appeared manageable. He would succeed. He had a strong back and hands that itched to carve out something he could be proud for others to see, even if those "others" were just the pair of strays he'd found.

Rand allowed himself a slight smile for the first time that day. "Excellent. I'll go into town to round up a bed for you and anything else you think we might need."

Though God only knew where he'd get the money. The thought of accepting help from the mother who'd recently come back into his life after twenty-some-odd years stuck in his craw. His relationship with her was…well, complicated. He didn't know yet if he could forgive her for leaving him in an orphanage.

Still, the simple fact was, except for putting some money by for repairs and to buy cattle in the spring, he'd thrown everything he'd gotten from the sale of the saloon into this piece of ground. That left his brothers. Cooper and Brett would give him anything he needed. They'd always been there for each other and always would be.

Whatever help he had to ask for, he'd make it crystal clear it was only temporary. A loan, not charity.

"We're not used to much," Callie insisted. "Like you, some blankets on the floor will do just fine."

"All the same, I planned to buy more furniture and a cow anyway, so I'm not doing anything special." Or was he? Rand only knew he saw their need and related to their plight. Didn't mean anything. "Meanwhile, look over the supplies I brought. Whatever's missing, I'll get from the mercantile. I'll bring in more wood before I go. Enough to keep you until I get back."

Her curt nod indicated the discussion was over. She rose, picked up their plates, and carried them to the wash pan.

Rand buttoned his coat and put on his hat and

gloves. He intended to bring in some water so she wouldn't have to go out.

The north wind sent a chill through his bones when he stalked to the woodpile he'd cut only yesterday. He'd done that first thing, knowing how fast a person could die during a norther. After he carried in several armloads, he filled a couple of pails with water.

Once he had his new cook and her son taken care of, and her list in his pocket, he hitched his horses to the wagon. It would be a miserable ride into town, but he didn't have much choice. Callie and Toby would have a bed before nightfall.

He didn't know from what or whom they were running. Memories of a woman—a friend from town, Jenny Barclay, whose husband had beaten her to within an inch of her life a year ago—swept through his mind. He recalled her dark bruises and the injuries that had laid her up for weeks. He had vowed then that he'd never let that happen to any woman again.

The next bottom-feeder who thought he could thrash his wife and get away with it had better run, because Rand would kill him.

Was Callie married? Seemed likely, since she had a son.

Despite the absence of any visible sign of abuse, he didn't discount that often scars lay buried deep inside, where no one could see. He knew more than a little about scars, how they puckered and left welts long after the wound closed. He sighed, shoving the painful darkness of that particular part of his life back into its hole. With some effort, he corralled his thoughts, bringing them back to Callie.

For sure, something had happened to send her and Toby out into the cold. Though he'd promised not to ask any questions, he cursed his damnable need to know. She aroused a strong curiosity, and he probably wouldn't rest until he figured out her story.

Besides, he couldn't effectively protect her if he didn't have any idea what had caused her life to intersect with his on this cold, wintry morning.

Rand set his jaw.

No matter what he had to do.

No matter the secret Callie kept.

No matter the circumstances that led her to his door, he'd keep her safe.

He'd stake his life on keeping that promise.

Two

THOUGH CALLIE QUINN APPRECIATED RAND'S KINDNESS more than he knew, she didn't trust him. She couldn't. Too often generosity had invisible strings attached.

He'd show his true colors eventually.

All men did.

They all betrayed. They wounded. They lied.

But for now, she'd take the shelter and food he offered. She had little choice. Toby was sick. Still, she intended to keep her eyes open. At the first sign of Sinclair going back on his word, she'd run. She would never forget the crucial mistake she'd once made. She could never make up for that, but she could make sure she didn't repeat the lack of judgment that had cost her everything.

She swallowed hard, forcing back a sob. Though seven years had passed, the gaping hole was still in her heart. Her hands shook when she smoothed back her hair and forced her thoughts away from that horrible night when her world ended.

As soon as Rand set out for town, Callie gathered the ingredients to make a mustard plaster. Toby's cough worried her. The boy was sicker than she'd let on to the rancher. But she wouldn't let sickness or disease, or even a thief in the night, take the only good thing in her life.

And God help her, she'd protect him from the man who vowed to snatch him out of her arms and see her dead.

She mixed together the flour, mustard, and water, her glance going to the pile of blankets where he lay in front of the fire. His forehead was burning up as fever raged in his small body.

When she had the concoction ready, she spread it on a clean flour sack and applied the poultice to Toby's chest. Remembering her mother's admonition from too many years ago to count, she watched closely for signs of blistering. After fifteen minutes, she removed the plaster and applied the same to his back. She planned to reapply it through the day.

After covering him with a blanket, she put a hearty soup on to cook, made with a few potatoes, carrots, and onions she found in a little root cellar below the kitchen. Once that was done, she strolled through the house.

Each room brought back memories of the time she'd lived there with her family. The bedrooms upstairs that had belonged to her, her twin sister, and her older stepbrother were in great need of care, with their peeling wallpaper and warped floors. She moved to where a window seat had stood and glanced out the window at the tall tree they'd climbed down one night to dance in the moonlight.

They'd felt loved and happy here, giggling and planning for when they grew up.

Turning away, she went down the hall.

The room where her mother had died was filled with ghosts. Sadness and gloom hung onto her like gray, clinging spiderwebs, resisting all her efforts to brush them off.

She didn't tarry there. The pain was too great. Returning to the first floor, Callie went around to a hidden closet under the stairs and opened the door. She and Claire had played in there on rainy days. The room had been their own private sanctuary where they could tell each other secrets and promise to spend the rest of their lives together as best friends.

Pulling a gold locket from beneath her bodice, she opened it and gazed at Claire's likeness. This was the only prized possession she'd been able to grab in her hurry to leave.

A sob rose up, strangling her.

Why hadn't she stayed away? She'd known it would be hard.

But she had things to do here before she moved on.

She mustn't forget she had secrets to dig up.

The sky had turned pitch black by the time Rand Sinclair returned. Callie was at the stove, sliding a pan of corn bread into the oven when the back door opened.

The tall rancher filled the small kitchen even before he stepped inside. His windburned cheeks told of his misery. Guilt washed over her. If not for her and Toby, he wouldn't have faced that long ride to town.

When he removed his hat, his startling eyes—so clear and bluer than a wild Texas sky—stole her breath.

"You must be frozen," she said, hurriedly pouring a cup of hot coffee she'd made earlier.

"Smells good in here." He removed his coat and gloves and hung his hat on a hook by the door. He took the cup she handed him and curled his fingers around it as though desperate for the warmth.

"I made soup. Let it simmer all day. Nothing fancy."

"It'll hit the spot." He sniffed the air. "Was that corn bread you just put in the oven?"

"Yes, I hope you don't mind."

"What a crazy question. I'd kill for a slice of hot corn bread." He sat down at the table. "Like I told you, I don't know how to do much more than boil water. Do you know how to make biscuits?"

Callie allowed a slight smile. He sounded like a wistful little boy, afraid to ask for too many favors. "I do. We'll have some for breakfast."

A wide grin covered his face. "You don't know how much I'm looking forward to morning."

"It'll come soon enough."

He took a sip of coffee. "How long until supper? I need to unload the wagon and put my horses in the barn as soon as possible."

"Probably twenty minutes or so. I'll help you and it'll go faster."

"I appreciate the offer, but it's too cold for you out there." He emptied his cup and set it down, then got his coat, hat, and gloves. "Better get to it. The prospect of hot corn bread will make me hurry."

She watched him go back outside, shivering from a sudden onslaught of frigid air that swept in through the open door. No one had cared about her in such a long time. Maybe, just maybe, he was an honorable man and truly what he seemed.

Was it possible?

He came back a few minutes later with packages and bundles teetering precariously in his arms. She flew to take some from him.

"I may need a little help getting the mattress inside if you don't mind." He laid the packages down on the floor.

"I'll be happy to."

"You stay inside. Keep the door shut until I bang on it. Don't want to lose all this wonderful heat."

Over the next twenty minutes she assisted, taking some of the load after he got the bedstead and mattress to the door. By then, the corn bread was done, golden and delicious. She set it in the warming oven while he took the horse to the barn.

Checking on Toby, she was relieved to find his fever had broken.

"I'm hungry, ma'am."

"I have some nice hot soup for supper. Do you think you can wait for Mr. Sinclair to come back in?"

He nodded. She smoothed back his sweat-drenched hair, giving thanks for the improvement. Overcome with emotion, she kissed his cheek. "I love you, little man. We're going to be all right. I'll make sure of it. I'm going to keep you safe."

"Love you too," he said quietly.

When Rand returned from the barn, she had the table set and the pot of soup and the corn bread sitting in the middle.

"Horses are cared for, and now I can hardly wait

for supper." He removed his outerwear and blew on his hands to warm them, taking the fresh cup of coffee she offered.

"We can spare a few minutes for you to thaw out by the fire. We don't have to eat right this instant."

"Oh no you don't, lady," he growled. "I'll not take a chance on eating cold corn bread. I'll warm up when that home cooking hits my belly. Won't talk me out of that pleasure."

Callie called Toby and they all took their places. She'd barely said "Amen" before Rand dove in. She watched in amusement, wondering at his enormous appetite. One would think he hadn't eaten in a month of Sundays.

With the rancher occupied, her gaze wandered over his hair, which was the color of worn saddle leather. The lamplight brought out golden glints that danced amongst the brown strands touching his collar. Dark stubble on his jaw lent toughness to his handsome face. The long fingers lifting a slice of corn bread to his generous mouth appeared far more suited to a banker or lawyer.

Like it or not, she was curious about him.

As though sensing the direction of her thoughts, he leveled his vivid blue eyes on her. Her mouth dried. To hide her discomfort, she quickly turned to Toby. "Do you like the soup?"

"Yes, ma'am. It's good."

"More corn bread, young man?" Rand asked.

"No, sir."

"You're still looking kinda peaked."

"He's better," Callie said. "I kept a mustard plaster on him all day. It helped break his fever. He's not coughing as much. I'm sure tomorrow will see more improvement."

"Thank goodness I found you when I did, even though you were ready to break both my legs with that big stick."

"You scared me." She felt heat creeping into her face. "You looked eight feet tall, standing there with your gun drawn. What did you expect?"

"Thought it was poachers. The Colt was a precaution. Never thought I'd find you and Toby in the shadows."

Callie laid down her spoon. "I'm grateful for this warm house and hot food. I'll try not to make you regret taking us in. Toby and I will stay out of your way."

"Now hold on a minute. My house is yours and you'll consider it that way. You're doing this old bachelor a huge favor. Most likely I'd have died from starvation if you hadn't taken pity on me."

The sincerity of his words wrapped around her. She could almost let hope into her heart. But that would be dangerous. Nibbling on her corn bread, she turned to the question she'd been dying to ask. "What did you do before you bought this parcel of land, Mr. Sinclair?"

"Owned a saloon in Battle Creek. The Lily of the West."

Laughter quickly rose, refusing to let her squash it. "You were a saloon owner? You've never operated a ranch before, have you?"

A wry grin flirted along the corners of his mouth. "Sounds ridiculous, doesn't it?"

"Pretty strange. So you don't know anything about cows?"

"Not much, although I used to live on a ranch when

I was a boy." He slathered butter on another piece of corn bread and took a big bite. "Figure my brothers can teach me what I don't know." Rand explained that his brothers Cooper and Brett were in the ranching business and that the best rancher ever born raised them. "What about you? Where did you live?"

Icy panic brought a chill to the warm room. Callie drew herself up. "You agreed that you wouldn't ask any questions. Not even a day has passed, and you're going back on your word."

"Let me get this straight. You can ask me anything you want, but I'm not allowed to find out even the most basic things about my new cook?"

"It'll be this way or we'll head out the door."

Rand gave a heavy sigh. "All right. I apologize, Callie. Didn't mean to pry. Just wanted to get to know you a little. I promise to watch it from now on."

Toby pushed back his bowl and asked to be excused. Callie's gaze followed him as he headed back to the pile of blankets.

"I accept your apology. This time. But I meant what I said." She rose and collected her and Toby's bowls. Then to dispel the tension, she said, "If you brought apples from the mercantile, I'll make a pie tomorrow."

"I certainly did. A pie would be most welcome."

Refusing to let her take his bowl, Rand rose and carried it to the wash pan himself. Callie watched him refill his coffee cup and return to his seat, stretching out his long legs in front of him. It was clear that this bachelor was accustomed to doing things himself. He didn't expect her to wait on him. She found that a relief as she set about washing the dishes.

"I'll finish this coffee, then set up the bed, but first—I brought you and the boy some things from town. Open the packages, Callie."

When she turned, she found herself staring into his blue eyes. "We don't need—"

"You darn well do, and I won't hear you arguing about it. Now, let those dishes go and find out what's in these packages. I'll help you with them later."

The man was awfully bossy. She was about to tell him what he could do with those packages when the sight of Toby lying listless in front of the stone fireplace stopped her. To survive the winter, the child needed a coat and warm clothes. Maybe that's what Rand had brought from town. She couldn't refuse those no matter how much she·wanted to.

Drying her hands on the flour sack that she'd made into a dish towel, she sat on the floor and tore off the brown paper wrapping on one of the packages. The fleece-lined coat for Toby made her breath catch in her throat. An answered prayer.

Sudden memories of her mother popped into her head. Before her death, Nora Quinn Powers regularly bought and took things to the needy in town. One year in particular, she purchased the most beautiful coat for a little girl who had next to nothing. It had a white fur collar and a muff. Callie, eight at the time, desperately wanted that coat. She'd caught her mother not looking and hid it in her room. A day or two later, she overheard her mother talking about how the sheriff had found the girl half-frozen. She never forgot the painful stillness that came over her. She'd raced upstairs and retrieved the coat, and from then on, she never begrudged anyone the help they needed. For years, she always added the girl to her nightly prayers and asked for forgiveness.

Now, as she clutched the new coat, she thanked her mother's ghost and the saloon-owner-turned-rancher for looking out for Toby when she couldn't.

Rand had also bought a soft wool dress in a pretty shade of nutmeg for her, and a coat as well. She unwrapped a woman's warm flannel nightgown, then shirts, pants, gloves, and a knit cap for Toby. Rand had even thought to add two bars of fragrant soap. The last package held a comb, brush, and mirror.

A pile of quilts, sheets, and pillows lay in a neat stack. Rand's generosity brought tears to her eyes. She thought of the miserable nights she and Toby had spent in the elements, too cold to sleep. This was a far cry from that.

Maybe, for such generosity of spirit, she could possibly endure a very bossy man with beautiful eyes.

"Thank you," she whispered.

"Just glad to help. Probably didn't get everything you needed. Never bought things for a lady before." A curious light came into his eyes as he shifted his feet and crossed them at the ankles. "But hopefully I got enough to get you by for now."

"That and more, Mr. Sinclair."

He quickly held up his hand to stop her. "My name is not mister. Thought we cleared that up at the start. My rule. I'm Rand. Got it?"

"Yes. This must've cost a fortune. I'll repay what you spent as soon as I'm able."

"Don't want paid back," he growled. "Your thanks are more than enough."

"Very well. You have my thanks." But no matter what he said, she wasn't through with the subject. She would find a way to repay him. One way or another.

"You're welcome."

"I need to put more salve on your burn."

"My hand is fine. Not much pain."

Callie took his good hand and led him to the table. "All the same, I'm putting more ointment on the burn," she said firmly.

"I know better than to argue with a determined woman."

"Good." She got the tin of thick balm and dabbed it onto the palm of his hand. It had already taken away much of the redness, though she knew it had to hurt.

Afterward, he tried to help her in the kitchen, but his fumbling presence only lengthened the task. Finally, she nudged him toward the bed he still had to set up in the room off the kitchen where she and Toby would sleep. He took the hint at last and disappeared.

In the midst of the quiet that followed came a horrendous crash. Looking in, she saw the iron bedstead lying over on the floor and Rand struggling to right it. He stood in the middle of a tangle of metal, muttering a string of cuss words and trying his best to keep her and Toby from hearing the colorful language. Callie covered her mouth to smother the laughter.

His care to keep from being heard touched her. His show of respect raised her opinion of him several notches.

Quickly she moved to offer her services. She

held the headboard while he attached the rails, then switched to the foot and did the same. With that secure, she handed him lengths of rope and watched him knot them back and forth across the open space. This would serve as a base for the unwieldy feather mattress. At last she took one end and he the other and they lifted the thick mattress into place.

A little later, surprise rippled over her when he threw a rag rug onto the floor beside the made-up bed onto which they'd spread quilts. "To keep your feet from getting too cold. Keep this door open to draw heat from the stove. I'll make sure it stays lit."

"Rand, you're a good man." Gathering tears that she refused to let fall blurred his face. "Keep your bed where it is by the fireplace in the parlor. It's too frigid upstairs."

His breathtaking blue eyes widened with surprise. He was silent for the space of a heartbeat, then cleared his throat. When he spoke, his voice was raspy. "As you wish."

Three

BREAKING DAWN SENT PINK LIGHT FLOODING THROUGH the windows the next morning, and Rand awoke thinking he'd died and gone to glory.

He raised his head and sniffed. The smell of ham and biscuits permeated the house. His growling belly told him time was wasting. If he didn't get busy, he'd miss out.

But he lay there a full minute, pushing aside the remnants of a recurring dream that had terrified him since he was a boy. He didn't know what the shadowy bald-headed man who seemed ten feet tall or the rocking wooden pony with the glowing red eyes meant or why they were lodged in the deep recesses of his brain. Maybe the dream meant nothing other than he was losing his mind. It instilled terror, that much he knew.

Throwing back the quilts, he pulled on his boots. Except for his gun belt, he'd slept fully dressed, so he made fast work of getting to his feet. After eating, he'd go pick up the milk cow he'd bought yesterday. A growing boy needed milk to drink.

Seconds later, he pushed through the kitchen door

and stopped, drinking in the sight. Callie stood at the stove, tending to breakfast. A smile curved his mouth. She wore the wool dress he'd bought because it had reminded him of her pretty amber eyes.

He didn't know beans about ladies' sizes, so he'd relied on Emmylou, the clerk, to help with that. The mercantile's selection hadn't been all that much to brag about, but the woman seemed to know what she was doing.

Now with a critical eye, he took in Callie's curves. The dress hugged all the right places and then some. The hips, waist, and...

Good Lord! His heart hammered in his ears worse than Brett beating on that Indian drum of his. Closing his eyes, he struggled for a long moment to push those thoughts from his head and gain control of his traitorous body. He couldn't, wouldn't, expect anything from Callie other than putting meals on the table.

When he had his thoughts firmly in hand, he opened his eyes and sighed. Being a bachelor made him miss out on a few things, not all of them physical.

A wife to wake up with.

Children to teach things.

Sharing the bounties of his life with a family. Having someone to grow old with.

But he couldn't marry, no matter how enticing finally having someone relying on him made it appear. He wasn't husband material. Never would be. Being lost and abandoned as a child had determined his lonely path. His adopted brothers, Cooper and Brett, had banded together with him and were the only family he needed. They wouldn't let him down. They wouldn't walk out on him as first his parents, then so many others, had.

He'd learned long ago that eventually, everyone walked away.

"Morning," he said, heading into the kitchen. His gaze found Toby sitting by the warm oven.

Callie handed him a cup of coffee. "Good morning."

When their hands touched, a bolt of something ran up his arm. He didn't want the contact to end. "Sleep well?"

"Like rocks. Both of us. Toby is not as croupy today." She reached down to brush the boy's black hair. "Biscuits need another five minutes, then we'll eat."

"I'll wash up." He set his cup next to his plate. "Toby, want to come with me?"

"Yes, sir."

Rand noticed some of the water he'd lugged in yesterday sitting on the back of the stove. He filled a washbowl on the counter and lifted the boy up, grinning as Toby splashed around. Give a youngster some water and he was in heaven. Though it had been Rand's observation that mothers generally had a conniption over the mess, Callie only smiled.

"How old are you, Toby?"

"This many." The lad grinned, holding up six fingers.

Rand whistled. "That's pretty big. You're a young man."

"Tomorrow I'm gonna be as big as you."

He laughed. "That so? That's awful fast."

"I know how to shoot. An outlaw's gun takes six bullets."

"Uh, I'm sure it does, Toby."

Callie blanched and whirled, her eyes slamming into his. "I don't know where he gets these things."

"There's no telling." Still, Rand filed it away. Questions buzzed inside his head like a swarm of horseflies as he calmly set Toby down and took his turn at the washbowl, but he set them aside for now. Rand mopped up the mess, keeping one eye on the oven door.

God forbid he miss the biscuits.

～

Callie collected the breakfast plates and took them to the wash pan. Rand had already gone out to feed the horses. He'd told her about a milk cow he'd bought and that he'd have to go after it. With the cow only a mile away, he would just walk the animal over.

Toby had tried to traipse out after him, but she'd put her foot down. The boy still had a bad cough. Besides, he appeared to be forming a bond with the tall rancher. That troubled her. If Toby became too attached, it would kill him when they had to up and leave.

Maybe at a moment's notice. She had to stay ready in case Nate Fleming found them here on this remote ranch. He was as mean and wily an outlaw as they came. He'd kept them on the run from Missouri to Texas, and it'd taken all her cunning to evade him.

She glanced out the door, thankful that it wasn't as cold today. The wind had died down, and the sun cast glorious golden rays across the landscape. Ever since she was a child, she'd hated gloomy weather, so she welcomed the warmth of the sunshine with a lighter heart.

Rand's trek after the cow would give her the

perfect opportunity to look for the key she'd buried when she was only eight years old. It went to an ornate metal box that had belonged to her mother. Callie recalled the day Mama had presented her and her sister each a key and said that if their lives ever needed to look up, to open the chest. Until then, she'd put it in a safe place.

Nora Quinn Powers had died that spring, shortly after Callie and Claire turned nine.

Despite her stepfather Edmund Powers's steadfast promise to continue living on the ranch, he'd promptly moved them to Kansas City. That had been the first in a long string of broken promises, disappointments, and heartaches that pierced all the way down to her soul.

But the most unforgivable of all had come when he up and married socialite Liza Masterson mere weeks after her mother's death. Liza made no bones about the fact that she abhorred Callie and Claire, while their stepbrother David could do no wrong. Liza had taken things, smashed expensive vases, and ripped the pages from Edmund Powers's favorite books, saying the girls had done it. The woman had laughed when Edmund punished them. Often when Callie and Claire had walked near, she'd reach out and viciously pinch them, leaving deep bruises. All because they reminded her of a daughter who ran away, choosing to live with strangers rather than her mother.

Thank God, Liza no longer wielded power over them.

Lost in her memories, Callie suddenly realized she still had dishes to finish and the kitchen to clean. She put some water on the stove to heat while she swept the floor. Then she made hot, soapy dishwater. As she washed the breakfast dishes, her thoughts drifted once more.

Finding her buried key and her mother's box occupied her thoughts.

She desperately needed her life to look up now.

Not only that, but she had to locate the chest before Nate Fleming found them. Ever since Claire succumbed to a mysterious malady two months ago, Callie had suspected Nate Fleming of poisoning her sister. She had no proof, though.

No denying Claire had had a weakness for Nate. The outlaw could be quite charming, and Lord knows a more handsome man never lived. Desperate to escape Edmund Powers and Liza, it hadn't taken Claire long to fall under Nate's spell, and they'd married shortly after.

In the beginning, Nate kept his criminal activities hidden from Claire. Then Toby was born. Having a son changed things. A year ago, he began taking Toby, then five, with him on jobs and teaching him the outlaw trade.

Callie would never forget the desperation in Claire's wild eyes as she'd begged, "Please promise you'll keep Nate from taking Toby. Raise my son to be a good, honest man, not a hunted outlaw like his father. Promise me."

"I vow on Mama's grave that I'll protect Toby with my very life. I'll keep him safe."

The minute Claire took her final breath, Callie had gathered up Toby, and they rode out before Nate even knew they were gone. Despite getting a head start, Callie had more close calls than she cared to count. By the time they'd reached this ranch, she was mentally and physically exhausted.

Her mind went back to her mother's treasure chest. Where on earth had her mother hidden it?

If Nate should find them before…

No, she wouldn't entertain those possibilities. She would succeed. Toby's life depended on whatever might be in that box.

While she waited for Rand to leave, she set the rest of the house to rights, putting things away and making everything neat and tidy. In the process of folding Rand's blankets and quilts, a metal ring with no fewer than two dozen keys on it clattered to the floor. It seemed a bit odd that he'd have so many things that required locking up.

But he *was* a former saloon owner. Maybe he'd forgotten to turn over some of the keys when he sold the business. She shrugged and laid them next to the neat stack of bedding, where he'd find them.

When she next looked out the window, Rand had mounted up in front of the barn. He sat astride a big, handsome blue roan that sidestepped and pranced around. Though she knew very little about ranch stock, she suspected it was prime horseflesh. In a moment of idle curiosity, she wondered about its name.

The horse was a perfect match for Rand. They moved as one. Both carried themselves tall and straight, as though proud of who they were and of the blood flowing in their veins. Though she could easily picture Rand sitting at a card table in some smoky saloon, the lamplight playing on his tanned face, she knew that whether he succeeded or failed at the ranching business, he would give it all he had.

There would be no half measures with this Texan, at least when it came to work. All or nothing. He should emblazon that motto on every surface of the ranch. A hunch based on years of experience told her that.

Betrayed by her stepfather too many times to count, abandoned by her stepbrother, David, when she needed him most, and left high and dry by a man she'd trusted had taught her well. She'd stared into Rand's startling blue eyes and he hadn't ducked his head or turned away. His eyes were honest and direct. She admired that about him. And then there was the care he took of Toby, making the little boy feel like the most special thing in the world.

Still, she wouldn't let him get too close. It could all be smoke and mirrors and she could be a fool.

Again.

Toby tugged on her skirt. "I wanna go out to play."

"First, we need to talk." Callie knelt down to his level. "Remember how I told you not to say anything about your father?"

The youngster nodded.

"It's very important that you don't say anything else."

"About outlaws an' stuff?"

"Yes. It wouldn't be good for Mr. Sinclair to know about your father."

"What if my papa hurts Mr. Rand? I need to warn him. Can I tell him about putting burlap on the horse's feet so the posse can't track 'em?"

"No, don't mention anything about what went on

when you were with your father. None of it. Forget
you ever knew those things. Your father isn't going to
hurt Mr. Sinclair. I'm not going to let him. Besides,
we'll be gone before your papa gets here."

Toby's face brightened. "I'm glad. Mr. Rand is real
nice. Now, I can go play?"

Callie hugged him to her. "I suppose. You can't
stay out too long, though. I don't want you to have a
setback, young man."

He patted her cheek and grinned. "I won't get sick."

"I love you so much." She bundled him into his
coat, gloves, and knit cap. Pulling on hers, she opened
the door. "You stay close, where I can keep an eye
on you."

Toby took off running as if she'd just let him out
of a dungeon after years and years of captivity. She
watched the silly boy for a moment, then looked
around, trying to rely on the faded memories of an
eight-year-old girl.

Where had she buried the key?

Under the big walnut tree beside the house, where
she and Claire had spent many hours playing during
the summer months?

Slowly, she moved in that direction. But it didn't
feel right.

Maybe around the barn.

Eighteen years could sure blur a memory. Wrinkling
her forehead, she tried to turn back the pages of time.
Panic struck her. What if she never remembered?
What if Nate had found her mother's box and taken
what belonged to Callie? She'd put nothing past a
man who'd stolen the coins off dead people's eyes.

She whirled to check on Toby's whereabouts and it hit her.

The woodpile. That was it.

It had been close to the house, and she'd been in a hurry that Saturday to go into town with her mother.

"Toby, come back this way, sweetheart. You're going too far," she called.

When the youngster heeded her request, she strode to the stack of wood and stared at the ground. She'd buried the key somewhere around the old chopping block.

All those years ago, she hadn't had anything but a piece of kindling to dig with, so she'd buried it pretty shallow.

The image of the distinctive brass key filled her mind. Most keys were round on top and rather plain, but this one was swirled and ornate.

"Toby, want to help me dig?"

He stumbled over his feet as he ran to her. "Oh boy."

She explained what she was looking for and handed him a sturdy piece of kindling. She grabbed another for herself. Within minutes, they'd dug several holes in the soft ground.

Nothing.

Empty holes popped up all around the stump. Finally she sat back on her heels. Her whole body went numb.

She'd failed.

Tears pricked her eyes.

The key that might have meant her future was gone.

Four

TWO HOURS AFTER RAND RODE OFF TO FETCH THE MILK cow, a sudden clip-clop of hooves coming toward them raised the hair on the back of Callie's neck. *Nate.* They didn't have time to make it inside the house.

Her panicked gaze swept the yard for a hiding place.

Behind the woodpile. Trembling, she hurried Toby around the stack of wood and whispered for him not to make a sound. They knelt down and Callie grabbed a stick of wood. She'd defend them with all she had. If Nate wanted a fight, she'd give it to him. She had no qualms about bashing his head in.

The horse stopped a few feet away, and she heard the creak of leather as a rider dismounted.

"Rand? You here?" a man asked in a deep voice.

"Where you at, Rand?" There were two of them.

Toby tried to rise and Callie jerked him back down, holding her hand over the boy's mouth. It wasn't Nate, but whoever they were might go away if they got no reply.

"Maybe he went after that cow he said he bought. Reckon we'll make ourselves comfortable until he shows up." The rumbling voice belonged to the first speaker. "It's too far back into town. Besides, I don't think he'll be gone long."

Callie's heart sank. They were stuck where they were. No way would she make her presence known. The fewer who knew she lived on the ranch, the better.

At that moment, the faint mooing of a cow reached her ears. The sound became louder and louder.

Finally she heard Rand call to the two men, "What're you doing here today?"

"Came to work, little brother. Looks like you could use the help of an army. But maybe we were wrong."

"Don't you dare leave. I'm not about to look a gift horse in the mouth. I ain't no fool," Rand said. "Have you met my help and her son, Toby?"

"Nope. The place appears deserted," answered the one with the deep voice. "I'd wondered why you came to me for a bed and a loan yesterday. Now it makes sense."

"Yep. Callie?" Rand hollered.

Lord, help. What should she do now? She couldn't pop up and say that she and Toby were huddling like a couple of frightened prairie dogs too scared of their own shadows. She chewed her lip and waited.

"She's probably out getting some fresh air," Rand said. "Let me put this cow in the barn and I'll show you what I have in mind, Coop. Brett, I especially want your ideas."

The voices moved away. Seizing her chance, Callie grabbed Toby's hand and made a beeline for the house.

Once inside, Callie's nerves settled. A short time later, she glanced out the window at the men as they came from the barn. These must be the brothers Rand told her about. All three were tall, but the one wearing the sheriff's badge stood about two inches taller than Rand, and the other one wore knee-high moccasins and a long feather in his hat. She searched her memory for what Rand had told her. Cooper Thorne was the sheriff in Battle Creek in addition to owning the Long Odds Ranch, and Brett Liberty owned the Wild Horse Ranch.

Besides having different last names, the brothers bore no resemblance to each other at all. Brett, with his dark coloring and manner of dress, was an Indian. Clearly they were not natural-born brothers.

Had they simply met up, desperate for someone to belong to, and claimed that distinction for themselves? She glanced at Toby. She could understand that impulse all too well.

∽

Rand laid out the plans for his Last Hope Ranch and its 350 acres, but his mind was on Callie. He knew she had cloaked herself and Toby in dark shadows somewhere. But then again, maybe she'd decided to light out the minute he'd turned his back. He prayed that was not the case. Whether she knew it or not yet, she needed someone to care about her. She might not be aware of it, but he'd already taken that job.

"I'll get rid of these weeds and trash littering the yard," he continued, jerking his attention back to repairs. "Fix up the barn and corral, patch the barn roof. Then I'll make the house and bunk quarters more livable. After that, I'll work on the fences."

"It'll take a heap of work for sure. A man will have to be awfully dedicated to his vision." Cooper pushed back his hat with a forefinger. "Is this really what you want? Are you happy here?"

"After all, you have to admit it's a far cry from living in town and owning a saloon," Brett added. "Sleeping till noon. Whiskey fumes seeping into your skin and pretty ladies coming out of the woodwork."

Rand ignored the bait. He refused to bite. But he did think it odd that his baby brother kept staring at the house with a strange grin on his face. With Brett's keen hearing, Rand wondered if he'd detected a noise.

"What's the matter, Brett? You hear war drums or something?"

"Nope." Brett dragged his attention back to the subject. "Go ahead with your big picture."

Leaning against a broken corral post, Rand studied his brothers and said quietly, "I know it doesn't look like much, but this is my chance, maybe the last one, to prove some things to myself. Yes, I can be happy here. It's peaceful. And it's away from my mother."

"Now we get to the heart of the matter. This is an escape," Cooper drawled. "We really can't fault you. You can't be in the same room with Abigail—or Clara, or whatever she's calling herself these days—for five minutes without wanting to kill her."

"The thing is, she let me rot in that orphanage. Then she waltzes back into my life almost twenty-five years later and acts all motherly and full of concern, like I can't possibly exist without her and her considerable money. Well, I don't need it and I don't need her."

"She thought you died with your father," Cooper pointed out.

"Her story, not mine," Rand snapped. "She could've tried to make sure. *No grave* should've been a hint."

To his way of thinking, Abigail Winehouse, famous opera singer that she was, never wanted to be saddled with a kid. So when she had a chance to tour the West, she'd jumped at it. Said good-bye to her five-year-old son, kissed her husband as if she hadn't been in too much of a rush, and taken off, never glancing back.

"I'd give anything to have a mother," Brett said softly.

"You can have mine and welcome to her."

Lost in his thoughts, the silence stretched. When Rand glanced up, he caught his brothers' wide grins. "What?"

"We'd like to know about this Callie woman now," Cooper said. "Did you get tired of being a crotchety old bachelor and tie the knot without telling your two brothers?"

"You don't have to hide her." Brett stuck a matchstick in the corner of his mouth.

Irritation that he wouldn't have felt a week ago climbed into Rand's chest. He thought back to over eight months ago when a mail-order bride, Delta Dandridge, had arrived on the stage announcing she'd come to wed Cooper. But his brother had been bound and determined to evade matrimony by whatever means.

Rand had teased him unmercifully. Somehow he failed to see the humor now.

"She works for me." He explained how he'd found her and her son hiding in one of the old buildings half-frozen and hungry. "I gave her a job, nothing more.

So put all your comments and suggestions away and let her be, or you'll answer to me."

Cooper's grin vanished as he quirked a dark eyebrow. "You know we're just giving you some brotherly love, don't you?"

"No need to get so defensive." Brett clapped him on the shoulder. "I'd like to meet her. She sounds real special."

She was, but Rand didn't share just how much with his brothers.

"What's her last name? She may be from around here. Part of my sheriff duties is knowing everyone who lives in these parts."

"Told me to call her Callie, just Callie, and made me promise not to ask any questions," Rand said quietly. "Clearly she's running from something." Most likely *someone*.

All that stuff Toby spouted about an outlaw's gun holding six bullets had been stuck in his brain since breakfast. Maybe Callie was married to an outlaw?

The possibility was like molten lead in his stomach, the strong feeling nearly knocking him to his knees.

"Well, things have a way of changing," Cooper said. "Give her some room and let her see that you have her best interests in mind. Once she realizes you're not going to hurt her, she'll come to trust you and share whatever fear drove her here."

Brett squinted off into the distance. "Scared people have trouble believing in the good in the world and think they're not worthy of all they're entitled to. Just go slow and easy."

It didn't take a genius to know his baby brother

was thinking about himself and Tolbert Early, a man who'd beaten Brett half to death when he was only eight years old. Justice had come last April when Brett finally killed the low-down varmint. Rand was glad he'd been there to witness it.

Cooper bent and picked up a small rock. After turning it over in his hand, he let it sail into the trees. "Everything will work itself out. Took Delta and me some time to trust each other with our secrets. But we finally did. I never thought in a million years that I'd be married to her, but look at me now. We're as happy as two bullfrogs sunning on a log."

"You say that now, but you went kicking and screaming all the way," Rand pointed out. "It wasn't until faced with the fear of losing her that the facts became crystal clear."

"Amen, brother." Brett grinned. "I think it's time to meet this mysterious woman of yours."

"Lord, I don't know if I'm ready for this." Rand cast a glance toward the house. Callie's fear swirled around him like dark swamp water where he stood. "Don't ask a bunch of questions and don't make her feel threatened. Don't embarrass me, either."

"Yes, Mother," Cooper growled. "We're grown men, for God's sake. I think we know how to behave by now. Delta even lets me out of the house occasionally without supervision."

"Any other instructions, Rand?" Brett asked quietly. "Just relax. We want what you want."

With a short jerk of his head, Rand led the way to the house. He opened the back door and called softly, "Callie?"

Toby came running, holding a bent stick that served as a gun. "Mr. Rand, I saw you with the cow. We were hiding."

"Well, I'm glad you came out." He picked the boy up and swung him around. "I'd have hated to lose you."

Callie hurried from the little bedroom. "Young man, do you always have to…" Her voice trailed when she drew up short. "I apologize."

Rand set the youngster down and moved aside to let Cooper and Brett inside. Toby stared at Cooper's badge, his eyes growing wide. The boy seemed to have trouble swallowing.

"These are my brothers I told you about, Callie," Rand said. "The ornery cuss with the badge pinned to his chest is Cooper Thorne. Brett Liberty is the other. He can skin a rabbit before you can even get the fire started."

Callie's face flamed. Rand thought she'd never looked more mortified. Or prettier, for that matter.

Cooper and Brett tipped their hats and said, "Ma'am."

Rand wouldn't have bet money on her accepting their token of politeness, but though she hesitated, she finally managed, "I'm pleased to meet you."

"Ma'am," Cooper said. "My wife Delta would love to have you come visit. She gets lonely out on the ranch and misses her friends from town. The Long Odds is only a mile north of here. We also own the Four Promises outside of town, dividing our time between the two. I know how women band together against the loneliness."

Callie nodded but kept silent.

Toby crept up to Brett and touched the fringe of his moccasins. "Are you a real Indian?"

"Toby! That's rude. Now apologize to Mr. Liberty."

"But I just want to know." Toby ducked his head, the words expressing his remorse apparently getting stuck in his throat.

Brett knelt to study the six-year-old. "When I was your age, I had such a burning curiosity of the world too. It's okay to ask questions. Yes, I'm an Indian. And you know what?"

Toby stared solemnly into Brett's eyes. "What?"

"I live in a real, honest-to-goodness tepee on my land called the Wild Horse Ranch. I raise horses."

"Really?"

"Yes. I'd like for you to come see for yourself, if it's all right with your mother."

"Could I sleep in it?"

"Don't see why not." Brett winked and dropped his hat onto Toby's head.

The boy struggled to look up at his mother from beneath the huge brim. "Can I, ma'am? I really want to."

"That's 'may I,' young man. And we'll see."

"Aw shoot! That means no."

Rand stepped in. "Don't look all down-in-the-mouth, little man. It just means your mama is thinking about if it's warm enough, that's all." He caught the look of gratitude Callie shot him and turned to his brothers. "Want some coffee?"

They agreed, and over the next two hours sat at the kitchen table neck-deep in plans. Rand made a list of how much lumber, nails, fence posts, shingles, and other materials they'd need. He deeply appreciated his brothers sharing their knowledge. They went out of their way not to appear bossy or speak over his head, presenting their comments as only suggestions. That they ultimately left it up to Rand to make his own decisions about things meant more than they knew.

This was what family did. Or should do. He thought of his mother, who tried to cram her wishes down his throat.

In the midst of it all, Toby climbed into his lap. A short while later, the boy yawned and fell asleep with his head resting against Rand's chest.

He had a vague awareness of movement in the kitchen and the quiet clink of pans, but he'd been engrossed in getting his dream down on paper before it faded to pay much attention.

Callie appeared at his elbow. "If you gentlemen will wash up, I'll serve lunch."

Cooper jumped to his feet. "I didn't intend to put you to all this trouble, ma'am. I meant to be out of your hair by now. Delta will have my hide. I promised to take her into town."

"It's no bother, Mr. Thorne. I have to cook for us anyway, and it's no hardship putting a few more beans in the pot."

"Thank you, Miss Callie," Brett said, pushing back his chair. "I leap at any chance I get to eat someone else's cooking. Get tired of my own."

Rand waited until his brothers headed out to the tank at the foot of the windmill to wash before waking up Toby. The youngster rubbed the sleep from his eyes and looked around as if wondering where everyone went.

"Thank you, Callie. I didn't plan on this. I'd have warned you if I'd known they were coming."

"I admit, they did cause concern at first. They're such big, tall men."

"I sure didn't expect they'd stay for lunch. I created extra work for you. I'm sorry."

"Don't be silly, Rand. You hired me to cook."

He wanted to say that he knew her fear of strangers and regretted springing his brothers on her the way he had. But when her eyes, the color of rich warm whiskey, turned on him, his brain refused to think of anything.

Except taking away the fear lurking there...and maybe figuring out how to kiss her.

Five

LATER THAT EVENING AS THEY ATE, RAND WATCHED Callie out of the corner of his eye. The lady was quite a distraction, sitting across the table from him with her reddish strands shimmering in the lamplight amid the darker brown of her hair. When her eyes met his, every nerve ending quivered, and it was all he could do to form a coherent thought. She did things to him no other woman had.

She'd warmed up the beans, fried potatoes, and made another pan of corn bread. His favorite meal. She'd been awfully quiet, not saying more than two words and keeping her eyes lowered to her plate.

Finally, when he managed to get his tongue to work and could stand the silence no longer, he spoke. "Whoever taught you to cook certainly did me a big favor. Everything you make is the best I've put in my mouth."

"The woman who cooked for us took me under her wing. I spent a lot of time in the kitchen, because it was the only place I could be sure my stepmother wouldn't go."

Rand digested that. He wanted to ask why she'd

avoided her stepmother, but he'd learned his lesson. No questions. "Well, I'm mighty glad your cook saw potential in you."

An uncomfortable silence fell over them. At last Rand said, "It's getting colder outside. Wind's turned out of the north and clouds have rolled in. Probably rain. Maybe snow."

Damn, couldn't he think of something better to say?

Callie looked up. "I'll keep Toby inside. I don't want him to have a relapse."

"A good idea. You're deep in thought, Callie. Anything you want to talk about?"

"Just woolgathering. I like your brothers, but I'm confused."

"They tend to boggle a person's mind, all right."

"You call them brothers, yet you all have different last names and you couldn't be more mismatched."

"You're right." Rand put down his fork and propped his elbows on the table. "We're not natural born, we're blood brothers. We all come from an orphanage where deep bonds formed that are unbreakable even today. We pricked our fingers and declared ourselves family. We're all each other have. Or in my case *had*, because my dear mother appeared from out of the blue several months ago, after all this time."

"I take it you're not especially pleased."

"Let's just say it's not easy to accept. I won't pretend that all is rosy, even though Abigail Winehouse might. I have certain things to work out."

"How would you feel if she up and left and you'd never see her again?" Callie asked quietly.

Rand frowned. He'd never considered that. How

would he feel? Happy, sad, relieved, or maybe abandoned again?

Memories of how he used to lie awake in the orphanage and dream of his mother one day coming to get him created trenches in his brain. Every part of his being had cried out for someone to belong to, to be loved by—to be special, to matter.

In a lot of ways, that was why he'd opted to buy a saloon instead of a ranch. He wanted to surround himself with people, ever looking, ever hopeful he'd find what he most yearned for.

His gaze found Callie. Kind of ironic that he hadn't discovered her in town but out on the ranch, where he'd never expected it.

But why exactly hadn't he looked for his mother after escaping from that orphan train with Cooper and Brett? Even though he was only eleven at the time, he knew she was alive somewhere. He had her name.

Why hadn't he wanted to find her?

He squirmed in his chair. Maybe he'd been afraid of what he'd find? That she'd reject him again?

Maybe he'd stayed away from her because the truth would've hurt too much. Part of him didn't want to examine these questions too closely.

The uncomfortable ache in his chest made him lose his appetite. He needed some fresh air. Without a word, he pulled on his coat and disappeared into the black night.

∽

Callie readied for bed a while later. Rand still hadn't returned. She suspected the question she posed to him about his mother had upset him. Whatever the problem was between mother and son went far deeper than even he had seemed to realize. She wished she'd kept her mouth shut and her nose out of things that didn't concern her.

But Rand intrigued her. She'd never known a more generous, caring man. It hurt her to watch him wrestle with some inner demon and not be able to help him.

What kind of mother would leave her son in an orphanage? Maybe the same conniving, spiteful kind as her stepmother, Liza. Icy fingers crept up Callie's spine.

Lord help him if this was true. She prayed that whatever was between the son and his mother could find resolution soon.

She knew what happened when it didn't come, the holes that hate and anger left. She'd said too much tonight. Except for Rand now, few had ever known why she hid in her stepmother's kitchen so often. In truth, the room had been her sanctuary. She thought of Cook and wondered about the dear lady. Lord knows, Liza made life in that house a living hell.

Callie prepared to crawl in beside a softly snoring Toby when she heard the back door open. The tension inside her eased. She'd be able to sleep now.

Rand had returned.

Blowing out the lamp beside the bed, she slid beneath the quilts. Memories of Rand's vivid blue eyes banished the cold from her body. She'd never felt this safe with any man before. It felt real nice. She'd waited a long time for someone like Rand. She didn't know what to make of it, so she forced herself to close her eyes and try to sleep.

A cold dawn came far too soon. She rose and dressed, dreading a trek outside for wood for the stove. Making coffee would be first on her list. She tiptoed into the dim kitchen and stumbled over something, nearly falling on her face.

An animal's sharp yelp sent alarm ricocheting through her heart. She grabbed for the first thing she could find—her broom—and wielded it like a club.

Rand's soft chuckle filled the room. She hadn't even seen him sitting at the table. He struck a match. When he lit the lamp, a warm glow spread over the kitchen.

"You gonna beat the poor critter to death with a broom?"

The growling way Rand had of talking sent delicious quivers along her nerve endings. Then a dog's velvety tongue licked her hand, bringing her focus back to what it *should* be on: the furred intruder in her kitchen. "Where did the dog come from? It wasn't here when I went to bed."

"She."

"She what?"

"You called our furry friend an it. She's a female."

Finally, Callie thought to put the broom away. "Begging your pardon. Where did *she* come from? If it's not too much to ask."

"Found her last night when I went out for some fresh air. She was bleeding. Looked like she'd tangled with a wild varmint. I doctored her a little and brought her inside, since it was far too cold to leave her out in the elements."

Callie knelt and inspected what appeared to be a

scraggly golden retriever. The retriever was covered with ticks and cockleburs. She'd evidently been out in the woods for a long while, maybe her whole life. The hound touched her cold nose to Callie's hand.

Staring into the dog's expressive brown eyes, Callie stroked behind the ears and crooned. "You're such a loving girl, aren't you? We'll get you cleaned up and brushed, just wait and see. Rand, she's so sweet."

"That she is," Rand agreed. "Broke my heart when I saw the whimpering, bloody mess shivering by the barn door."

"How old do you think she is?"

"Doubt if she's more than a year."

"What's her name?"

"She hasn't told me that yet. She's pretty shy. But she did say that she likes it here."

"Ha, ha. You're a funny man."

Rand squatted down beside Callie, resting on the back of his heels. "Thought I'd let Toby do the naming honors."

Only a whisper of distance separated them. With Rand so close, she could smell the fresh air that lingered on him, the faint fragrance of coffee and… shaving soap? She hadn't expected that, and it caught her by surprise. A quick glance from beneath her lashes revealed that he'd indeed shaved. This was the first time she'd gotten an unobstructed view of his firm, square jaw.

The solid warmth of Rand's shoulder brushed hers, and a heated flush climbed to Callie's face. His very kissable lips were much too close.

Getting to her feet before she succumbed to

temptation, she glanced around the kitchen. He'd already brought in wood, a low fire burned in the stove, the coffee was made, and a half-full cup sat on the table where she'd seen him sitting.

In the next room she noticed a fire in the fireplace and the pile of neatly folded blankets.

"You haven't been to bed, have you?"

Sighing, Rand got slowly to his feet and retrieved his coffee cup, taking a swallow. "Had too much thinking to do. I'm surprised you didn't hear me roaming around all night."

Anger at Rand's mother rose. What she'd done, whether she meant to or not, had come near to destroying her son. What was she like? Callie couldn't help but wonder.

"You didn't have to do my chores." She yanked a skillet off the shelf beside the stove. "Some hired help I am."

"It wasn't any trouble. I was already up." He refilled his cup and set the empty pot to the side. "Besides," he said, grinning, "I left the cooking for you. Wouldn't even dare make a mess of that."

"Good. Now sit down and stay out of my way."

"Yes, ma'am." Still grinning, Rand dropped back into his place at the table. Ruffling the dog's ears, he said, "You hear that, hound? We've just been given a boot to our backsides."

Grabbing the empty coffeepot, Callie filled it with water and put more on to boil just as Toby wandered into the kitchen, rubbing his eyes.

The boy noticed the new resident right away. His eyes widened. "A dog! Oh boy! Can we keep him?"

"Her," Callie and Rand said at the same time.

"I want you to think of a good name for her," Rand said. "Something real good. Not like Yellow Dog or Outlaw or Bullet."

Toby squinched up his eyes and glanced around the kitchen, thinking hard. "Biscuit!"

The dog gave a sharp bark and ran up to the youngster.

"Well, I think she knows her name." Rand grinned. "Couldn't have thought of a better one myself."

Callie's heart filled with love as she watched Toby. He'd needed something to get his mind off his rotten outlaw father. A son needed a father, but not one like Nate. No kid deserved a parent like that.

It suddenly occurred to her that perhaps Rand's mother had left him because she thought herself wrong to raise him. But surely she hadn't been as unworthy as Nate. No one was.

Nate Fleming had robbed every train, bank, packhorse, and stagecoach he came across, killing anyone who got in his way. He'd bragged that everyone in his family since 1764 had followed the lawless path. It all started with a pirate grandfather who plundered and murdered up and down the eastern seaboard. Even his mother and his sisters had embraced the outlaw lifestyle. His mother, Big Foot Lucy, had established quite a reputation before the law ruined her promising career.

None of them tended to live past the ripe old age of thirty-eight, either succumbing to bullet wounds or a hanging, whichever came first.

Nate had another think coming if he thought she'd let him drag Toby down with him. Her nephew would get a chance to amount to something. Callie would see to it. She would have, even if she hadn't pledged that to her sister.

Some things were just right, and this was one of them.

"Toby, don't get too close to Biscuit until we get these ticks and burrs off her," Callie said firmly.

"I'll give her a bath after we eat and get her cleaned up real good," Rand promised. "Until then, mind your mama."

"Awww, yes, sir." Toby sat down at the table. Biscuit's nails clicked on the floor as she padded over and rested her muzzle on Toby's leg, looking just as dejected as the boy.

Callie turned back to getting breakfast on the table for her hungry men. But when she realized she'd counted Rand as part of her family, a stillness came over her. She raised her gaze and fell smack into Rand's blue eyes. The seriousness with which he studied her created a warmth that didn't come from the cookstove.

What was this thing between them?

Or was she simply seeing something that wasn't there?

Lord help her if she knew.

Putting away the confusion, she turned to something she understood—cooking up hot, nourishing food for Toby's and Rand's bellies.

Rand rose, pulled on his coat, and announced he was going out in the raw, overcast day to milk the cow.

By the time he came back in, she had plates of ham, eggs, and biscuits on the table. In short order, she had them fed and agreed that Biscuit could have her bath in the warm kitchen as soon as she finished the dishes.

A damp chill hung in the air despite the fire in the stove.

A chill that went all the way down to her bones.

A strong premonition swept over Callie, terrifying her to the marrow. Evil stalked them like some wild beast, intent on feasting upon their carcasses.

She couldn't stop it, not even if she ran as far and as fast as she could.

Death and disaster would hunt her down.

Nate was coming.

Icy edges of fear gnawing into her veins told her so.

Six

THE NEXT FEW DAYS, CALLIE LOOKED FOR HER MOTH-er's treasure box every chance she got, but still the hiding place eluded her. If only her mother had told them where she was putting it.

On this day, Callie started a systematic search the minute Rand went outside to tear off rotted boards from the barn in preparation for repairs. With the two horses, a cow, and now a dog, he needed a place for them that wasn't about ready to fall down. He'd already put in an order for some lumber. The new sawmill in Battle Creek would have it cut and ready for pickup in a week.

She thought it smart of him to order only what he needed a little at a time. But then, Rand was not missing anything in the brains department.

Her search for the treasure chest resumed in the downstairs rooms. She checked for loose floorboards and fireplace bricks. Then she began running her fingers along the walls for hidden compartments. Having no furniture yet made it easy, especially with Toby outside with Rand and Biscuit.

When nothing came to light, she stood back and tried to put herself in her mother's shoes. She doubted the woman would've buried it outside, because of the heavy rains that summer. Due to the soggy ground, they'd had to wait three days to bury Nora Quinn Powers. She remembered how impatient her stepfather had been, the way he'd railed at everyone.

Looking back now, she realized the reason he'd fought the delay had been because he intended to marry Liza as soon as possible. That meant he'd known the socialite months, maybe even a year, before his wife died.

And he'd had the nerve to chastise and lock Callie in the basement for three days for letting Marcus Wolfforth kiss her after he'd given that louse Andrew Jameson permission to come courting. Fury swept through her.

She ran to her room and jerked on the coat that Rand had bought. She had to find her mother's grave. She wouldn't waste another second.

Marching to the barn, she stopped to gather Toby. "Let's go for a walk."

"Where to?" The boy squinted up at her.

Callie's breath caught in her throat. He was the spitting image of Nate Fleming, right down to the same mannerisms. Even had his father's way of walking. Toby would be very handsome one day.

Dear God, just don't let him be an outlaw.

Rand leaned against the side of the barn, watching. Though the breeze carried a chill, he'd removed his jacket and now wiped beads of sweat from his forehead. The muscles in his upper arms strained his shirt.

Riveted by the sight of both boy and rancher, she struggled to get her thoughts back on track. "Exploring. Who knows what we might find. At the least we'll have an adventure."

"Can Biscuit come?"

"Absolutely. I'll bet she's an expert at finding hidden things."

"Don't go too far," Rand cautioned in a low voice. "I've noticed a lot of mountain-lion tracks lately."

"Thanks. We'll stay close."

Toby laid down the hammer and they set off. A faint recollection of the house being visible from the gravesite gave her the general vicinity. While they trekked through the trees, she kept a sharp eye out for predators, both the wild and the outlaw kind.

Again, relying on an eight-year-old's faded memory proved quite a task. She'd scoured several areas before Toby accidentally stumbled over it. With a cry, he landed face-first in a pile of dead leaves and dank earth. She brushed him off while Biscuit licked his face as though checking for injuries.

Though Edmund Powers had promised to put a headstone on the grave, the only thing marking it was the cross fashioned from rocks that she and Claire had laid on top of the burial spot.

Tears pricked her eyes and trickled down her cheeks. Her mother deserved more than to be forgotten and betrayed by a faithless husband.

Kneeling, she ran her hands lovingly over the crude marker.

Toby stood watching. "Ma'am? Why are you sad? It's only some dumb ol' rocks."

Callie wished she could explain, but the youngster wasn't old enough to understand yet that his grandmother's bones lay beneath the soil. She smiled up at Toby. "I know, but they're arranged in a pretty cross."

"Who did it?"

"Your mother and I."

"She did? Why?"

"To mark the spot so we could find it." Callie got to her feet and draped an arm around the boy's shoulders.

"I'm sad too," Toby said. "I miss Mama."

Callie kissed the top of his head. "So do I."

"Aunt Callie, why do people have to die, anyway?"

"I wish I knew. I wish I knew." A strangled sob rose.

Then the brush rustled. Something was coming into the small clearing.

Her heart pounded as she looked around for a weapon.

"Get behind me, Toby." She pushed him away from the danger, though a mountain lion would make quick work of her and get him anyway. Still, she'd give her all to protect him.

Relief swept through her when Rand emerged from the thicket with a rifle.

She turned and brushed away the lingering tears before she faced him.

"Got worried about you," he said, peering curiously at her. "Is everything all right?"

"We're fine. Thanks for coming."

"We found a cross," Toby piped up.

"You don't say." He moved around Callie to look at it. "I didn't know this was here. Wonder who put it there?"

"My mama an' aunt."

Callie could've strangled the boy. Toby looked so pleased with himself and what he'd divulged. "It's nothing. We'd better get back. I just remembered I was going to bake a pie for supper."

"A pie! Oh boy!" Toby gave a whoop and a holler.

"Come then. The day's going fast," she said, moving toward the house. When she noticed Rand wasn't behind them, she turned. "You coming, Rand?"

"I'll be along. Want to check for signs of mountain lions." He was staring curiously at the grave though and not looking for wild-animal tracks at all.

She kicked herself for not being more careful. He was too smart. The truth she'd sought to hide was most certainly going to be uncovered.

And she didn't know how to stop it.

❧

Rand's gaze followed Callie. Only when she disappeared from view did he turn back to the grave. He'd heard everything. No wonder Toby always called her ma'am and not mama. He wasn't her child—the boy was her nephew. Though she hadn't exactly lied, she'd let him think that the boy was hers. Probably to protect them.

So, who was Toby's mother and how had she died?

And who rested in this grave?

He'd seen Callie's tears, though she'd been quick to turn away. The person buried here was very special to her.

Did that mean that Callie had once lived here on this land?

This grave and the fact she'd picked the Last Hope

as a hideout told him that it was very possible. And the possibility existed that she might even have a claim to the property. He wasn't sure how he felt about that.

He knew he wouldn't fight her for it. If this land belonged to her, she could have it.

It bothered him that she wouldn't confide in him, though. How could he protect her and Toby with his hands tied behind his back?

A deep sigh rose. Maybe he should talk to Cooper and Brett about the matter. A person without anything to gain out of this dilemma could assess it more calmly.

Over the next hour, he built a makeshift fence around the plot. It simply seemed the thing to do. When he got back to the house, he laid his rifle within reach and resumed removing the rotten boards from the barn. He didn't see any sign of Callie or Toby or the dog. Probably in the house. Thoughts of hot apple pie for supper made him work faster.

His mind kept returning to what he'd learned and he wondered what he should do. Confront Callie or pretend he hadn't seen or heard anything?

If he told her what he knew and suspected, he was sure she'd run. She'd certainly threatened to if he started digging.

The pretty lady had his back up against the wall. She held all the cards. What was worse…she knew it. *Damnation!*

He caught movement out of the corner of his eye and reached for the rifle before he recognized Brett. "Howdy, brother. A whole ranch full of prime horse-flesh and you're walking?"

Brett grinned. "Needed the exercise. Gettin' fat."

Rand took in Brett's lean body. "Yeah, I can see that. I do think I see a fat head up there."

"If that's supposed to get my goat, you need to try again."

The leather bundle strapped on Brett's back and the long poles his brother dragged behind him drew Rand's curiosity. "What's that you're hauling? Did you decide to become a nomad?"

Brett removed the bundle. "This is for young Toby. I recalled how special mine is to me when I got it last year after deciding to embrace my roots. Thought I'd set it up here in the yard for him to play in. Pretending to be an Indian is a sight better than playing outlaws."

"I agree. But if you think his mama will let him sleep out here in a tepee, you need to lay off the peyote."

"Miss Callie does seem awful protective."

"Probably with good reason." Rand told him about the grave and what he'd learned. "I'm not sure what I should do now."

"Nothing. Let her come to you. If you go to her with demands, she'll blow up like a mule with a belly full of green apples. Most likely she'll leave."

"I wish she'd trust me."

"She does, she just doesn't know it yet. If the lady didn't, she'd never have agreed to stay for even a little while."

"How did you get to be the smart one, Brett?"

"When I decided you, Cooper, and me would become a family."

"Oh no, I decided that. You can't take the credit. And I'm also the best-looking."

Brett raised a dark eyebrow. "Says who?"

"Says the one who hasn't decided he's fat."

Toby barreled out the kitchen door, trailed by Biscuit. "What'cha doin'?"

"Hi, pardner." Brett ruffled Toby's dark hair. "I brought you something."

"What is it?"

"Your very own tepee."

"To keep?" Toby's eyes widened and his big grin spread.

"Maybe. We'll see how it goes. If you mind your elders, you can keep it. If not, I'll have to take it back."

"I'm the best boy in the whole world."

Brett's grunt seemed to say that time would tell as he arranged twelve long poles on the ground and began tying the tops of three together with a length of rawhide. "Where do you want to put this, Rand?"

"Let's move it over by the woodpile, where it's out of the way." He was going to be the only white man with an Indian tepee on his ranch. How had this sorry state of affairs come to pass? But he wouldn't say no. It meant too much to Brett and to Toby.

Callie came from the house looking fit to be tied. "Hello, Brett. I hope this isn't what it looks like."

"Miss Callie, I wanted something special for Toby to play in, that's all. If you draw the line at him sleeping out here, that's all right. It's up to you to decide when and how often you want the boy to use it." Brett gave her a smile. "I'd never undermine you."

"This could be very magical to a child," Rand said gently.

"Please, ma'am?" Toby begged. "I wanna be an Indian."

Biscuit gave a loud whine and spun around in a circle as though she too was adding her two cents' worth.

"Please?" Toby persisted.

When she lifted her eyes to Rand, he gave her a lopsided grin and a wink. Getting tangled up in her warm whiskey gaze could be quite pleasurable, he found.

"Oh, all right." Callie threw up her hands. "But I won't have you sleeping out here, young man. You'll play in it only when I give you permission. And you'll have chores to do each day before you can play. Understand?"

"Yes, ma'am."

"It's too dangerous out here at night anyway, with that mountain lion hanging around," Rand said. "I'll keep an eye on him during the day. I don't want you to worry."

Toby hugged Callie, then threw his arms around Brett's waist. "Thank you. I'm glad we came here."

Brett returned Toby's hug, then knelt to rub Biscuit's head. "Now tell me where you got such a fine-looking animal."

Rand stood watching the pint-sized squirt relay what little facts he knew. He already loved this little kid. Whatever had happened to them, it made him happy that he could help bring a light to the boy's eyes. He remembered how dull they'd been when he'd first found them in the run-down bunkhouse last week. His mind turned back time to the days following his, Cooper's, and Brett's escape from the orphan train. To avoid detection, they'd slept during the day and traveled by the light of the moon, eating food whenever they found some or managed to kill a rabbit or squirrel. Cooper was always the one to watch over them and fight when things called for it. He'd once tried to kill Tolbert Early in a bathhouse for attacking Brett.

Toby had that same protective instinct. Rand only prayed he could help the boy stay a boy a while longer. Once he became a man, he could never go back.

"Where are you, brother?" Brett asked.

"Just thinking that you'd best explain what we need to do."

With Biscuit supervising and pretty much getting in the way, they all pitched in erecting the tepee, which was made from buffalo hides.

Working side by side with Callie proved to be the best part. Each time their hands touched, a current ran up Rand's arm. He couldn't imagine what might happen if the touching involved a bed and the scent of night around them. He'd probably just explode faster than a load of nitroglycerin. Likely find pieces of him three states over.

The haunted look had begun to fade from her eyes a little, and she wasn't as tense and anxious as when they first arrived.

Maybe, just maybe, the fear would be gone soon.

And then he intended to kiss the daylights out of her.

Of course he'd go slow. He closed his eyes and watched it play out in his head.

He'd start by kissing each eyelid, then move to her shell-like ears and trail kisses down her long slender throat.

Tiny nibbles at the corners of her mouth.

Trace the seam with his tongue.

Breathe her fragrance.

Whisper tender words.

Only then would he press his lips fully against hers and take all that she wanted to give.

And then...

"Rand!"

It took a minute to sink in that someone was trying to get his attention. "What?"

"Where did you go?" Brett asked. "I need you to help me get these sewn buffalo hides around this tripod and cone I've made. Of course, if you'd rather take a nap—"

"Just show me what to do," Rand snapped.

As they worked, Rand's gaze kept straying to Callie's soft, round curves. The woman was going to be the death of him yet.

Even so, he was realizing he'd die a happy man if he could only get a taste of her lips.

Seven

CALLIE PAUSED IN THE SUPPER PREPARATIONS TO GAZE through the kitchen window. This was the part of day her grandfather used to call half-light or in the gloaming.

Strange disquiet grated along her nerve endings. Like the sky, her life was in the gloaming and had been since that fateful night she lost her reason for living, stuck between moving forward and the dark shadows of pain and fear strangling her.

Last year, she'd attended a reading of "In the Gloaming" by Meta Orred, a well-known Scottish poet, and two short lines came to her now: *When the winds are sobbing faintly / With a gentle unknown woe…*

The words had brought foreboding then as they did again now. Even through the thick windowpane, she could hear the breeze brushing the naked limbs of the trees, wailing, warning, wishing.

Lost in her thoughts, she was startled when Brett entered with his hat in his hands. He'd left Rand and Toby outside. This was the first time she'd been alone with Rand's brother, and she didn't quite know what to say.

She stuck with a safe subject. "Will you take supper with us, Brett?"

"I'm sorry, Miss Callie, but I need to start heading back, since I walked over. Have chores to do. Didn't mean to be here this long. I just wanted to thank you for your hospitality."

"You should be thanking Rand, not me. I only work here."

"All the same, even a dyed-in-the-wool bachelor who lives in a tepee knows who rules the roost. Rand is a lucky man."

"I wouldn't know."

"I would." Brett stood with his feet braced apart. He seemed a little uncomfortable. "I want you to understand that I never meant to push the tepee on you. I'm sure you could've wrung my neck."

"True, I wasn't thrilled. But I can see how much it means to Toby. He can use more reasons to smile and laugh and be a boy. Thank you for giving him that."

"Ma'am, I hope you don't take this the wrong way. I know you're running from something, something that terrifies you."

When she opened her mouth to speak, he held up his hand. "No, please let me finish. I recognize the signs. Just know that you can tell me anything, and it'll stay between us if that's the way you want it. You can trust me. I'll also never let anything or anyone hurt you or Toby. That is my solemn promise."

Sudden tears sprang into Callie's eyes and her bottom lip quivered. "You don't know how much I thank you," she whispered.

The big Indian covered the few steps between them

and engulfed her in a stiff hug, the kind between new friends. Then he nodded and left as quietly as he'd entered. She knew he'd meant every word. Brett Liberty would fight for her if she gave the signal.

Though Rand hadn't voiced it, she knew he would also. She'd seen quiet commitment in his eyes and in the little things he did. No one had cared about her welfare in such a long time.

She regretted that he'd caught her at the grave. How much had he overheard? If she stayed, she'd have to tell him about Nate and the fact that she once lived here. Very possibly she'd have to face his anger for not trusting him enough.

Also, if she stayed, she would only bring trouble to Rand's door. Nate would surely kill him when he came. She wouldn't let that happen. The price for his generosity and kindness would not be death.

But if she left, which seemed more likely each day that passed, where would she go? Who would take them in? Would anyone?

She cursed Edmund Powers, who'd turned her out and left her without funds.

Unshed tears blurred her vision. Having to leave this quiet sanctuary would kill her. Having to leave the man whose laughing blue eyes buckled her knees would rip her heart to shreds.

How had she come to care so deeply for him?

～

Over the next few days, Callie devoted her time to searching for her mother's box. When the weather permitted, Toby spent nearly every second that she allowed him out in his tepee with Biscuit. That boy loved both the tepee and the retriever dearly.

She and Rand had come up with a list of simple chores for Toby before he could play. Gathering the eggs, sweeping the porch, feeding and watering his dog, and hauling in one bucket of water a day provided valuable structure for him. On a ranch, everyone had to contribute to the running of it. She and Claire had had chores. Sure, they'd griped and complained, but having tasks to do had shaped them into the women they became.

She had moved upstairs to begin searching the upper rooms when she saw two heavily laden wagons pulling up to the house. Immediately, her muscles clenched in alarm. Rand came from the barn to meet them.

Only when she saw his wide grin did she relax. He evidently knew these men. She hurried downstairs.

Rand opened the door as she came into the kitchen. "The furniture is here. I would count it as a favor if you would help supervise the placement. Women seem to have a gift about these things."

"I'd be happy to. But surely you have an idea where you want some of it."

"Nope. Wherever you decide will suit me fine."

Callie quickly glanced out the door for Toby, making sure he wasn't in the way, then busied herself. Pretending she was lady of the manor, she told the men where to put the sofa, settee, and sideboard. A tall chest with a mirror, a wardrobe, an oak washstand, and one of the largest beds she'd ever seen went upstairs into the room that would be Rand's.

Rand carried in a rocking chair. "I don't know

where this came from, as well as some of the other pieces. I certainly didn't order this rocker or sideboard, but Homer flat refuses to lug them back into town. I guess this chair belongs to you now, Callie."

It was odd how he kept forgetting she didn't plan on being there long. Or maybe he deliberately refused to think of her as temporary. It seemed to be some sort of crazy dance they silently did.

He couldn't remember.

She couldn't let herself forget.

❧

Rand stared at Callie during supper that evening. She was a mystery. For someone who kept herself and her feelings sternly in check, why had she let his brother Brett hug her? He'd watched the brief display of affection and wondered at Brett's ability to break through her granite resolve. Rand certainly hadn't gotten anywhere, and he wished he knew his brother's secret. Frankly, it stuck in his craw.

Maybe the fact that they were both quiet people had something to do with it. He intended to find out next time he saw Brett.

They finished eating and Rand helped Callie with the dishes. "Sit with me in the parlor, Callie. Try out your new rocking chair."

"I suppose I can do that."

A short time later, Rand added more wood to the fire and sat down on the cowhide sofa. He ran his hand across the buttery soft leather. This didn't fit in with the peeling wallpaper and rough planks on the floor. Nowhere in his memory could he recall buying anything this fine. It and the matching settee were beyond his means.

An uneasiness drifted over him.

Of course. His mother.

Abigail had interfered again. He'd bet his last dollar. Tomorrow, he meant to straighten her out. But tonight he was going to enjoy his makeshift family. Rand closed his eyes and let contentment wash over him in waves. He'd never had a real home before, and though it was a bit strange, it was definitely nice.

Toby and Biscuit sprawled on the floor in front of the fire that crackled and popped. Both appeared to be tuckered out.

Callie's rocker creaked softly with each back-and-forth movement. "Rand, please feel free to rearrange the furniture if I didn't put it where you wanted."

"I'm one hundred percent satisfied. You did a great job. Like I said, women seem to have a knack for this."

"Since you have a bed now, you'll probably want to sleep upstairs."

Was that a hint she preferred him up there? Maybe she'd feel safer. "I reckon so."

"Good. I'm sure the bed will be far more comfortable than the hard floor. And warmer also. I took the liberty of spreading your quilts on it."

"Thank you. I intended to put the tall chest and mirror in your room. You need it far more. I'll move it."

The stubborn tilt of her chin appeared. "You will not. I manage just fine."

"You're a stubborn woman, Callie." But, oh, such a pretty one. Those eyes the color of warm whiskey could do things to a man. Right now, they were heating his blood and making his heart pound like hundreds of stampeding horses.

"I daresay you're equally bent on getting your way."

"You never let me have the last word, do you?" he growled.

Her mouth spread in a smile. "Not if I can help it."

Rand leaned forward, propping his elbows on his thighs. "Callie, are you happy here?"

"Yes. It's nice. How about you? Do you miss the lively atmosphere of the saloon? The most excitement you have here is watching the logs turn to ash in the fireplace."

"I wouldn't trade this for anything. I have no regrets. I found everything I ever wanted." He hoped she couldn't read between the lines or else he'd scare her into leaving. That would devastate him.

He couldn't imagine how lonely it would be without her.

On some gut level, he realized Callie could be the woman for him if, or when, he ever got over his fear. His mind knew it and his heart for damn sure knew it. But he couldn't get past his vow to keep his heart walled off against the pain. He couldn't risk it.

One day his worst nightmare would happen. He didn't delude himself. She would leave.

The thought that kept plunging icy, paralyzing fear into him was the thought of waking up one morning and finding that Callie had taken Toby and vanished.

If that happened, he knew the loneliness would descend like a flock of vultures.

"Rand," Callie said softly. "Toby's fallen asleep."

"I'll carry him to bed." He rose and lifted the sleeping boy. Biscuit looked up and chuffed, then went back to sleep.

Callie went ahead and turned down the bed. Rand laid him down and pulled the covers over him, then Callie leaned to kiss Toby's forehead. They both stood in the doorway watching the youngster sleep.

Her scent wrapped around Rand like a warm blanket.

"Between that tepee and Biscuit, Toby is in pure heaven," she murmured. "Thank you."

Emboldened, Rand slipped his arm around her waist. Having her so near, touching her, was pure torture. He took the fact that she didn't slap him senseless as a sign she didn't object.

When she glanced up into his eyes, he brushed a light kiss across the warm lips that drove him wild with desire.

She melted against him as he drew her closer. For a brief moment, she rested her head on his chest. Rand kissed the top of her silky head, breathing in her fragrance. He'd found out what heaven was like.

But Callie quickly stepped back as though remembering where she was. "We can't do this, Rand. I can't."

"Sorry. Got carried away." He raked his fingers through his hair, calling himself every name he could think of. His impatience had ruined his chances.

She moved into the kitchen and pulled out a chair. "I made it clear this arrangement is only temporary."

Finding a cup, Rand poured the last of the coffee and sat down. "I hoped you'd reconsider."

"I'm still going to leave. I can't stay."

"Promise me one thing."

"If I can."

"All I ask is that you won't slip out without saying good-bye." He struggled to keep the thickness that was strangling him out of his voice. "Please…for God's sake, don't let me wake up one morning and find no sign of you anywhere. Can you do this one thing?"

"I may not have time—"

"Let me help you. I can fix whatever the problem is."

"No one can fix it," she said sharply. "No one."

"If you'll just tell me, we can work it out together. Cooper is the law in Battle Creek, and Brett is an excellent tracker. Let us help." He knew he was begging, but it didn't matter.

Nothing mattered except making sure he kept this complicated, maddening woman in his life. Dear God, he had to unlock her secret before it was too late, before she walked out.

Callie made him feel he deserved to be loved, that he wasn't a failure, that he could measure up to the man he wanted to be like—Isaac Daffern, his mentor and friend.

"I know what it's like to run." Rand covered Callie's hand with his. "When I was eleven years old, the orphanage put some of us on an orphan train bound for Nebraska. Cooper and Brett were on it too. Right outside a little town in Illinois, we jumped off the train. Keeping one step ahead of the people who were searching for us, we walked for weeks to Hannibal, Missouri. There we got jobs in a bathhouse."

Rand paused, remembering the events. "A man, Tolbert Early, attacked Brett, who was only eight, for taking his watch. Which he didn't, of course.

Cooper shot Early and we ran for our lives. That sheriff was out for blood. We were lucky to have escaped his clutches. Sometimes in the dead of night, I still recall the fear and terror. Until Early showed up back in the spring, Cooper swore he'd killed him. A rancher by the name of Isaac Daffern saved us back then. Took us in and gave us a home. He taught us how to be men and how it felt to have a father. We worshipped Isaac."

"What happened to Isaac?"

"He got sick. Doctors called it influenza. When he died, he left each of us four hundred dollars in his will. Cooper and Brett bought their ranches. I bought the saloon."

"And Tolbert Early, the man who attacked Brett?"

"Brett killed him after he kidnapped Delta Dandridge."

"Cooper's wife?"

"Yes, only they weren't married at the time. We were lucky to have saved her. If ever evil saturated every nook and cranny of a person's heart, it did Tolbert Early's."

All the color drained from Callie's face, leaving it a sickly hue.

"I've frightened you," he said. "You don't have to worry though; he can't hurt you. He can't hurt anyone. His vile, worm-eaten bones lie under six feet of dirt."

"I do have to worry. Early wasn't the only evil person."

Her whispered words drove a chunk of ice into Rand's heart, cutting off the ability to breathe. "What do you mean?"

She wearily brushed her hand over her eyes.

"Sometimes discipline turns to abuse. I've said too much."

No, she hadn't said nearly enough.

Who was this villainous person and why was she so terrified of him? What had he done?

Rand fought with the need to pull her against his chest and wrap his arms around her. He would protect her until blood no longer ran in his veins.

Whoever wanted to harm her would have to go through him.

And he'd go through hell for her.

Eight

CALLIE TOSSED AND TURNED ALL NIGHT. THE FEATHERY kiss Rand had pressed to her lips had somehow seared into her brain. She didn't seem able to get it out.

One would think she'd never been kissed before, never known the scent of a man, never felt a man's hand on hers. Though certainly nothing comparable to Rand, she'd once had all that. But Richard Farrington had left her high and dry, as had Marcus Wolfforth, off to see the world, he'd claimed. She'd once thought she might have a future with one of them. Recently she learned that her stepfather had paid to make both men vanish.

Her thoughts turned to Claire. Her twin had been the wild one, attracted to the wrong kind of man. Claire had yearned for excitement and danger, and Nate Fleming certainly supplied a steady diet of that. By the time Claire saw through the outlaw, it was too late. She was in his clutches. At least she'd done what she could to save Toby.

Forget danger and thrills. Callie would take someone steady like Rand any day. This tall rancher was different from anyone she'd ever met.

And his kiss, little more than a brush of his lips, had ignited a fire inside her. She couldn't imagine what a full-fledged kiss would do, though she longed to find out.

Only she couldn't, wouldn't, let that happen again. She had to keep these dangerous desires from rising to the surface. They were employee and employer. She'd do well to brand that on her memory. He was her boss. She was his cook. Nothing more. Period.

But no matter how hard she tried, she couldn't forget the warmth of his lips and the heat of his body that had banished the chill from hers.

There was no getting around the fact that she enjoyed being with Rand. She'd never known anyone who appreciated the smallest things, like hot biscuits and apple pie and putting a smile on Toby's face. She didn't like just one thing about him; it was the hundreds of small things that someone else might not notice.

With a smile on her face, she finally drifted to sleep.

Around midmorning the following day, Callie heard a knock on the front door. For a minute, she stood frozen. Not once since she'd started living in Rand's house had anyone ever come to the front door.

Rand had left early, saying he probably wouldn't be back until suppertime. He'd taken the wagon, so she assumed he'd gone after the lumber he'd ordered, although he hadn't said as much.

Twisting her hands, she hesitated, torn between running out to get Toby from the tepee and hiding or seeing who the person was.

But Nate wouldn't waste time knocking; he'd simply kick the door in and take whatever he came for. She forced herself to relax. Finally, smoothing her hair, she went to see who it was. A regal, dark-haired woman dressed in finery stood there.

"I'm sorry," the caller said in a throaty voice. "I'm wondering if I have the right place. Is this where Rand Sinclair lives?"

"This is his ranch, but he's not here at the moment."

"Oh dear. I'd known it was a long shot, but I really wanted to speak to him. I'm his mother, Abigail Sinclair."

"Won't you come in, Mrs. Sinclair?"

"Abigail. Please. I haven't been Mrs. Anyone for a very long time. I'll only stay a moment to let my horse rest before I head back to town."

Callie led Abigail into the parlor and motioned her toward the cowhide settee. Callie took the rocker, letting her gaze rest on the mother who created such conflicting emotions in Rand.

Even though more than a few streaks of gray ran through her dark hair, Abigail Sinclair was stunningly beautiful. Callie put her age somewhere around mid-forties. Her visitor's long, slender fingers removed her leather gloves while her sweeping glance took in the squalor of the peeling wallpaper and warped floor.

"I'm sure you're wondering who I am and why I answered Rand's—Mr. Sinclair's—door. I'm Callie. I cook for him and keep his house."

Finally, Abigail gave Callie her attention. "I see. I'm sure he'll need a housekeeper when he gets this ranch going. I didn't realize it was in such poor shape. But the furniture is nice, real nice."

Callie's dander rose. She wanted to show the disapproving woman the door and tell her Rand was doing the best he could. About everything. "He understands he has a lot of work in front of him, Abigail. It'll take time to fix it up. You should see how hard he works. From daylight until dark every day."

"My dear, you certainly don't need to sell me on my son. He takes after his father. I hate to say that stubbornness is a Sinclair trait. Jack has been gone for twenty-three years now, but I'll never forget that man. Rand was only five when Jack passed." Abigail ran her fingers over the smooth leather of the settee and sighed. "I can make things so much easier for Rand, if he'd only let me."

"A man has to have his pride, even if he has little else," Callie said softly.

"Pride has its limits. It can't repair a roof or put up a fence." Deep sadness seeped into Abigail's voice. "And it sure can't mend the past."

Callie opened her mouth to comfort the woman when Toby ran into the house, not stopping until he reached the parlor. "Ma'am, come quick!"

"What is it?" Shards of fear pierced Callie's heart. She jumped to her feet and hurried after Toby.

"A big kitty. The biggest I ever saw." Tears rolled down his cheeks. "It'll kill Biscuit. Please don't let it."

She slowly opened the back door. The hackles on Biscuit's neck stood up straight as deep growls rumbled from her throat. She'd faced off against the mountain lion Rand had warned them about, positioning herself between the cat and the door to the kitchen. No one had to tell Callie the dog would give her life protecting Toby.

Dear God, don't let it come to that.

"Get out of here right now," Callie yelled. "Scat!"

The lion barely spared her a glance. Callie looked around for something to throw. Spying the firewood stacked beside the cookstove, she grabbed the largest piece and threw it at the beast as hard as she could.

The missile fell off to the side, but the lion took off running, with Biscuit giving chase. Toby pushed by her and ran after the dog before she could stop him.

"Toby, stop! Come back here." Callie's skirt got tangled up in her legs and she nearly fell down the back steps. In her frustration, she came near to ripping the garment off. If Toby were to die…no, he wouldn't. She wouldn't let him.

Suddenly she was aware of Abigail Sinclair beside her, pressing a small palm pistol into her hand and apologizing. "It's not much more than a peashooter, but it's better than nothing."

Callie gripped the weapon and charged after Toby. She'd gone only three hundred yards when she saw Toby and Biscuit heading back. Her knees buckled now that the danger had passed. Hugging her nephew, she ushered him into the house along with Biscuit and Abigail Sinclair.

Handing the derringer back to Abigail and thanking her, Callie herded them back into the parlor. Toby gave Callie no argument when she ordered him to stay inside. She should have her head examined for letting him outdoors without anyone to watch him.

That was too close a call.

She stood with her arm around Toby. "Abigail, this my...son, Toby. Son, say hello to Mrs. Sinclair."

Toby's shy grin broke through his dirt-streaked face. A feather drooped from behind his ear. "Howdy, ma'am."

"I'm very happy to meet you, Toby," Abigail said. "You're a very fortunate little boy."

"I'm Indian," he announced proudly.

"I see. I suppose that explains the feather and the tepee out back." Abigail's eyebrows rose as her glance shifted to Callie.

"Toby likes to pretend. And Rand's brother, Brett, bears responsibility for the tepee." She didn't miss Abigail's frown of disapproval.

"I might've known." Abigail's eyes darkened.

Callie finally remembered her manners. No reason why she couldn't be civil. "In all the excitement, I completely forgot...would you like a cup of hot tea?"

"As a matter of fact, that would be nice."

Excusing herself, Callie filled the teakettle and got two cups from a shelf that was nothing but a painted board stuck on the wall. She checked the cups for chips or cracks. When she reached for the tea, she realized that Abigail stood in the doorway. Rand's mother took in the small room.

"I'll have it ready in a moment," Callie murmured. She was glad she'd cleaned the house that morning, especially the kitchen.

"You don't have a pump inside?" Abigail asked sharply.

"Rand—Mr. Sinclair—hauls in water."

"I'll have to speak to my son about that."

"Really, we get along just fine the way things are."

The water seemed to take a blessed hour to boil. Abigail moved on, wandering through the house, muttering to herself and shaking her dark head. Finally, with the tea in hand, Callie shepherded the woman back to the parlor, where Toby and Biscuit played in front of the fire.

Abigail took a cautious sip. "This certainly hits the spot. I became quite chilled on the ride out."

Callie couldn't say the same. She was sweating. For some reason she wanted Abigail to be proud of her son and not so critical about everything, choosing to see only the house's shabby appearance. She yearned to grab Abigail and shake her good, tell her that love was a thousand times more important than the way something looked.

Before she could form a response about the weather, the front door banged when it hit the wall.

Rand glared. "Mother, what are you doing here?"

His hard, brittle voice could've stripped whitewash off ten miles of fencerow.

Callie had leaped to her feet when the door flew open and now stood in indecision between mother and son. "I'll just go about my business. You two need to talk." She started toward the kitchen and turned. "Shall I fix lunch?"

"No," Rand said without taking his eyes off his mother. "She won't be staying."

Minutes later, Callie heard them move outside. Her heart broke for Rand. He'd been through so much and deserved a mother's love.

But was Abigail Sinclair capable of giving that?

∽

Rand firmly took his manipulative mother's arm and propelled her outside where their voices wouldn't carry. He had things to say that called for privacy.

He hated that she always made him so angry he could spit nails. Frankly, he didn't know how to cope with her. At times she was the loving mother he'd always yearned for. But those periods were short. It was never long before her self-centeredness came out again and she'd make everything about her.

The jealousy she had toward Cooper and Brett irked Rand more than anything. His brothers had been with him through thick and thin. It was a sight more than she'd done. He knew he could count on them. With Abigail, he'd learned she'd first have to determine how it might affect her before she committed.

Abigail pulled away, straightened her wool her-ringbone jacket, and jerked on her kid-leather gloves. "I'm happy to see you also. You don't have to man-handle me."

"Why did you come, Mother?"

"Is there any law against seeing where my son is living?" Abigail patted her hair.

"You know there isn't. It's all well and good, I suppose. I was on my way into town to talk to you anyway, but I happened to remember something and turned around. It's time we had a chat."

"I can't imagine what about."

"Men delivered my furniture yesterday, and lo and behold, it wasn't what I ordered. I know you switched it out. Don't bother denying it," he ground out.

"What is so wrong about a mother wanting the best for her son?" Abigail huffed.

"I'm done with your constant interference. Nothing I do is good enough to suit you." Why couldn't she spend her days telling George Lexington how to run his establishment? She'd started stepping out with the hotel owner six months ago. Rand had thought overseeing the extensive hotel renovations would keep Abigail busy and out of his affairs. He was wrong.

"I simply want to make up for all those years when—"

"When you let me rot in an orphanage because your career meant more to you than your son," he finished. "You can't make up for that. It's too late."

Though an opera singer by profession, the fledgling actress in Abigail came out. One thing about his mother was that she never did anything in half measures. She flung her outstretched arms toward the heavens as if she were taking a curtain call. "I only had one shot to get what I wanted. If I hadn't done what I had, I would've ended up a nobody, working as some common saloon girl. I left you with a friend who was supposed to look after you. How was I supposed to know Margaret would let your father have you the minute I turned my back? I couldn't very well leave you with him, considering his addiction to gambling. He was always chasing the next big win that would put him in a bracket with all the rich blue bloods he sought to be like. He was gone for days or weeks at a time, forgetting he had a wife and child. My friend Margaret promised to watch after you."

Rand hauled her hands down and held them so they couldn't fly up again. "We've gone over this until I'm sick of it. Excuses can't undo mistakes. Drop it.

I'll run my life the way I see fit. I'm capable of making my own decisions."

Tears trickled down Abigail's cheeks. "You're living in squalor. I can make things so much easier for you."

"Here's the thing, Mother." His voice softened. "I don't want it easy. I want nothing more than to find satisfaction at the end of the day, knowing I did the best I could. Everything doesn't have to be done all at once. I want to be a man, a strong one that won't fold when the going gets rough. The only way I can do these things is if you quit this infernal interfering. It has to stop. Now. Today. If not, then I can't let you be a part of my life."

She sniffled, then wailed, "I'm trying. It's not easy for me, either."

Rand reached inside his lined wool jacket, took out a handkerchief from his pocket, and handed it to her. "We're from two separate worlds, you and I. You're used to the finest of everything. I'm used to making do with whatever I can get. I'm happy with what I have. That's not to say that I don't want better. I do. I'm just content to get it a little at a time."

"Will you please keep the furniture? It's all I ask. I promise to curb my impulsiveness. I swear I will."

He glanced at the house. The cowhide furniture was really quite something. And that big four-poster bed was much better than the simple brass one he'd chosen that would have had his feet dangling off the end.

"Can't you consider the furnishings a housewarming gift?" she pleaded.

Rand thought of all the reasons why he should tell her

to take them back. In the end, he couldn't. He saw how much it meant to her. "I suppose, but no more. I mean it. Do you understand? Hands off my life. Agreed?"

"Yes."

He helped her into her buggy. "I'll ride along with you into town. Just let me thank Callie for making your tea and tell her I'm leaving. I'll be right back."

The quiet house seemed empty, and for a minute panic swept over him. Had his mother run Callie off? He had no idea what Abigail had said to her. His mother was capable of anything. Her claws might've come out along with her jealousy, which seemed to happen pretty often toward the people in Rand's life.

Then he heard the soft rattle of pans and relaxed.

Smiling, he headed for Callie's domain. "I'm off again. I want to make sure Mother gets back to Battle Creek safely. I'll bring back some knitting needles and yarn. You look like a knitter."

"Thank you. I'd love it." Callie's eyes met his. "Why did you come back so early?"

"Had a feeling something was up. Glad I did. Besides, I forgot to see if you needed something from the mercantile."

"Some potatoes and carrots if they have some. I think I used the last yesterday."

Rand twirled his hat between his hands. "I apologize for my mother. Please don't let her upset you. Sometimes she says things without realizing how it sounds."

"The only thing that bothers me is how she affects you. I wish she could be what you need. But there is something more. You should know we had an encounter with the mountain lion a little bit ago.

Biscuit chased it, and Toby, fearing for the dog's safety, ran after them. Your mother gave me a derringer. Though I didn't have to use the weapon, I was grateful to her."

Alarm tightened in his chest. "Don't let Toby outside. And when Biscuit needs to do her business, tie a rope to her neck. It's time I took care of this cat."

"Until you do, I'll fear for Toby every time he steps outside."

Rand wished he could draw her into his arms and whisper comforting words. But she'd made it clear she didn't welcome his touch.

Nonetheless, he brushed her cheek with his fingers.

The contact seared him.

Dear God, in his dreams he already had her in his bed. How could he bear living in the same house, breathing the same air, and be unable to offer the slightest affection?

He'd die from sheer torture.

Nine

FOR THE NEXT THREE DAYS, CALLIE SAT WAITING patiently for Rand to come home. She needed to know he was all right.

After his mother's visit, he'd gathered Cooper and Brett and they'd gone to hunt down the mountain lion. Said he wouldn't return until he killed the dangerous beast.

She took advantage of his absence to dive into her search. There wasn't a place she hadn't looked. Maybe someone else had found the chest her mother hid. She could come to no other conclusion. Panic rose up. She desperately needed whatever was inside.

When your life needs to look up, open the box. Her mother's words echoed in her head.

The chest was simply gone. Lost.

Finally, on the fourth morning, Rand rode up to the house and dismounted.

Callie breathed a sigh of relief and ran out. "You're back."

He slid his Winchester from the scabbard and gave her a tired grin. "Got any corn bread, woman?"

"Not until supper."

"How about coffee, then?"

"I can make some real fast."

Rand came inside, hung his coat and hat beside the door on a nail, and sat down at the table. "You're a sight for sore eyes."

Heat rose to her face. She could say the same about him. But she wouldn't.

They were cook and employer. Nothing more. She'd started repeating this to herself several times a day. And often in the dead of night when the house got quiet and still and thoughts of him kept her awake.

Callie got the coffee on and sat down across from him. She watched him wearily rub his eyes. "Did you kill the lion?"

"Late last night. Thought he'd outwitted us."

"I'm glad it's over."

"That makes two of us. We won't have to worry about him getting Toby or Biscuit anymore."

As though hearing his name, Toby ran into the kitchen and threw his arms around Rand's neck. "Mr. Rand, you're back."

"So my head tells me, but my body still feels like it's in the saddle."

Biscuit whined and jumped up on Rand's leg, wanting her share of attention. He ruffled the dog's ears with affection.

By the time the coffee finished boiling, Rand had given a blow-by-blow account. The hunters had experienced too many dangerous scrapes. The scariest had been when the lion leaped from a tree onto Brett, and Rand and Cooper couldn't shoot for fear of hitting their brother.

"Is Mr. Brett okay?" Toby asked with wide eyes.

"Clawed him up pretty good, but he's fine."

"I'm glad it didn't kilt him. Or you, Mr. Rand."

"Me too, boy. Me too." Rand tousled Toby's dark hair.

Callie looked up and fell into his blue eyes. He flashed her a crooked little grin that made her stomach pitch and twist as though it were a wild bronco determined not to be ridden.

Faster than a fire sweeping across a prairie, her mind leaped to the brush of his lips across hers the night before he left. To cover the uncomfortable tightness in her chest, she asked him if he was hungry.

"What I want is a bed," he murmured low.

Dear heavens. Why would he talk about anything like that in front of a youngster? Maybe he was too tired to know how it sounded. But he was sure staring at her like he knew.

"A nap would do you good," she said briskly. "I can take care of your roan and put him in the barn. Toby will be thrilled he can go outdoors now. I'll keep him outside for a bit. The house will be quiet."

"I appreciate your offer, but I'll wait until bedtime, if it's all the same. Need to feed and water old Blue, and he can stand currying. I'll get to it." He rose and went to take his roan to the barn. Toby tagged along after him, talking a mile a minute.

The boy dearly loved Rand. It showed in the way Toby tried to adopt Rand's walk and the rancher's way of talking.

With them out of the kitchen, Callie turned her attention to her job. In a quandary about supper, Callie inventoried the options and settled on chicken and dumplings. That is, if Rand would take care of the chicken part. She tapped her bottom lip with a finger. They only had eight layers and one cantankerous rooster that refused to stay in the coop. They couldn't kill one of those.

She needed to discuss the situation with Rand. Maybe he felt up to hunting. She'd seen some grouse and turkeys in the woods. If Rand was too tired to shoot one, it would be potato soup and corn bread.

When she stepped into the barn, she heard Toby say, "I'm real sad. My mama lives in heaven now. Aunt Callie said Mama's lookin' over me though. She ain't gonna let anything happen to me."

"I'm sorry, Toby," Rand said in a gentle tone. "It hurts when you don't have your mama's arms around you anymore. I used to want that more than anything."

"Did you ever cry? I do sometimes. 'Course, I cain't let Aunt Callie see me. Makes her real sad on account of my mama bein' her sister."

"It's all right to cry, boy. And, yes, I still do. Doesn't make you less of a man. No matter what anyone says."

Callie stood out of sight in the shadows, waiting to hear more. She didn't have to wait long.

"What happened to your daddy?" Rand asked.

She sucked in her breath. That low-down, promise-breaking traitor! Callie charged toward the stall.

But not before she could keep Toby from saying, "My papa might be in the hoosegow, whatever that means, on account of he robs banks an' stuff. Sometimes he kills people. He's real mean."

"Tobias Matthew!" Callie yelled. "I told you not to go spilling secrets. You disobeyed me. I oughta…"

She came face-to-face with Rand. This made it official. One hundred percent of the men she knew had betrayed her. She should've listened to her gut. It was always right. But, darn it, she'd so wanted him to be different. She'd desperately needed to be able to trust again.

"Hold it, Callie," Rand said, standing in the stall door. He put up his hand. "I won't let you in here."

"Where's Toby?"

"I won't let you talk to him until you simmer down. The youngster deserves understanding, not anger."

"You're telling me how to raise him?" Callie snorted. "You promise-breaking tinhorn."

Rand inhaled and drew himself up as though she'd struck him. Pain darkened his blue eyes. "I have not broken my word."

"What do you call it, then? You agreed to not ask questions."

"You never said I couldn't ask Toby," he said stiffly. "Only you."

Toby peered from around Rand's big body. His pinched white face and the tears trickling down his cheeks broke her heart. What had she done? She was no better than Nate Fleming. The anger left as fast as it had risen. She sagged when her knees buckled.

Gentle hands held her steady. "It's going to be all right. I promise. I'm here and I'm going to help you. We'll get through this together. You can count on me. Please trust me."

Callie leaned against Rand's broad chest as his

soothing hand ran up and down her back. It felt so good to be held. Maybe she should trust him. After all, he was right. She hadn't made him promise anything in regard to Toby.

After several minutes, she stood back. Kneeling, she reached for Toby, brushing away his tears. "I'm sorry for yelling. Sometimes grown-ups mess up real bad. Can you give me another chance? I promise to do better."

Toby threw his arms around her neck and kissed her cheek. "You ain't mad at me?"

"Nope. Not even a tiny bit. I was wrong to order you not to talk about your mother and father." She kissed Toby's forehead. She loved this little guy more than she'd thought possible.

"I love you, Aunt Callie."

"I love you too, sweetheart."

Biscuit whined and put his paw on her knee.

"Do you love Biscuit?" Toby asked.

"I sure do."

"She wants a kiss too."

Callie glanced up at Rand, who'd propped himself against the bars of the stall. His raised eyebrow challenged her. "All right, Toby, I can do that." She leaned to kiss Biscuit's snout.

"I'll bet Mr. Rand wants one too," Toby persisted. "You hollered at him just as much as me."

For the love of Pete. Heat rose to her face. This had turned into a big, complicated mess. But she deserved it for throwing such a temper tantrum. She'd known the ball of yarn was unraveling—she just hadn't known how fast.

She got slowly to her feet. "I'm sure Mr. Rand will be satisfied with a handshake. That's what grown-ups do."

"Nope." Toby shook his head. "A kiss."

Rand's grin stretched from ear to ear. "You heard the boss, Callie."

"Oh for heaven's sake." She couldn't have moved if her life depended on it. That didn't matter though. Rand certainly seemed quite limber on his feet. And very eager, to boot. "I really need to see about supper."

"It can wait," Rand persisted softly. "You brought this on yourself. If you back out now, you'll lose credibility with Toby. Do you want that?"

Callie's mouth dried. "No," she whispered.

One step and he stood nose to nose with her.

Good heavens. She struggled to draw air into her lungs. A niggling suspicion told her this would not be a mere brush of the lips this time. She realized a part of her would be incomplete if that was all she got.

Rand reached out. With agonizing slowness, he took her face between his big hands then crushed his lips hungrily to hers. Sizzling spirals of heat rose and spread through her body, leaving a scorched path. She couldn't breathe and she didn't care. The yearning inside overpowered everything.

The knowledge that she needed Rand more than food or air or refuge swept over her.

Immediately, her stomach did that twirl-and-dip thing that had her clutching the front of his shirt to keep from falling.

Dear God, she'd never felt so alive, so wanted, so desired.

Her pulse raced as the loud throbbing in her ears drowned out everything, including the voice of reason.

She forgot where they were and the fact that Toby looked on.

She forgot the danger.

She forgot everything in the strong need for this man that rolled over her like a midnight tide crashing to the shore.

Her hand slid around his neck and into his silky brown hair. She couldn't deny this attraction between them. The power of it shook her to the depths of her being.

Biscuit's bark and Toby's clapping brought her back to reality, and she quickly pulled away. She had to get a grip on herself.

Cook and employer, she sternly reminded herself.

Callie's face flamed. She whirled and sought the refuge of her kitchen, safe for the moment from temptation.

❧

Rand watched her go, wishing for one moment longer with Callie in his arms. But he understood. It wasn't right to show such affection in front of a child.

He owed Toby a debt of thanks, for if the boy hadn't insisted, Callie's lips would never have met Rand's again.

Some day he meant it to be behind a bedroom door. He'd carry her to his bed and take his time. Little by little, he'd unleash the simmering passion that burned beneath her cool exterior. She would know what it was like to be cared for.

But did he have enough time before she left? With what Toby had spilled, Rand knew the odds were stacked against him.

Slowly, the pieces were falling into place. He'd learned they were running from an evil man. After the boy told him his father robbed banks and trains and could possibly be in the hoosegow, Rand now knew beyond a doubt the father was an outlaw.

Though Rand still had no name, chances were pretty good that Toby looked like his father. The next time he went into town, he'd ask Cooper to look at all the wanted posters for a black-haired male. Rand just might figure out this puzzle without asking Callie a single question.

He sure hoped so. If he didn't learn fast, he could lose them, either to a bullet, or they'd disappear deeper into the shadows where he couldn't find them again.

Wishing he could convince Callie that staying put on the Last Hope Ranch was the safest thing, he finished the roan's currying. He left Blue on his bed of fresh hay to rest in the stall, and he hurriedly put everything away.

The longing to be with her had been an ache in his gut for days. He couldn't wait to sit across the table from her.

About that time, Callie called them in to supper. He collected Toby and washed up.

The meal of potato soup and corn bread hit the spot. Rand ate three bowlfuls. He didn't think much when Callie disappeared into the kitchen. When she returned with bowls of hot peach cobbler, he thought he'd died and gone to heaven. As he dove into the delectable goodness, he thought it was the best pie he'd ever eaten.

Afterward, Toby wandered off with Biscuit. Rand sat at the table sipping on a cup of coffee, watching Callie set the kitchen to rights for the next day. He took out his ring of keys from a pocket and idly examined each one.

Keys gave him power. At the orphanage, one caretaker had locked him in a dark cellar with the spiders and creepy-crawlies and left him overnight to punish him. He determined then and there he'd never be without a key again. Over the years he'd collected two dozen. He figured if one didn't fit a lock, another one might.

If only he could unlock this complicated woman with one of his keys. Were it only that simple. If so, he'd have one made to fit the special lock she'd placed around her heart.

He had all kinds of keys, square ones, plain round ones, one with a fancy scroll, one with a rectangular top, but not one would fit the secrets she'd locked away.

"You seem lost in thought." Callie folded her flour-sack dish towel and sat down at the table. "Anything I can help you with?"

"Afraid not much anyone can do. Just thinking about these keys and remembering a time long ago."

"When you were at the orphanage?"

He nodded and told her about the horror of being locked in the cold, dank basement. "I couldn't see my hand in front of my face."

She laid her hand on his arm. "I'm sorry. I thought I had it bad after my mother died. I can't imagine what you had to endure. No wonder you're so angry at Abigail."

"I'd rather not talk about her." He propped his elbows on the table and released a long sigh. "That night I vowed to never be so powerless again. So I started collecting keys." His eyes met hers as he reached for her small hand. He began to caress her fingers, drawing little circles on each digit.

"You mentioned your mother, Callie. From what you said, I assume she died when you were very young. I'm not asking you to confirm or deny it. I can figure it out just like I put two and two together about that grave in the woods. I know she's buried there."

Callie sighed. "You might think this is a game of some sort, but I assure you it's not. I have reasons for keeping secrets, even if you don't happen to agree."

His eyes searched hers. "Secrets are fair pickings. I won't break my promise. I won't ask any questions. I only wanted to ease your mind a bit. I built a fence around the grave. Right now, it's only a makeshift one out of what I could scrounge at the time. Eventually, I'll put up a sturdy wrought iron fence around it. I won't have my cows trampling it."

Sudden tears shimmered in her eyes. "Thank you. As long as we're confessing to things…I apologize for yelling and slinging accusations at you today. I probably sounded like some crazy woman. I won't let it happen again."

"I can take care of myself. It was Toby I was worried about," he said quietly.

"That stings worse than anything. I know what it's

like to have voices raised at you when you're nothing but a kid. I'll never do that again to Toby."

"Good." He drained the last swallow from his cup and grinned. "The boy is quite a conniver, though, I must say."

Callie colored a becoming rosy hue. "Yes, he is. About that kiss…"

"I don't regret it. It's something I'll remember for a long time." Like for an eternity. "It meant a lot to Toby that we make up."

"It wasn't seemly. You're my employer. I'm nothing but a cook here. Don't forget that."

Nothing but a cook? She was so much more than that. She'd never be a *nothing* anything.

"You appear to be worrying about that enough for both of us."

"Someone has to remind you. You keep forgetting. Cooks don't go around kissing the men they work for."

"So you have experience in this matter, do you?" he teased, just to watch the color flood back into her face.

"You know what I mean, mister," she said sternly.

She rose. Walking to the door, she crossed her arms as though protecting herself from something, looking out into the gathering shadows. Biscuit padded into the room to her side and whined to go out. She opened the door and stood on the top step. He wondered what she was thinking. He might never know.

Rand separated the fancy scrolled key from the others, wondering what it had once gone to. He was still pondering that when Callie returned and sat at the table. She was like that key in a lot of ways. It didn't belong with the others and neither did she. The beautiful woman with eyes like warm whiskey was definitely special.

When she glanced at the key, her eyes suddenly widened and she got very still. "Where did you get that one?"

"Found it lying outside the day I came to look the property over. Kinda pretty, don't you think?" It crossed his mind from the look on her face that the key might possibly belong to her.

"Yes."

"Maybe you have an idea what it goes to, Callie."

"It reminds me of one I used to have a long time ago."

"What did your key unlock?"

"I'm not sure," she hedged. "My mother gave it to me."

He could tell she knew more than she was saying. "Do you still have it?"

Her eyes were riveted on the key. "I lost it. Why all the questions about one old key?"

"Reckon I want to figure out what it went to. Puzzles interest me."

"Do you mind if I look at it? Just for a minute."

Rand handed the keys to her and watched her instantly pick out the scrolled one. Sadness crossed her face as she ran her fingers over the metal, feeling each groove. A distant light came into her eyes.

"You seem to know something about this key."

Callie jerked and dropped the keys as though they'd singed her. "No. I've never seen it."

Refusing to meet his gaze, she picked them up and handed them back.

Rand sighed and rose, sticking the metal ring back in his pocket. Wouldn't serve any purpose to keep insisting. She'd talk about it when she got ready. He changed the subject. "Will you sit with me in the parlor?"

"You haven't slept in three days. Don't you want to find your pillow?"

"In a bit. First, I want to rest and let this house calm my hungry spirit." And to spend some quiet moments with the woman who could steal his good sense. But he didn't tell her that.

His thoughts flew to their kiss in the barn. He'd aimed for a light one to satisfy Toby, not a kiss so long and deep. But when his lips pressed against hers with such longing, he'd lost his head. He'd been a prisoner of a body that demanded more.

Callie shook her head. "I really shouldn't. It's not proper. I'll just get my knitting and sit in here."

"I suppose this is all about reminding me that you're a hired hand and I'm your employer, and never the twain shall meet."

When her amber eyes met his, her tone became hard. "Like I said, nothing can come of pretending. It doesn't change the facts."

Rand frowned. "Not even if I request your company? I don't wish to be alone." Indecision marred her pretty face. He watched the play of emotions and at last the tiny smile of surrender coupled with her soft sigh.

"In that case, I will keep you company."

He held out his hand and they moved into the cozy room, where he could admire the woman whose kisses were like honey and dream about all the things that made his heartbeat race.

He didn't exactly know how it happened, but she moved her rocker in front of him so that her knees touched his and had yarn strung between his hands before he could turn around. He watched her roll it up into a neat ball.

"What kind of wallpaper would you like for this room, Callie?"

"I think a light gold color, since the cowhide furniture is a rich brown. Not a floral. Just a pretty, understated, elegant design. Like a diamond pattern. The St. James Hotel in Kansas City has a very lovely wallpaper that I always admired."

"Then that's what we'll have. Anything else?"

"Maybe a picture or two. I used to paint a long time ago. I wish I had some of the prettier ones I did."

"So do I." Rand watched her make a ball with the skein of yarn. He loved the comfortable silence. When Callie took the last strand, he leaned back. "You can paint some more pictures. Give me a list of the supplies you need and I'll fix you right up."

When Callie dragged the chair back into its spot, it felt as though she'd moved to the next county. So close, yet so far. He longed to have her next to him, to feel her warmth.

"That was a long time ago, Rand. I doubt I'd remember how."

"Doesn't hurt to try."

"I admire some of the views of this land. If I could get them down on canvas, it would be my gift to you for letting Toby and me stay."

"I will cherish anything you paint."

The sound of her laugh made him smile. "Better wait until you see my fumbling attempts."

In the quiet that followed, Callie's knitting needles clinked softly together. Rand couldn't take his eyes off her.

She was the woman he hadn't let himself look for his whole life. And she was right here in his house, sitting by his fire, filling him with a fierce longing that he'd never experienced before.

By some silent agreement, they didn't talk about all the things they wanted to discuss. That was okay with Rand. They had time for that.

Toby had fallen asleep again with his arm around his dog.

Rand rose and lifted him. "I'll tuck this tired boy in bed and then I'll turn in myself. You coming?"

Callie glanced up and gave him a tiny smile. "I think I'll knit just a bit longer. Thank you for taking care of Toby."

When he passed her, he lightly touched the top of her head, then let his hand drift to her shoulder. "Good night, then."

"Good night, Rand."

He turned and glanced back, sealing the memory forever in his mind. The creak of the rocker. The fire casting off a warm glow. His lady knitting with a look of contentment on her beautiful features.

This was like a dream. And he didn't want to wake up.

This could all be his. If he only knew she'd stay.

Ten

SINCE FIRST HIS MOTHER, THEN THE MOUNTAIN LION, had interrupted Rand's plans, he didn't go into town after the load of cut lumber until Saturday.

He'd had to do some tall talking, but Callie and Toby went along.

With his heart hammering, he helped her up onto the bench of the wagon. She put Toby between them. Rand didn't get a chance to say much on the ride; Toby did all the talking, while Callie took in the countryside.

It appeared everyone had come into Battle Creek that Saturday. Traffic crawled through the crowded streets. That was fine with him, though. Each driver had to maneuver around a small burial plot right smack in the middle of the street. He'd known many a person who clipped the wrought iron fence that surrounded it.

"Mr. Rand, why did they bury those people in the middle of the street?" Toby asked.

"Those graves were there long before the town. They say the men were government surveyors who were massacred by the Indians. We'll probably never know for sure."

"Mr. Brett's an Indian. Does he kill people?"

"Toby, that's not polite," Callie gently scolded.

"Nope, he doesn't kill people," Rand answered, pulling up to the busy mercantile. He turned to Callie. "I'll let you out here so you can do your shopping while I load the lumber. Get whatever you need and have John Abercrombie put it on my bill. All right?"

"I can do that."

"Oh, don't forget to stock up on canned peaches. I want plenty."

Setting the brake, he jumped down to help Callie and Toby to the ground. When he put his hands around Callie's waist, tingles ran the length of his arms. "Get something for you and the boy too," he said gruffly, "not just stuff for cooking. See if he has those paints and whatnot that you need to begin painting those pictures."

She nodded without saying anything.

After making sure they were safely inside the store, he followed the pig trail to the new lumber mill. When he, Cooper, and Brett had moved here almost eight years ago, only a handful of businesses lined the main street. Now, thanks to Cooper's wife's efforts, the town was thriving. Delta Dandridge Thorne had made such a huge difference after she arrived last March. They proudly sported a church, a schoolhouse, the lumber mill, and a seed library that had been Delta's personal idea. A second hotel would open in a matter of weeks. Rumor had it they were getting an opera house and a small clinic.

But the single thing that had attracted more people and businesses was Delta and her women's club called the Women of Vision. Soon after they had set to work painting and hammering and fixing the run-down buildings, the rest of the town began to pitch in. Now, everyone reaped the fruits of their labor.

All except one holdout—the Lexington Arms Hotel. George Lexington had dug in his heels and refused to refurbish his hotel or fix up the exterior.

But after Rand's mother, Abigail, had struck Lexington's fancy, the man had recently begun making repairs. Rand suspected Abigail had laid down the law. Or maybe it was because a second hotel was slated to throw open its doors soon. Whatever the reason, Lexington had been working feverishly to get his establishment in better shape. He'd seen the writing on the wall.

Rand pulled up to the lumber mill and hopped down. A few minutes later, he began loading his order. He didn't want to leave Callie in town alone longer than he had to.

∽

Callie gave her order to Mr. Abercrombie, who resembled a scarecrow. He was reed-thin and his skin stretched so tightly over his face, the bones seemed on the verge of breaking through. But his twinkling eyes held a kindness that put her at ease.

While she waited for her purchases, she strolled around the store looking at everything. She was surprised to find some paints and brushes, even canvas. Excitement swept over her. She'd always loved the peace and fulfillment painting gave her. Selecting what she needed, she laid them on the counter with her other things.

Over a dozen other women were also browsing. Some spoke to her. She answered back very politely without encouraging conversation. Callie glanced down at her bare hands, embarrassed. No decent woman wanted to be caught without gloves. Rand had said to get something for her and Toby. The glove display was at the front of the store by the window. She picked up a pair that fit and happened to glance out the window at the people walking past.

The saliva dried in her mouth and her heart pounded in her chest.

Nate Fleming strolled down the street without a care in the world. No mistaking the black hair that glistened under the sun's rays or the way he walked. That swagger belonged to no one else. He'd always acted as though he owned the whole world and everyone in it, but now he seemed even more arrogant and ruthless.

As though sensing someone watching, he spun around. She ducked into the shadows, praying she was quick enough. A few minutes later, he moved toward the mercantile door.

Her stomach churned. She couldn't let him find her and Toby. She got her nephew and moved to the back corner of the store, where she hid behind a tower of feather mattresses.

"Toby, don't make a sound. I beg you."

"I won't, Aunt Callie. When we get through playing hide-an'-seek, can I have a peppermint stick?"

"Yes, darling." She kissed his forehead. "Remember, not a peep."

How long they huddled there, she didn't know. It seemed like a year or more. Finally, she peeked around the mattresses.

Walking by, Mr. Abercrombie noticed her and came over. "Can I be of assistance, ma'am?"

Callie kept her voice low. "Is there a tall, dark-haired man still in the store? He wears a pearl-handled Colt strapped low."

"Is he bothering you? I'll send someone for the sheriff."

Vivid recollections sent chills up her spine. Nate had gunned down one lawman in cold blood for daring to try to arrest him. Callie had watched it all, then she had run behind the nearest tree and relieved her stomach. She refused to put the sheriff of Battle Creek, who happened to be Rand's brother, in Nate's sights.

"Please, don't involve the sheriff. If you could be so kind as to... Do you have a back door?"

"Yes, but really, Sheriff Thorne needs to know the man is a threat. He can protect you."

Nate's callous voice echoed in the store as he spoke to a clerk, demanding she wait on him immediately. He could be extremely cruel when he didn't get his way. She prayed for the clerk's safety.

"Thank you all the same, Mr. Abercrombie. If you could show me the back door, I'd be forever in your debt. Mr. Sinclair will return for the packages soon."

Toby jerked on her skirt, whispering, "The peppermint stick."

"Oh, and can you please add a peppermint stick and these gloves to the purchases?"

"My pleasure. Please be safe, ma'am."

"You also. Be on your guard against him, Mr. Abercrombie. He's very dangerous."

The minute Nate turned his back to them, she took Toby's hand and slipped out the rear exit. Callie didn't take a deep breath until they were in the alley.

Ignoring the chill in the air, she carefully made her way across the street. Three barrels stood against the side of the building. She made a space for Toby amongst them. "You stay here out of sight. I'm going to find Rand."

Toby trembled beneath her hand. "I'm scared."

She kissed his cheek. "You'll be fine, sweetheart. I promise. I'm not going to be very far away."

Nate emerged from the mercantile. He stood on the wooden boardwalk, his piercing evil eyes scanning the street. Callie sucked in a breath, pressing against the side of the building. When he turned in the direction of the saloon, she left the hiding place and went to seek Rand.

Nate Fleming had destroyed her sister, and he would do the same to Toby if he had a chance. Dear God, she'd keep his innocent son out of his clutches no matter what she had to do. Toby would have an opportunity to grow up into a sensitive, honorable man.

Now that she knew with certainty the outlaw was here, she'd have to leave the ranch and find another sanctuary.

Tears pricked her eyes. She wished God would tell her how she'd be able to leave Rand.

After loading the lumber, Rand swung by the sheriff's office.

Cooper glanced up from behind his desk when Rand strolled through the door. "Looks like you could use a strong cup of coffee, little brother."

"I can use more than that, but coffee would hit the spot." Rand plunked down in the chair opposite the desk. "Need help with something."

"Let me get the coffee on and we'll parlay."

A few minutes later, Rand relayed what he'd learned and his hunch that the desperado would most likely have some of Toby's features. They were poring over the wanted posters when John Abercrombie stormed in.

"Have a problem at the mercantile," Abercrombie said.

"What kind of problem?"

The store owner told them about the hardened, dark-haired man and the woman and little boy who were hiding from him. "You must know her, Rand, because she said to put her purchases on your bill. She was desperate and afraid. When I told her I'd send for you, Cooper, she begged me not to. I helped them escape out the back door."

Cold foreboding came over Rand. He jumped to his feet. "It has to be Callie. He's here."

Long strides took him to the door. Grabbing his hat, Cooper was right behind him. They left Abercrombie standing there with his mouth gaping.

A few women milled around the store, but no men. Where had Callie gone? Had the outlaw gotten her? With his heart pounding, Rand went outside and surveyed the street.

"Any sign of her?" Cooper asked, joining him.

"Nope."

Just then, a boy darted from the building across the way and threw himself at Rand. Rand hugged Toby close. "Where's your Aunt Callie?"

Toby dragged his sleeve across his nose and shrugged. "Don't know. She made me hide an' went to find you."

"Is she hurt?"

"I don't think so, but she's real scared."

"Okay, let's you and me go get her."

Before they stepped off the boardwalk, a stranger ambled by on a tall midnight horse. He wore all black, even his hair. The rider stared at them with the coldest, deadest eyes Rand had ever seen. Toby ducked behind him, clutching Rand's jacket with trembling fingers.

The boy had recognized the man. This had to be the outlaw who terrified Callie. From the corner of his eye, Rand watched Cooper's hand steal to the Colt on his hip and slide it out.

If the outlaw so much as blinked, he'd be dead before he ever left the saddle.

Rand hid Toby from view until the stranger rode on. "It's okay to come out now."

Cooper knelt in front of the boy. "Do you know who that was?"

Toby nodded. "He's real mean. He hit Mama lotsa times an' made her cry."

"Is that your father?" Rand asked tightly.

Again Toby nodded with big tears in his eyes.

Rising, Cooper turned to Rand. "You find Callie. I'll take care of this. I won't have him terrorizing my town."

"Maybe I should come along," Rand suggested.

"Nope." Cooper pulled his hat low on his forehead. "If I can't take care of one measly stranger, I don't need to be sheriff. Go find Callie."

"Maybe she's over here." Toby tugged on Rand's hand.

Rand and Toby went up and down the street and they finally found Callie hunched down next to the side of the Three Roses Café, shaking like a leaf in a stiff gale.

She flew into his arms. "I didn't know how to find you, and Toby was gone when I came back."

"You're all right now." Rand held her tight. "I'm here. Anyone harms you, they're going through me."

"Can we go home now? I need the safety of the ranch."

Rand's heart lurched when she said "home." That she thought of the Last Hope Ranch that way meant so much to him.

"About to suggest that very thing." He needed to find out more about Toby's outlaw father, but it probably would be better to wait until he got her to a safe place. "You wait here. I'll pick up our purchases from the mercantile and we'll head home."

Inside the store, Rand collected the things Callie had bought. He went out to find Cooper standing beside the wagon.

"I need to talk to Miss Callie," Cooper said. "Where is she?"

"Waiting where it's safe. Good luck getting her to talk. Damn, Cooper, she's scared really bad."

Battle Creek's sheriff blew out a frustrated breath. "All the more reason to find out who this outlaw is. I sympathize with your cook, but I can't very well protect her or the town either until I know his name."

"I take it you didn't have that little *chat*?"

"Nope. Couldn't find the rotten cayuse. Don't know where the hell he went."

"Hop in. We'll drive the wagon around to her. Just be gentle. Have a care for what she's going through."

"Yes, Mother." Cooper climbed up. "Believe it or not, I've never browbeat a woman in my life or locked her in a dungeon."

∽

A few minutes later, Rand took Callie's hand and squeezed. "Give Cooper the man's name and we'll get out of town."

"I can't. I don't want—"

Cooper put his arm around her shoulders. "Miss Callie, this is important. You know better than any of us how vital it is. I have to keep my town safe. It's what I get paid to do."

"He'll kill you," she whispered. "I can't let that happen. I won't do that to your wife or to Rand."

"Miss Callie, I assure you I can take care of myself."

"You don't know him."

"I've known men like him my whole life," Cooper said quietly. "Now how about it?"

"Please, Callie, so I can take you home," Rand said.

Callie looked from him to Cooper. "Nate Fleming.

You'll have no trouble finding his wanted poster. He has a price on his head in four states."

"Thank you," Cooper said. "Leave everything to me."

Rand swung Toby up into the wagon box, then did the same to Callie. Waving good-bye to Cooper, they left Battle Creek behind them.

A mile down the road, Toby leaned his head against Rand's shoulder and fell asleep, exhausted by the events in town. Rand put a protective arm around the boy and sighed. Nate Fleming had better not manage to track down his prey at the Last Hope. The man would find a bullet waiting for him.

Rand would die trying to keep his patchwork family safe.

Eleven

THE MINUTE CALLIE STEPPED INTO HER ORDERLY kitchen, she took a deep, cleansing breath. She'd done lots of thinking on the ride back from town. And with Toby asleep and Rand lost in his own thoughts, she hadn't had many interruptions.

It was time to leave.

Nate Fleming had seen to it that she had no choice. He was ruthless and determined to get his son. It didn't matter to him how many people he had to kill to achieve that.

Unshed tears clogged her throat.

The reality of her intense protectiveness of Rand jarred her. She'd do anything to save him. Even if it meant standing in front of a bullet. Even if it meant…

…abandoning him like so many others had. She was no better than his mother. The thought of bringing him more pain was unbearable. Dear God, he didn't deserve her betrayal.

Her heart ripped apart at the thought of leaving this man who'd come to mean so much to her. But she simply had no other option.

Tonight.

Rand's impassioned plea echoed in her mind. *Please…for God's sake, don't let me wake up one morning and find no sign of you anywhere. Can you do this one thing?*

She wouldn't go back on her word. Yet neither could she face him as she walked out of his life. Sweet Lord, what to do?

Shrugging out of her coat, she set about getting supper. She'd cook him something special first. Then she'd leave.

One of the purchases in town had been a smoked ham. She'd slice off nice, big chunks of that and panfry some potatoes. Biscuits, and a peach pie to finish off the meal.

Toby was outside with Biscuit in the tepee. Suddenly her throat tightened. How could he leave that dog behind? Yet they couldn't take her with them. For someone who'd arrived without anything, they sure had a lot to break free from now.

She glanced out the window. Rand stood with his head bowed, one foot propped on the broken corral fence. He seemed a million miles away. When he shifted and stared at the house, she saw tears glistening on his face. A sob broke from her mouth. She was the cause of those tears.

This kind, generous rancher had been her beginning, and now he was going to be her end.

∽

After supper, Rand stood by her side, helping with the dishes. He'd been so quiet, and for a man whose appetite knew no bounds, he'd eaten very little.

Their hands brushed as she handed him a wet plate. Sparks of heat went through her. His long, slender fingers mesmerized her. They could wield a hammer with skill, hold a child's hand, or wipe a tear as easily as they probably had dealt a round of poker in his saloon. She loved his hands.

"Would you take a walk outside with me?" Rand's quiet voice broke and told her he knew.

"Some fresh air would be nice." Maybe it would help her say what she had to.

They finished and she went to tell Toby where they'd be, only to find him snoring softly with his arm wound tightly around Biscuit. She kissed his forehead and returned to the kitchen.

"Toby's asleep already."

"He's tired. Seeing his father took a toll on him." Rand helped her with her coat and grabbed a lantern. "We won't be long in case he wakes up."

"Thank you."

The cold air had her clutching her coat together and a light mist fell. It seemed heaven was crying also. Her shoes crunched on the frozen ground. Rand held her arm as he directed her to a seat on a log inside Toby's tepee.

"I know you're planning to leave." The words came out bruised and hoarse as he took her hand. "Likely as soon as I go to bed. I wish I could change your mind. But I won't try to stop you. I understand."

Callie couldn't look at him. If she did, she'd be lost. "It's really for the best. Nate will find us here. Can't you see? I have to leave."

"It's what he expects you to do. It's the most

dangerous decision you can make. Callie, I can protect you here. I can't keep you safe if I don't know where you are. I don't think my heart can take the worry and the constant fear of not knowing."

"So I'm supposed to twiddle my thumbs and wait for him to find us? Believe me, he *will* find us," she whispered, her heart breaking. "You don't know how ruthless and cunning he can be. He's the most dangerous, deadly man I know. I can't watch him kill you and know I'm the cause." She couldn't live with herself.

Rand caressed her cheek. "I may not know him, but I know others like him. Cooper, Brett, and I rid the world of Tolbert Early. We can rid the world of Nate Fleming. Give us a chance."

"I haven't had anyone to stand up for me in such a long time."

"You have me. You'll always have me, no matter what."

Callie leaned into him, borrowing his strength. His strong, steady heart beat softly against her ear. When his arms went around her, she snuggled into the sweet haven. "I'm so tired of being scared, of jumping at shadows, of waiting for him to strike."

"Running away from here will not change any of that. In fact, it'll only make everything worse. Tell me the rest of what you're keeping from me. Trust me with your secrets. There's no reason to hold back any longer."

She knew he was right. It was time to come clean.

"Start with your name," Rand gently prodded.

"Callie Quinn. My twin sister, Claire, was married to Nate Fleming. Toby is her son, and unfortunately, Nate's also. Before Claire died two months ago, she made me promise to take Toby and run, to keep Nate from getting him. The man is a natural-born killer. He views Toby as his property to do with as he sees fit. I'll not let him destroy my nephew."

"He won't get Toby, or you, as long as I'm breathing." Rand's declaration held gritty hardness. "Even if Fleming should get lucky, I'll rise from the depths of hell and strike him down."

The level of Rand's protectiveness brought stinging tears.

"Answer me this…did you live on this property at one time?" Rand's breath ruffled the top of her head.

Callie moved out of his arms. "Yes, until I was nine years old. It was the only safe place I knew to come."

"I'm glad you did. Do you think Fleming knows about this ranch?"

She chewed her lip. "I can't be sure. But even if Claire mentioned it, a person would have to know precisely where to look in order to find it."

"Callie, I have to ask. Do you have a claim to this land?"

"No. My conniving stepfather, Edmund Powers, tricked my mother into signing over the deed to him. Edmund sold the ranch as quickly as he could. It wouldn't surprise me if he'd had a buyer lined up before she was in the ground."

"I've known men like him. I'm sorry he hurt you."

"Edmund won't get another chance. He's out of my life." And good riddance. He could take his Liza and all her money and pursue his political aspirations.

"I just have one more burning question." His fingertips softly brushed her cheek.

"What's that?"

"May I kiss you?"

Tingles at the prospect danced up her spine. Instead of answering, she leaned close and boldly pressed her lips to his. One last kiss to take with her.

"Oh no you don't, lady," he protested. "We won't hurry this one. If a memory is what you want, it's what you'll get."

Rand appeared in no rush to take what he wanted. He seemed to savor each second of their private time together just as she did.

Sliding his hand behind her ear, he pressed his lips to each eyelid. Then he moved slowly downward, leaving a trail of kisses along the curve of her cheek and jaw. The sweet agony of his maddening assault released a flurry of quickenings in her stomach.

She rested her hand on the hard plane of his chest, inhaling the fresh scent of the rain and fragrant woods beyond that swept into their shelter.

Closing her eyes, Callie branded each precious second on her brain for after she left.

Rand.

He'd given her more than a place to live. He'd given her a glimpse of heaven.

Every brush, every graze of his lips arose in her a yearning for more.

Just as she thought she couldn't stand another minute of the delicious torture, he got to her softly parted lips. Teasing little nibbles at the corners of her mouth, his tongue lazily inching along the seam made the heat simmer in her veins, then flood into the core of her being.

Rand put a finger under her chin and tipped her face up. When he finally captured her mouth, the pure pleasure and searing hunger stole her breath. His gentle, tender care made her breath hitch.

The very air seemed electrified. Her heart fluttered wildly as she became caught up in the storm of passion that bound her. The quiver of his muscles beneath her hand told her the kiss had affected him also.

With a moan, he slipped his tongue between her lips, and she tasted the sweetness of the peaches that lingered there.

As his mouth settled firmly on hers, he crushed her to his chest. She was safe with Rand's arms around her. Like a butterfly inside a cocoon. Shy and a bit uncertain, she let her hand stray to the soft strands of his hair. Then, breaking the kiss, she buried her face against his throat.

Why hadn't she met him sooner, before she'd made a mess of her life? She only prayed she didn't add more mistakes.

This tall bachelor made her feel things no other man had. Callie cupped Rand's strong jaw with her palm. There was nothing weak or soft about this saloon owner turned rancher. *Solid as a rock* described both his character and his body.

"You know you can't leave now," Rand said gruffly.

"You make it very hard. I'll only agree to stay for a few more days. Beyond that, I can't promise."

Rand nodded. "Fair enough. I'll just have to see what I can do to persuade you. I'm a fair hand at that according to my dear brothers, who aren't shy about voicing their opinions."

"I need to get back in the house. Toby will be scared if he wakes up."

Putting an arm around her, Rand helped her into the kitchen as though she was something to cherish.

Cook and employer, she repeated to herself.

But the words were weak and held little meaning.

Nate Fleming built a fire outside Battle Creek and looked up at the bright stars. He'd be comfortable in a room at the hotel if that sheriff hadn't given him the evil eye.

He'd recognized Toby standing with the sheriff and the other man. No mistaking his flesh and blood. But why Toby was with them, he didn't know. He'd seen no sign of that uppity twit, Callie, who had stolen Toby and turned the boy against him.

He thanked his lucky stars he'd remembered Claire telling him she'd once lived outside Battle Creek. He'd come to the right place.

Finding them might take a little digging, but he would ferret them out. Toby was his, and he wouldn't stop until he got him back.

His wife hadn't understood the importance of carrying on the family tradition. But then she'd been a huge disappointment all the way around. He'd thought her stronger than she turned out to be. She had no stomach for disciplining Toby. A boy needed to be taught to fear the rod. Nate didn't consider applying a firm hand as a beating. Sure, he left marks. That was the way it was done. A boy had only to look at his welts to remember not to cross his sire again.

Nate set the coffee to boiling and stretched out on his bedroll. He thought of all the things he'd do to Callie when he caught her—and catch her he would.

What he had in mind would take time. He'd haul her to the gang's hideout. First, he'd put ten lashes on that proud back. Break a few fingers. Twist her arms. Then he'd really have some fun. Maybe he'd bite her like he'd done his obstinate wife when she refused to do his bidding. It irked him that he'd never broken Claire's spirit.

He'd take his time with Callie and the results would be different.

After he got her warmed up, he'd let his brothers have their turn. They were family and they had revenge of their own to heap upon her head. And when she was a bloody mess, they'd take turns applying a piece of hot metal to her. She'd wear his brand. She'd belong to Nate for the rest of her life. They'd ruin her pretty face good. No other man would ever look at her.

She'd beg them to kill her, but he had other plans.

Once he'd broken her, he'd keep her around to cook and to pleasure him. Anytime, anywhere. Taking out the makings for a smoke, he rolled a cigarette and lit it. He blew a few smoke rings and smiled. Yes, ol' Nate was going to make Callie Quinn very, very sorry she messed with him.

Once he got her out of the way, he'd turn his attention to Toby. He would have to work hard to undo all of the Quinn sisters' bad influence. First he'd change the boy's name. He'd always hated that god-awful wimpy name. Change it to something like Bart or Black Jack. Something fitting for an outlaw.

And then he would teach the boy how to kill.

In the end, Toby would be his son. All his. No one could stop that from happening.

After a cup of hot coffee, he made a plan. He'd sneak back into town and get rid of that meddling sheriff. Then he'd look for the man who'd shielded Toby from view. Something told Nate he'd find Callie Quinn there.

His plan was foolproof.

All he had to do was be patient.

Twelve

THE NEXT MORNING AFTER BREAKFAST, RAND AND Toby went outside to work on putting new lumber on the barn. Callie doubted the youngster would be much help, but the boy loved spending time with the tall rancher. He needed the security Rand offered.

Nightmares had plagued Toby. During the night, he'd sat up in bed several times screaming, "Don't let him get me! Save me!"

Callie wished her calm words of assurance had come from her heart. But they hadn't. Nate terrified her as much as he did Toby.

It surprised her when she rose to find Rand sitting grim faced in the kitchen with his Winchester resting on the table a few inches from his hand. He also wore a gun belt with his Colt in the holster. From the looks of it, he'd sat up the entire night guarding her and Toby. He didn't have to say a word. She knew he would make this his routine. Rand would battle the dark shadows that would reach out and grab her and snuff out her life. He would fight to the death for her, for them.

When that brilliant blue gaze met hers, her knees had buckled and she had to clutch the back of a chair to steady herself. She knew he was remembering the kiss last evening.

The kiss that had plundered her ability to think straight had carried Rand's heart with it. The intensity of it still pulsed inside her. Afterward, lying there in bed, she'd burned with desire for more, and she guessed he felt the same way. She suspected she'd never tire of his kisses, but she also knew where her desires would lead.

And she wouldn't go down that path.

Callie rose and stacked the dirty plates. Rand's key ring lay on the table. He'd forgotten to stick it into his pocket.

Sitting back down, she lifted the ring and flipped to the scrolled key. She recalled hers had a nick near the hole, some kind of imperfection in the metal.

Rand's key bore a nick in the same place.

She was positive this was hers. What to do about it? Explain everything to Rand? She knew he'd give it to her in a heartbeat. But then she'd have to tell him what it went to.

It might be better to leave the key where it was for now. It was safe. When she found her mother's treasure chest, she could tell Rand about it then. No sense heaping more onto his shoulders. The man had enough to handle.

With that decided, she got up and put a pan of water on the stove to heat so she could wash the dirty dishes.

While she waited, she straightened up her kitchen.

In the quiet of the house, it seemed she clearly heard her mother's voice whispering through the familiar rooms. *Don't run. Make a stand here. This is the place.*

Stunned by the clarity of the thought, Callie sank into a chair. Why not? She glanced around her at the house that had sheltered her long ago, and again now. This was her home. The one where loving memories surrounded her. She'd had love here, climbed her first tree, learned to ride a horse and to read and write. The marks on the wall in the kitchen had measured Claire's and her growth. Little nicks she'd carved in the banister to record her time here still remained. Strength slowly seeped into her.

Yes, the time had come to make a stand and fight. Right here on the Last Hope Ranch. Rand was right. Running would only get them killed. At least here Rand and his brothers presented a formidable force. They would protect her and Toby.

Glorious calm washed over her. She was at peace now that she'd made the decision and knew it was right.

Hurriedly, she washed the dishes. She needed to be out helping the man who was willing to brave the scorching flames of a dragon's breath and slay him for her. She couldn't wait to tell him.

❧

Rand found that having Callie beside him, holding the boards while he drove in the nails, was quite a distraction. He'd already hammered the dickens out of his thumb and forefinger several times. He could barely feel the throb, though. Each time he looked at her, such an overpowering longing for another taste of her lips came over him.

"Want to take a break?" she asked. "I have something to talk to you about."

"I can sure stand to wet my whistle." His heart sank. It could only mean bad news. He laid down the board he'd just picked up, and they walked to the water tank at the foot of the windmill. With Toby in his tepee playing, they wouldn't be disturbed.

"When are you leaving?" His low voice was thick and unsteady.

"We're not. We're staying right here. It came to me this morning that running is not the solution. I'm making a stand. Here on this land. For better or worse."

"Thank God." Rand picked her up and swung her around. "Best news I've heard in a month of Sundays. What changed your mind?"

"Put me down first." She laughed. "You're making me dizzy."

Before he set her on her feet, he held her close against him for a long moment, feeling the beat of her racing heart.

"My mother changed my mind. I knew she would tell me to stay. It's time to draw a line in the sand."

"And here I thought it was my strong powers of persuasion. I told you I had a gift." Rand's grin vanished. "It's the right thing to do, the safest thing for you and Toby. I heard the boy's screams during the night. Terror can play havoc with a person's sleep."

Callie nodded. "I want in on all of it. Don't you dare shut me out. I need to know where every gun and knife is and how to use them."

"Agreed, if it'll help you relax. But let me do the worrying now. All right?"

The sound of horses and the creak of a wagon coming down the lane to the house reached his ears. "Callie, I don't know who this is. Get behind me until I find out."

She quickly did as he told her, pressing against his back. Rand sent a glance toward the tepee, willing Toby to stay put.

As the wagon rounded the side of the house, Rand relaxed. "It's all right. It's Cooper and his wife, Delta."

He could feel the tension leave Callie's body as he tugged her out from behind him. He put an arm around her waist.

"Whoa." Cooper stopped and set the brake. He jumped down and helped Delta from the seat. It took some delicate maneuvering due to Delta being in the family way.

Cooper had told him the babe wasn't supposed to arrive for about three more weeks, but from the look of things, Delta might not make it.

Rand didn't miss how Cooper's hands lingered on his wife, lovingly brushing her large stomach before he paid them any notice.

After the introductions, Rand turned to Cooper. "Did you catch Nate Fleming?"

"Not yet." Cooper shoved his hat back from his forehead. "That's one of the reasons I drove out."

"Besides, I thought it was time I paid a visit and met Callie," Delta said, taking her husband's hand. "Don't forget it was my idea to come, dear."

"How could I forget, darlin'—you've been

badgering me for days." The love in Cooper's dark eyes when he looked at Delta belied his gruff tone.

His brother was a very lucky man. Deep love radiated from both their faces. Rand always got kind of misty-eyed around them, listening to them calling each other darlin' and dear. He was starting to see that maybe he shouldn't fight so hard against making a life with someone. His gaze sought Callie's. If only he could be sure she wouldn't abandon him and take his heart with her in the end...

"I need to ask Miss Callie a few more questions." Cooper turned to her. "Do you mind?"

"Not as long as Toby stays out of earshot," Callie replied. "He had upsetting dreams all night." She explained Nate's true relationship to Toby and her.

"Would Fleming have a hideout around here, someplace near where he could stay out of sight?"

"I don't think so. His main stomping grounds are in Missouri and Kansas. Before now, I've never known of him to travel to Texas, although I'm certainly no expert on Nate Fleming's comings and goings."

"Maybe he lit out, decided things were too hot in Battle Creek." Distracted, Cooper's gaze followed Delta as she lumbered toward the back steps to the house.

Rand noticed that his brother didn't pay them any mind until Delta had lowered herself to the top step.

"You're wrong, Sheriff—Nate Fleming doesn't run scared. He's right here. He won't leave until he gets his hands on Toby. Don't ever underestimate him. And please be careful. He has a preference for shooting men in the back. Especially lawmen," Callie ended, her voice fading to a hushed stillness.

"She's decided to make her stand here at the ranch, Coop," Rand said. "We may need your and Brett's help."

"You can count on it."

Rand kept his arm around Callie's waist as Cooper asked more questions in an effort to learn all he could about this outlaw in their midst. Her pale face became pinched and drawn as she gave them as much information as she could. From the picture she presented, Rand knew they hadn't ever seen a man as ruthless and cruel as Nate Fleming. Finally, Rand halted the questions.

"Callie, why don't you and Delta have some hot tea and a nice talk?" Rand suggested. "Coop and I will finish up the barn."

After Cooper helped Delta into the house, the men busied themselves sawing and hammering with some talking worked in.

They spoke more about Fleming, then Cooper abruptly changed the subject. "Rand, you remember Emily? She married one of my ranch hands, Joe Winters."

"Of course I do. She worked at the Three Roses Café. I recall she had a baby a few months ago. A shame about Joe getting killed in that accident. What about her?" Joe had been a real likable fellow and had worn his Indian heritage proudly. Two thousand pounds of bull crushed him right before the baby was born. He never got to see his daughter. Rand couldn't think of anything sadder.

"The doctor told her to start settling her affairs. She only has a few days to live. Doc says she has a tumor growing in her brain and it's already stolen her vision. Already, she can't care for her three-month-old. She asked me and Delta to take little Wren and raise her."

"And are you?"

"Can't. With Delta giving birth to twins—"

"Twins?" Rand grinned and gave a whoop.

"Yep. Gonna be two of the little rascals. Can you imagine?"

"Not even for a second. I should've known Delta would find some way to be different. Congratulations, big brother. If I had something, we'd celebrate with a snort."

"Thanks. Sure takes some getting used to. Sometimes I lie awake at night and try to picture myself as a daddy. Anyway, we can't take on the care of three babies. I won't let Delta shoulder that load."

"I'm sure Emily will find someone."

"No one she trusts has stepped up so far. Most folks have trouble accepting a half-Indian baby. If Emily doesn't find Wren a home, the babe will have to go to the orphanage." Cooper drove a nail into the wood with one powerful blow. "You know what that can be like."

Memories of the place where he spent years of his young life crossed Rand's vision. The poor food, the darkness, the whippings…the cellar. He shivered. No matter what, he'd see Wren would not have to face that nightmare.

"I'd take her, but I doubt Emily would want a bachelor raising her daughter."

"You could get married."

"Yeah? And just how would I do that, Mr. Big Brother Sheriff? Going to wave your magic wand and make me a different person? You're not a magician."

"Don't have to get so damn dramatic about it, or

so bullheaded either." Cooper grinned. "I see how you act around Callie, how you look at her when you think no one is paying attention."

"You know why I can't ask her," Rand snapped. "Everyone except you and Brett always leaves. Remember Jolene, my first love? And Beth, my second? And Patrick, my closest friend, who left the saloon one night with my money and didn't bother coming back? Not to mention my mother, who couldn't remember she had a child. And then there's another list of the ones who upped and died on me."

"I remember. It was Brett and I who picked up the pieces and put you back together," Cooper said quietly.

"Then what in God's name do you expect? Just last night, Callie told me she's leaving. I argued against it and some of what I said must've sunk in, because just before you came she told me she was going to make a stand here and fight. But once we remove the threat, she'll be gone. She'll walk out just like all the rest have. My heart can't take another blow. It hurts too much."

"Nothing in life is guaranteed. If you want to live, really live, you have to take a chance. I did and I'm not sorry. I can't imagine my life without Delta. She adores me." Cooper waggled his eyebrows comically.

"I'm not you. Have you forgotten our talks over the years?"

"Nope. Only thing I seem to have forgotten is how god-awful stubborn you are." Biscuit came from the tepee, stretching and yawning. Cooper knelt down to rub her belly. "Wren needs a home, a family, not some stinking orphanage."

Rand wrinkled his brow in thought. Cooper was right. But Callie wasn't going to stick around. She'd said so plain as day.

She would soon walk out of his life and take his heart with her. There was nothing he could say or do to stop her.

∽

Callie poured the tea and set out a small tin of cookies she'd made. "Rand never told me you were in the family way. When is your baby due?"

"Babies. We're having twins. They're due to arrive in three more weeks—that is, if I can make it."

"Oh how wonderful! You must be so happy. I was a twin. Claire and I were inseparable. Drove our mother crazy."

"I'm a little frightened of giving birth, but Doc will be there to help me."

She *should* be frightened, Callie thought. Callie had been in Delta's position once, years ago. She would never go through that again. She couldn't.

"Do you have names picked out?"

"Afraid not. Cooper and I can't agree. His choices are Henry and Henrietta, George and Georgia, Max and Maxine. These are the best. The other suggestions I won't repeat. I know he's just saying this to get a rise out of me after I told him no matching names. Besides, we could have two boys or two girls, not one of each. I like Claire and Callie though. Very pretty."

"Thank you. Claire succumbed to a mysterious illness, so it's been especially difficult. I kind of feel adrift now, like a ship without a rudder."

"I'm so sorry," Delta murmured and touched her arm. "I was an only child, so I've been alone my whole life. I always wanted a sister, someone to share secrets with."

"I don't know how I'd have made it without Claire. I just hated it when she married Nate Fleming. I warned her how dangerous he was. She didn't see the monster she married until it was too late. He made sure she couldn't seek help. On her deathbed, she begged me to take Toby and run. I didn't hesitate."

"I'm sure you love Toby like your own son. He's lucky to have you." Then Delta told her about Emily Winters, a young widow who was dying, and how she was frantically searching for someone to take her baby daughter and raise her.

"That's heartbreaking," Callie exclaimed, clapping her hand over her mouth. "I wish there was something I could do."

"Actually, maybe you can. How about you and Rand taking the baby?"

"Raise a child together, two unmarried people? That would not be an ideal situation for Emily's daughter. Besides, I will leave once Nate is caught."

"Plans can change. You could wed. You'll never meet a more gentle man. He'd take care of you and your nephew and protect you."

True, Callie had never known anyone more honorable, steadfast, and caring. But she would never marry. She couldn't.

Fear drove searing pain into the depths of her being. She was broken.

Rand could never know her secret. Callie's hand

trembled as she set her teacup down. "I'm sorry. I'd like to help, but this is asking too much. Besides, it's too dangerous for us until Nate is caught." And then after he was, what? She'd most likely thank Rand for his hospitality and go...where exactly? She hadn't a clue. It would require some thinking.

But why would she continue to stay? The torture of being so near yet unable to plan for a future with Rand Sinclair was becoming unbearable.

"What happened to Emily's husband, if I may ask?"

A shadow crossed Delta's face. She told Callie about Joe's Indian roots and the prejudice he'd encountered. How Cooper hadn't hesitated in hiring him on at the Long Odds. How a bull trampled and killed him. "He never got to meet his daughter or kiss his wife good-bye. It devastated all of us, but it shattered poor Emily."

"How horrible, and now she's dying as well. I hate to think of that poor baby growing up without a mother and father." It reminded Callie of Toby's situation. She knew what it was like, too, how lost and alone she and Claire had felt after their mother died.

A child deserved a home.

And love.

It tore at her heart that she couldn't offer that. She couldn't marry Rand. Not even for the sake of a child.

If she'd only learned but one lesson during her life, it was that one mistake was enough. Heaping another on top of it would only compound the problem, not make anything better.

They'd have to find another solution.

Little Wren Winters would not pay for Callie's cowardice.

Thirteen

THAT NIGHT RAND SAT IN THE PARLOR, MESMERIZED by the way the firelight danced and cavorted on Callie's hair. The crackling flames playfully brought out the reddish glints in her chestnut strands.

She seemed content in her rocker with a sock of Toby's that she'd been darning. It didn't take any effort to picture her with a babe in her arms.

Ever since Coop had told him about Emily Winters's dire situation, he hadn't been able to get that soon-to-be-motherless babe from his mind. He sure hoped someone would take the little thing. The babies in the orphanage were rarely picked up and hugged or even spoken to. They lay in their cribs and cried until they had no tears left.

Rand tightened his jaw. He would not let that happen to Wren. Not even if he had to raise the child by himself, though he didn't know if Emily would agree to that.

Toby rolled over and sat up. The boy appeared deep in thought. "Aunt Callie, how come I don't have a brother or sister?"

Callie's startled gaze slammed into Rand's. The question had caught her totally unaware, as it had him. He shrugged and lifted an eyebrow.

When she spoke, her voice was quiet. "Your mother wanted to fill a whole house with children, but she took ill. If she could've recovered, I'm sure she would've given you that brother or sister you want. What brought all this on, Toby?"

"The sheriff an' Mr. Rand were talkin' about this little baby that needs a home. Cain't it come here? I'd take care of it an' love it an' teach it to be an Indian."

Rand covered his mouth to hide a grin while dodging Callie's glare. Clearly she blamed him for this. Finally, he said, "Toby, there's more to it than that. There are lots of other things to consider."

"Like what?"

"Well, a child needs a family."

"We're a fam'ly."

Now what? He couldn't promise that they would always be together. Callie would waste no time packing up one of these days after the law caught up with Fleming. They didn't have anything to bind them to each other except fear of the outlaw.

And passionate moonlight kisses. He couldn't forget those if he tried. But kisses weren't enough.

Even if he felt he could offer marriage, Callie would be better off without him. That was the hard, honest fact. After all, what would she want with a struggling rancher who was more at home in a saloon? Or a broken-down ranch that needed so much work before it ever saw its first cow?

A woman like Callie deserved a fine home and a

husband who could give her nice things. Rand could offer her nothing.

But maybe if he kept working hard and fast, she wouldn't leave before he got the ranch put together the way he wanted. Maybe if she saw the home this place could be, she'd stay then.

That she'd decided to make a stand here on the Last Hope was a sign that maybe, just maybe, he had a shot.

If time didn't run out on him first.

Two days later, Callie was hanging up the last of the laundry on a line Rand had strung from the barn to a tree. Toby played in the tepee, whooping and hollering, and Rand worked on the roof of the house making repairs.

At the sound of a buggy coming down the lane, Callie turned.

Cooper's wife, Delta, and another woman pulled up. Callie waved. She liked Delta. They already had an easy friendship. Rand scrambled down from the roof and offered Delta assistance, which she seemed glad to accept, since her rounded body wouldn't allow for too much bending.

"It's too dangerous for you ladies to be riding across the countryside with an outlaw on the loose," Rand scolded good-naturedly.

Delta put her hands on her wide hips. "Rand, you know I always carry a gun. I'm a sheriff's wife, and Cooper always makes sure I'm prepared for trouble. I'm fully capable of handling whatever comes."

"Yes, ma'am. I sure wouldn't want to cross you."

"Are you taking advantage of the sunshine, Delta?" Callie asked. "It's such a pretty day."

"Guilty as charged." Delta laughed and reached to take an infant from the other woman. "Emily Winters and I wanted to come see you."

Rand helped Emily from her perch. It was apparent the frail woman had lost her sight. He made the introductions, and Emily clung to Callie's hand as though she was the only thing saving her from a pool of quicksand.

"Let's go inside to the parlor. I'll make tea." Callie cast a curious glance at the small bundle Delta held. No doubt Emily thought Callie would change her mind once she held the baby girl. She had no desire to look at the child, and she sure wasn't going to hold Wren or let her into her heart.

No. Not now, not ever.

With Rand taking tender care of the ladies, he got them situated in the parlor. "If you'll excuse me, I need to get back to my leaking roof," he said. "Plus, I don't want to leave Toby outside alone."

Delta spoke up. "Emily would like a word after we finish our tea."

"Callie can come get me." With that, he went out the kitchen door.

"What's this about?" Callie worried with the pocket of her apron. "I thought we made it clear we can't take the baby."

"My time is near," Emily whispered with tears running from her sightless eyes. "I have nowhere else to turn. I have to find a home for my daughter."

The impassioned plea deeply touched Callie. She gripped the young mother's hands. "Emily, I'd love to be the answer you need. I truly would. But I just can't. I'm sure Delta told you about the outlaw trailing me. He would like nothing better than seeing me dead and my nephew in his clutches. It's too dangerous for the baby. I won't take a chance Fleming might succeed. And besides, I plan to leave once this is over. Rand has been very kind to open his home to Toby and me, but he's only a friend."

"I understand." Emily's shoulders drooped.

"I'll see about that tea." Callie went to fill the teakettle and get it on to boil.

"Callie, come quick!" The urgency in Delta's cry struck fear.

Flinging down the tin of tea, Callie hurried to the parlor. Emily Winters lay on the floor twitching and convulsing.

"Here, take the baby." Delta thrust the infant into Callie's arms. "The doctor told me what to do. I have to keep Emily from chewing her tongue until this passes. Can you get me a soft cloth?"

The warmth of the baby's small body wrapped around Callie. She closed her eyes and braced herself against the pain.

Finally, she got control of herself. Racing to the kitchen, she grabbed the dish towel and ran back. Once Callie delivered it, she went to get Rand. He scrambled into the house, his face white.

"It's Emily. Delta's trying to help her."

Rand hurried to the parlor with Callie right behind. In the midst of it all, the baby's squalls echoed throughout the house. While Rand helped the stricken woman, Callie rocked sweet little Wren.

A song from long ago sprang to Callie's mind and she began to softly sing. Either the rocking or the singing or both soothed the infant, and she closed her eyes. One tiny fist clutching Callie's finger was all it took for the tears to flow.

How in God's name could she turn away such a perfect little girl who desperately needed someone to cherish her, to calm her fears when nightmares came, and to teach her how to become a young lady?

After what seemed like hours, the convulsions stopped. Rand gently lifted Emily to the sofa. Quiet sobs broke the stillness. He glanced at Callie and wondered at her outpouring of grief for a woman she'd only just met. He went to her side and rested a hand on her shoulder.

"Are you all right, Callie?"

"I'll be fine."

"Help me understand."

"Please, just see to our guests. We'll talk about this later."

Rand sighed. It was clear she wouldn't discuss it. He had no choice but to drop it for now. "I'll be here whenever you get ready."

Delta placed a wet cloth on Emily's forehead and gave him a weak smile. "Thank you, Rand. You were a big help. These episodes are becoming more frequent with each new hour. This is the second today."

Time was not on Emily's side, it seemed. Deep sadness seeped into Rand's soul. "How are *you* holding up, Delta? Cooper told me Emily lives with you in the main ranch house."

"I'm managing fine. Cooper helps some, but between running our ranches and being sheriff, he has little time." Delta covered her patient with a blanket and lowered her wide girth onto the settee. "I'll do whatever I have to for Emily. She has no one else."

"I understand how difficult it is and wish I had an answer." Rand knelt in front of Callie, handing her a handkerchief he took from his pocket. "It's all right, Callie. Emily is sleeping now."

"I'm so sorry," Callie said, wiping her eyes. "I should've been more help."

He laid a hand on her knee. "Do you want me to take the baby?"

Momentary panic filled her beautiful eyes. "No. Please let me hold her."

"All right," he said gently and sat down next to Delta. "How long does Doc Yates give Emily?"

"A week, maybe. It's close. That's why it's really important to find a home for Wren. It would sure ease Emily's mind. I wish I could keep the baby, but Cooper said I'll have more than enough when the twins come, and I agree."

Callie nuzzled the babe's cheek. "May I have a word with you in the kitchen, Rand?"

"Sure." Puzzled, he watched her hand little Wren to Delta, then followed her to the next room.

"We have to take the baby," she burst out. "We're Emily's only hope."

Rand placed his hand to the side of her face, searching her whiskey-colored eyes. "I feel the same way, but it's only right for the baby's sake to have two parents, and I can't marry you."

"Can't or won't?"

"Both. Remaining a bachelor is the way it has to be. Trying to fill another jagged hole in my heart is too hard and takes too long. Everyone I care about always ends up walking away. I have to protect myself from that hurt." It killed him to deny her. The only way to protect himself was to hurt her. If only it could be another way. She was asking too much of him. Couldn't she see that?

"Surely not everyone has done you wrong."

"I'll be glad to furnish proof. I once asked a young lady by the name of Jolene to marry me. We were nineteen years old. She said she would, so I made all the arrangements. She never showed up for the ceremony. Cooper saw her with another man, loading her trunk into a wagon. They drove out of town and she was gone. No word to me, no pretty excuses. She didn't even have the courtesy to tell me she'd changed her mind."

"That was one woman, and she didn't deserve you."

Rand shook his head. "She was just the first. Beth was the second and far more cruel because she told me I was going to be a father. Only she forgot to tell me that she was already married—to the mayor of the town, and the child was his. There were others who betrayed my trust, but I'm sure I don't need to go down the list." He wiped away the remains of a tear from her eye and softened his voice. "Our arrangement is only temporary. You said so yourself. I can't go through this again."

"I will agree to stay by your side and raise Toby and this baby." Callie rested her palm on Rand's chest.

"Trust me when I say I'll never abandon you. Please, give me a chance. That's all I ask."

"Let me get this straight. After insisting that you're only here for a few weeks, you're now saying you want to make this your home?"

She swallowed hard. "Yes."

"Why? Why the change of heart?"

"I realized a few minutes ago that it's time to put the ghosts of the past to rest and to do what is right and good."

"What assurance do I have that a week, a month, or a year from now you won't decide that you've made a mistake and pack up?"

"I have nothing except a solemn vow. What about you? Would you be able to make a life with me?"

He wouldn't survive the next time someone walked out of his heart. "I honestly don't know. I must be crazy for even considering this for one second."

Callie laid her head on his shoulder. "We're a sorry pair, aren't we? Seems life has done its best to drop us to our knees."

"We are and it has." He smoothed her hair. "Forget this crazy plan."

When she lifted her head, a light blazed in her amber eyes. "No. I think we can make this work if you're willing. You're a gambler. What odds do you give this hand so that a motherless babe will have a good life?"

Rand allowed a tight smile. "I wouldn't push in all my chips. At the moment, I only show a pair of threes."

"That's something to build on, isn't it? Who knows what cards we'll turn over next."

"It's possible, I reckon."

"Sometimes a person has to take a leap of faith and hope for the best. I'm the last one I thought would do this. But when I held Wren in my arms, I knew I couldn't let her go. Very soon she will have no one. I can be a good mother. I know it. I see you with Toby and know you want to be a father. We can make a happy home."

Shoving his hands through his hair, Rand blew out a loud breath. "I just don't… I know what you're saying is true and all that, but I'm not the marrying kind."

Callie clutched the front of his shirt as though she were falling. "I'm certainly not either. This scares the life out of me, but I can't turn my back. Can you? If not us, who *will* take Wren?"

Could he turn a blind eye and close off his heart to a babe who needed him? "Put that way, I guess that means I'm in. We'll simply have to trust each other and try to make this work." God help him if he was making another mistake.

"I need you to agree to one thing."

A sinking feeling settled in the pit of Rand's stomach. "What's that?"

"I can't share your bed. We'll have a marriage in name only."

He narrowed his eyes. And here she was already drawing away. "Fine. Then I can't offer my heart or speak words of love."

"It might not always be this way. One day, after we've both put our ghosts to rest, who knows? Can you live with that?"

"I find the terms of your agreement acceptable.

You just have to do one thing for me. It's a small thing, really."

A wary look crossed her face. "What is your request?"

He tucked a loose strand of hair behind her ear and stared deep into her eyes. "You have to kiss me every night before we go to bed. This make-believe marriage should have some benefit." Just as a building started with one board and nail at a time, maybe their marriage could begin with one kiss at night. Yet what kind of structure would it be, when everything was all said and done? Would it crumble and fall down around them? "Can you do that?"

"That's reasonable. Thank you, Rand. When will we tie the knot?"

Quick as possible, he supposed. Emily was fading fast. "It's too late to go into town today. I'll ride out first thing in the morning and make arrangements with the new preacher. Tomorrow afternoon? Is that suitable?"

"Yes. Let's have the ceremony at Delta's and Cooper's so Emily can be there. It will mean a lot to her."

Rand glanced down at his arm. She probably didn't even realize she'd laid her hand on him. But he'd felt it instantly because the warmth seared the skin beneath his shirt.

"That's the perfect place, Callie. I'm glad you thought of it. Want to seal the deal with a hug before we tell Delta?"

"I have no objections to a hug."

"Come 'ere then, Wife." He tugged her up against him.

Folding his arms around her, Rand let a ragged sigh escape. They still had things to prove to each other. He only prayed they wouldn't regret their decision.

Maybe one day they'd slay all those ghosts of their pasts she'd talked about. All he needed was a chance and plenty of patience.

⚜

Callie tried to pretend not to feel the quivers that came from the warmth of Rand's hand on her waist as they strode into the parlor. Acknowledging his touch would confirm the deep waters she'd stepped off into. Yet she didn't have enough imagination to block what his nearness did to her.

Her heart went out to him. The glimpse he'd given her into his painful past made her aware of all she'd promised. This marriage would bind them. There would be no going back. She could never leave him. Her life was with him now.

Please, dear God, don't let it be a mistake.

Delta was ecstatic at the news. "Thank you both. Now Emily can pass on in peace. And how wonderful that you want her to be at your wedding." She turned to Callie. "We have some planning to do, my dear, if we're to pull this off so quickly. We're about the same height and size. Well, not the size I am now." She laughed. "Let me rephrase that. You're the size I used to be six months ago. I insist you wear my wedding dress. It's a lovely creation of satin and lace."

"Thank you. You're too kind. That's one detail off my mind. The dress I have on is the only one I own. I'd never want to embarrass Rand."

"Nothing you do will ever make me hang my head," Rand declared firmly. "You could wear a burlap sack and I'd still marry you."

Emily roused and sat up. They told her the news and watched the most glorious smile brighten her face. "You're the answer to a prayer. I know my daughter will be in safe hands."

"I'll leave you ladies to finish making the arrangements," Rand said. "I need to get back to my patching job."

When he came back in, Callie and Delta were chattering like a couple of magpies. It seemed they'd discussed everything down to the tiniest details.

Toby sat near Callie, holding the baby and smiling to beat all get-out. The thrill of being a big brother was written all over his face. Rand couldn't wait to see what happened when the baby got colicky and cried all night.

Exhaustion seemed to have taken a toll on Emily. Rand knelt down in front of the sightless woman and took her hands. "We're going to cherish Wren and see that she grows up into a beautiful and happy young lady. And we'll tell her all about her brave mama and how much you loved her."

Tears rolled down Emily's pale cheeks.

A few minutes later, Rand helped both women into the buggy and put the baby in her mother's lap. He led his horse from the barn and hugged Callie. "I'm going to make sure they get home safely. I won't be long."

"Rand, I told you I'm perfectly capable of getting us back to the ranch." Delta pulled a small gun from her dress pocket, then lifted a Colt Walker from under the seat in the wagon box. That cannon would put the fear of God into even the most hardened criminal.

He laughed. "All right. I take your word. Just don't let Cooper kick me halfway to Galveston."

"I can handle my husband." Delta waved good-bye and flicked the reins.

Toby stood with one hand on Biscuit and the other clutching Callie's dress. She slid her arm around his thin shoulders.

Rand glanced back as he returned his roan to the barn and a mist came into his eyes.

His wife.

His son and soon-to-be baby daughter.

His family.

All he'd ever dreamed of was about to come true. One more day and his lonely heart could settle.

But he couldn't afford to relax yet. He knew how quickly minds could change…how fast life could turn on a man when he thought nothing could go wrong.

Fourteen

TOMORROW WOULD BE HER WEDDING DAY.

Callie lay awake all night. What had she done? How could she marry Rand?

If he...

A sliver of cold fear ran through her. She'd let him believe that the sleeping arrangements would eventually change, that she would fulfill her wifely duties one day. She'd already betrayed his trust, the very thing she'd vowed to never do.

But her path was set and she couldn't turn back. When she'd held little Wren in her arms, she knew she had to give the babe a home and love. It was as simple as that.

Even as she questioned the agreement to marry, she hungered for the baby in her arms again. That was worth her promise to kiss Rand each night before they went to bed.

The thought of Rand's kisses made her heart beat faster. Yet how long would he be satisfied? How long before he grew tired of the arrangement? And what about the wedding ceremony? Vowing to love and cherish someone she barely knew gave her the jitters. What if she froze up? What if she couldn't get the words out?

Though Rand was as different from Nate Fleming as night from day, what if she ended up as miserable as Claire?

No, it could never be that bad. It was unfair to compare.

A thin ribbon of light came from under the door, assuring her Rand was on watch. She was safe from everything except her overactive mind.

If only she could be the wife he wanted. She'd give anything if she could. Both of them would be forced to confront their paralyzing fears one day.

She sighed and rolled over, praying for strength and a double helping of courage.

∽

A cold, gray dawn greeted Rand.

"Great, just great," he grumbled, climbing from beneath the warm covers. He'd wanted the day to be perfect for Callie. "Nothing I can do to change it, though."

While she made breakfast, he milked the cow and collected the eggs. Stealing eggs from the hens technically fell under Toby's chores, but the boy hadn't gotten up yet and the day was wasting.

Rand's tongue tied in a knot when he sat across the table from Callie. What did one say to a woman before her wedding? *Did you sleep well? How about this weather? Do you have nervous jitters, or worse, cold feet? When are you leaving me?*

"We're going to make this work, Callie," he said instead, reaching out to cover her hand. "I'm not saying we won't have challenges, but whatever comes, we'll get through it. You and me. Together."

"I know." She licked her dry lips and met his gaze straight on. "I've always heard where there's a will there's a way. I'm just nervous. We don't even know each other. What if you grow to hate me?"

"That will never happen." He flashed a grin. "On the other hand, you may want to throw something at me and run out of this house screaming when you discover my bad habits. Cooper and Brett threatened to shoot me. Said I snored so loud, I could wake a stone-deaf garden rake."

She allowed a bit of a smile. "I've seen no sign of that. For all you know, I do the same...or worse. We're not perfect people. No one is."

"I want you to move to one of the upstairs bedrooms. The one you're in is too small. I'll buy more furniture of course. I want you to have whatever you need. Your comfort means a lot to me." He heard Toby shuffling around in the next room. "I'll never hurt you—you can count on that. I'll move heaven and earth to keep you and Toby and Wren safe."

Callie's hand curled inside his. "As long as we're being honest, I vow to never give you cause to curse this day."

Rand withdrew his hand when Toby stumbled to the table. The sleepy boy seemed awfully happy about something. Rand didn't have to wait long to find out.

Toby pulled out a chair and leaned close. "Will you be my papa?"

"That would give me great pleasure, but since you already have a father—"

"I ain't claimin' him. I want you."

"I'll have to speak to a lawyer. Maybe I can adopt you and make you my son. I can't think of any greater joy."

"Me neither. An' Aunt Callie can be my mama an' Wren can be my sister."

The boy appeared to have everything figured out and orderly in his world. With his chest swelling near to popping the buttons off his shirt, Rand reached over and mussed Toby's hair.

This was going to work out. It had to. Four lives depended on it. One, then two strangers, had formed a family. Now they'd added another. His tight circle was growing.

He was already counting the minutes to bedtime so he could kiss Callie again. He might manage to wrangle two kisses in one day if he played his cards right. One before the preacher and one later, in private.

∾

The sun broke through the clouds that afternoon, banishing the chill from Callie's bones. Cooper had picked up her and Toby in a handsome surrey for the ride to his Long Odds Ranch for the solemn ceremony. Rand would meet them there with the preacher.

The news that Emily had taken a turn for the worse during the night cast a pall over the day. Cooper didn't know if she'd be up to attending.

"Delta has packed up most of the baby's things,"

Cooper said in that deep voice of his. "Wren will go home with you and Rand afterward."

Panic rushed over Callie. She didn't have enough experience. She'd never cared for a baby all by herself. What if she didn't know what to do? What if she caused Wren harm?

Her blood stilled. What if Nate killed the infant when he came to settle up with her?

Callie twisted her hands in her lap. "Delta didn't have to do that. I could've gotten everything together."

"She didn't mind. My wife is a whirlwind of nervous energy these days. She hates the thought of turning over Wren's care to someone else and has concerns about the impending birth of our babies."

"Maybe we should leave the infant where she is for now."

Cooper's honest gray eyes met hers. "No. Delta's exhausted. She needs to rest up for the delivery. We haven't been able to prepare for our own babies yet."

"In that case, we'll relieve you of Wren."

"You're getting a good man, Miss Callie. Rand is top-notch. He just needs someone to believe in him. He carries a lot of hurt, and I think you might be the one to heal him."

"I'll do my best." Yet Callie didn't know how she'd do that with the limitations she'd placed on their marriage. What she'd done wasn't fair to the man who was used to being abandoned.

The remainder of the ride passed in silence. The Long Odds Ranch was most impressive, from the massive crossbar they passed under to the dwelling itself. The two-story frame ranch house appeared to have a fresh coat of white paint. A wide porch stretched across the front. It put Rand's humble dwelling to shame. That was all right, though. She knew one day Rand would have his fixed up every bit as nice.

Rand's blue roan and wagon was tied to a hitching rail in front alongside another horse she didn't recognize. He'd made it. She'd had a fear in the back of her mind that he'd leave her standing at the altar.

His words sounded in her ear. *I can't offer my heart or speak words of love.*

No one ever had. Still, she couldn't help wishing for it. Just once. Just to know that she mattered that much to someone…to Rand.

She shut her mind from the pain and disappointment as Cooper halted near Rand's big roan. Brett and Rand strode from the house. Rand wore a big grin and beat his brothers to her side.

Placing his hands around her waist, he pulled her against him as he swung her to the ground. He held her for several heartbeats and whispered in her ear, "I couldn't wait to see you, my wife. You look exceptionally beautiful today."

"I pray we're doing the right thing," she murmured.

But the fact the sun's rays warmed her face helped dispel some of her jitters. Marrying on a cold, gray day was definitely bad luck. She needed good omens, not bad.

When he offered his arm, she slipped her hand in the crook of his elbow and together they strode toward their future.

❧

Nate Fleming shrank into the brush near the road and watched Callie Quinn and his son go into the house. He wished he could get closer, but the ranch hands near the entrance kept him from it.

Hate welled up. He'd started to shoot the sheriff in town but decided to trail him a little first. He was glad he'd waited. The lawman had led him straight to the twit who'd stolen Toby from him. Killing the sheriff on his own land was much more fitting anyway.

And then when he got done with him, he'd turn his wrath on his former sister-in-law.

Soon he'd have her in his clutches.

⁂

After Rand delivered Callie upstairs, he found his brothers having a powwow outside. "What's going on?"

"Better tell him, Brett," Cooper said.

Brett made no attempt to dodge the question. "Been scouting the area and I've seen troubling signs."

"Go on." Whatever it was, Rand needed to know.

"Lots of tracks, hooves and boots both, in the woods across the way. Remnants of a campfire. Looks like someone has been hunkered down for a while. Waiting for something."

"Who do you think it might be?" Cooper asked.

"Could be someone just passing through. Don't know."

"Guess we'll know soon enough if it's Fleming." Rand clamped his back teeth together and stared off into the distance. Things would not bode well for the outlaw if he tried to take his family.

⤶⤷

In Delta's bedroom on the Long Odds Ranch, Callie slipped into the borrowed creamy satin wedding gown. She'd never seen anything so fine despite the fact that she'd once owned some beautiful clothes. She thought of Rand waiting downstairs and tried to quell the butterflies in her stomach.

Neither had spoken much. Her heart ached for this man who'd been horribly hurt by life and the people he trusted. They had that in common. They'd both walled off their hearts until nothing much remained except fear and loneliness.

How were they going to make this work?

Callie finished getting ready, then gave herself one last look in the mirror. She didn't recognize herself in this gorgeous dress. Smoothing her hair, she left the room.

When she saw Rand standing at the bottom of the stairs, her breath caught. He looked so handsome in a frock coat.

His eyes lit up. "I've never seen a more lovely, utterly breathtaking woman," he said when she reached him. "You look like an angel. I'm a very lucky man."

"Thank you. I've never seen you in such finery."

"What do you think?"

"I'm going to have to make another rule. I don't want you wearing these clothes in town or the women will be flocking around you, displaying their feminine charms. You're all mine now, Rand."

His grin made her heart skip several beats. "Suits me just fine. Are you ready?"

When she nodded, they went to join the others.

"Do you take this man to be your lawfully wedded husband?" the young preacher's voice boomed.

Callie swallowed hard past the lump in her throat. She glanced down at Rand's strong hand, his tanned fingers curled around hers.

"Look at me, Callie," Rand said softly. "We can stop right now if you don't want this."

She shook her head and turned to the man of the cloth, who waited for a response. "I do."

The rest of the ceremony was a blur. She must've said all the appropriate things, because it moved forward like a well-oiled wheel.

"You may kiss your bride, Mr. Sinclair," the preacher concluded.

Her heart stopped as Rand raised her veil and lowered his mouth to her slightly parted one. His tender kiss promised a safe port in a raging storm, security when the night pressed around, and easy affection.

Then, when she thought he'd end it for propriety's sake, he crushed her to him and with a heated fury deepened the kiss.

It left her breathless and shaken. Her face flamed at his boldness.

Beside her, Toby clapped and hollered. Brett, who looked quite handsome in a beaded leather shirt and pants and his tall moccasins, was first in line to congratulate her.

"Welcome to the family, Miss Callie." Brett enveloped her in a hug. "Rand found himself a beautiful wife. I'm tempted to steal you away from him."

A threatening rumble came from Rand's throat.

"Oh no you don't. She's mine, little brother, and don't you be forgetting that."

Callie laughed and broke free. She made her way to Emily Winters, who had slumped over into the chair. The woman looked so frail and tiny. Callie knelt down and took her hand. "Are you all right, dear?"

"Need to lie down," she whispered.

Cooper lifted the woman in his arms and carried her up the stairs. Callie and Delta followed. They tucked her into bed and sat down beside her. Callie watched as Delta laid an open locket that had Joe's picture inside on Emily's pillow.

"The angels are here," Emily murmured. "See them? They're beautiful. My Joe. And Mama. It's been so long."

With tears blurring her vision, Callie went to get the baby. Something told her the woman would never see another sunrise. When she returned, Emily's breathing had become increasingly shallow. She laid little Wren on her mother's stomach.

Emily's hand crept out from beneath the quilt. The baby clutched it for all she was worth. It was as though she were trying to keep Emily from leaving, to pull her mother back from the death that hovered so near.

Wren didn't make a sound. She lay there very still, her bright little eyes following some unseen movement in the room.

The lanky preacher was in attendance along with Callie, Delta, Cooper, Rand, and Brett. Callie found comfort in Rand's arms. She cried while he held her, then let him wipe her eyes.

As the sun set in the western sky amid vibrant

purple and orange hues, Emily Winters breathed her last on earth and went to join her heavenly father. Only then did Wren break from her trance and begin to wail.

Emily had held on as long as she could. Finding a loving home for her daughter had freed her. Callie was determined to be the best substitute possible.

One day she'd tell Wren about the woman who'd given her daughter life and how bravely she'd faced the end.

Rand and his brothers were putting the baby's things into the wagon when a sudden shot rang out. The bullet pierced the crown of Cooper's black Stetson.

They dove to the ground. Because of the wedding, they'd removed their weapons. Rand had never felt so vulnerable.

"Who the hell would try to kill me on my own damn land?"

"Gotta be Nate Fleming." Rand raised his head and looked around.

"I haven't seen hide nor hair of him since that first day."

"Just because you haven't seen him doesn't mean he wasn't there," Brett reminded him softly. "You know that."

One of Cooper's ranch hands peered out from behind the wagon and pitched him a rifle.

Rand scanned the tree line, where Brett had seen signs of someone. If he were Fleming, that's where he'd hide in order to take the shot. A second later, an orange flame spat from the shadows. This time the bullet lodged in the side of the wagon.

"He's in the trees, Coop."

"I saw." Cooper sprang to his feet, followed by Rand and Brett. By that time, it seemed every hand on the ranch was there. All released a fierce volley of firepower.

Minutes went by and nothing moved. Cooper cautiously stole toward the place where the shot had come from. Rand walked on one side of him with the pistol that one of the men had pressed into his hand raised and ready to fire. Brett flanked him on the other.

Whoever had crouched there had fled. Remains of a cigarette lay in the dirt. And nearby was a playing card.

The king of diamonds.

Rand sucked in a ragged breath. Someone had burned the eyes out.

Cooper picked up the card. "He left this for a reason. What the devil is it supposed to mean?"

"It's possible that he views himself as some sort of king. Someone superior to others. And maybe the eyes are burned out because he doesn't want people to see what he's doing." If evil existed anywhere, it did in Fleming. The outlaw made Tolbert Early look like a choirboy.

God help him, he'd keep Callie safe if it took every last ounce of strength he had. No one would harm her. Not this day or any other.

Taking painstaking steps, Brett appeared to be following the tracks. Soon the trees and undergrowth swallowed him.

"Well, he for sure knows where I live. I'm betting he knows the way to your home too, Rand." Cooper pocketed the card. "We've gotta keep our women out of the crosshairs."

"Yep. For a fact. What are we going to do about the man in the meantime? We really have too much ground to cover." The reality of the situation frustrated Rand.

Cooper stared into the distance. "We learned the hard way from chasing Tolbert Early how difficult it is to find one man in the bush when we have no leads. Don't even have a direction to start. Besides, I have a feeling if we were to take out after him, he'd double back and get Callie and Toby. Maybe Delta too."

Brett crouched on his heels, staring at the ground. "He wants us to play into his hands. For now, we must defend ourselves and the ones we love. We have no choice."

"I agree," Rand said. "I'll keep my guard up for any sign of him."

"If he comes into town, I'm arresting him on the spot," Cooper declared. "And if he doesn't come peaceful, I'll shoot him."

When they got back to the house, Delta and Callie were waiting on the porch. Both women's eyes were red rimmed.

Callie hurried toward Rand. "We heard shots. What was it?"

How was he going to break this to her on their wedding day? Rand swallowed hard. "Someone in the woods fired at us. Can't be sure who. He was gone when we got there."

Cooper reached into his pocket for the card. "Does this mean anything to you?"

"Oh God, no!" Callie gave a cry and clasped her hand over her mouth. "He's here. It's Nate."

"How can you be sure, sweetheart?" Rand asked gently, wishing he could take away her fear and put happiness in its place.

"It was his way of warning a person he was coming after them. He left one for me before, when I tried to help my sister get away from him."

"Reckon that settles it." Cooper took the card from her shaking fingers and slipped it back into his pocket. "From now on, Delta will have an escort every time she goes outside. I won't leave her unguarded for a moment. I'd suggest you do the same, Rand."

"I plan to, brother. I'll also keep a closer eye on Toby."

"I want you to teach me how to shoot, Rand." Callie's voice shook a little, but she put a good helping of determination in it.

It was a heck of a thing to have your new wife ask you to teach her to shoot on her wedding day. Still, if she wanted to learn, he'd darn sure teach her.

And anything else she wanted.

Fifteen

EMILY'S FUNERAL TOOK PLACE ON THE LONG ODDS Ranch the following day with the ranch hands forming a protective circle around them. No one would get through. They buried her high on a hill next to her husband.

In the midst of singing "Rock of Ages," a mourning dove flew down and rested on Emily's burial spot. The sight made Callie's voice waver as the words tried to get past the lump in her throat.

She gazed at Rand's bowed head and wondered what he was thinking.

They'd stayed at the Long Odds because of fears that Nate would ambush them in the dark. "I won't put you or the children at risk," Rand had declared, putting an end to the discussion.

Rand gave her the bed and he slept in a chair. Several times in the night she'd awakened to find him staring out the window into the blackness. He didn't have to tell her he was looking for the trouble that was riding hell-for-leather straight at them. The foreboding hadn't helped in getting the rest she'd needed.

He'd disappeared before dawn, and she hadn't seen him until it was time to walk up the hill to the little cemetery. He'd carried something wrapped in a piece of burlap.

Slipping her hand inside his now as they stood beside the mound of fresh dirt covering the rough wooden box, Callie leaned close, borrowing from his warmth. "I'm sorry, Rand. Losing a friend is very difficult."

"Nothing harder," he said low, wiping his eyes. "Never thought when we buried Joe that we'd bury his wife a few months later. Guess we never know."

"That's why it's terribly important to live each day with no regrets."

His crystal gaze made her breath catch. "Do you have any about marrying me?"

"No, we did the right thing, Rand." It surprised her that she didn't have a moment's hesitation. "I shudder to think what would've happened to little Wren. We'll give her the love she needs so she can grow up strong and healthy."

A shadow crossed his face. He pulled free from her touch. "At least we can do that, if nothing else."

His black mood frightened her a bit. She'd never seen this side of the easygoing man she'd married.

As the last of the mourners began the trek down the hill, he removed a wooden cross from the burlap sack. It had Emily's name carved into it along with the appropriate dates. Rand stuck it deep into the soil and ran his hand across Emily's birth date.

"What is it, Rand? What are you so angry about?"

"I'd cuss a blue streak if you weren't here."

"Why?"

"I'm fighting mad that we married solely for the sake of a child. How can we give her a proper home and the love she desperately deserves when our marriage isn't real?"

"I don't know. All I can say is that I'll be by your side as we figure everything out."

"Then, there's this damn funeral. Emily and Joe are gone. Other than Wren, what do they have to show for their life here? And there's the problem with my mother. But the thing that angers me most is that when the time comes for me, I have no dates to put on my marker. Most everyone knows when their life began. Not me. I don't have a beginning. Near as the people at the orphanage could determine, I was around five years old when I came. I can't recall celebrating a birthday."

"You could ask your mother," Callie said gently, her eyes smarting. Cooper was right about the deep hurt that had festered into almost unmanageable pain. If only she could do something to help. But she seemed to have heaped more on top of the old wounds.

"Don't you think I have? Claims she can't remember, that she was sick for months following my birth and nearly died. She says my father wrote it down in the family Bible, but by the time she returned home from her tour out West, someone else lived in our house and they'd gotten rid of all of her belongings, including the Bible. She was gone for over a year."

How very sad not to know when you were born. It must be an awful feeling. Some people believed a birth date was tied to a person's purpose in life. To not have one stole clarity. Rand must feel only half a person. Callie was only beginning to understand this complicated man she'd married.

"What about your father? You were with him for the first years of your life. Didn't you celebrate a birthday?"

"Can't remember one time. Once my mother left, my father didn't want to celebrate anything. That is, when he was around. Most times I rarely saw him. I stayed with a friend of my mother's until she got tired of me."

"Then we'll simply give you a birth date. Do you have a favorite month?"

He brushed her cheek with a finger. "This one."

"January? Why?"

"It's when I met you. When my life changed. When I found meaning. You're my beginning, Callie."

"Oh, Rand." Tears clogged her throat. She didn't know what to say. That she meant so much to him brought meaning to her life also…in addition to an enormous responsibility. Therein lay a problem.

"I can see that I've overstepped my bounds. Guess it's time to load up the kids and go home, Mrs. Sinclair. Where I can make a fool of myself in private."

When he turned away, Callie grabbed his arm. "You're not making a fool of yourself. What you said touched my heart and left me speechless. I'm proud to be your beginning. I declare that henceforth your birthday shall be January 1. We'll celebrate it every year."

A grin curved his mouth. "Thank you for understanding and not fearing you've tied yourself to a madman."

She tucked her hand in the crook of his elbow. "Let's go home."

Rand kept his Winchester in his lap while his sharp eye scanned both sides of the road as they made their way toward the Last Hope. He released the breath he'd held when at last they turned onto the property.

Toby had chattered nonstop. The boy was enthralled with his new little sister and asked fourteen million questions. His main concern was how long they were going to keep Wren. He hadn't stopped grinning since they'd assured him it was a forever kind of deal.

"Just like me?"

"Yep, just like you," Rand said.

Not even lye soap and a wire brush could've scrubbed the grin off the lad's face. The grin still persisted when they pulled up to the house. Biscuit raced from the barn to greet them, and the last thing Rand heard was Toby telling the dog all about Wren and how they had to protect her.

Over the next hour and a half, he moved everything from Callie's room by the kitchen to the bedroom upstairs across from his. Then he added the baby's cradle, crib, and the dozens of other things Cooper and Delta had thrown into the wagon.

Rand could've sworn they were still tossing things into the back as they pulled out. He'd never seen so much stuff in his entire life. The child had more clothes than the law allowed.

When they got everything arranged, along with the tall chest of drawers from his room, he draped an arm around Callie's shoulders. "Will this do?"

"It's perfect. Simply beautiful." She moved out of the circle of his arm and laid Wren in her cradle. The infant gave a deep sigh and smiled in her sleep as Callie covered her with a fleece blanket.

Watching it all, Rand thought his new bride had never looked so lovely. If Fleming hadn't thrown a pall over everything, she would be beaming. It was clear she already loved Wren as though the babe were her own child.

Though he longed to have Callie in his bed so he could reach out and touch her and keep her from leaving, it gave his soul peace to know she was so near.

∾

The shooting lessons commenced once Rand had everything in the house to Callie's liking. They bundled up Wren and brought her outside in a basket. Toby parked himself beside the babe with one hand holding hers. Biscuit found a rabbit to chase and disappeared into the woods.

"Are you ready, Callie?" Rand walked back from a stump where he'd placed an old peach can and picked up the rifle.

"As much as I'll ever be."

He noted her wide eyes and the way her hand trembled. "There's nothing to be afraid of. I'll teach you everything you need to know. First lesson is how to work this lever."

Callie nodded and licked her dry lips. He showed her how to pull it down and back up. "This does two things. It ejects a spent cartridge if you've already fired and also gets a new one in place for the next time. You try it." He handed the weapon to her.

Though she was nervous, she did as instructed. He

was so proud of her. It took courage to tackle something very clearly out of her area of expertise.

Next came loading the chamber with cartridges. "Watch out or they'll pinch your finger," he said. "Slide each one into the slot."

After she'd loaded several rounds, he instructed, "Settle the stock firmly against your shoulder so it won't bruise you. Now raise the sight—this V-notched piece of metal on the barrel. Get your target in the center of it." Standing behind her, he put his arms around her and helped bring the rifle to her shoulder.

When her soft curves settled into the indentations of his body like clay into a mold, his heart thudded against his ribs.

His mind went haywire every time they breathed the same air, but her present closeness and the fragrance of her hair scrambled his train of thought, and it took off across the country regardless of where the tracks were. If she'd asked his name, he would've mutely stared at her.

"I don't know if I can do this, Rand. Maybe I'm making a mistake."

"You can do anything you set your mind to. You need to know how to defend yourself and the children in case I'm not around."

"All right."

"Steady now," he murmured in her ear. "Get that can in your sights. Take a deep breath and squeeze the trigger nice and easy. Don't be afraid of the kick. I've got you."

Flame and smoke shot from the barrel and sent her falling back into his arms. It took him a minute to breathe again and let her go. He wanted to prolong the moment.

At last he released her and glanced at the target. The bullet had missed the can. It took several more tries to hit the blasted thing, and each time she fell against him, the contact jarred his senses. Maybe, just maybe, he could have what he desired more than anything. Over and over they practiced until Callie said she had to cook supper.

"You did really well. I'm very proud of you."

"Do you truly think so? You're not just saying that?" She handed him the Winchester.

He took it, stroking her arm. "Would I lie? None of my other students can light a candle to you."

Callie laughed. "How many students do you have?"

"Well, just you, but I'm not telling a fib. You're a natural. And you got over your fear right away. I daresay Fleming had better keep his distance. You'll fill him so full of holes, his own mama won't know him."

"She's dead. Judge Isaac Parker hanged his mother in Fort Smith, Arkansas, along with two more of Fleming's kin."

The calm, matter-of-fact statement struck Rand like a load of buckshot. In that moment, it hit him what they were dealing with. Fleming was no run-of-the-mill outlaw. And he wasn't going to give up and go away. Men like him weren't bound by time or distance or anything else.

Fleming would get what he came after.

Unless Rand stopped him.

Ice formed in his veins. He'd do whatever he had to. Make no mistake about it.

As Callie cleared the table that night, Rand held
Wren, playing with her. The child seemed to know
exactly what he was saying and tried her darnedest to
talk back.

"I think we'll soon have to call this child Magpie
instead of Wren," he announced. "She's going to be
a talker."

Callie turned from the dishpan. "I like that nick-
name. She's very intelligent, that's plain to see. Do
you think she knows what happened to her mother
and misses her?"

"Not for me to say. I wouldn't dispute the notion,
though. The bond between a mother and child is
extremely strong."

"Yes, it is." Her voice held a strange quality. Maybe
she was referring to herself and her mother.

When Callie dried the last dish and put it away,
they moved to the parlor. She tossed a quilt onto the
floor and Rand laid little Wren on it. Toby and his
dog immediately plopped down beside the babe, one
on each side. Rand pitied anyone who ever tried to
harm the child.

He sat down on the sofa and let the scene soothe
some of the raw places inside. The crackling fire,
the creak of the rocker, the soft click of the knitting
needles all melded into one word—*home*.

He'd finally found somewhere to belong. Nothing
or no one was going to take that away.

"Did you lock the doors, Rand?" Callie asked.

Though the question seemed innocent enough,
Rand knew the reason for it.

"Sure did. You and the children are safe. I'll check again before we go up to bed if that'll ease your mind."

"Will you sleep with a gun?"

"Plan on it." He rose and went to her, laying a hand on her hair. "I wish I could take away your fear, darlin'. Wish I could take away the darkness, make all your days sunshine and happiness. Wish to God I could make your world brighter so you'd smile more. I dearly love your smile, the sound of your laughter."

"I will when it's over and I can put the past where it belongs. I'm sorry I've involved you in this mess. I'm so afraid of what Nate might do to you."

"I'm a big boy. I can take care of myself." In addition to looking after all the ones he loved, he added silently.

"I know you can." She patted his hand. "Look over there. The trio's asleep."

Toby had one arm around the baby. Even in sleep, he was protective.

"That boy dearly loves his new sister. And I love them both. We're gonna be happy here, Callie."

"I know I roped you into marrying me and I'm sorry."

"I'm not. And you didn't *rope* me into anything. I could've said no. This is what I've dreamed of my whole life." He just prayed it lasted.

"Even when you were swilling whiskey, dealing cards, and doing God knows what else in your saloon?"

The twinkle in her eyes made him happy. That she could tease meant she wasn't going to let anyone rob her of the chance to be lighthearted on occasion.

"Yep, even in my whiskey-swilling days." Warmth pooled low in his belly. It would soon be time to collect his nightly kiss. Anticipation hummed inside him like the drone of bees.

Those kisses were going to be his ruination, and he cursed his weakness. Even so, there was no way in hell he'd stop giving them.

They sat for a while lost in their own thoughts, then each carried a child upstairs and tucked them into bed.

"Don't worry, Callie. I'll watch over you. Get some rest." He tugged her against his chest, wondering if she could hear his heart beating wildly. The woman didn't know it, but she had more power in her little finger than he had in his entire body.

His *wife*.

"I have no fears as long as you're with me," she whispered, looking up at him.

Rand slid his hand beneath her hair and lowered his mouth. The kiss was full of raw hunger and need. A raging desire so unbridled it strangled him rose up. He wanted to pull her against him and caress every inch of her body until he put out this fire that seared everything in its path. His hand slipped to the swell of her breast to touch her gentle curves. He couldn't get enough of this woman he treasured.

He'd tried to resist loving her, but with each passing minute, it became clear he fought a losing battle.

A low moan rose from his chest.

One day he'd get brave enough to undo a few buttons and feel her silky skin. A tremble weakened his knees.

Dear God, if he lived to be as old as Methuselah, he'd never tire of kissing her.

He hadn't been wrong in saying she was his beginning. And somehow he knew she'd also be his end.

Sixteen

THE WIND THROUGH THE TREES SEEMED TO WHISPER the words, *Prepare, prepare.*

Though they hadn't glimpsed Nate, something told Callie he was watching. Waiting. Ready to pounce. Often when she went outside, her skin prickled.

So more shooting lessons had followed. Now that they were caretakers of another small life, Callie wanted to make sure they were as ready as they could be for whatever came.

With much practice, she developed some skill with both a rifle and a pistol, at least enough to be familiar with the weapons. She'd begun carrying a small derringer in the pocket of her dress.

The cold piece of metal brought a sense of security.

Now, with sunlight spilling in through the windows, she sat rocking Wren, who filled her with unbelievable joy. Rand and Toby were outside. Her mind drifted to past mistakes and regret.

Her biggest—Richard Farrington—crossed her mind. Dear, sweet Richard. He had fought his demons right alongside her. She'd met him the year she turned eighteen. From the start, their friendship had formed out of the fact they were two lost souls looking for a way through the muddled maze of their lives.

One night, they met beside a clear stream behind her stepfather's house. Though eight years had passed, she still recalled how the moonlight reflected on the water, the sound of Richard's sobs, the feeling of utter despair.

"My mother is gone," Richard had cried. "Found her hanging from a tree out back."

He'd cut her down and then found the note saying that she couldn't take any more. His mother had been a widow, and the struggle to keep going simply drained the life from her.

Callie's attempts to comfort went too far. They spent the night in each other's arms. Before dawn, despite the fumbling gropes and awful pain, she had become a woman. A couple of months later, she discovered she was with child. Calling her a slut and an utter disgrace, her stepfather, Edmund Powers, sent her to live with his crone of a sister outside Jefferson City. Claire went with her. Away from their step-parents' eagle eyes, her twin met Nate Fleming and married him to spite Edmund. He'd been livid that she would defy him and promptly told both Claire and Callie they were dead to him.

Richard Farrington disappeared, and she'd learned only six months ago that Edmund had hired some thugs to beat him senseless and put him aboard a ship bound for the Orient. She never saw or heard from him again.

Callie had the baby five months later. A girl, she was told by her stepbrother, who, carrying out his father's instructions, ripped the infant from her arms. Only one brief glimpse, one precious moment with her little darling, and David took it all away. No matter how much she and Claire begged, David refused to tell her where he'd taken the babe.

To this day, she didn't know what had happened to her.

Not even if her baby angel was alive. A tear slipped down Callie's cheek. What she'd give to see her child again.

As she cradled Wren's small body that fit so perfectly into her arms, she remembered the trauma of the childbirth and the terrible darkness that had overtaken her afterward. Such horrendous pain and blood loss. The doctor told her she'd almost died. She'd felt so adrift, she'd almost wanted to.

She could never take the chance of that happening again.

That one night, because she'd simply wanted to make Richard happy, altered the course of her life forever and ruined any chance of being a true wife to Rand.

And, oh God, how she wanted to.

But the pain, the enormous loss, and now the fear kept her in a stranglehold.

A shuddering sigh rose from deep inside, pushing aside the painful memories that cut to the quick. Callie caressed Wren's coal-black hair, inhaling the babe's sweet fragrance. She'd made many missteps in her life, but agreeing to be a mother to little Wren wasn't one of them.

If she did this right, maybe it would begin to heal

the past in some small way and she could finally make peace with what had happened.

The kitchen door opened and she smiled. Rand had shown her how it felt to be truly loved and cherished. Their nightly routine of enjoying each other's company in the parlor, then kissing before they went to bed was something she looked forward to from the moment her feet hit the floor in the morning.

Some nights he kissed her twice, but she didn't let him know she noticed. Each kiss seemed to hold a promise that he'd always keep her close to his heart, no matter the restrictions she placed on him. A huge part of her wished she could be the wife he needed, sleep beside him, and take comfort from his nearness.

But Rand wouldn't want a woman who was so broken. He deserved a whole wife. Children meant everything to him. She could never give him a biological child.

So she had to silently endure the torture of Rand's nearness and try to tamp down the desire that flowed like molten lava through her veins.

Rand entered the parlor and laid his large hand on her head. "I love watching you holding the baby. Makes something turn over inside of me. You're a wonderful mother."

"Flattery can get a man in trouble, you know that?"

He grinned. "I'll risk it. Just came in to tell you that Cooper and Brett are here with a small army. We're starting work on the house." He paused. "We sorta have to feed 'em. Do you think—"

"I'll take care of it, Rand. I don't mind."

"Thank you." Before he went back out, he slid his hand down her hair to her shoulder.

"Is Toby in your way?" she asked.

"Nope. I like having the boy around."

"If he gets bothersome, send him in the house."

A quick nod and Rand went back out to the work crew. Callie kissed the baby and laid her in the cradle. It would take a lot of food to feed all those hungry men. She had no time to waste. Thinking of the past wouldn't set it to rights. Nothing could. Too much water under that bridge.

With the feel of Rand's touch still lingering on her hair, she pulled out her pots and pans and set to work.

All the kissing and touching had awakened a powerful need inside her. How easy it would be to slip into Rand's bed. But first she had to figure out a way past the barriers she'd set.

And find the words that would destroy his love.

He should know what kind of wife he'd gotten.

❧

Callie had just fed the workers lunch and was cleaning up the kitchen when a knock sounded at the front door. After pushing the window curtain aside for a glance, she opened it for Rand's mother.

"Abigail, how nice to see you. Please, come in."

The woman squared her stiff shoulders and forced a smile. "I hope I can have a word with you if it's convenient."

"Of course." Callie motioned Abigail inside. "Rand is out back. I can call him."

"I'd rather you didn't just yet."

Something told Callie this would be a trying afternoon. She prayed for patience. Seating Abigail on the settee in the parlor, she took the rocker. "What's this about?"

"I had to hear through the tittle-tattle going around town that you and my son have wed. It made me look like a fool."

"I apologize. We had to plan it very quickly." Callie told her about Emily Winters and the circumstances that led to the marriage. "We'd have loved to have you there but had no time to assemble guests. We never meant to cause you embarrassment."

Abigail drew her gloves off slowly. "I fail to see why you couldn't have waited a few days. Rand simply didn't want me."

"That's not true." Callie moved to the space beside her and took her hands. "Your son loves you. You gave him the one thing he'd wanted his entire life—a mother. But Rand is no longer a little boy. He's a man. He doesn't need his nose wiped for him. Forgive me for saying this, but you're both trying too hard."

"I suppose you're right. It's just so difficult." Abigail gave a wry smile. "Impatience has always been my shortcoming. I want everything yesterday. Delays eat a hole in me. It nearly killed me when I kept silent so long, pretending to be a grieving widow. So many times I wanted to blurt it out. But fear of Rand's rejection was a strong deterrent. And now look at us, look at what it got me. He can barely stay in the same room with me. I should never have passed through Battle Creek."

"I think it might help to relax and stop wearing

your feelings on your sleeve. You're not going to change Rand. The more you try, the further you'll push him away. I want you both to have a happy, comfortable kinship. He truly needs you and I think you also need him...maybe more than you know."

"I suppose I could try to mend my ways." Abigail pulled her hands free and adjusted the frothy hat of silk, lace, and feathers that had probably cost a pretty penny. "Now, I'd like to see my new granddaughter."

Callie suppressed a groan of frustration. In one breath Abigail said she'd try to change and in the next she was back to demanding. "I'm sorry, but Wren is asleep right now."

"Can I just peek at her then?"

"I won't deny you that. I moved her cradle into the kitchen, where it's warm, while I worked."

Abigail followed her into the next room. She leaned over the cradle and touched the babe's dark hair. "She's beautiful."

"Yes, she is." Before Callie could stop her mother-in-law, she picked up Wren. So much for promises. The infant's eyes flew open in alarm and she screwed up her face to cry.

"There you are," Abigail crooned, cradling the infant in her arms. "Isn't this much better?"

For whom, Callie wondered? Wren had been snoozing peacefully.

Abigail scowled. "This baby needs to be held. Lying on a hard bed will make the back of her head flat. A mother knows about these things."

Callie let the slight go and chuckled. "You have no idea how rare it is for her to lie in her cradle. If

Rand's not holding her, Toby is wagging her around like a favorite toy."

"That child is not old enough to hold a baby." The woman shifted Wren to her shoulder and patted the small back. "I won't have him hurting my granddaughter."

Anger rose. "Look, Abigail, we always take the safety of the children very seriously."

"Oh dear, I've done it again, haven't I? I just wanted to hold her in my arms for a moment."

Callie sighed. Abigail was never going to change, so she might as well accept her, faults and all. "Would you mind taking care of your granddaughter while I finish up the dishes and get some supper on? It would be a tremendous help."

"I'd love to." Beaming, Abigail kissed the babe.

"She likes to be rocked. I'll join you in a while."

While she washed the last of the dishes, she looked out to see where Toby was. She found him with Brett. Someone had rigged a belt around Toby's waist and it had a hammer hanging from it. He spied her and waved, making the drooping feather fall from his hair where he'd stuck it. No doubt that wide grin he wore would be permanent. She'd never seen the sweet boy happier, and that brought a smile to her heart.

Rand came to the door and opened it to whisper, "How about a kiss now in preparation for our good-night ritual? It's good to prime the pump, so to speak. Wouldn't want rust to form."

"I'm not some pump to be *primed*." Though she glowered, inside she glowed like a beacon guiding ships to safety. She waggled her finger. "I agreed to

one each night. Don't go trying to change the rules,
mister. Besides, your mother is here."

His grin vanished. "What does she want?"

"Two things. She had her feelings trampled on
because we didn't tell her about the wedding, and
secondly, she wanted to see her granddaughter," Callie
said, keeping her voice low.

"Guess I oughta come in and say hello."

She followed him into the parlor, intending to act
as a buffer in case they needed one. As they neared,
she heard their visitor singing a beautiful lullaby. Rand
stopped and stiffened. His face froze.

"What is it, Rand?"

"I've heard that song before. Nothing. It's nothing." He touched her cheek with a fingertip and they
moved on.

When they entered the room, Abigail looked up
with big tears in her eyes. "Rand, I love this precious
little girl. She's stolen my heart."

"She has mine too, Mother."

"I never knew how special being a grandmother was."

"Just don't go spoiling her."

"I most certainly can if I want to," she huffed.

"Relax." Rand shoved a hand through his hair
and then jammed his hat back on. "I didn't mean it
as an order."

"I put tea on," Callie said, hoping to defuse the situation. Rand and his mother were like oil and water.
One word could set tempers flaring. She prayed for
the wisdom to know what to say. "How are things in
town, Abigail? Did the new hotel open? The Texas
Cattleman's, isn't it?"

"Yes. It's slated to welcome patrons next week. Mr. Lexington is quite beside himself with fear that they'll steal his business. He's working night and day to complete the renovations to the Lexington Arms. Of course, with rumors of that horrible outlaw running rampant, the citizens are on edge. I keep my doors locked."

"That's an excellent idea," Callie murmured. Everyone should take extra precautions against the stone-cold killer.

"You shouldn't have driven out, Mother—it's not safe. I worry about you traipsing across the countryside."

Rand seemed to have said the magic words, because Abigail beamed. "It's nice to know you care. I'm very careful and I always keep the derringer in my pocket loaded. Besides, George Lexington rode out with me. I left him at Cooper's Four Promises ranch so he could check on a nephew who just hired on. I'll pick George up on the way back."

"Coop is here working on the house. He will escort you back to the ranch. Let him know when you want to leave."

"I will, son."

The remainder of the visit went well. Abigail was in good spirits. Maybe the key was knowing that someone you loved cared about you. It certainly seemed the case. Callie filed that away for future reference in dealing with her difficult mother-in-law.

⌘

For the remainder of the day, the lullaby his mother had sung to Wren played over and over in Rand's head. It seemed so familiar. Where had he heard it?

Suddenly bits and pieces of a memory of sitting in someone's lap filled his head and how the sweetness of the song had soothed his fears. It had been Abigail. She *had* loved him. When had that changed? When had Abigail decided that her career was more important than her son?

Rand laid down his hammer. He almost wished the memory had stayed buried, because that would be a lot less painful than having to face the truth: he hadn't mattered enough.

Memories held such power. They could bring happiness, they could devastate, or they could hold him in a steely grip that bound more securely than chains.

Take the dreams he kept having that instilled sheer terror. The one last night had shaken him to the core. He stood all alone in the dark, surrounded by trees. Suddenly, a horse galloped straight for him. Its glittering eyes glowed an eerie red. The animal rose on its hind legs above him and let out a horrible noise. Rand couldn't escape. There was nowhere to run. Just before it came down on top of him, he woke up.

The nightmare had left him drenched in sweat and struggling to catch his breath. What did it mean? Why did nightmares plague him now? For God's sake, he wasn't a child anymore.

"Everything all right, Rand?" Cooper laid a hand on his back.

Rand jerked and picked up his hammer. "I'm fine. Just thinking."

Brett glanced up. "We can stop for a bit if you want."

"Won't get anything done if we don't keep after

it." Unable to explain his troublesome thoughts, Rand pushed the memory and dream to the back of his mind and dove into his work.

By the time darkness moved across the land like a stealthy invader, Rand was ready to call it quits. Every bone and muscle ached. They'd completed the outside of the house. Tomorrow they'd all return and start on the interior. He couldn't wait to get it fixed up for his new bride.

He and his brothers had discussed when to stock the Last Hope with cattle and decided to do it within the month. Cooper was giving him thirty head for a wedding gift. Brett would kick in ten of the best horses in Texas. Then they mentioned that a nearby rancher named Otis Crenshaw needed to sell off his herd numbering around three hundred. Otis was going back east to live out his days with his daughter and son-in-law.

The price was right at two dollars a head, far cheaper than the going rate because of the need to settle things quickly. Since Rand could only comfortably run around a hundred cows on his spread, Cooper agreed to buy the remainder for his and Delta's second ranch, the Four Promises.

Rand's dream was all coming together. Excitement hummed inside. He'd never thought it would happen.

Before Cooper left, he gave Rand the news that Nate Fleming had left the area. Seemed the sheriff in Corsicana had telegraphed that Fleming had robbed a stage between there and Fort Worth yesterday. Maybe the outlaw had decided to cut his losses and move on. At least it appeared that way. Rand wasted no time in telling Callie. Her radiant smile made his chest swell.

That night after supper, he brought in some wood for the fireplace and threw on a couple of logs. As he rose, an envelope on the mantel caught his attention. He opened it to find five hundred dollars inside along with a note.

> *Dear Rand,*
>
> *Before you fuss, this money is for my granddaughter. Use it to buy whatever she needs. I won't have her going without. We can all use a little assistance now and again. This will help you get on your feet. I won't hear another word about it.*
>
> *Abigail*

Rand cussed a blue streak under his breath. His mother would be the death of him. He didn't know what to do about it yet. If he kept the money, it would only encourage her to persist on the same path. He'd learned that if he gave her an inch, she'd take a mile. But the fact was he could use it. The renovations had eaten up the cash he'd set aside and he had to buy more furniture for the house. Toby needed his own room.

Rand put everything back into the envelope and laid it on the mantel. He'd sleep on it. Maybe he'd dream of an answer.

Wren let out a cry from her cradle. Sounds from the kitchen told him Callie was finishing up the dishes.

He picked up the babe. "Hey, little one. What's your problem? Need something in your belly? Tell your papa and I'll fix it."

Toby had been lying on the sofa. He sat up. "She ain't hungry. That's her poopy cry."

The boy seemed to have something there, because a reeking odor reached Rand's nose. Strange how the boy had a gift for knowing these things.

Rand held the child away from him and looked around for…he didn't know what exactly. Definitely help of some sort, preferably a small army. He wasn't about to ask Toby what to do. Nope. Not because he didn't think the six-year-old had answers—he most assuredly did—but because Rand was the father, and fathers were supposed to solve problems.

No, he wouldn't need Callie. He could do this. After all, it was a small job. It'd be easy.

"I do believe you're right, Toby. I guess I'll take her upstairs."

"Aunt Callie changes her down here. The diapers are in that box next to the cradle."

"Oh." Rand found a stack of folded cotton triangles. He got one and laid the baby on a quilt on the floor. Her cries got louder and more insistent. "Hold your horses, little girl. I'm doing my best here."

Filling his lungs with a cleansing breath, he unfastened the safety pin that held the contraption. The stench hit him square in the face and nearly made him lose his supper.

Good Lord!

He'd better hurry. He turned his head to the side and took another breath. Wren squalled and began to kick and squirm, getting it on her feet, on Rand's hands, on the quilt. With any luck, the wall escaped. Thank goodness he hadn't bought the new wallpaper, though.

Now that he had the diaper off, what next?

With a hasty plan in his head, he managed a downward swiping motion with the soiled diaper and wadded it up in a ball. But he couldn't put the clean diaper on until he washed off the remnants, which clung like thistle to a horse's tail.

Wren wailed.

Suddenly, a wet cloth magically appeared in his line of vision. Toby stood holding his nose. In his outstretched hand he clutched the damp rag. "Hurry. I cain't breathe."

Overwhelming gratitude filled Rand. He took the offering and finished the job, but not without twice jabbing his finger with the safety pin.

Finally, he picked up his sweet baby girl, who smelled much better. "There. It's all done. No more poopy crying, you hear?"

He shot a glance at the offending diaper, which stunk to high heaven. Maybe he could pay Toby to go throw it outside far, far away from the house. He glanced at Toby and received a firm shake of his head that said he wasn't about to touch the thing. It might as well have been a rabid animal.

A giggle came from the doorway. Rand turned to see Callie. Her laugh told him she'd witnessed it all.

"You could've helped, you know," he said.

"Yes, but I wanted to see how you handled the initiation. Congratulations. You're now a father, Mr. Sinclair."

Rand grinned. "I couldn't have done it without Toby's help. He's quite a little man. Thanks, Toby. I owe you one. For a minute there, I thought I might have to turn the job over to you."

Toby shook his head emphatically. "I ain't doin' it. I ain't never ever doin' that."

Callie laughed and handed Rand a bottle. Picking up the soiled diaper, she thankfully took the stinky ball of cloth from the room.

With it gone, Rand could breathe much better. He sat in the rocker and watched Wren greedily suck on the bottle. He pressed a kiss to her forehead.

This was a heck of a life he now had. And he wouldn't trade it for all the tea in China.

The protective fierceness rising up left him shaken. No one was going to steal his happiness.

Soft footsteps announced Callie's return a few minutes later. What they had might not be perfect, but it fulfilled him in ways he'd never thought possible.

One day, she'd see the love he had to give.

But tonight...tonight they'd begin to get to know each other a little more.

Seventeen

AFTER THEY GOT THE CHILDREN TUCKED INTO BED, Rand and Callie sat by the fire for a bit. He remembered the envelope on the mantel and rose to get it.

Callie glanced up from her knitting. "What's that?"

"Money my mother left. Five hundred dollars. I found it when I came in after supper."

"What are you going to do?"

"Don't know yet. Wanted to talk it over with you. She left a note also. Said the money is for *her* granddaughter because she wasn't going to see Wren doing without. Like we're depriving the babe. It's a bunch of malarkey." Rand searched Callie's face as she put down her knitting and gave him her full attention. She seemed deep in thought.

"Maybe she just wants to help. Maybe she's not as controlling as you might think. She has her faults, but she really does seem to care. Could be Abigail just doesn't know how to show it."

"My mother appears to have an ally."

"I saw her differently today for some reason."

Rand stared at the envelope. "The fact is, we really could use the money."

"Then take it. Let her have her joy."

"It sticks in my craw that she's constantly butting in, but if I don't take this, she'll just go behind my back and try something else."

"Will you let your pride get in the way of accepting what you need? That money would make life easier for you."

"I'm afraid she'll use it to control us."

"What would you do with it if you don't keep it? You know she won't take it back."

"I could donate it to an orphanage. I've given money before to a big one in Fort Worth. What do you think I should do?"

Callie put her knitting into the cloth bag and tucked it away. "You need to resolve your differences with Abigail or you'll only continue to be at odds. Go see her and lay all your cards on the table. Find a way to get past this for your sake and for hers. Maybe all she wants is to know she's helping."

"I suppose." Rand let out a troubled sigh and rested his elbow on the mantel. "I didn't know when I married you that I was getting such a wise woman. If we're keeping the money, I'm going to buy you a new dress."

Her eyes met his and her color rose. "I've got everything I need right here."

"Let's call it a night. What say we go to bed, Mrs. Sinclair?" Her lips were calling him and he couldn't wait to taste them.

Each shared moment, each touch, each kiss moved him closer to his goal. One night he'd have his beautiful bride in his bed beside him. That is, if he didn't lose his mind first.

❦

Over the next week, the ranch was a beehive of activity. Rand, his brothers, and the extra men worked hard making repairs to the house. A group outside put new fence posts in the ground and started getting the land ready for cattle.

Callie loved watching Rand work. Everything about him fascinated her, from his enthusiasm to the love he showered on Toby and Wren. She'd long since given up the search for her mother's treasure chest. Her life didn't need to look up any more than it already did. She was content. With Nate so quiet, she had everything she wanted.

Except being able to let him have her body.

Each time she thought she might be able to give herself, fear rose up, putting a stone wall between them.

Now, as her eyes sought the lines of his tall, familiar form, her guilt became unbearable. She had to find a short reprieve. Fresh air, the sky overhead, and her paints would bring calm.

After lunch, Callie brought Wren outside. She put the baby in a basket and set up her easel. She knew exactly what she wanted to paint.

As a girl, she'd always been partial to the way the sun filtered through the canopy of evergreen trees, creating lacy images on the ground below. She'd made up stories out of the dancing lights and shadows. They'd become valiant knights on horses slaying dragons, and pretty maids in need of saving. Now she prayed she could capture what her mind saw.

Toby bounded out the kitchen door with his faithful dog. "What'cha doin'?"

"Painting. Would you like to try?"

"Naw. I'll just keep watch over my sister."

"Is something bothering you?" It wasn't like the boy to leave the men. He usually wanted to be right in the thick of things with his heroes.

"I don't wanna go away. I wanna stay here with you an' Mr. Rand an' Wren."

Laying down her paintbrush, she took his hands. "Honey, you're not going to have to leave."

"Cause we're a fam'ly?"

"Yes, that's exactly right. We belong together. What brought this on?"

Toby shrugged and dragged his sleeve across his nose. "I'm scared. What if my papa comes and makes me go with him?" Tears formed in his dark eyes. "He makes me do bad things."

Anger swept through her. She had no idea what Nate had made him do, but she knew what he was capable of, and that terrified her. She pulled Toby to her and hugged him. "Can you tell me what kind of things?"

"Stuff. I don't wanna talk about it."

"Okay, honey, you don't have to. Just know that Mr. Rand and I will take good care of you and keep you safe. Your papa isn't going to get you. We promise."

"Or Wren either?"

"Nope. You're both safe."

The baby girl let out a cry. Toby wiggled out of Callie's arms and leaned over the basket. The way he patted Wren's back and talked to her formed a big lump in her throat. The boy took his role of big brother seriously. It was plain to see he loved Wren with all his heart. Callie suspected that as soon as the infant learned to toddle, the two would indeed be inseparable.

After watching a moment to make sure her services weren't needed, she picked up her paintbrush. Within minutes she became lost in her work. She didn't look up until the men came from the house.

"There you are." Rand let his hand rest on her shoulder. "I wasn't sure where you'd gone. We're done for the day." He leaned down to look at the painting. "That's pretty. I would've bet a whole stack of chips you still had talent. I'm happy to see I was right."

Callie shrieked and quickly dove in front of the canvas. "Rand, you're not supposed to look yet. It's not finished."

"Could've fooled me."

"Where did the boy go?" Brett asked. "I missed him not being underfoot. I won't leave without telling him good-bye."

"He was here a bit ago." She told them about Toby's worries that Nate might take him. "Wren cried and he got her quiet. I imagine he got bored babysitting and took off to the tepee with Biscuit."

"Probably so." Brett walked to Cooper's wagon and helped him load some things into the back.

"Want to see what we got done to the house?" Rand asked.

"I'm dying of curiosity." Callie covered the painting with a cloth, picked up the baby, and took Rand's hand.

He led her through the downstairs rooms. "I still have to find that wallpaper design you want for the parlor, but we fixed the floors. Got the kitchen in pretty good shape too."

"I saw. I love everything." She met his gaze and felt warmth blaze a path inside her as only he could do. The man she'd married could heat her blood with nothing more than a glance. If they ever reached a point where they did more than kiss and touch, they'd probably burst into flames.

God help her, Rand Sinclair tempted her to forget everything and crawl into his bed. Maybe she would some night.

The thought startled her, yet the truth was there.

"Well, that's about it. We'll start upstairs in the next few days." His hand rose to touch her face. He moved closer.

A cry from outside ruined the moment and they jerked apart. "Rand, you better come quick."

They raced outside, where Cooper met them. His face had drained of color. "Toby's gone. He's not in the tepee and we can't find him anywhere."

⁂

"Maybe he snuck upstairs and is playing up there." Rand refused to accept the worst. He had to rule out everything before he would let himself consider that Nate might've snatched him.

Callie whimpered and put her hand to her mouth. "I wasn't watching him. I should've paid more attention. I should've…"

Rand's arm slipped around her shoulders. "Don't blame yourself. We were all busy. I never thought this would happen with so many workers on the place. Don't worry, sweetheart, we'll find him."

They searched all through the house, but there was no sign of the boy. Rand and Callie went back outside.

Brett came from the woods. "Found tracks leading away from here. Looks like a child and a dog."

"No adult ones?" Rand asked the question that was in all their minds.

"Not that I could see. Of course, we can't rule anything out. There are tricks. If a man doesn't want to be tracked, he can tie burlap to his feet. I'll keep looking. Just came back to get my horse."

Cooper grabbed some lanterns and quickly selected five of his best men. "Stay here and keep Mrs. Sinclair and the baby safe. The rest of you come with me."

"Rand, I need to be out there looking," Callie said, clutching his arm.

"Darlin', as much as I'd love to have you help search, Wren has to have someone caring for her. Besides, Toby might return. Could be he chased after Biscuit and hasn't been taken after all."

"I pray that's the case. Go find our son. Bring him home."

"I'll not come back without him. If anyone can find him, Brett can." He kissed her cheek and went to saddle his horse. He hadn't a moment to waste. Darkness would arrive soon, and night predators would stalk the woods, both the two-legged and the four-legged kind.

As Rand was about to leave, Callie ran from the house with a burlap sack and a wool blanket. "For Toby when you find him. He'll be cold even though he has his coat. And here's some bread, cheese, and ham for you and the men. Save some for Toby."

Rand drew her against him and kissed her. "I'm going to fix this. Go inside now and keep the doors locked. Cooper's men will protect you."

Tears running down her face pierced him when he looked back a few minutes later. He hadn't kept his promise. He should've tried harder to watch over the boy. Fact was, he'd gotten too comfortable and let down his guard.

That had been a mistake.

～

Following Brett closely, Rand felt the hair on the nape of his neck rise. The woods closed around him like hundreds of sentinels guarding its secrets. He inhaled the dank smell of rotting leaves and fallen timber. Heavy shadows created a multitude of hiding places. The hoots of an owl and the yip of a fox probably chasing his supper added to the haunting scene.

They found the place where someone had recently tied a horse. Fear knotted Rand's stomach. It seemed to point to Fleming. Yet he couldn't be sure. Toby wouldn't willingly go with the man who gave him nightmares.

About two hours into the search, Brett knelt on one knee to peer at the earth. A scowl darkened his face.

"What is it?" Rand asked.

"Toby and his dog definitely aren't alone." Brett showed him and the others the faint boot print of a man. "Whatever he has on his feet slipped to the side and the tracks of a horse are becoming clear."

Fleming did have Toby.

Rand's gut burned with white-hot anger. He clenched his fist. When he caught up to the outlaw, he'd take pleasure in exacting retribution. For now, he wouldn't rest until he saved the boy who'd snuck into his heart. Every second Toby spent with Fleming was one more they couldn't get back.

The silvery moon rose over the treetops, reminding Rand that he hadn't eaten. He divvied up the food among the men. They ate in the saddle as they resumed the search.

Cognizant of how far voices could carry in the woods, no one spoke. They didn't have to. Rand knew their minds were on rescuing Toby, and they wouldn't stop until they had him, not even if they had to chase Fleming all the way to hell and back.

About midnight, Rand heard a dog's frantic bark. Prickles of warning crawled up his spine. He leaned forward in the saddle.

Brett held up a hand and spoke low. "Don't, brother, it might be a trap."

"I've got to." Rand spurred his roan into a gallop toward whatever awaited. Whether it was Biscuit or not remained to be seen. The dog could be hurting. He had to save it.

He and the others rode for almost half a mile. The barking got louder and louder. At last Rand rounded a stand of trees, and there in the moonlit clearing was Biscuit. She was tied to a tree. He drew his Colt, scanning the shadows for any movement. Sliding off his horse, Rand knelt down beside the dog. Biscuit whimpered and licked his face while he cut the rope holding her.

Brett, Cooper, and the rest of the searchers kept watch while he checked the dog for injury.

"Near as I can tell, I don't think she's hurt," Rand announced, aiming the light from the lantern.

"Appears she's been tied to the tree for a while. The rope rubbed her neck pretty bad in her effort to free herself. Probably tied her up so she wouldn't give the jackal's position away."

Without a word, Brett peered closely at the ground all around the clearing. Rand knew if anyone could piece together the facts, Brett would.

At last his baby brother spoke, "Toby grows tired. He rested here by the tree."

Laying a hand on Rand's back, Cooper said, "We'll get him back. The mangy devil will grow too tired to travel and have to stop. Then we'll pounce on him quicker than a barn cat on a mouse. Ready to move out?"

With a quick nod, Rand started to lift Biscuit onto the horse.

Brett stopped him. "Let me have the dog. She might lead us to them. It's worth a shot. Your decision."

Without further discussion, Rand handed Biscuit over to his brother. Brett knelt down and rubbed the animal's ears. "Go to Toby, girl. Go find him."

The dog appeared to understand. She took off like a shot. Everyone scrambled onto their mounts and followed. Rand prayed they wouldn't be too late. He feared Fleming might kill his son to keep them from having him.

Rand had promised to bring Toby home safe, and by God, he'd find a way to keep his word. Somehow.

Failing his wife was not an option. He wouldn't be able to face the pain in her eyes. It would hurt too much. She asked so little of him. He would put a smile back on her lips.

Like a jolt, he remembered the words she'd spoken as she said good-bye. *Bring our son home.*

With his mind on hitting the trail, her statement hadn't registered until now.

"Our son," he whispered the words his heart had longed to hear into the night.

It was true. Toby was their son in every way that mattered except the legal one. He vowed to contact an attorney as soon as possible. Cooper told him one had come to Battle Creek a few days ago, looking for a place to hang his shingle. Hopefully, the lawyer was still around. If not, Rand would go all the way to Fort Worth for one if he had to.

No mistake, he would make Toby his son.

A little ways down the trail, the breeze died and it got deathly still. Not a nighthawk, an animal, or a blade of winter grass moved. Rand's senses sharpened to a fine edge. He scanned the shadows.

The whisper of something unseen warned him.

He was halfway out of the saddle when a shot shattered the eerie silence.

Eighteen

THE BROTHERS SCATTERED LIKE A WAD OF BUCKSHOT. Rand's Colt was in his hand before he ever remembered drawing it.

Where had the blast come from?

Beads of sweat rose on his forehead as he peered from the tree he'd dived behind. Nothing.

Damn, he wished daylight would come.

Though dense timber surrounded them, they were more or less sitting ducks. Fleming had eyes on them. They had to figure out from which direction the gunfire had come and fast.

In an effort to keep pace with the racing dog, they'd become separated from Cooper's ranch hands. It was just the three of them now. Three to save the little boy who meant so much to Rand.

From the corner of his eye, he watched Cooper and Brett crawl into some thick brush. Maybe they'd seen the flash of powder or the haze of smoke in the aftermath.

What had happened to Biscuit? Had Fleming killed the dog?

Instead of joining his brothers, Rand waited,

scanning for signs that might tell him where Fleming held Toby. Minutes ticked by.

Then he saw what he waited for.

Slight movement twenty yards ahead made his heart slam against his ribs. He heard the faint whimper of a child.

If he tried to race across the small clearing, Fleming would cut him down before he got halfway. No, he had to be smart.

Slowly, Rand backed away from his hiding place. One sound, one slipup, and he would alert his enemy. Using tactics he'd learned from Brett, he painstakingly made an arc through the woods and came up from behind.

In the thin slice of moonlight, he saw the figure of a man hunched down with one hand over Toby's mouth.

He'd found the murdering piece of scum. But he couldn't get a clean shot without hitting Toby.

A calm stillness swept over Rand as he stood. He gripped the Colt tighter and ordered, "Drop it, Fleming."

Rising, the outlaw swung and fired. The bullet slammed into a nearby tree.

Rand cursed the fact he couldn't return fire. "Let the boy go and fight like a man."

"He belongs to me. I'm his father, his kin. You ain't nothin' but a two-bit cowboy, trying to act like some big shot. I'll kill you where you stand."

As Cooper and Brett stepped from the brush to flank Fleming, the outlaw suddenly hoisted Toby tightly to his chest and moved deeper into the shadows.

"Pitch your weapons into the trees and back away, or the boy dies," Fleming snarled. "Quick now, or I'll put a bullet into his head."

Tossing his pistol would leave Rand defenseless, but he wasn't about to gamble with Toby's life.

"Indian, that means you too."

"I don't carry a gun," Brett said.

"Never heard of a man who doesn't have a weapon of some sort. You strike me as a knife carrier."

Without a word, Brett removed his knife from his moccasin, laid it on the ground, then kicked it away.

"A real father doesn't want any harm to come to his son," Cooper said, throwing his Colt out of reach. "You don't seem to much care about his welfare."

"I do what I hafta do. I ain't of a mind to go to jail. Appears you boys just got bested."

Coupled with the darkness and the hat pulled low onto Fleming's forehead, Rand couldn't see the man's expression, but he knew the outlaw was smiling, pretty satisfied that he had the upper hand. Rand glanced around, searching for something to use as a weapon. They'd promised Toby they wouldn't let Fleming get him, and somehow, someway, he had to keep that vow.

Biscuit suddenly leaped from the brushy cover with a vicious snarl and clamped down on Fleming's arm with her powerful jaws.

"Get this mutt off me!" the outlaw screamed. In the struggle to free himself of the sharp teeth, he released Toby. Then a shot rang out and Biscuit fell to the ground with a high whine. Thin wisps of smoke curled from the pistol as Cooper launched himself on Fleming. The two men went down. Just as Brett scrambled toward them, Fleming rose with his gun pressed to Cooper's chest.

"I'll kill him," the outlaw yelled.

Rand's gut clenched as he searched for a plan to keep *Cooper* alive.

"He hurt my dog." Sobbing, Toby raced toward his beloved fallen dog.

"Toby, wait," Rand yelled. But the boy didn't heed.

Before he could say more, Fleming pulled the trigger again.

An empty click. No burst of orange flame. No dead brother lying on the ground.

The outlaw was out of bullets.

Intent on seizing the advantage, Rand rushed forward as Cooper drew back and slammed a fist into Fleming's face. A grunt followed the crunch of bone.

Fleming staggered backward, then cradling his bloody arm, he sprinted into the inky blackness.

While Cooper and Brett gave chase on foot, Rand knelt beside the whimpering canine, trying to ascertain the severity of the wound, cursing the thick blackness.

In the midst of pounding hoofbeats, the other men arrived. They quickly dismounted and someone brought a lantern over. Rand found that the bullet had grazed Biscuit's neck. The dog had narrowly missed a severe injury. Rand gave Toby the good news. Lord knew the lad could use some.

"We lost you," a man by the name of Greely said, crouching down beside Rand. "I hate the woods at night. It's creepy. Wish we could've stayed up with you. Looks like we would've caught the guy if we'd been here."

"We tried our best. Next time he won't be so lucky. We'll get him." Before Rand finished binding the dog's wound, Brett and Cooper returned.

"Fleming got away," Brett said. "He made it to his horse, and the night swallowed him. Pressing on would've been too dangerous in the dark."

Rand got to his feet and, with a narrowed gaze, stared in the direction Fleming had disappeared. "Brett, I'd count it as a favor if you'd see that Toby and his dog get home."

"It's a bad idea to go after Fleming alone."

"Don't have a choice. He'll be back, and when he does, he'll rain hell down on us. I have to protect my family. Best to go after him while he's wounded."

Brett turned to Cooper. "Talk some sense into our brother."

"I happen to agree, and as a duly sworn lawman, I'm going with him."

Shrugging, Rand laid a hand on Brett's arm. "It's the only thing to do. It's up to you to get Toby home. Tell Callie I'll be back as soon as I can. Will you stay with her?"

"I will keep her and the children safe, never fear."

"Thanks." Rand clasped Brett's hand. "I wouldn't entrust their care to anyone else."

After instructing his men to go back to the Long Odds in case Fleming doubled back and harmed Delta, Cooper and Rand mounted up. Though Rand hated parting company with their posse, he knew Cooper had to protect his wife.

Thank God, it wouldn't be long until daybreak.

Rand was cold and hungry and tired, but the burning desire to see Fleming behind bars kept him going. He didn't care how long it took—he would put the outlaw where he couldn't hurt anyone else.

By the time the sun came up, Rand and Cooper had covered many miles. They paused on a hill overlooking a farmhouse. Wisps of lazy smoke curled from the chimney.

The saddle creaked when Rand leaned forward. "Don't see a horse in front. Hopefully Fleming bypassed them."

"Wouldn't bet on it. He's hurt and he needs grub. Horse could be around back," Cooper pointed out. "I say we circle the house from a distance and see if we spot anything suspicious before we approach."

"You're the lawman. Sounds like a good plan."

Under cover of the wooded hills, they made a circular turn about the small homestead. No sign of a horse or that Fleming had holed up inside.

"I'll ride down and knock on the door," Cooper said.

"Like hell," Rand spewed. "You ain't going to leave me cooling my heels up here. I know you're the lawman, but if it's all the same, we'll go down together." Besides, he could smell the coffee boiling. A cup of brew with a plateful of eggs would make the gray day much more agreeable.

Without waiting for a reply, Rand cautiously inched his way down to the cabin. He kept a steady hand on his Colt and an eye on the rough-hewn dwelling.

Ten yards from the structure, the unmistakable click of someone cocking a pistol stopped him in his tracks.

⁓

Callie was dozing at the kitchen table when Brett rode in a little after dawn. Seeing Toby with him made her heart sing. She clasped the boy to her, then checked him over from head to toe. Satisfied that Nate hadn't harmed him, she made a bed for Biscuit and watched as Brett gently lowered the dog.

Toby planted himself beside the beloved pet. "How's my baby sister? I missed her."

"Wren is just fine," Callie assured him. "She missed you too."

"I was real sad when my father shot my dog."

She laid a hand on the top of his head. "I'm sorry."

"Why does he have to be so mean?"

Meeting Brett's dark gaze, she wondered what to say. How did you tell a boy his father was rotten to the core and that he had not a speck of decency or love in him?

"I don't know, honey. I wish I did. But Biscuit is going to be good as new. It's only a scratch."

Once she had coffee boiling, Callie took the weapon Brett pressed into her hand and went out to gather the eggs. If worse came to worst, she could rob the nests at gunpoint.

"Nate Fleming is miles and miles away," she grumbled under her breath. Besides, with five of Cooper's men milling around the yard and barn, Nate wouldn't dare try anything.

Though she griped about Brett's concern for her safety, she knew he had her best interests at heart. Lord knows, Nate would take great joy in ending her life if he could.

The wind buffeted her about, nearly knocking her off her feet. Her breath fogged in the misty air as she unlatched the door fashioned of chicken wire and stepped inside. While she collected the still-warm brown eggs, thoughts of Rand swirled in her head.

Where are you? Are you hurt? Please be careful.

It terrified her that he'd ridden on with Cooper to try to catch Nate. They didn't know the outlaw like she did. They hadn't seen the trail of blood he'd left behind him.

Taking care not to bump the basket, she left the cackling chickens, fastening the door behind her. For a moment, she leaned her head against the wire enclosure, blinking back tears.

How would this end? Would Fleming let Rand live when so many others had lost their lives?

Inhaling a calming breath, she stuffed her fears to the back of her mind and hurried into the house out of the cold wind. Once she'd fed Toby and Brett, she tucked Toby into bed. "I want you to sleep a while."

"But the sky is blue. I can't sleep until it gets black."

"Just try. Close your eyes and maybe sleep will come."

Callie hadn't made it to the door before the boy was asleep. She paused in the hallway, listening for the sound of Rand's footsteps, remembering the fragrance of him and the wild Texas land that he always brought inside with him. Going to the door of his bedroom, she gazed at his bed. A quiet sob rose.

"I miss you, Rand," she whispered brokenly. "I wish I could tell you. Please come home. I need our nightly kisses, your arms around me. One of these days, I'll hold on to you tight and never let you go." She let the stinging wind that clamored to get inside carry that promise to her husband.

❧

Rand swallowed hard. Had Fleming gotten the drop on them despite the care he and Coop had taken? His heart hammered inside his chest.

"State your business," a male voice barked.

Cooper stepped forward and stated his name. "I'm the sheriff over at Battle Creek. This is my brother. We're trailing a dangerous outlaw and his tracks led here."

The door opened and a grizzly bear of a man stepped out. His long, shaggy hair whipped about in the breeze. He kept an ancient pistol that must've been used to fight at the Alamo trained on them.

"We don't mean any harm, mister," Rand said. "Just wanted to know if you've seen him. His name is Nate Fleming. Has coal-black hair and rides a big black gelding. Has a wounded arm."

The pistol lowered. "Might as well come on in. This place is busier than a town durin' a hangin'."

Sounded like Fleming had been there, all right.

Rand and Cooper removed their hats and followed the man through the door. A tiny woman stood at the cookstove. She turned and her smile showed a big gap in her teeth.

"Howdy, ma'am," Rand said.

"Would you care for some coffee, young man?"

"If it wouldn't trouble you none. I smelled it all the way up on that hill yonder." He rubbed his hands together to warm them. "It's mighty chilly out."

Cooper gave her a nod. "I'll take some too, ma'am, long as you're offering."

The farmer motioned them into chairs at the table. "Name's John Abel. That's my wife, Rebecca. She's a right fair cook."

"About that outlaw—" Cooper began.

"Nope, I ain't talkin' about outlaws 'n' such on an empty belly," John declared. "We eat, then we jaw."

Though it chafed to have to wait, Rand gratefully accepted a cup of hot coffee that Rebecca handed him. The couple appeared starved for company, the way they latched onto Rand and Cooper, but every second spent cooling their heels meant Fleming was getting farther away.

He had to admit that the plate of eggs, sausage, and flapjacks was a welcome sight, though. Rebecca truly did know her way around a cookstove. He and Cooper dove right in, happy to trade time for a hot meal.

At last, John finished and pushed back his plate. He lit a pipe and puffed on it for several minutes. "Now, about that jackanapes you're lookin' for. Reckon he pounded on our door just as we were gettin' out of bed 'fore daybreak. Forced his way in. Rebecca made coffee and bandaged his arm. Looked mighty bad too. Kept a gun on us the whole time. Thought for sure he might kill us, but he hopped on that big black gelding of his and lit out."

"Which direction did he go?" Cooper asked, leaning forward.

"Due east. Toward the train tracks."

Rand squinted, thinking. "Did he talk about boarding a train?"

"Nope."

Cooper drained his cup. "Did he tell you anything?"

"That he was trying to get his son back," Rebecca spoke up. "Said a woman stole him. That true?"

"Yes, ma'am, it is." Rand didn't try to color the facts.

"The woman who took him is my wife, and she was only upholding a deathbed promise to the boy's mother. Fleming isn't fit to raise a barn cat, much less a son."

"Some aren't," she agreed. "I saw the measure of the man. Better watch out for that outlaw, though. He's itching to get even. Seemed a nice enough sort at first, but he got this real mean look in his eyes when he thought we didn't see."

"Appreciate the warning, Mrs. Abel. You're lucky he didn't kill you in cold blood." Cooper turned and shook the farmer's hand. "Thanks for your hospitality. If you're ever in Battle Creek, stop in and say hello. Reckon we'll push on. Got a lot of ground to cover."

Rand braced himself for the cold, biting wind, then followed Cooper out the door. What he wouldn't give to be back home with Callie and the kids. He had a lot of good-night kisses to make up for, and he chomped at the bit to get started.

Kisses, he'd found, had the power to heal his battered spirit. This bit of time without the added pressure of lovemaking seemed to be what Callie needed.

His kisses allowed them to gently explore each other. To trust.

His darling Callie. His life had totally changed the moment he first laid eyes on her. She'd given him much more than hot food in his stomach. When he got back, he'd tell her just that.

❧

The two men rode hard and fast. Rand gritted his teeth with frustration. They'd wasted too much time with the Abels. If only they'd kept riding, they could've caught up to Fleming and would already be headed with him to jail.

Except they hadn't known which way he went. They'd needed John Abel. Pushing forward as hard as they dared was their only option.

Just as he thought things couldn't get more miserable, cold rain began to fall. Driven by the wind, raindrops stung his face and hands and at times hampered his ability to draw air into his lungs.

To take his mind off the conditions, Rand thought of Callie, remembering every little detail about her.

The way her breath hitched right before he placed his mouth on hers.

The way her smile lit up all the dark places inside him.

And the way she could make a man feel like the richest person on earth.

Yes, he'd waited a long time for her to come along.

Only one other woman had come close to holding a candle to her—Rachel Madison. Rachel had arrived in Battle Creek with her father in a traveling medicine show. Like Callie, she'd caught his fancy right away. Her infectious laugh and zest for life touched everyone around her. But Rachel had contracted scarlet fever soon after their arrival. Doc Yates had done what he could for her, but she passed on without ever knowing how much she meant to Rand, or the plans he was making for their future.

A shudder rolled over Rand in a huge wave. Was fate against him? Would Nate take Callie from him too, just when he'd opened his heart again?

He urged the blue roan into a faster gallop.

Nineteen

IN THE DISTANCE, RAND COULD MAKE OUT THE
Houston and Texas Central Railway train idling at the
water stop ten miles outside of Corsicana.

Fear gripped him. What if Fleming managed to
get aboard?

They hadn't come this far for the outlaw to slip
through their fingers now. Rand needed to end
Fleming's bitter reign of terror and put him behind
bars where he couldn't kill anyone else.

Everything in Rand cried out for justice. He set
his jaw and tried to cajole a little extra from his horse.
But Blue had no more to give. Rand had pushed him
too hard. Sensing his faithful animal's exhaustion, he
slowed to a walk. It would accomplish nothing to kill
the roan.

Cooper did the same. Thick lather covered both
horses.

"Damn!" Rand dismounted and kicked a tuft of
dried grass.

"I ain't giving up," Cooper said, his deep voice
strong. "Besides, we don't know for certain that

Fleming came this way, that he aims to get on the train.
The man could've changed course after he left Abel's."

"No, but I feel in my bones we're on the right
track." Rand picked up the reins and began walking as
fast as he could in the driving rain. Maybe they still had
a shot. Maybe it would take longer than normal for the
train to take on water. Just maybe the conductor would
see Fleming sneak on board and throw him off.

With hope hammering in his heart, Rand increased
the length of his stride. "Come on, Coop, get the lead
out. We'll make the train."

⁓

Callie brushed back loose strands of hair and gazed
from the kitchen window into the distance. The
ominous gray skies hung low, threatening to burst
any minute. Rand would be out there exposed in this
storm because of her and Toby.

She bit back a sob.

Where was he? Had he caught up with Nate? Was
he lying hurt…or dead…somewhere?

Toenails clicked on the floor and Biscuit stuck a
cold nose to a hand that had dropped limply to her
side. The dog's whine seemed to offer sympathy and
to say that everything would be all right.

Kneeling, Callie threw her arms around the retriever's neck and buried her face in the soft fur.

Toby looked up from where he and Brett sat at the
table, playing some kind of game using pebbles. "She
gives real good hugs when you're sad, Aunt Callie. I
sure do miss Mr. Rand. Do you think my old papa
ain't gonna let him come home?"

It was odd how easily a child could declare something and it was so. Though Toby hadn't exactly put it into words, Rand was his new papa and nothing would change it.

"Don't you worry about that," Callie said firmly, getting to her feet. "Nothing or no one will keep him from coming back to us. He holds you and Wren in a secret place inside his heart."

"I'm glad," the boy said, sniffling.

She met Brett's dark eyes. She knew he chomped at the bit to be out there with his brothers, helping them locate Nate. Though he didn't let it show, she knew he simmered with frustration. He gave her a sudden smile that revealed his white teeth. He was going to steal some woman's heart one day. She prayed the woman would truly appreciate this special kind of man.

"Young Toby, I have an idea. How about we go out to the tepee and pretend to be Indians?" Brett said, getting up.

"Can I, Aunt Callie?"

"I think that would be a very good idea. What fun." When Toby ran to get his coat, she turned to Brett. "Thank you for helping keep his mind occupied. You're a godsend."

"It's little enough. Wish I could do more." He put an arm lightly around her. "Never count Rand out. I learned a long time ago not to bet against him. Every blasted time I did, I lost. He'll be walking through this kitchen door before you know it, wanting to know where the hot biscuits are."

Callie laughed and leaned her head on Brett's

shoulder. "You are right about that. I don't know what I'd do without you to remind me about these things."

She helped Toby into his coat and buttoned it up. After he and Brett sprinted for the tepee, she stood looking at the rain that had begun to fall. She'd only been married a week and already Rand had snuck past all her defenses and staked out a corner of her heart.

Imagining a life without him was impossible. He had the power to give her everything she'd longed for, if only she'd let him.

How long could she keep holding back, refusing to give him what he needed most?

And how could she deny the thing she most wanted to give?

∽

Rand and Cooper's walk to the train seemed to take a lifetime. Rand's breath came in shuddering gasps. He kept his gaze anchored on the billowing smokestack, willing the iron horse to remain stationary.

One foot in front of the other.

Just fifty yards to go.

Please let us get there in time.

Lightning split the heavens in jagged zigzags. Two seconds later, thunder crashed, shaking the ground. Rand stumbled and went down to his knees. Struggling to his feet, he plunged on, trying to keep pace with Cooper, who'd taken the lead.

Forty yards to go. Little by little, they got closer.

They could do this. Rand got his second wind.

"You're not gonna get away, Fleming," he shouted into the rain. "We're coming for you."

Thirty yards.

The train made a groan and the iron wheels began to turn. Rand's heart plummeted. They weren't going to make it. Still, he kept going foot by precious foot. If either he or Cooper could swing aboard, they could stop it and jerk the outlaw off.

He dropped Blue's reins and made an all-out mad dash. But he came up short.

The train gained momentum and rumbled down the tracks just out of reach. Fleming moved out to stand on the small platform on the back of the last car, holding onto the railing…grinning.

"You better run, you sorry piece of cow dung," Rand yelled at the top of his lungs. "We'll catch you, just wait and see."

"Hell and be damned!" Cooper kicked at a rock sticking out of the ground. "Reckon we'll rest the horses for a while, then ride into Corsicana. I'll wire the sheriff down in Mexia and tell him to stop the train. We'll hope Fleming doesn't jump off before then."

"Well, one thing about it, he won't have a horse." Rand motioned to the big black gelding standing beside the tracks. "At least we have one thing in our favor."

"About time. Plus we know which way he's headed."

With water running off the brims of their hats, they took cover from the storm under the big water tank and settled down to wait for the horses to recover. The rain would thankfully help cool them down. Brett would have his and Cooper's hide for riding the animals so hard. Horses meant everything to Rand and Cooper, but to their brother, they were sacred. That they hadn't seen any choice in the matter might not appease him.

"We almost made it, Coop," Rand said. "Another five minutes and we would've had Fleming."

"Should have our butts kicked for letting Abel talk us into breakfast. I knew better than that." Cooper leaned back and pulled his wet hat down over his eyes.

"Yeah, but I'd sure like to have another plate of those flapjacks right about now. Mrs. Abel was almost as good a cook as Callie." Rand's thoughts again turned toward home. He picked up a piece of wood that would make a good spinning top and took out his pocketknife. "You know, Coop, I'm a lucky man."

"How's that?"

"I have everything I ever wanted. My own land, kids, and a pretty wife to ease a man's loneliness. I never thought I'd be so happy. I've got it all, and I'll be damned if Fleming's going to ruin it."

"We've got him on the run and we'll keep him running."

"I don't mind dogging him until his tongue lolls out. Long as we keep him going away from us, he can't hurt the people I care about. But I won't be satisfied until we lock him up. No one's safe until he is."

"Your tongue seems double-jointed today, the way it's flapping around. Can't you see I'm tryin' to get some sleep?"

"You're awful gripey."

"Well, you're talking my ear off. Give it a rest."

The water tank stood high enough so that a man of Rand's height could just barely stand under it, minus the hat. He rose and stood looking out at the deluge, which showed no signs of stopping. Then his gaze shifted down the tracks in the direction the train had gone.

A muscle worked in his jaw. Somehow, someway, he'd catch up to Nate Fleming.

When he did, there would be hell to pay.

Callie put the kettle on for some hot tea. It seemed just the thing to lift her from her doldrums. She'd just fed and rocked the baby to sleep. Brett and Toby were still out in the tepee. They'd come in for lunch, then gone back out. She didn't know what they were up to, but Toby had blurted out he had a secret.

With the water on to boil, she got down the tin. When she opened it, a small folded piece of paper lay on top of the tea leaves.

What on earth?

Curious, she unfolded it and saw the neat letters.

Dearest Callie,

You are my rock. Only you can soothe the ragged edges of my soul. You are seen. You are my life, my everything.

Your patient husband

Tears that were hovering right beneath the surface flooded down her cheeks. She clutched the note to her chest and had a good cry.

She'd married an amazing man. He had the ability to make her feel cherished, caress her heart even when he was miles and miles away. He really did "see" her. Nobody had since her mother was taken from her. Nobody.

Her heart sang. She was Rand's life, his everything.

Whether or not she could soothe his spirit raised questions. It flattered her that he thought she could. While she waited for the tea to steep, she went off to locate a pencil and paper. Then she sat down to think of what to say.

The minute she finished her cup of tea, she took the pencil in hand.

My Dear Rand,

You make me very happy. I never thought I could ever find a man like you. Your kisses each night make my heart soar. When I close my eyes, I dream of you. Never stop kissing me.

Your ever-faithful wife

She folded the paper into a square. Now where to put it so that he'd find it? At last she decided to leave it on his pillow. Buoyed by excitement, she flew up the stairs. She felt like a kid again.

Before she left the note, she lay on his bed and put her head on the pillow. This was where she yearned to be. Next to her husband, sleeping in his arms, breathing his scent.

One day she'd find a way to be brave enough to face her fears. She promised. Maybe he could overlook the inability to face her terror. Hope rose. He'd already looked into her heart and seen the woman she wanted to be.

In the meantime, the note would have to tell him the things her heart was unable to say.

&

That night after supper, she sat with the children and Brett in the parlor. She smiled, watching her husband's brother hold little Wren. The two looked so much alike, with their raven hair and dark eyes. They shared the same heritage. Sadness filled her that the babe would never know her ancestors.

"Brett, will you teach Wren your ways when she gets old enough to understand?"

His sad eyes met hers. "I wish I could, but I have no knowledge of the Indian culture. Since I was raised with the whites, I don't even know which tribe I come from. I think she may be Comanche. But I will help all I can. Maybe we can figure it out together."

"Thank you." A person needed to know where they came from, especially those who straddled two worlds.

Sitting beside Brett, Toby held the baby's hand. He couldn't be near her without touching her. "How old is Wren?"

"She's three months old," Callie answered. "Why?"

"Was I cute before I got to be a number?"

"What do you mean, sweetheart?"

"She's not even to a one yet. My number is six."

The mind of a child moved in mysterious ways. Toby could say the cutest things. "Honey, you were a very precious baby. Everyone remarked on how cute you were."

"Did my mama love me?"

Callie moved from the rocker to sit beside him on the sofa. She pulled him into her arms. "You were the apple of your mother's eye. She loved you more than anything in the whole wide world. She risked her life for you."

"Sometimes I get really scared. It's hard to remember what she looked like. I don't wanna forget her."

"Just remember that we were twins. She looked a lot like me, except her hair was curly, where mine is straight."

"Yeah, but what did her face look like?"

"Wait right here. I have just the thing." Callie raced upstairs and rummaged through her meager belongings. Finally she pulled out a gold locket that had Claire's picture inside.

Toby looked up expectantly when she returned.

"Here is something I've been keeping for you. I think it's time you had this." She pressed the locket into his hand.

Tears swam in his eyes when he opened it. "It's her. That's my mama."

"Yes, honey. This picture was taken when she was looking at you. See her smile? Now you can quit worrying about forgetting what she looked like." Callie kissed the top of his head.

Toby stared at the image a long time. "My mama's in heaven, where she's safe."

"That's exactly right. Heaven is a beautiful place where nothing bad can happen."

"Is she happy there?"

"I'm sure she's very happy. She's not in pain anymore."

He looked up. "When my old papa gets put in the calaboose, will she come back?"

Callie's arms went around him. "No, sweet boy. She can never come back. When you're in heaven, you stay there. But she'll always be with you inside your heart. She's watching over you and making sure nothing happens to you."

"Wren's mama is up in heaven with my mama?"

"Yes."

"She's gonna be so sad when I tell her about her mama and that she had to go away for a long, long, long time. I bet she cries like me. Sometimes I cry when I'm sad."

"It's good to cry."

Brett spoke up in his quiet way. "Tears cleanse the soul and wash away the sadness. Never be ashamed of your tears, young Toby."

Suddenly he wiggled out of Callie's arms. "Almost forgot."

He reached under the sofa and pulled out something wrapped in one of his shirts. "This is for you, Aunt Callie. Uncle Brett showed me how to make it. Open it."

First, Rand was the papa he'd chosen, and now Brett was his uncle. What next? She loved seeing how children put order in their lives.

She pulled away the fabric and sucked in her breath. Toby had fashioned a heart out of woven narrow strips of leather. A small blue feather dangled from the side. "It's the most beautiful thing I've ever seen. I'll always treasure it. Thank you, sweet boy." She kissed his forehead.

"He did all the work himself," Brett said. "I only cut the strips and showed him what to do with them."

"I messed up a little bit over here." He pointed to the imperfection that made the gift even more precious to Callie.

"I'd never have noticed if you hadn't shown me. So this was what you and Uncle Brett were working on all day."

"Yep. An' he's gonna teach me how to make stuff with pretty beads when he gets to go home for them."

Callie couldn't trust herself to speak. She'd had two very unexpected, wonderful gifts on a day when her heart was heaviest.

Life was full of surprises. And so much love, it spilled out all over the place.

Twenty

RAND RODE IN BEFORE DARK TWO DAYS LATER. HE couldn't wait to see Callie. She must've been watching from the window, because she flew from the house.

With a leap, he dismounted and swung her around. "You're a sight for sore eyes, woman."

"I was so worried about you, Rand, afraid I might never see you again." Her voice was breathless and quivery as if she held back tears.

"Just try getting rid of me." Setting her on her feet, he held her so close, he could feel the wild beating of her heart. "For two cents, I'd kiss the daylights out of you right here. I've missed our nightly ritual."

He lowered his head, but before he could press his lips to hers, Toby raced from the house.

"Mr. Rand, you're home." The boy launched himself at Rand and hugged him around the waist while Biscuit barked and jumped. Rand handed him the wooden top he'd carved. "Oh boy. Just what I wanted."

Then Brett came out holding little Wren and was joined by Cooper's men. With a ragged sigh, Rand decided kissing his wife would have to wait.

He told the ranch hands that Cooper had ridden

on home and wanted them to meet him there. They hurried to the corral to get their mounts and saddled up, ready to get back to their own bunks.

Later, over plates of beans, potatoes, and ham, Rand told his family about the chase to capture Fleming. "He slipped through our fingers. Not sure how. Best we can figure, he got off the train somewhere between that water station and Mexia."

"He won't get far walking," Brett said.

Rand put down his fork. "I doubt he'll be afoot for long. I won't let down my guard." He turned his attention to Toby. "Anything new happen around here while I was gone?"

"Uncle Brett showed me how to make things an' we played lotsa games. He's real smart."

"*Uncle* now, is it?" Rand teased.

One of Brett's rare smiles formed. "Apparently."

Callie rose and came back with a hot peach pie. "I think it's nice, and Toby needs all the family he can get."

"Won't get any argument out of me. That pie sure smells good. Can't wait to get some in my mouth. I'd crawl through a patch of thorny thistles on my belly for one of your pies. Heck, I'd do it for anything you cook, darlin'." Rand loved the rosy glow that colored her cheeks. Staring into her warm, whiskey-colored eyes, he boldly winked.

That made her all flustered. He loved that too, the fact that he could get her in a fine dither.

His hand brushed hers when he took the piece of pie she cut. He'd never been struck by lightning, but he was sure it felt similar. Lord, he'd like to sweep her into his arms and carry her up to bed.

Heat crawled from Rand's belly as he attempted to keep his thoughts on the conversation. During a lull, he glanced at the clock and swore the hands hadn't moved since he sat down at the table. Time was creeping like cold molasses.

&

While Rand and Brett talked low in the parlor after supper, Callie knitted. They'd already put the children to bed, so she had ample time to watch her husband. She couldn't put her finger on it exactly, but something about him had changed.

Or maybe…

Was it she who was different?

She was mesmerized by Rand's long, slender fingers as he motioned with his hands when he spoke. It wasn't hard to imagine them caressing her body.

Delicious excitement swept the length of her. The only one who'd attempted such intimacy with her had been Richard Farrington that night so long ago, and he'd failed miserably. Richard had been nothing but a clumsy boy.

Rand Sinclair, on the other hand, was all man.

A very virile, desirable man.

He knew exactly how to make her feel like a woman, treasured and valued. The night before he left, he'd kissed her, then his fingers had moved over the curve of her breast as though memorizing every inch beneath her bodice.

Dear Lord, how would his hands on her bare skin feel?

Was it wrong to want to be touched yet refuse to make love? Didn't one thing lead to the other?

No, she decided. She could welcome Rand's warm touches, knowing that he wouldn't take advantage. He had too much honor to go back on his word.

Besides, the caresses made her melt. Each time he ran his fingers over her, she glowed inside like a million twinkling stars.

It was uncanny how he seemed to read her thoughts. He stopped midsentence and met her gaze. Then his grin crinkled the lines at the corners of his sky-blue eyes.

Her breath caught in her throat. One of her knitting needles fell from her slack fingers onto the floor. Her face grew hot as she quickly retrieved it. What an imbecile.

The note she'd left on his pillow waited upstairs. What would he think when he read it? She groaned. Whatever had she been thinking? He'd probably take it as a sign that she wanted to consummate their marriage.

Her pulse raced. Did she?

Yes. But then her old fears rose, and she knew she couldn't.

If only she could forget the horrible darkness of that time and instead focus on the happiness inside the wild beating of her heart.

Before she could argue with herself any further, she flung aside her ball of yarn and knitting needles. She had time to run upstairs and get the note. Yes, that's what she needed to do. Before it was too late. Before he saw the words she'd written.

Your kisses each night make my heart soar. When I close my eyes, I dream of you.

She'd said too much, given away her feelings for him. Rand's stare made her flush. "Brett, my wife seems to be signaling that it's time to turn in. We can finish our discussion tomorrow."

Then Brett looked at her too with a knowing glint in his dark eyes and got to his feet. "Yes, it's been a long day for everyone. Since you're back, I'll be moseying on after breakfast. Need to check on my horses and do a few things. Good night."

"Why don't you sleep on the sofa? It'd be a lot more comfortable," Rand said.

Brett shook his head and grunted. "I'll take young Toby's tepee. Don't want to get too soft. I don't rest unless I can breathe the night air and smell the ground beneath me."

"Well, suit yourself." Rand stood and turned to Callie. "I'll lock up behind him. Don't go upstairs yet."

She nodded and stuffed her knitting back inside a cloth bag she kept beside her chair. Tingles danced up her spine. A few more minutes and his lips would be on hers.

Good heavens, one would think she was a schoolgirl, not a twenty-six-year-old woman.

With her thoughts in a tizzy, she moved across to the oil lamp. Blowing it out, she went to wait at the bottom of the stairs.

Before she knew it, Rand's arm slid around her waist and he murmured in her ear. "I have counted the minutes until bedtime. Thought it would never get here. Are you ready?"

"Yes. Wren will awaken wanting fed before long."

He guided her up to the second floor. Outside her door, he tugged her tightly against his chest. Her pulse quickened with some ancient, undeniable hunger.

"I hope you're not in a hurry, because I intend to catch up on things. By my count, I owe you a whole passel of kisses. You're all I thought about while I was gone."

"I don't—"

"I do. Tonight I intend to exercise my rights within the guidelines you laid out."

Callie relaxed and leaned into the solid wall of his chest, letting her soft curves mold to the contours of his lean body. His rugged look, framed by the shadows, spoke of danger, but she wasn't afraid of the man she'd married.

She ran her fingers lightly across a firm jaw that sported three days' worth of growth. "I missed you. I missed this. I'm glad you're back."

"That makes two of us," he growled, his breath softly fanning her face.

Lowering his mouth, he slanted a kiss across her lips lightly at first, then allowed it to deepen with raw urgency until she could barely breathe. Or think. Or hear above the pounding of her heart. She wanted nothing more than to feel his lips and his hands touching her.

Sliding her hand beneath the soft hair at the nape of his neck, she parted her mouth slightly. When his tongue dipped inside, she faintly tasted peaches. She'd never felt so much need well up inside. She needed Rand like she'd never needed anything. How could she have lived this long without him?

A second later, he removed his mouth from hers and murmured, "You drive me crazy, woman. Would you mind if I unfasten some buttons of your dress?"

"How many?" What a dumb question, but her brain had deserted her. The tingles doing backflips and twirls up and down her spine had made forming coherent thought impossible.

"Three. Or four. You have so many." He flashed a fleeting grin. "I have the greatest desire to feel my wife's skin. Will you welcome me?"

"Yes," she managed to whisper.

The air was cool on her flesh as he undid the four buttons she'd allotted. But he didn't stop. She covered his hand with hers. "You said four, and that's what I agreed to."

"I never was much good at arithmetic." He took her hand and kissed each of her fingertips.

She surprised herself when she moved his hands back into place so he could resume. She wanted this man who would risk his life to protect her from all harm. Desire flowed in her veins.

By the time he finished, her dress lay open to the waist. Even the middle of summer wasn't this sultry and hot. He pushed aside the fabric and untied her chemise.

He first stroked the swell above her breasts before moving lower to touch the rigid peaks of her nipples. He brushed them before taking one between his thumb and forefinger. She gasped with unexpected pleasure as heat raced from her stomach along each nerve ending.

If he hadn't supported her, she'd have gone to her knees. Unable to do more than sag limply against him, she gripped the front of his shirt and surrendered to the press of his kiss to the pulsing hollow at the base of her throat.

Delicious quivers swept over her in waves, each one more powerful than the last.

His ragged breath ruffled the hair at her temple. "You are so beautiful. You captivated me the moment I saw you hiding in that old run-down bunkhouse. Thank you for taking pity on a lonely old bachelor. Our marriage saved me."

"We seem to be bound by something larger than physical desire," she agreed. "After seventeen years, I've truly found a place to belong. A home."

"Me too."

Before she could mention the note he'd left in the tea tin and her reply, Rand's lips hungrily found hers again. The searing kiss sent spirals of pleasure into every secret corner of her being. It seemed as though the heat of a raging fire burned within her, rendering her incapable of logic. An achy yearning spread.

She didn't know how many times he kissed her. She lost count the moment his lips had first touched hers. Time and space ceased to exist, and it didn't matter. Nothing mattered. She wanted to stay in Rand's arms forever.

He'd woven some sort of spell over her, one that had made her totally lose herself in him. She was nothing but liquid bone and muscle.

And her soul was finally at peace.

Rand thought he'd gone over a cliff, the way his stomach pitched. His heart hammered in his ears as waves of excitement raced through him. He nuzzled Callie's slender neck, traced the curve of her jaw, buoyed by her reception of his caresses.

Her fingers moved to the buttons of his shirt, and

once she'd released them, she laid her small hand on the hard plane of his chest.

Overcome by the pleasure of her shy touch, he bent to kiss her breast, taking the peak into his mouth. He tried to slow down, but the rising heat from below flooded his head, driving him. Still, he forced himself to stop, to ask the question he knew he should.

Taking a ragged breath, Rand murmured in her ear, "Do you want more, Callie? All you have to do is say the word."

"I…can't. Not yet."

"Then we'd best end this here before I forget that I'm a gentleman. Temptation is a two-edged sword." He helped her button her dress, then watched helplessly as she slipped into her room, shutting the door behind her.

On unsteady legs, Rand turned and moved to his bed as though in a trance. He'd gone too far tonight; he knew that. But, damn, he wanted her. She was in his blood, his thoughts, and had taken up residence in his heart. It was sheer torture living in the same house and not being able to show her how much she meant to him.

Where was this all going to lead? Somewhere or nowhere?

A scrap of paper resting on his pillow seemed odd. He picked it up, held it to the light, and read the words Callie had written.

Your kisses each night make my heart soar. When I close my eyes, I dream of you. Never stop kissing me.

He hadn't imagined her softening. It was real, and the note confirmed it.

They had to talk. He stalked across the hall and stood before her door. But his honor wouldn't let him turn the knob. He would never force her to admit her feelings. She had to reach the reality herself.

He pressed his hand against the smooth wood.

⁂

A sob caught in Callie's throat as she leaned against the door. Dear God, she wanted to take everything Rand had offered. The mass of feelings stirring in her heart for this good, kind man had her living for a glimpse of his sinful grin. He could do things to her body that awakened each nerve ending, made her stomach whirl and dip, and had her dreaming of sleeping beside him. Not that they'd likely get much slumber. She envisioned running her hands over his bare arms and chest, then lower, leaving a trail of kisses in her wake.

With tears lurking behind her hot eyelids, she touched her swollen lips, remembering every detail of this special night.

Something had shifted within her. Rand's kisses and warm fingers on her skin was one of those defining moments separating yesterday and tomorrow. She'd crossed an invisible line, and there was no going back. She wasn't the same woman she'd been yesterday or even a few hours ago.

Rand had forever branded her as his.

Turning, she spread her fingers and laid her hand on the door, imagining that Rand was on the other side.

"I love you, my cowboy. Please don't give up on me."

Twenty-one

THE FIRST RAYS OF DAWN CREPT LIKE A THIEF THROUGH the window. She groaned at the unwelcome intrusion on her dream in which Rand was making sweet love to her. His hands should be immortalized in verse, for they could make her body sing.

She thought of rolling over to see if she could recapture the dream, but Wren's babble came from the crib. No more evading reality. She rose and quickly dressed.

Lifting Wren into her arms, Callie went down to the kitchen. She lit the lamp and saw a square of paper with her name scrawled across it propped against the sugar bowl. Her heart beat faster. Putting Wren in the cradle she kept downstairs, Callie picked up the note and read:

My Darling Callie,

You are the star that guides me like a beacon in a blinding storm. I've been lost for such a long time. Thank you for saving me. Thank you for making me the happiest man alive.

Forever yours, Rand

With tears clogging her throat, Callie kissed the note. He asked for so little, this husband of hers. It was time she became a wife in the truest sense.

She needed to tell him her secret.

Today. No more stalling. No more walls between them. Just honesty. She owed him that much. Having made that decision, her heart felt lighter as she stoked the fire and put the coffee on.

The twinkle in Rand's crystal blues when he came down a few minutes later sent Callie's heart into a frenzy. "Good morning. Did you sleep well, darlin'?"

"Better than I have in a long time." She'd slept without fear or worry. A deep, restful sleep. Maybe it was due mostly to the fact that her bones had liquefied...

...and that she knew Rand was just across the hall, keeping watch over her and the children.

"I didn't hear Wren cry during the night." He picked the babe up and came to give Callie a kiss.

Something had definitely shifted, and it wasn't just with her. She liked this new morning ritual.

"That was because the little darling didn't wake up until daylight. It was a first for her, and I'm not sure what to make of it. Maybe there's something wrong."

"Sounds more like something right to me. She's happy and content with us." He paused. "Thank you for the note you left on my pillow. Funny thing, I dream of you too, even when my eyes are open. I think we're gonna make it, Callie."

"I loved the note you put in the tea tin, and the one here on the table." She'd memorized the words and written them on her heart.

You are seen. You are my life, my everything. And the new one that said she was his guiding star.

Unlike her, her husband had quite a way of voicing his thoughts. The notes might just be *her* best way of communicating things she couldn't say.

Besides the kissing and touching, that is.

Toby and Brett came from different directions into the kitchen, stopping further private conversation.

The men went out to do their chores, leaving Callie to get breakfast on the table. She hummed as she worked. Coming here to the Last Hope had changed her life in more ways than she could count. This was where she belonged.

Still, what would happen after she told Rand the truth? Would her revelation take all this away? *Please, God, don't let that happen.* Rand would never be satisfied with a wife who couldn't share his bed.

How could a man live with only half a wife?

By the time Rand, Brett, and Toby returned, she had hot food on the table. Her heart turned over at the sight of her note-writing husband and the boy who looked up to him as a father.

Though Rand became immersed in plans with Brett to catch Nate Fleming, his eyes kept seeking her out, grazing the area where the buttons of the dress met her neck. Knowing the direction of his thoughts, her face grew hot.

Memories of the liquid pleasure she'd felt when his mouth sought her bare skin flooded her senses. He'd quite easily persuaded her to lower her guard, opening her dress—and what was worse, he took delight in it.

If he didn't stop looking at her now, Brett would notice and she'd die of mortification.

Still, her heart raced each time she recalled Rand's velvety touch on her bare skin, the feel of his mouth on hers. She glanced through the window at the brilliant sunrise and sighed.

How would she fill the time until they came together again outside her bedroom door?

She could already feel his tender touch that had awakened her to untold joy—and renewed fear.

≈

Rand had never had a more tasty breakfast. Callie had outdone herself as usual. Or maybe it had something to do with their blossoming relationship.

At last he laid down his fork and pushed back his plate. "I have to go into town to see an attorney and totally clear the air between me and Mother, and I don't want to leave you and the children here by yourselves. We'll make a day of it, do some shopping. I'm sure there are things you need both for yourself and the house."

"I don't relish the thought of going, but neither do I wish to stay behind. I'll get Toby and Wren ready."

Brett stood. "I must go too. Have lots to do myself."

Toby got out of his chair and tugged the tall Indian's hand. "Don't forget to bring the beads when you come back."

"I won't. In the meantime, you keep practicing what I showed you." Brett laid a hand on top of Toby's head. It was clear the two had developed a special friendship. His brother had given a little boy something lasting.

Rand saw him off and hitched the wagon while Callie was inside making sure the children were presentable. He saw Callie through the kitchen window and grinned. He couldn't have asked for a better wife and silently thanked Emily Winters for providing the reason to marry. Callie was pretty, and smart—plus she had the silkiest skin he'd ever felt.

His trousers became uncomfortably tight just thinking not only about last night, but all the nights yet to come. Soon he'd persuade her to share his bed, he felt it in his bones. Then he'd go to heaven every night after and take her with him. He'd never imagined marriage could be this satisfying. He adjusted his pants before Callie noticed. He groaned. Anyone would think he'd never even stolen a first kiss with a girl.

She stepped from the house just then with a basket full to overflowing, probably with things Wren might need or thought about needing. The way the newly born sun caressed Callie's face and hair aroused the familiar ache he'd just fought to tamp down.

In a desperate attempt to hide the evidence, he rushed forward to relieve her of the load. By the time he'd helped her and the children into the wagon, he'd gained control.

The ride into Battle Creek was pleasant. A cold breeze blew, but thankfully no rain fell. Rand had brought plenty of blankets to keep them warm. He reached to tuck a loose corner around Callie's knees and gave her a smile. They seemed to have turned a corner last night, and it bolstered his hope that he could kindle something inside her so strong that it would overcome whatever it was she feared.

Fear and dread were two overpowering emotions. They held people prisoner until facing them was the only way to break free. He felt the same dread about having this talk with his mother but knew he couldn't avoid it any longer.

He let his thoughts drift to what he was going to say.

And what exactly was that?

He hadn't a clue. He only knew they had to get some things out in the open so the bitter taste in his mouth would go away. It was time to let go of old hurts. He had a new life now, and a wife that excited and amazed him.

Reaching across Toby, he laid his hand on hers. "You're awfully quiet. Anything you want to talk about?"

She smiled, and he felt like she'd given him the moon and stars. Such a simple thing, yet it meant so much. He didn't need riches, fame, or glory. All he needed was Callie beside him and the hope that filled his heart that she'd keep writing her notes and letting him open her dress.

"Thank you for your concern, Rand. Actually, there is something I need to discuss with you, but it can wait until later."

Whatever it was must not be too serious. He hoped it didn't have anything to do with his love for kissing and touching her. He'd gotten a sample of her simmering passion last night. Like a breathtaking rose, her petals were just beginning to open. When she came to realize her full potential, she'd be something to behold.

Thinking of that caused his heart to hammer in his ears.

Callie Quinn Sinclair had definitely livened up his dull, boring life. He felt like shouting it out to the world.

The sound of hooves coming fast behind the wagon jerked him back to his senses. Though he didn't think Nate Fleming had a chance in hell of returning so soon, Rand laid a hand on the Colt in his gun belt.

A rider came up beside him. "Mister, I'm lookin' for the town of Battle Creek. Is it nearby?"

Rand took in the stranger's trail-worn clothes, unshaven jaw, and graying hair beneath a bowler hat. The silver-studded saddle on the magnificent white gelding didn't fit the rider. "Straight down this road about two miles. Can't miss it."

"Obliged." The traveler tipped his hat to Callie and galloped on.

Something about the man unsettled Rand. Maybe it was the ugly scar on his cheek. "Callie, did you recognize him?"

"No, but then I didn't look at him very closely because of tending to Wren. Why?"

"I don't know. Just a feeling I've got, I reckon." He'd make sure to talk to Cooper when he got to town. He wouldn't soon forget the fancy white horse and its trappings...or the stranger who rode it.

Forty-five minutes later, Rand hardly recognized Battle Creek. The town was a whirlwind of activity for a Wednesday—or any other day, for that matter. Throngs of people and wagons of all kinds made it difficult for Rand to maneuver down the main street. He wondered what was going on. The banner stretching overhead finally provided a clue:

Battle Creek Winter Festival and Dance, January 31st

Oh yes, he remembered Cooper telling him that Delta and her women's club, the Women of Vision, had garnered support for a winter celebration. Rand had so much admiration for Delta and her group of visionaries. They'd accomplished things that down-right astounded him. For a minute, he wished he and Callie lived in town. She'd probably love to be a part of something really beneficial.

Though the festival wasn't going to get into full swing until Saturday, folks from all around had begun gathering in, desperate for a break from the monotony of winter. A joyous mood filled the air from the street musicians on every corner to the smiles on the pedestrians' faces. One couple danced on the sidewalk.

"Why are those people so happy?" Toby asked.

"They're glad to escape their loneliness, even if it's just for a few days," Rand explained.

"Oh. Are you an' Aunt Callie gonna dance?"

Rand looked at Callie and winked. "We just might."

The only place he found to leave the wagon was with a handful of others in the dead grass in back of the jail. He swung Toby to the ground, then handed him the baby to hold. Rand put his hands around Callie's waist and lifted her from the seat.

He brushed her lips before he set her on her feet and watched the high color rise. "With so many people in town, it's going to be difficult keeping Toby in your sights. I'd take him with me, but I need to talk to my mother alone. I'll come get him after I'm finished, all right?"

"He'll be fine. I'll see to it."

Toby suddenly hollered. Rand looked to see what was wrong and had to bite back a laugh. Wren clenched the boy's lip with one hand and was trying to stick a finger up his nose with the other.

"Here, let me help you." Rand took the babe and kissed one chubby cheek before passing her to Callie. Now that he'd rescued Toby, he returned to their conversation. "If you run into any trouble, head for the sheriff's office. Cooper will be there. He'll keep you safe."

"You have more things to occupy your mind than my welfare. Now go. You said yourself that Nate is afoot. It'll take him time to get here. Besides, he won't show up in Battle Creek. He'll come to the Last Hope."

Pulling her close, Rand spoke low. "Darlin', nothing is more important to me than your welfare." He pressed a kiss to the back of her hand. "Furthermore, I intend to dance with you before we leave."

He tucked her brilliant smile into a secret place in his heart and walked her and the children to Abercrombie's Mercantile.

Then as he strolled toward his mother's home, his thoughts returned to the stranger he'd seen on the road. He should've shared his niggling concerns with Callie, but he hadn't wanted to steal the joy from her face when he had nothing to go on.

Lord knows, his gut had been wrong before.

Abigail Sinclair was loading a basket with the

luscious fried pies she'd become known for since she arrived in Battle Creek four years ago. She'd kept her face covered with a heavy black veil back then and called herself Clara. Only after Tolbert Early shot Rand had she revealed her true identity both as his mother and the famous opera singer, Abigail Winehouse.

She looked up when he entered her kitchen. "Hello, Rand. You're just in time to carry these for me."

"I need to talk to you first if you don't mind."

"Oh dear. You're displeased with me again." She went to the mirror and set a plumed hat on her head. "What did I do now?"

Gently, he took her hands and led her to a seat in the parlor. "Why didn't you look for me all those years ago?"

"I told you, I thought you had perished. By the time I returned, a whole year had passed. Folks relayed that my friend Margaret, to whom I had entrusted your care, left town without a child in tow. After months of looking, I tracked her down. She said Jack came and got you shortly after I left. He told her he was taking you on an adventure to Peterville Flats, a town forty miles away. It's all a mystery to me, but that's where he died. Several people there confirmed that they had seen a small boy with Jack."

"But you never found a child's grave," he argued.

"That is true."

"So there was one for my father?"

"Sadly, they never recovered any bodies at all. If not for two men who reported seeing him float downstream, I wouldn't know that he'd drowned.

I bought a tombstone, had both your names carved into the granite, and put it next to the river. I wanted someplace to go to talk to you."

Now that was creepy, knowing his name was etched on a stone somewhere when he walked around very much alive. "I want to believe you, Mother. I really do, so I can put an end to this right now. This town, did it have a wooden pony with blue spots up on one of the buildings, possibly a saloon?" The fragment of a buried memory teased the edges of his mind. "The horse rocked back and forth, and its eyes glowed."

"Yes, I did see that. It was a saloon called the Painted Pony. But how did you know?"

"I'm not sure. Still trying to figure that part out."

"Son, I did the best I could. I'm not perfect, but I would never have done anything to harm you in any way. I loved you so much. I still do. You can't imagine my immense joy when I discovered you were alive. I'm so sorry I waited such a long time to reveal myself." Abigail touched his arm.

"I wondered about that. Why you waited."

"At first I just wanted to get to know you without the pretense or expectation that often comes when you find you're family. I saw the real man you'd grown into. You were so confident and happy. Then I was afraid you wouldn't want me, didn't need me. The longer time went on, the harder it was to break free. I became trapped in the fabricated life I'd built. I couldn't face the questions, the judgment. But I've always loved you, even when you thought I didn't care and had turned my back on you. It's why I've done what I have, why I bought the saloon—" She stopped abruptly, biting her lip.

"You bought the Lily of the West? You?" he exploded.

"Don't be angry. I wanted to give you your dream," she said in a small voice. "You weren't supposed to find out."

"How else should I feel, Mother? You can't leave anything alone. You always have to try to fix things. You can't trust me to be a man."

She wrung her hands. "I'm doing the best I can."

"You can't buy my love, you have to earn it," he said quietly. "Don't you see?"

"Can't we start over?" Tears filled her eyes. "I don't know how to be a mother. I'll learn, if you'll give me time."

The anger left. For the first time, Rand saw a glimpse of the woman who'd tucked him into bed, given him a kiss, then sung him to sleep. She truly did love him. He knew that now. It was time to forgive and forget, wipe away all the pain. He accepted that she would always be a little self-centered and meddle in his affairs, but he wasn't perfect either. Not by a long shot.

He went and put his arms around her. "Starting over sounds good. You'll have to teach me how to be a son. Won't be easy, when I've been on my own since I was eleven."

"We'll do it together. One of these days, I want to hear how you survived after escaping that orphan train. From what little I know, Cooper looked after you, and I owe him a huge debt." She lowered her eyes and smoothed her dress. "And about the money…it's customary for a parent to give things to their child."

"Within reason," he grudgingly admitted. "Just don't make a habit of it. I want to do things for myself."

"You always were independent from the time you were born." She gave a deep sigh. "You insisted on dressing yourself and putting on your shoes when you could barely teeter around on your little legs. I had my hands full with you."

"Don't expect that to change." Rand went to stare out the window. He wondered if he should mention his dreams of a shadowy figure throwing his father onto the thin ice of the river. Had it really been just a bad dream like so many others in his childhood… or real? He'd buried so many things deep inside his mind…

Still, the nightmares were too real. They had to be memories or else he wouldn't know about the blue-spotted pony with glowing eyes.

"Tell me how you know about the Painted Pony Saloon, Rand. It's odd that you remember it."

Rand turned. "How could I not? That horse rocking back and forth with those glowing eyes would stick in any child's memory. It had a crank on the side that someone could wind up to make it move. I was there, Mother. And I think it has to do with something I might've seen."

"Tell me and we'll figure it out together."

"For years I've had these terrifying dreams, but now I know I had to have been recalling events that actually happened. I seem to remember Father hiding me in some thick underbrush and telling me to not make a sound. I recall fragments of a man telling Father something about giving him enough time to pay what he owed. They argued, then the man told a bald-headed giant to get rid of Father. I watched this man who seemed eight feet tall pick up my father and hurl him onto the ice. I watched it break, and Father disappeared. I never saw him again."

Abigail clamped her hand over her mouth. "They murdered him. They murdered my Jack."

Twenty-two

ALTHOUGH CALLIE SPENT A PLEASURABLE HOUR IN THE mercantile looking at everything, her thoughts were on Rand. She prayed he would get things straightened out with Abigail so he could find peace. She hated to watch this animosity with his mother eat him alive.

Toby tugged her skirt. "Can we go? I wanna play."

"Just a few more minutes," she said absentmindedly, her attention on a vibrant blue yarn. She could knit a muffler for Rand.

Intent on finding the right shade of blue, she suddenly missed Toby's hand on her skirt and panicked. When she whirled, she froze. The scarred stranger in the bowler hat who had asked the way to Battle Creek was handing Toby a piece of licorice.

"Toby, get back here," she said sharply. "Don't talk to strangers."

"I ain't. He just gave me some candy."

The candy giver's smile only served to increase the pounding of Callie's heart.

"Forgive me, ma'am. I should've asked first. I saw how impatient the boy was and wanted to help so you could finish looking at that pretty yarn. You have a nice pair of young'uns."

She tried to still her racing heart. She hated this distrust of every stranger. "Do I know you, mister?"

"Oh, I truly doubt that, ma'am."

It was time to cut this short. She didn't know who the scarred man was or what he wanted, but she couldn't afford to take chances. "Toby, thank the gentleman."

As soon as the boy dutifully followed her request, Callie hustled him out of the store. She almost had to drag him, because he kept stopping to look at the street musicians. Then, when a juggler caught his attention, Toby tried to pull away. He cried when she wouldn't let him stop and watch. By the time she reached the jail and safety, she was out of breath.

Cooper took the baby from her and helped her to a chair. She sat on the edge with worry knitting her brow.

The stranger could be one of Nate's brothers. She didn't know, because she'd only seen them once a long time ago. It would be like Nate to telegraph them to come help him steal Toby.

Dear God! She swallowed a strangled sob.

How could they hope to win against an army of cutthroats?

❧

Chills raced the length of Rand. Even though he'd reached the same conclusion, hearing his mother put into words that his father was murdered made the hair on his neck stand up. "Who were those men I'm remembering, and why did they take his life?"

"I can't answer the who, son. Jack owed so many

people. He simply couldn't control his gambling addiction, not even when I begged and pleaded. Evidently, one man refused to give him more time to repay a debt." Abigail stifled a sob. "Tell me all you saw."

"After the tall man got rid of Father, the two men yanked me up from the brush and said they were going to take me where no one would ever find me. And they did."

"You didn't remember any of this before now?" Abigail rose and moved to the window beside Rand. He put his arms around her, and it seemed the most natural thing in the world that they would take comfort in each other.

"I only had tiny pieces, but I thought they were from a long-ago nightmare. The whole picture emerged as we talked."

Abigail leaned to look up at him. "Does this fix things between us once and for all?"

He suddenly realized that he'd blamed her all this time for something that wasn't her fault, that he was taking out his fears of being unwanted and abandoned on her. True, she'd left him behind to pursue her career, but she hadn't known he was in an orphanage. She'd truly believed him dead. And then after she stumbled onto him as she passed through Battle Creek, she'd stayed, giving up her career and travel. He was sure it cost her a lot more than money. The renowned singer left all the fame and became a lonely, reclusive widow named Clara.

For him. Because she wanted to be a part of his life, even if it was from the fringes.

"It does. I see the past clearly now. I apologize for

refusing to believe you, for thinking you never cared about me. I haven't been a very good son. Can you forgive me?"

She patted his face and stared into his eyes. "You were only protecting your heart. In those years when you didn't know who I was, I saw how much you cared for people and how you welcomed the drunks who had no family into your upstairs living quarters when the weather was bad because you were afraid they'd freeze to death outside. I saw how you stood up for Jenny and her son Ben when Hogue Barclay beat them. And I saw the money you sent the orphanage in Fort Worth. You know what else?"

"What?"

"I am so very proud of you, proud of the man you became."

"Thank you, Mother. You don't know what that means to me."

They strolled toward the kitchen. "Are you still angry at me over buying the saloon?"

Rand swatted at the plume of her hat, which was tickling his nose. He kissed her cheek. "Nope. We're good. Now, about those pies. Mind if I eat one before we deliver them?"

"I made peach, your favorite, hoping I'd see you today."

"In that case, I'll have several." He put his arm around her. "Thank you, Mother."

∽

Rand had just finished his pie when Abigail, who stood at the sideboard, turned sickly pale and swayed. He jumped up and helped her into a chair.

"What's wrong, Mother?"

"It's… I'm feeling a little faint. I think I'd like to lie down."

"I'll help you upstairs, then go for Doc Yates."

Abigail waved her arm. "Oh for pity's sake. There is no need for a fuss. I'm fine. Everyone gets a bit light-headed now and then. Now, be a good son and help me to my bed." Once upstairs, she shooed him away. "Go. Callie and the kids need you. I'll rest a minute and be good as new. No worrying over me. I forbid it."

A smile curved Rand's mouth. She seemed her typical self. Maybe it was nothing, just as she said. "All right, then. I'll run on. But only if you're positive."

"I am. Now go."

Leaving the house, Rand dragged his thoughts back to the man in the bowler he was searching for. He'd about given up, when he spied the white horse at the hitching rail in front of the Lily of the West. Pushing through the batwing doors, he stood, searching each face for one with a long scar. Only the stranger wasn't there. Disappointed, he turned and strolled toward the mercantile, where he'd left Callie. Even though it hadn't been long, he couldn't wait to see her.

But when the clerk told him she'd left rather hurriedly, fear gripped his heart and wouldn't let go. Remembering his instructions to go find Cooper if she felt threatened, he raced toward the jail. He found her sitting across from Cooper's desk, clutching a handkerchief.

"Missing your family?" Cooper asked. He held Wren while Toby played at his feet. "I'm getting in plenty of practice for the twins."

Before Rand could answer, Callie leaped from the chair and into his arms. "I think we have big problems. I'm so scared."

"Tell me what happened. Is it Fleming? Is he back? Did you see him?"

"No." She told him about running into the strange man they'd passed on the road and the way he'd offered Toby licorice. "He complimented me on the children. When I asked if I should know him, he said he doubted it. That scar on his face gave me chills. He seemed to take undue interest in us, you know? I got the children and came straight here, like you told me."

"That's good, darlin'." He smoothed back her hair. "You stay here with Coop. I need to find out who this stranger is and what he wants."

Nothing seemed to make sense.

Cooper rose, cradling the baby in the crook of his arm. "Rand, I live in hopes that one of these days you'll remember who wears this badge. But since you know what this man looks like, I'll stay here with Callie and the children. We shouldn't leave them unprotected. I'll go through the wanted posters and see what I can find. I need to know who's in my town before all hell breaks loose. Sure would make my job easier if I had a name to stick on him."

Callie laid her head on Rand's shoulder. "He could be one of Nate's brothers. I wouldn't know, since I never saw them. What if he sent this stranger? How can we fight...?"

"Darlin', don't borrow trouble. Cooper will keep you safe until I get back."

"If you latch onto him, bring him to me," Cooper

ordered. "At the end of your Colt, if you have to. I'd like a chat with him. On days like this, I sure miss having a deputy. Wish the mayor would agree to let me hire one soon."

Rand nodded and opened the door. He needed answers and he meant to get them. The sooner the better.

❧

Returning to the saloon, Rand marched to the long bar. "Pettibone, did you notice a man in here wearing a bowler? Has a scarred face."

"Sure did. Had to throw him out on account of him accusing a fellow at his table of cheating. Created quite a ruckus, so I showed him the door. Told him this is a peaceable town."

"Did he give his name?"

"Nope, at least not that I heard. Wish I could be more help."

"You did fine," Rand said. "If you think of anything else, let me know. And if he comes back, send someone for me or Cooper pronto."

Outside the saloon, Rand's gaze swept up and down the street, taking in the celebrating men and women. Now what?

He decided to make a pass through the crowd, hoping for a glimpse of him.

Rand pushed back his black Stetson with a forefinger and started down the boardwalk. He knew these wide-open spaces offered a great hiding place for those who wanted to stay lost.

As Rand ambled down the street, he wished he had Cooper beside him. He could use another pair of eyes, and Cooper was a top-rate lawman. He'd inherited the job very suddenly after Sheriff Strayhorn suffered a heart attack six months ago. Doc Yates had been unable to save him. Battle Creek lost a beloved friend that day. Then Strayhorn's deputy took over the lawman duties in Waco so he could be near his sick mother, leaving them desperate.

Cooper refused the job at first offer, but he'd seen how badly the town needed law and order. Everyone knew it was only temporary, though. He'd turn over the reins to a replacement faster than greased lightning whenever they found one.

Rand passed the mercantile, the newspaper office, and the Lexington Arms, keeping his eyes peeled for the stranger in the bowler. He should probably gather Callie and the kids and head for home before too much longer. It would not be wise to let darkness overtake them.

If trouble rode toward them, he wanted to be able to spit in its eye and take its measure.

Then prickles crawled up his spine. He whirled and found himself face-to-face with the mysterious stranger.

"I see you found Battle Creek all right, mister." Rand's hand flexed above the handle of his Colt. The man's eyes flicked to it before glancing up. "You got family here?"

"Let's just say I have my reasons for coming." The strange-colored eyes became hooded as though he was used to trouble finding him.

"I didn't get a chance to introduce myself earlier. I'm Rand Sinclair."

"I know. Reckon I might've heard of you."

"Care to elaborate?"

"Not particularly."

Impatience rippled through Rand. For a second, he considered shooting the stranger for being so vague. But then Cooper would probably make him clean up the mess before locking him in jail. Likely wouldn't serve anything but bread and water, either.

"You know my name—what's yours?"

"Unfortunately, I don't think it's none of your business." The man smiled, unruffled by the questions.

Heat crept up Rand's neck. Clearly, Mr. No Name wasn't going to tell him anything. "I'm guessing Fleming must've sent for you."

"Don't know what you mean, Sinclair."

"Whether you do or not, Sheriff Thorne would like a word if you don't mind."

"Is this concerning the misunderstanding in the saloon?"

Rand decided two could play this game. "Guess you'll have to find out for yourself. Now come along. I'm not asking." He readied to draw his Colt. One way or another, the man was coming and he *would* answer a few questions.

"Are you a deputy or something?"

"*Or something* just about fits."

"I haven't done anything wrong. I'm a peaceable man, minding my own business."

"Then you don't have anything to worry about, do you?"

No Name smiled. "I hope this won't take long. I have things to do."

"Then we'd best get moving."

Keeping a wary eye on the man, Rand marched him to the sheriff's office. Cooper rose from behind his desk and ordered the mysterious stranger to take a seat.

"What's this about, Sheriff? I haven't broken any laws."

Rand listened to the exchange. They were finally going to get to the truth. But before the stranger would quit hedging, the baby began to fret and drew his attention. His gaze sought Callie's, and he smiled as she tried to soothe the child, but to no avail. Rand needed to get her and the children away from here. Cooper could handle things.

She gave him a grateful smile when he took Wren and suggested he take her to a quiet place. His old friend, Mabel King, owned the boardinghouse, and he knew she'd be happy to have the company.

Out on the sidewalk, Toby pointed toward the juggler. "Can I watch the man throw those plates up in the air an' catch 'em? Please?"

"I reckon, but just for a minute."

It didn't take much to satisfy the boy who was so curious about everything. They watched until the baby began to fuss; then Rand ushered them down the street to Mabel's. He wasn't wrong. The middle-aged woman's face lit with joy when he explained the situation and asked for her help. She bustled to the kitchen to fill Wren's bottle and had a fresh-from-the-oven cookie for Toby when she returned. Seeing that they were in excellent hands, Rand kissed Callie's cheek and said he'd be back soon. Two more things to do and they'd head home.

He'd speak to that lawyer Cooper told him about, then find out what Cooper had pried out of the stranger.

Rand ruffled Toby's hair and knelt down beside him. "I need you to watch over your ma...aunt and Wren for me. Think you can do it?"

Toby grinned. "Yep. I ain't gonna let anyone hurt 'em."

"That's my boy."

Letting himself out, Rand gazed at the milling crowd. Then his eyes drifted to a man hanging up a shingle across the street. It read Micah Jones, Attorney. Just the person he wanted to see.

Micah Jones looked more like a riverboat gambler than a lawyer. He wore a boiled white shirt and red garters on his upper arms. His brocade vest and shock of thick gray hair completed the image of a man who lived life on his own terms.

"Could I have a word with you, sir?" Rand asked.

"Jones is my name, and problem's my game," Micah boomed. "None are too big or too small. Come into my office."

Once inside and face-to-face, Rand immediately liked the lawyer's intelligent brown eyes. He explained the circumstances with Toby and Wren. "I want to make them my children."

"Then we'll just make it happen. The baby will be easy. The boy will be a little more difficult, since his father still lives. From the sound of it, the man doesn't need a child."

"No, sir, he doesn't."

"I'll fill out the necessary papers and put them before the county judge in Corsicana. You may have to make an appearance before him and relay your reasons for the adoption. I'll know more as we go along."

"How much will this cost?" Rand thought about the five hundred his mother had given him. This would be a good use of the money.

Micah Jones scratched his thatch of gray hair and made it stand on end. "I can't see it costing more than fifty dollars, all told."

Rand reached into his pocket, pulled out the fee, and laid it on the scarred, beat-up desk. "I want to get this resolved as soon as possible. I hope you'll understand."

The lawyer pocketed the money. "I'll start on it today."

Shaking Jones's hand, Rand opened the door. He was anxious to hear what Coop had found out. As he stepped onto the boardwalk, he plowed into Cooper.

"What did you find out from the stranger?"

"Rand, you barge through life like you're on a bucking bronc, hanging on for all you're worth," Cooper said, straightening his crooked tin star. "Never ask me how things are at the Long Odds or how Delta is these days. It's pretty rude, if you ask me."

A long sigh left Rand's mouth. "How's the ranch?"

"Fine."

"How's Delta doing?"

"Fine. About ready to explode and crankier than all get-out." Cooper took a sack of lemon drops from his pocket. "Want one?"

"Nope." Though Rand chafed at the delay, he knew better than to try to hurry his brother. Finally, he couldn't stand it. "Well?"

"Relax. The man is no cause for concern."

"Why the hell not? He scared Callie half out of her wits."

Cooper's gaze scanned the growing crowd. "Tom Mason is his name. He's a retired Pinkerton and claims he's looking for someone."

"Are you buying that wagonload of manure? Because I'm sure not. I'll bet everything I have he's connected to Nate Fleming."

"Damn it, Rand, settle down and listen. You always were the impatient one, the one who always thought he was right, the one who never could stand to wait more than three seconds for anything. You don't listen to reason, either."

"I didn't come to town for a character assessment." Seething, Rand leaned against a post that held up the overhang from the establishment's roof. "What about this Mason? Who's he looking for?"

"Brett. Mason wants to find our brother."

Twenty-three

ALARMS WENT OFF IN RAND'S HEAD AS HE DIGESTED the information. "You didn't tell him where Brett is, did you?"

"Nope." Cooper stuck the sack of lemon drops back into his pocket. "Want to check him out first, make sure he doesn't mean our baby brother any harm. It's my job to see to it, and I will."

"Why is it your job? I'm just as capable as you."

"I know that, but number one, I'm the sheriff, and number two, I'm the oldest and I've always looked out for you and Brett. Figure I always will."

"I'm a bit old for a nursemaid," Rand said dryly. "Stop treating me like I'm still wet behind the ears."

"Don't mean to. Just a habit, I reckon."

"Well, try to break it." Rand lifted his hat and shoved his fingers through his hair. "Why would Mason be looking for Brett, anyway?"

"Wouldn't say. Insisted it was confidential."

"Horsefeathers! What do you think, Coop? If Mason is who he says, what business could he have with Brett?"

"I took the fellow's measure and I'm inclined to believe him. Probably has to do with Brett's horses—heard about the fine stock on the Wild Horse and wants to buy some. Or maybe he wants to pay him some money. Hell, I don't know. I'll ride out and ask Brett if he can shed any light on this."

Rand pushed away from the post. He had a lot to do and he didn't have time to waste. "I'd watch that man, Coop. Don't let him near Brett."

Cooper bristled. "You want my job, Rand?"

"Nope."

"Then quit telling me how to do it."

Leaving seemed an excellent idea. Rand wove through the crowd toward the mercantile, where he picked out a pretty new dress for Callie, a deep rose with a row of lace around the collar. Then he ordered some furniture for the room that would be his son's and the pretty wallpaper Callie had chosen earlier.

After adding various and sundry other purchases to the bill, he told John Abercrombie he'd be back to get them later.

"I'll have 'em ready." The mercantile owner waved and moved to the next customer.

Lively music greeted Rand when he stepped onto the boardwalk. He stopped for a moment to watch couples who broke into dance. He'd promised a dance to Callie, and he meant to do just that as soon as he fetched her from Mabel's.

With anticipation of holding Callie in his arms, Rand turned his boots toward the boardinghouse and his family.

Minutes later, he strolled into Mabel's. Callie's smile

warmed his heart. She was so pretty, sitting there in the parlor with the sunlight streaming through the window bringing out the auburn streaks in her brown hair. The baby lay beside her on the settee, happy as a lark. Busy playing at Callie's feet, Toby looked up and grinned. The boy was playing with the top Rand had made for him and was getting the hang of keeping it spinning.

"Look, Papa, I can do it real good."

Papa. The word settled in Rand's heart like silt drifting to a riverbed after it had been disturbed. This woman and these children were his whole world. He wouldn't want to keep living if something happened to them.

"You sure can, son. You make me very proud." Rand turned to Callie. "We should probably head home soon. I have lots to tell you on the way."

Callie gathered little Wren and stood. "Did you get everything done that you came for?"

"Yep." He took the baby from her and settled the child in the crook of his arm. "We'll just swing by the mercantile and collect our purchases on our way out."

She nodded and turned to Mabel King. "Thank you for your hospitality. I enjoyed getting to know you."

Mabel hugged her. "Stop by the next time you come to town, dear. I'll have some tea waiting for you. And I'd like to introduce you to my sister, Jenny Barclay. She has a boy about Toby's age. Ben and Toby will make quite a pair."

"I'd love to meet Jenny. She sounds lovely."

Rand's arm slid around his wife's waist. "Thanks for giving Callie and the children a place to rest. We'll see you next time, Mabel."

Outside the house, Rand herded them toward the street musicians. "I promised to dance with you, Mrs. Sinclair, and I aim to do just that. Besides, if we don't show our appreciation, the fiddlers will get their feelings hurt."

Callie colored. "Have you forgotten about the baby?"

"I haven't forgotten about anything." He aimed Toby toward a bench in front of the Lexington Arms Hotel and plopped Wren in the boy's lap. "We won't be long."

Then he swung Callie into the thick of the dancers, her skirt swirling around his feet. The waltz seemed to be made for them. He held her close and breathed her fragrant hair. "I've wanted to do this ever since I laid eyes on you. Your body moving against mine as music swirls around us. I can feel your heart beating."

Unshed tears swam in Callie eyes when she glanced up at him. "Rand, I don't know what you expect of me…of us. I'm sure to be a disappointment."

He lifted her hand to his lips and kissed it. "Darlin', you'll never let me down, no matter what you do. I'll always be proud to call you my wife. I know you're keeping something back, something that terrifies you. Just know that whatever it is, I'm not going anywhere. And neither are you. Trust me with your secret."

"I just need a little more time."

"I'm a very patient man where you're concerned." He kissed her forehead. "My heart and my arms are always open."

The last strains of the waltz drifted into the air like smoke through a keyhole. Rand sighed. "Guess we'd better mosey along home."

When they went to collect the children, Rand could barely see Toby over the group of youngsters around him. Rand heard his son announce to the gaggle of pint-sized minions that he had to take care of his baby sister on account of his aunt and papa were keeping the fiddlers from getting sick of playing music and going home.

Then Toby announced to his subjects, "My baby sister grows her own teeth too. All by herself. One of these days when she's big as me, she'll be able to chew and everything."

What a boy. Rand's heart swelled inside his chest. Somehow or another, the county judge had to approve the adoption. Rand refused to consider that he wouldn't.

They collected their purchases from the mercantile and took the road toward the Last Hope Ranch.

Toby had hopped into the back of the wagon at the mercantile with the packages and sacks of sugar, flour, and meal. The boy didn't fool Rand. Toby would look through everything for the stick of candy John Abercrombie had thrown in. Rand didn't mind, though. That would give him private time with Callie. He noticed she sat closer to him, and that made his heart beat faster.

"What did Cooper find out about the stranger?" Callie had Wren sitting up in her lap. "I'm about to die of curiosity."

Rand told her what Coop had learned about Tom Mason. "If that's to be believed."

"What does he want with Brett?"

"Don't know."

"Sounds like you don't trust this man."

"Nope." Rand pushed back his hat to scratch his forehead, then told her about his talk with his mother. Callie tucked the edge of a blanket around the baby and reached for his hand. "I'm so glad you got everything ironed out, Rand."

"Me too."

Callie's laugh filled the breeze with music, lifting his spirits. "Sometimes life knows just what to give us to make everything better."

"Yes, it does." Rand recounted how his repressed memory came back and the conclusion that his father was murdered.

"What a horrible thing for a little boy to witness. Your mother truly had no idea what happened to you."

"I can see that now. She didn't just go her merry way with never a care like I'd always thought."

"I'm glad you made your peace. What did you learn at the lawyer's office?"

"Micah Jones thinks adopting Wren will be easy. I may have to appear before the judge and plead my case for Toby. At any rate, we've got the ball rolling. Soon they'll belong to us."

"Oh, Rand, that's great news." The baby began to fuss, so Callie put her on her shoulder and patted the small back.

Rand swiveled in the seat to glance in the back. Toby had been quiet far too long. The boy was sitting on the edge of the wagon with his feet dangling off the end, happily eating the peppermint stick he'd found in the purchases.

Just then, the wagon ran over a big rock and the

child flew out, landing in a clump of winter grass. Callie screamed. Rand pulled on the reins and leaped down, barely giving the wheel that was lying to the side a cursory glance.

"Toby, are you hurt, boy?"

High-pitched laughter filled Rand with relief. The boy couldn't be hurt too badly if he could laugh. The lad sat up. "Whooee! Can I do that again?"

Callie appeared at Rand's side, clutching the baby. "No, young man, you cannot. You could've been seriously injured. Are you sure you didn't break anything? Rand, check his arms and legs."

Before Rand could follow her request, Toby popped to his feet. He wiggled both arms this way and that, then his legs. Rand was hard-pressed to keep a straight face. The six-year-old looked like he was trying out for a part in a traveling sideshow of some sort.

"He's fine, Callie. He thought it was fun." Rand draped an arm around her shoulders.

"Well, I'm not fine. He scared ten years off my life." She jiggled the baby up and down to keep her from fussing.

Rand turned toward the tilted wagon. "If everyone is all right, I have some work to do."

After situating Callie and the children over to the side, he looked around for a sturdy piece of wood to use for a lever. A substantial tree limb would work, he decided.

Everything was going well. Using the big rock that had caused the whole mess of problems to start with and the tree limb, he got the wagon raised.

"Callie, I'm going to need your help. Can you hold

the wagon up with this limb while I put the wheel back on?"

She passed the baby to Toby and came to assist. Being so slight, she had to drape herself over the makeshift lever and apply all her weight. But she finally managed.

Rand turned to get the wheel when a loud crack rent the air a half second before something slammed into his head, knocking him to the ground.

He plunged into a deep, dark cavern.

⌘

Callie stared in horror at the snapped piece of wood in her hand and then at Rand's prone body at her feet. "Rand!"

She knelt and put her ear to his chest to see if he was alive. Only she couldn't hear over the pounding of her own heart. Dear God, had she killed him?

"Rand, please wake up." She patted his face and felt the knot on the back of his head. Blood covered her fingers when she finished her examination. Though she didn't know for sure, his injury seemed serious. She had no doubt that she could get him into the back of wagon, but without a wheel, it couldn't go anywhere. Trying to still the panic that lodged in her throat, she got a blanket and covered him.

How would she get him home?

Her stomach clenched tight as she glanced up and down the road.

"Is Papa gonna wake up?" Toby's voice quivered.

"Sweetheart, he's going to be just fine. Don't you worry."

"Can we go home soon? I'm scared of the dark."

"I know. I'll have you home before night sets in." She looked at the growing shadows, wondering how she'd keep her word. Maybe she and Toby together could put the wheel back on. She had to try something.

Telling Toby to watch after his sister, Callie went searching for something else to use as a lever while staying within sight of her children. After several minutes, she located a small downed sapling that might work. She dragged it back to the wagon. Emptying out the basket she'd brought from home that morning, she laid Wren into it. Then she carefully explained to Toby what she needed him to do.

Positioning the sapling just right took a few tries, but her confidence grew when she finally raised the wagon. "Toby, honey, I know that wheel is heavy, but see if you can get it on."

The boy grunted and strained but finally had to give up. "I cain't. I'm sorry." Tears bubbled up in his eyes.

"It's okay. You did the best you could." She lowered the wagon and placed an arm around his shoulders. Rand gave a moan and moved his hand.

Callie scrambled to him. "Lie still, Rand. You're hurt. Toby, can you get me some water from the wagon?"

While she waited, she smoothed Rand's hair and tried to reassure him as much as herself. "You're going to be just fine. You simply took a blow to the head, and it knocked you out."

Rand worked his tongue and finally managed, "Fleming?"

"No, you were putting the wheel back on the wagon and the limb broke, flying up and hitting you."

He tried to rise. "Have to fix. Dark."

Callie held him down. "You're not able. I'll think of something."

Just then Toby brought the water canteen. Removing the stopper, Callie held the vessel to Rand's mouth. "Drink this. You'll feel better."

The clip-clop of a horse sounded. The bend in the road prevented her from seeing the rider, and that sent a frisson of alarm arcing through her. Closer and closer the form came, like a dark vulture bearing down on them.

They had nowhere to go.

She grabbed Toby. "Get into the wagon under the quilt and don't make a sound. Hurry!"

Sliding Rand's Colt from his holster, she cocked it. She'd shoot anyone who even thought to do her family harm.

Twenty-four

STANDING PROTECTIVELY ABOVE RAND, CALLIE stead-
ied the Colt and stiffened her spine, ignoring the
bunched nerves that screamed for her to hide. But
she'd never been a coward—it wasn't her way.

The white horse came into view first, and the
person sitting astride the animal was nothing but a dark
figure. She knew how to shoot, and she'd make sure
to aim for the heart.

As the rider drew closer, she recognized the stranger
whom Rand called Tom Mason. Though Rand said he
was an ex-detective, she didn't lower her guard. Too
often people claimed to be something they weren't.

Mason halted and leaned forward in the saddle. The
scar on his cheek was white against his skin, which
said it'd been there a while. "Reckon you can use my
help, Mrs. Sinclair. Mind if I fix your wagon before
you shoot me?"

When she hesitated, Rand attempted to get to
his feet, only to fall back, murmuring, "Let my
family be."

"Don't believe you're in any position to bargain,

ma'am. Your man's hurt, and I'm sure your children are close by." Mason's kind gray eyes flicked to the tilting wagon. He appeared harmless enough, but was he? "It'll be dark soon. You've gotta trust someone."

Yes, but who? Danger seemed to lurk around every corner.

Finally, Callie lowered the weapon. "A woman can't be too careful. I'd be obliged if you help with the wheel, then be on your way."

"I truly mean you no harm, Mrs. Sinclair," Mason said with a smile.

Callie saw the sincerity in his eyes and suddenly found herself liking the strength of his jaw. It was possible she'd been wrong about him. "Maybe not us, but we have a bone to pick with anyone who seeks to do Brett Liberty wrong. We'll put a shield around him that you'll never penetrate. Just so you know."

"I don't suppose you want to tell me where he lives."

"I'd sooner shake hands with the devil."

"Ma'am, he's in no danger from me."

"Then why are you hell-bent on finding him?"

"Afraid I can't say. That's between Mr. Liberty and me."

Toby flew down from the wagon and began flailing Tom Mason with his little fists. "Leave Uncle Brett alone."

To Mason's credit, he simply stood there silently, taking the blows.

Though Callie wanted to land a few well-placed hits herself for good measure, she pulled Toby off. "Stop it, sweet boy. Let him help us fix the wagon so we can get home and tend to your papa."

"Oh, all right," Toby grumbled, giving Mason the evil eye. "But I ain't gonna like it."

Mason smiled. "Fine son you got. Quite a fighter."

Callie swung to Mason. "I apologize. As you see, we're very defensive of Brett."

Rand pulled himself to a sitting position and Callie handed him the Colt. "Mason, you ever harm him, I'll hunt you down."

"Don't worry, Sinclair, I know better than to take on this bunch. Can't help wondering though…why did the boy call Liberty uncle? By my records, the man has no kin."

"You figure it out," Rand answered shortly.

"All righty." Mason grinned. "Reckon I'd best get this wheel back on before one of you kill the Samaritan."

With everything already in place, it didn't take Mason—with Callie's small assistance—very long at all. The ex-Pinkerton dusted off his hands and helped Rand into the back along with Toby. Callie wrapped them both in the warm quilts, then, at the baby's soft cry, moved to change her daughter's diaper.

"Can you handle the team, ma'am?" Mason asked. "I can—"

"I'll manage from here just fine," Callie said, cutting him off. She finished tending to Wren and got the baby situated on the seat beside her for the remainder of the trip. "Thank you, Mr. Mason. I'm very grateful you stopped."

"No ill will?" The scarred man mounted his white gelding.

"Just saying I appreciated the helping hand, no more."

"You're a tough woman, ma'am. I'd hate to be on your bad side."

"You already are, Mr. Mason." She said it pleasantly enough, but the way Mason jerked his head up told her he'd gotten her message. "You have a restful evening now…wherever that might be."

Thank goodness the Last Hope wasn't far. Callie flicked the reins and got the horses moving without looking back at Tom Mason. The long shadows darkening the road made her nervous. Anyone could hide in them and she wouldn't see the danger until it was too late.

Though the horses plodded slowly toward the ranch, she gave thanks for making each bend in the road safely. By the time the house came into view, it was pitch dark, and tension knotted Callie's shoulders. Biscuit came to meet them, barking and wagging her tail near off. Toby leaned over the side of the wagon, calling to his faithful companion and telling the dog about all the sights in town, especially the juggler.

"You should'a seen that man throwing those plates in the air an' catchin' 'em." Biscuit gave a sharp bark back.

Callie parked by the kitchen door and set the brake. Wren was fast asleep. After telling Rand she'd be right back, she carried the baby into the house and lit the lamps. Toby and his dog were right behind her. With the children safely inside, she went back out and climbed into the wagon bed.

She touched his face lightly, willing his eyes to open. "Rand, we're home. Do you think you can stand?"

"I can walk." He sat up and groaned. "Have a god-awful headache, though."

"Let's get you inside." She helped him from the wagon and up the three steps into the kitchen. He collapsed into a chair at the table, where he sat breathing hard. The short walk had taxed his strength. She didn't know if she could get him upstairs to his bed or not. It might be best to spread some quilts on the floor in front of the fireplace.

While he rested, Callie and Toby went out to unload their purchases. She filled the youngster's arms and gathered the remainder. Then, while he watched over Rand and Wren, she drove the wagon to the barn and unhitched the team. Though the cold night air promised a hard freeze, sweat covered her by the time she finished feeding and bedding down the horses.

The stressful day was about over. Before she went into the house to fix a bite to eat, she took a moment to roll her shoulders in an effort to relieve the tense muscles. A million stars dotted the black canvas overhead.

She remembered her vow that morning to tell Rand about her past and tear down the wall between them. Now it seemed unlikely that she could tonight with Rand injured.

Soon, though.

A person with a head injury requires constant monitoring, she could have sworn she heard her mother say as clearly as though Nora Quinn Powers stood there. *Don't let him go to sleep or he might not ever wake up.*

The admonition gave her chills. Callie had forgotten about the danger. She looked up at the sky. "Thank you, Mama."

Hurrying inside, she found Rand slumped over with his head on the table—asleep. "Rand, wake up. You have to wake up." She shook him until he roused.

"Sleepy," he murmured, trying to push her away.

"I know, but you can't. You have to stay awake until the danger has passed. Would you like something to eat? I'll bet you're hungry."

At his nod, she scrambled some eggs and sliced fresh bread from the loaf she'd made yesterday, all while keeping an eye on him. She didn't even have to call Toby to the table. The hungry boy came running and plopped down in his chair.

Ten minutes later, Rand had eaten almost all of it before pushing his plate away. He seemed more alert than she'd seen him since the accident.

After Toby finished and wiped his mouth, Callie asked him to help her get Rand up to bed. Though her husband, stubborn man that he was, leaned heavily on her, it turned out that Rand pretty much climbed the stairs under his own steam. A heavy weight lifted from her chest.

Stripping off his boots, holster, and clothes down to his long johns, she got him into bed and turned to Toby, who stood behind her. "I need you to sit here next to Papa and keep him awake while I clean up the kitchen. Do you think you can do that?"

The boy nodded, then asked, "But how?"

"Talk to him. Talk about anything and everything. If he starts to close his eyes, shake him real good."

"Okay."

She stood outside the door for a minute as Toby launched into a recap of their day in town. "I loved the people that played the music. When I get big, I'm gonna play a fiddle an' throw plates in the air an' catch 'em at the same time. But my favorite thing was dancin'. When I grow up, I'm gonna dance like you an' Mama did an' make her smile. She was so happy."

Callie smothered a sob. He'd just called her Mama. The child was still putting order in his life the only way he knew. It deeply touched her, as did the fact that he wanted her to be happy. They had to make his dream, and theirs, a reality. Somehow, someway.

"Yes, son," she heard Rand say. "She was happy."

Leaving Rand in excellent hands, she turned her attention to Wren, who was awake and looking around. When she saw Callie, the sweet baby smiled big, showing her toothless gums, and excitedly kicked her little legs. Callie picked her up and nuzzled her chubby cheek. Her heart burst with love for the child. She'd never felt as needed as she was in that moment.

She just prayed Rand got better so they could talk. It had taken her so long to make up her mind to clear the air, and now that she'd come to the decision, she couldn't. Every second dragged.

"Please, darling husband, you have to get better," she whispered.

⁓

Later, while she sat beside Rand holding his hand, the quiet of the house settled over Callie. The children were fast asleep, the doors bolted, and she was with the man she loved.

He gave her a sinful grin. "If you insist on keeping me from getting a wink of sleep, crawl into this bed beside me." His eyes darkened, daring her. "I don't bite, you know. And nothing would fix me up like feeling your soft curves pressing against me."

"Rand, you're talking out of your head, dear. Do you have a fever?" She leaned in and laid one hand on his forehead.

"Darlin', you have no idea."

"Are you sure you're not milking this injury a tad?" When she took his hand again, his fingers curled inside hers.

"I'll never tell." His tired grin made her heart leap. "But would you please rid me of this damn headache as long as I'm only pretending? You put your cool hand on my head again, and I know it'll go away. Now, I think we were discussing you stretching out beside me."

Lie in bed with Rand?

The daring thought sent quivers of excitement running through Callie like leaves on a tree in a summer breeze.

Dear God, how she yearned to curl up next to him, fit the curves of her body to his.

What would it hurt? She'd be fully clothed.

Before she could stop herself, she rose. When he moved over to make room, she lay down beside him.

The scent of the wild Texas land enveloped her. Rand was everything she'd ever wanted, ever hoped for, ever dreamed of. She snuggled against him as his arm came around her.

"Thank you, Callie. Now, you're home." He kissed her hair.

She lightly dragged her fingertips across the side of his face. "I don't deserve you, Rand. You're good and kind and decent."

"I hear a *but* in there someplace," he said, frowning.

"I know you have feelings for me. No one kisses the way you do without a fire blazing inside. Something is stopping you from going further. Darlin', don't you want us to have more, have a real marriage?"

"Yes." Her quiet admission seemed to open the padlock around her heart. It was time.

"Tell me what you're holding back. Trust me with your secret. I simply want to understand, nothing more."

With his arm anchoring her, she took a deep, shuddering breath and let it all pour out. She told him about her mistake with Richard Farrington that night so long ago and the resulting pregnancy at eighteen.

When she got to the hardest part of her secret—where her stepfather ordered his son to steal the baby from her—she broke down in sobs.

"I only held my angel girl for a few minutes, and then David, my stepbrother, was pulling her from my arms. I held on as tight as I could, but I lost consciousness. When I came to, Claire had a black eye and deep bruises. Claire had fought them both with everything she had, but it was no use. She stumbled downstairs, but they'd vanished into the blackness. Gone just like that. My sister said Edmund swore that night that if we tried to find the baby, he'd kill her."

Tears trickled down her cheeks and Rand tenderly wiped them away, murmuring, "It's all right, darlin'. Let it all out."

"My heart shattered in a million pieces. I don't know what they did with her, and it has tormented me every second of every day. I should've tried harder to find her. I shouldn't have given up."

"You had no choice. Don't you see? You protected your baby. You could do little else."

"For weeks I thought about killing my stepfather, but then I wanted to kill myself more."

"Why did your stepfather hate you and your sister so much?"

"He didn't at first. But when he married socialite Liza Masterson, it all changed. With her nonstop lies and hate, she turned Edmund Powers against us. She said we were evil, would never be worth anything, and he believed her. Then later, we challenged his authority at every turn. Claire married Nate to show Edmund she could. When I became pregnant, Edmund believed I'd done so to spite and embarrass him like Claire had."

Rand put a finger under her chin and raised her face. "I understand everything clearly now. Why you carried this deep sadness that no sunlight could reach. Why you reacted so strongly when Emily Winters came and begged us to take Wren. But you can't blame yourself. You did the best you could to find her, of that I'm certain. The overwhelming love for your daughter lay beneath every action."

She searched his eyes, afraid of the hurt she'd see there. "I didn't want to tell you this, but I ached to be a real wife. There's more, and it's what I've been so terrified to tell. This may change everything, but you need to know exactly what you've gotten. If you send me away, I understand. You're such an honorable man, and I—"

"I will never send you away." He lifted her hand and kissed the soft underside of her wrist. "Just trust me. Let's get rid of the secrets between us so we can move on."

"I'm broken, Rand. There is something wrong with me." The tortured words hung thick in the air. Her heart stilled as though waiting for a blow. She looked away, fearful of what his face would reveal. "I'm only half a wife. I almost died during my daughter's difficult delivery. I was bedridden for months afterward. I still remember the pain of the birth. Of losing her." A sob broke free. "I'm terrified of making love and maybe experiencing all that again, and that is why I made you promise that I'd never have to share your bed."

He caressed her cheek with the pad of his thumb. The immense gentleness must be how the brush of angel wings felt. Raising her face, he stared into her eyes. His fingers slid to her mouth and traced the curve of her lips.

"I'm sorry you've never known the joy of becoming one with someone. I'm sorry that you've only had pain. Given what you've endured, it's no wonder that you're frightened. Making love can bring great pleasure, though. If you're willing, I promise to be very gentle and vow to never force you to do anything. And should you get with child, I vow to guard you and care for you and never let anyone take our children from us."

She smoothed back a lock of hair that had fallen onto his forehead. Gazing into his blue eyes, she saw love shining in the depths, a love that he'd once vowed to never speak of. She trusted him more than anyone. He held her heart in his hands. Deep commitment in the lines of his face said he'd stand with her no matter the outcome of this night. Now it was time to share all of her with this wonderful man.

"I know you will. You've demonstrated that. Maybe it's time to let go of my fear and face up to the thing that scares me most. I know you'll take your time and let me find my way."

"You can count on that, darlin'. I promise to take it slow and easy, and if I hurt you in any way, I'll immediately stop. But why did you decide to take this step? I'm curious."

"You've filled me with so much yearning that I can't stand another night apart. I've been miserable because I want it all. I want all of you, not just your kisses." She stroked the side of his face. "I want to shower you with every drop of my love."

"Do you think we should hold off until you can visit with Doc Yates to make sure you have no physical problems? I would never do anything to hurt you. Losing you would be the last straw. I can't imagine what it would be like to live alone again, nor do I wish to find out. Maybe we should just lie here in each other's arms for now. And kiss, of course. I can't be near you without needing your lips on mine."

Callie shook her head. "I don't want to waste one more second. Life doesn't come without risk. I want you, Rand Sinclair. All of you. No half measures."

"Lord knows I sure don't want to keep a lady waiting."

Delicious shivers danced up her spine. "Make me feel—"

He silenced her with a burning kiss that stole her breath. When he finally removed his lips from hers, he covered her face and neck with kisses. Someone had taught Rand very well how to make a woman feel cherished.

Happiness curled inside her chest. She'd known her husband was a keeper but hadn't been aware of the extent of his commitment to her, to their marriage, until now.

In the soft lamplight, she saw a shimmer of tears in his eyes. She gently kissed each eyelid.

When he spoke, his voice was hoarse. "I convinced myself that I didn't need anyone, but I find I cannot live without you, Callie. You are my life. Never be afraid to tell me anything. I'll not judge. I meant my wedding vows. I want permanence. I want a forever marriage, and I'll accept nothing less."

"I'm sorry I didn't trust you enough. I just didn't want to ruin what I'd found here."

"Darlin', nothing on this earth will ever make me turn away from you." He rose on an elbow and tenderly smoothed back her hair. "As soon as we send Nate Fleming to the hangman's noose, I'll find your angel girl. Even if I have to kill Edmund Powers, I *will* get her back for you. That's a promise."

Twenty-five

DRUGGING HER WITH HIS KISSES, RAND UNFASTENED her dress one button at a time. He whispered in her ear, left a trail of kisses down her neck, and removed her clothing piece by piece until she lay bare.

He quickly shed the long johns she'd insisted he wear while recovering. Finally, with no barriers between them, he pulled her to him, crushing her breasts against his chest.

Touching the expanse of all that satiny skin made the heat from his belly spread through him like wildfire, consuming everything in its path.

But he wanted more. Lots more.

He needed to be inside her, feel her warmth around him, feel the hum of her body, and taste her desire.

Running a hand down the shapely curve of a long leg, Rand pressed his lips to the inside of her thigh and watched her satiny skin tremble.

Her shivery moan fed his hunger for her. With each touch, each caress whispering his love, he returned to her luscious mouth, pouring out his heart into a kiss that was long and deep.

Under feathery touches that encompassed every inch of her, he had her feverish body straining for release, toward the completeness that comes from giving all you have to the person you love. He just prayed she was ready for all he yearned to give her. He longed to show her that lovemaking wasn't anything to fear but something to savor.

Raking his teeth gently across her breast, he drew the tip into his mouth. Slipping his finger into the soft folds between her legs, he stroked. She responded with moans, plunging her hands into his hair and tugging him tightly to her.

He wanted Callie more than he wanted anything else on earth. As he'd written in the note, she was his life.

Callie Quinn Sinclair was his everything.

He'd never known what it was to love someone with all his heart and soul and mind.

When the slick wetness told him she was ready, he moved on top and eased into her. The pleasure stole his breath, his mind, his purpose. Fighting the desire to give passion free rein, he stilled his body until he regained control.

"Are you in pain, Callie?"

"No. Please don't stop. I never knew this could feel so good."

A few moments later, he began moving again and found that she instinctively matched his rhythm. His wife was a constant surprise—all proper on the outside and a tigress within.

He felt the beginning quickening of her release. She cried out, pulling him to her. The waves became stronger, rising ever higher. When he could stand no more, he shattered into a million pieces, becoming fragments of his old self.

As they came back together, he was reborn into a stronger, more determined man. Panting, he collapsed on top of her—then, not wanting to crush her, he rolled off to the side.

A fine sheen covered their bodies, the proof of their love.

Though Rand had been with countless women during his life, Callie truly was his first. She was certainly the only one who mattered. The others had been merely women to pass the time with.

After several minutes, he rose to plant a kiss on her eyelids. "Thank you, Callie. I lock your gift into a special place in my heart."

She'd suffered greatly, had her babe ripped from her arms. He made a solemn vow. No one would ever take anything else from her. If they tried, they'd find themselves six feet under and providing the worms with food.

Callie settled beside the hard planes of his body and laid her palm on his face. "I never knew what lying with someone could be like. Is it always like this?"

Resting his chin on the top of her head, Rand smiled. "Only with someone you love, I'm told."

"Do you love me, Rand?"

His old self would hedge. But the new one answered forthrightly and without reservation. "I once foolishly told you that I'd never give my heart to you. I was wrong. You had it a long time ago. Darlin', I love you more than my own life."

She raised up and kissed him long and hard. Rand

accepted what she gave and felt a familiar stirring inside once more. But he needed a bit of rest first.

They belonged together. Their lives were like a canvas that was only half-painted. Love would complete it in glorious, vibrant hues.

"I love you too, Rand," she murmured against his mouth. "I have for a while, but I wouldn't let myself say the words, because I felt unworthy of you." She laid her head on his shoulder. "We're going to be all right, aren't we?"

Rand smoothed her hair. "Yes. We're going to be better than all right. I'm going to fill your life with so much happiness and love that you grow dizzy from it."

"That sounds like a promise."

"It is, darlin', and I aim to deliver."

⁓

Later, lying there with Callie in his arms, listening to her soft breathing, Rand thought back on all he had learned and shook with rage. A powerful yearning to knock Callie's stepfather's teeth out rose up inside. Rand wasn't going to let Edmund Powers or his son, David, get away with such a heinous, unspeakable crime. They would answer to him. Before he got through with them, they would know what exacting retribution was and that Callie would always be protected from the likes of them. It was all Rand could do to keep from springing from bed and saddling Blue.

"My daughter would be seven years old now," Callie said softly. "She wouldn't remember me. I guess it's the mother in me, but I like to think that she's happy wherever she is. Just once before I die, I'd dearly love to see her."

"Never fret about that. You *will* get your wish just as soon as I can make it happen." Rand hated the gruffness of his voice. The anger coloring it was too strong to hide. "Tell me, why did you come back here when you were running from Fleming?"

"My mother's treasure chest. She hid the chest somewhere on this property, and I came for it. Mama never said what was in the box, but she told me and Claire, when our lives needed to look up, to find and open it. I thought it might have some money inside, and I needed something to sustain Toby and me."

He shivered with longing as she brushed back a stubborn lock of hair from his forehead. Though they'd just made love, he felt the heat already building again.

"I never knew the greatest treasure would be finding you."

Rand lifted her hand and kissed her fingers. "And I you. Until you came along, I had given up on love and family, focusing instead on protecting my heart. You gave me purpose. I take it you were unable to locate the box."

"I searched everywhere with no luck. Even the key that went to it was missing from where I'd buried it by the woodpile. You have it on your brass key ring. The fancy scrolled one you found."

"Why didn't you tell me? I would give it back in a heartbeat."

"I know, but it does me no good without a lock to put it into. I think Edmund must've taken the treasure box. It's the only conclusion I can come to."

They discussed that, then Rand told her that Toby had shared a secret of his own while sitting beside him. "Remember what Toby said about his father making him do horrible things?"

"I recall that very clearly, and how troubled I was."

"He told me how Nate forced him to kill small animals, then later used him to gain unsuspecting victims' trust, luring them into a trap where Nate robbed and gunned them down. That's a big burden for a little boy to carry. I assured him that he would never have to do anything like that ever again. Not as long as I'm alive."

"I'm sure that relieved Toby's mind. Thank you, Rand." She raised her head from his shoulder and kissed his cheek, her soft breath brushing his.

"Darlin', keep doing that and I'll have to forget all about my aching head."

"I'm sorry. I know you're not feeling well."

"Hey, don't apologize. You can kiss me all you want. I can be dead and buried, but one kiss from you and I'll pop right up from that dirt. You should patent your kisses as some kind of new medicinal tonic. Make a fortune."

Her eyes twinkled. "I'll bet you tell all your ladies that."

Rand kissed the tip of her nose. "You're the only lady in my life and the only one I'll ever want, both in this lifetime and the next."

Slowly, he traced every line, indentation, and curve of her body and committed them to memory. He felt a raging storm coming and he didn't know what, if anything, would be left once it passed. He wasn't leaving anything to chance.

He knew from experience how fragile and fleeting good fortune was.

Closing his eyes, he drew Callie's sweet fragrance deep into his heart.

The depth of his love for her shook him to the core. If this was to be their only time to lie together, he didn't want to forget a single detail.

Callie kept close watch over Rand for the next two days and slept beside him at night. It grew increasingly hard to keep him from getting up and doing chores. She only managed, with Toby's help, by keeping him distracted and entertained.

On the third day, she woke to find an empty bed. From the height of the sun outside the window, it was well past daybreak. Rand had left her sleeping. He must be seeing to the needs of the children. She threw back the covers, intent on dressing and rushing downstairs. Her men, as well as the baby, must be starving.

Despite the compulsion to leap up, she lay there a moment, remembering the night spent in her husband's bed. Rand didn't hate her for what she'd kept from him. He loved her, showing her in his touch, his kisses, and the light in his eyes.

"You're a lucky, lucky woman, Callie Sinclair," she murmured.

She stared up at the cracked, leaky ceiling of the partially renovated room. Over in the corner came a strange glint. She rose and moved closer.

There, in a nook where the wall and ceiling met— revealed thanks to the renovations—was a box of some kind. After throwing her clothes on, she pulled a chair beneath the space. Climbing up, she carefully lifted the box from its hiding place.

A layer of dust and cobwebs covered the top. Wiping it clean, she stared at the initials. *NQ*. Nora Quinn. This was her mother's treasure chest. Callie's fingers trembled. She'd found it.

Giving a happy cry, she stumbled down the stairs to the kitchen, where she drew to a halt, stunned at the sight. Flour covered every inch of the counter in addition to the floor. In the midst of the floury mess everywhere was a raw egg with the broken shell and a large puddle of milk.

"Good morning, darlin'." Rand grinned, looking up from his attempt at making biscuits. Toby stood beside him, and both had flour on their faces and hair. "Before you get mad...we're making breakfast for you. Our first effort seems to have failed, but I have confidence we'll get the hang of it."

"I'm helping," Toby said happily.

"I'll clean everything, don't worry." He came closer, dropping bits of dough to the gooey mess beneath his feet. Leaning in, he kissed her. "I love you, Callie."

"I love you too, Rand. And I appreciate the thoughtful gesture, truly, but you should've woken me." Her gaze swept to the baby, where she lay in her cradle. Rand had tied a bottle to Wren's hands using a strip of flour sack and had it propped on a wadded-up shirt. It took every bit of self-control Callie had to keep from erupting into gales of laughter. Her sweet, darling, blue-eyed husband.

"What is that you're holding?" Rand tried to wipe

away the flour he left on her face, but Callie could feel he'd only smeared it all over her.

She glanced down, remembering her find. "It's my mother's treasure box I told you about last night. I found it tucked into a corner of your bedroom ceiling."

"You don't say. Wonder what's in it?"

"Haven't a clue. Let me assist with this breakfast, then we'll see if we can find the key." She gently shooed him outside to wash off, cleaned Toby as best she could, and set to work.

An hour and a half later, she took the treasure box from a shelf where it had silently beckoned and set it on the table in front of Rand. He took out his ring of keys, selected the scrolled one he'd found on the property, and slid the teeth into the lock. The lid came open.

"There you go, darlin'." He pushed the chest to her. "See what your mama left inside."

Callie lifted out an old Bible and peered underneath. There didn't appear to be anything else inside. She opened the Bible and found a tintype of a beautiful woman with white hair. She had a ring on her finger and wore an ornate brooch on her dress. A piece of paper under the likeness simply stated, "Your legacy."

"Who is that?" Rand asked.

"I think it's my grandmother. I saw one picture of her a long time ago. She died before I was born."

"Anything else in the box?"

She felt around and discovered the bottom was loose. "I think this has another layer."

Taking the chest, he lifted out a piece of thin board. Nestled on a cushion of black velvet lay an emerald ring and an emerald-and-ruby brooch.

Callie's breath caught. "These must be worth a small fortune."

"They're certainly stunning," Rand admitted. "But what do they signify?"

"Rand, these must've belonged to my grandmother and probably her mother before that. They're the same as the ones in the image."

"Could be, darlin'."

Lifting out the jewels, Callie discovered several sheets of yellowed paper. Unfolding them, she saw it was a property deed. "Rand, where do you suppose this land is located?"

He took the deed from her and studied it. "It's the section right next door. Seems you own it, my dear."

"If that's true and this is legal and binding, I'm giving the deed to you." Callie touched his face and stared into the eyes that could make her knees as weak as milk toast.

"Darlin', that's sweet, but this belongs to you. I can't take it."

"Don't you want it? You can triple the size of your land."

"I'll tell you what. In this marriage, there is no yours and mine. This land will belong to both of us equally until it passes to our children."

"I like that."

"But the ring and brooch belong only to you."

When she opened her mouth to argue, he added, "Put it away for the children if you want. Or your daughter, when I find her."

She tipped her head back for his kiss, wondering what she had done to deserve a man like Rand. Whatever it was, she meant to keep on doing it.

Toby appeared in the doorway and sighed loudly. "Do you always have to kiss?"

Callie stared at the boy who tried so hard to be a man. He was holding Wren by an arm and part of her dress. The child was kicking her legs like a runaway chicken and wearing a slobbery smile.

"Toby, one of these days you're going to like kissing girls very much." Rand slipped a hand around Callie's waist and murmured so that only she could hear. "I hope you intend to sleep with me for always, because I have lots more ideas for staying awake. Besides, I really shouldn't be left alone with this head injury. You never know what'll happen."

The mention of sleeping with him permanently made her heart pound with excitement. It was exactly what she wanted, but she hadn't known how to broach the subject. "I can do that. I wouldn't want you to fall into a coma."

"Then you'll move into my bedroom?"

Callie laid a hand on his broad chest. "I've wanted to for a long time, but I didn't know how to tell you."

"Don't wait next time. You can tell me anything. All right?" Rand lowered his head and placed his lips on hers for a kiss that curled her toes.

"I love you, Rand." She leaned back and gazed into his beautiful eyes, truly grateful that their paths had crossed. She couldn't imagine being anywhere else. She'd never known such contentment. Though their marriage seemed just about perfect, Callie had learned the hard way not to get too comfortable.

Things were going too well. Her luck couldn't last.

Twenty-six

THE NEXT MORNING, AFTER ANOTHER UNFORGETTABLE night spent in Callie's arms, Rand rose and started out to do his chores. Making love to his wife consumed his every thought, every second, and every fiber of his being. She was more addictive than the opium he'd seen others use. He couldn't get enough of the feel of Callie in his arms, with her shapely legs entangled in his. Though they'd only just risen, hunger for more ravaged his body.

He gave a sigh. It was a long time until dark. He forced his mind to the business he meant to do in town. He needed to check on the adoption, make sure his mother was all right, and see about the validity of the deed they'd found. Then he'd come around by Brett's place and find out if Tom Mason had found him.

When he opened the door and stood on the top step, his blood froze.

Lying at his feet was a playing card—the king of diamonds.

Like the one Cooper had found on the day of Rand's and Callie's wedding, the eyes were burned out.

Nate Fleming was back.

Rand rested his hand on the handle of his Colt and scanned the property and tree line for movement. Though he didn't see anything, the hair that stood on the back of his neck warned him that Fleming was watching.

Toby started out the door only to have Rand stop him. "Get inside and stay away from the windows. Tell your mama trouble's come to call."

Though the boy's face turned sickly white, he nodded and stepped back, shutting the door.

Slowly, Rand moved toward the barn, every muscle on high alert. He had a feeling that this time they wouldn't be dealing only with Nate Fleming. The outlaw had likely brought reinforcements.

This would be a fight to the finish. Rand clenched his fists. He was ready to be done with the murdering scum.

A few yards from the kitchen lay a slaughtered wild animal. The killing had been so vicious he couldn't tell what kind of critter it was. Its eyes were burned out, head almost totally removed, and the body halfway skinned.

The warning wasn't lost on Rand.

His flesh crawled. The man they were dealing with would kill without a second thought. He already had. Fleming would have no qualms about snuffing out any life, especially of those who crossed his path. He'd kill all except Toby.

Briefly, Rand thought of riding to get his brothers. But he wouldn't leave Callie and the children, and it was too dangerous to remove them from the security of the house. They would simply be asking for disaster to strike.

He forced himself to keep walking. He had to check on the livestock. If Fleming killed the horses, they'd be stranded here at his mercy.

The barn was quiet and dark when he swung open the door and stepped inside. Though sunlight streamed in from the entrance, Rand took down a lantern from a nail and lit it. Then he searched every corner of the structure, finally satisfied no one hid in the deep shadows.

Blue nickered from his stall, as did the horse named Crow Bait next to him. The cow was alive and well also. That was a relief. He'd expected to find the animals dead. He turned to go when he heard a sound and found a dark figure filling the doorway.

"Keep your hands where I can see them," Nate Fleming ordered. "You got something that belongs to me."

"That's a matter of opinion. Get off my land." Rand itched to draw his weapon but knew Fleming would gun him down before he cleared leather. He narrowed his eyes, watching, waiting.

"In my own good time." The outlaw jerked Rand's Colt from the holster and flung it.

"There's nothing for you here, Fleming."

The glittering eyes hardened. Nate lifted his pistol and pressed the black barrel into Rand's cheek. "Here's the thing. I'm willing to be reasonable. Give me my son and the worthless woman, and I'll let you live."

"Afraid I can't do that. The woman is my wife, and Toby is my son now. He doesn't want any part of you.

You see, I know how to treat a boy. Fear and abuse have no place in my house."

"You've turned him against me. If not for your lies, Toby would run to me."

"You're crazy. You've lost, Fleming. Now get off my damn land."

"I got ways to make you reconsider."

White hot anger swept through Rand. "I'll never turn Callie and Toby over to you."

"Are you sure you have the heart for this battle?"

"I have plenty of heart. Soul too, and my spirit is steadfast. It's your thinking that's flawed."

"How's that, sodbuster? You call yourself a rancher, but you don't have anything but one measly milk cow."

Rand ignored the attempt to goad him. "You've never gone up against a man like me, Fleming. I'm one who won't lose, one who will fight to hell and beyond to protect the people he loves. One who intends to put you where you'll never hurt anyone again."

Just then, a skirted figure came up behind the outlaw. Cold sweat broke out on Rand's forehead. Why hadn't Callie stayed in the house?

"You should listen to my husband, Nate," Callie said, jerking the lever of the Winchester down and up like an expert.

Fleming's eyes widened a little as he angled to face her. His finger tightened on the trigger.

"We're not afraid of you," Callie said, "so toss your six-shooter to the side."

Rand stood transfixed, praying that Fleming wouldn't knock the rifle from her hands.

Sweat trickled into Nate's eye. He blinked, trying

to clear his vision. "If you want it, girl, you're gonna have to come get it. I know you don't have the stomach to shoot."

She reached behind her and pulled the door shut to keep any of Nate's allies from being able to get the jump on her. "That's where you're wrong. I have a lot to avenge. Though I can't prove it, I know with all my heart you killed my sister."

With Fleming's attention occupied, Rand waited for an opening. If only he could grab the outlaw's gun. At least he'd removed his weapon from Rand's face. Angling his body in order to keep an eye on them both, Fleming kept his pistol leveled on Rand. "I have your daughter, worthless woman. You'll never see her if you shoot me," Nate spat with an ugly sneer.

Rand watched Callie's knees give way as pain crossed her face. "Don't listen, darlin'. He'll say anything to get you rattled."

His voice seemed to bolster her. The Winchester wavered a little before she regained her grip. "You're lying. I don't believe you."

"She's a cute little girl. Looks just like you. Gonna be real pretty like her mama. She's seven years old now. Sweet little Mariah. We've gotten real acquainted—'course, we're just gettin' started. Claire used to tell me the sad story. The way she caterwauled, you'd think the whelp belonged to her. Didn't take any doin' to find Mariah. Once I stuck my gun in that weasel Edmund Powers's face, he was real quick to spill his guts. So was his son, David, right after he wet his pants. After I killed them both, I sent my brother Virgil to fetch her from the old lady.

She's outside now." Fleming's eyes glittered with a strange excitement.

Callie's whimper sent chills up Rand's spine. He knew that Nate had too many facts for it to be a bluff. "You lay a finger on her child, and I'll make you wish you were never born," Rand threatened softly. "Shoot him, Callie. Don't worry about me. Make it count."

"You oughta know that my brothers are nearby watching. Never fear, Callie. I'll break Mariah in real slow," Nate snarled.

Rage darkened Callie's eyes. Rand could see that she was beyond reasoning. Without another word, she squeezed the trigger. The bullet caught Nate's arm as he swiveled. The blast sent the outlaw's gun flying.

Rand lunged, grabbing Nate around the neck. The two went down, rolling over and over until they ended up against the grain bin. Rand absorbed vicious blows to the face. Even though he tasted blood in his mouth, he slammed his fists into Nate Fleming's jaw.

A normal man would've stayed down, but not one eaten up with hate and the need to kill. Fleming scrambled to his feet with fists raised. Rand lowered his shoulder and drove into the man's stomach, propelling him backward.

Grappling with the wily adversary, Rand kept swinging. When he knocked Fleming to the ground, Rand sprang toward his Colt, which lay three feet away, straining to reach it. Grabbing his legs, Fleming yanked him back.

Rand swiveled, gouging his eyes. Delivering a harsh uppercut, he threw the man face down onto the dirt floor.

Just as he crawled onto Nate's back and yanked his opponent's arms behind him, Nate yelled, "They've got me! You know what to do."

Shots instantly rang out from beyond the barn, peppering into the new wood.

"Release my brother if you know what's good for you," a voice yelled. "The girl dies if you don't."

"Ow, let me go! You're hurting me," cried a young girl.

Rand froze. It had to be Callie's daughter. Slowly, he released the outlaw and stood. He had no choice. Nate held all the cards.

For the moment.

That didn't mean Rand was giving up. His mind was working. He'd made a solemn promise, and nothing short of death would allow him to break it.

Twenty-seven

THE SOUND OF RAND'S AND NATE'S HEAVY BREATHING echoed inside the barn on the Last Hope Ranch. Callie struggled to take in air herself. How could things go so wrong?

Her precious daughter, whom she'd never thought to see again, was here outside, but in the clutches of evil men to whom human life held little value.

And Callie could do nothing.

Nate sprawled on the dirt floor, exhausted and bleeding from where she'd shot him.

Like someone moving through a thick fog, Rand stumbled to Callie and held her. Though she was grateful for his strong arms around her, ice seemed to float in her veins. She doubted she'd ever be warm again.

Every muscle, every instinct, told her to run to Mariah and save her. A mother should shield her child, not huddle frightened in a barn. Yet she realized that Nate's brothers would send a bullet into her heart the minute she stepped out. That wouldn't help her baby girl.

Or the two precious children in the house. They

were alone and she couldn't get to them. Toby must be so frightened.

"What are we going to do, Rand?" she whispered, eyeing Nate Fleming. "We have to protect the children."

She couldn't do anything about Mariah's situation right now, but she could save Toby and Wren.

"I'll get you to them."

"How?"

"I've got a plan. But first I'm tying Fleming. See if you can find something to stick into his mouth."

Heartened, Callie looked around while Rand got a length of rope and tied the outlaw's hands. She came back a few minutes later with a piece of the cloth Rand had cleaned his gun with.

Seeing what was about to happen, Nate began hollering, trying to escape. Rand held him down while Callie stuffed the oily fabric into his mouth.

"What's goin' on in there?" Nate's brother hollered. "Send Nate out before I lose patience and hurt this little girl."

Callie covered her mouth to smother the cry that rose.

"Hold on to your bloomers," Rand replied. "Make no mistake, you hurt that girl and I'll put a bullet into Fleming's brain before you can swallow spit. I'll uphold my end of the bargain, long as you do the same."

"We can't just let him go," Callie said, grabbing his arm. "He's our only leverage."

"Sweetheart, if I don't get you to the house and protect the children, they'll go in and take them." He smoothed her hair and kissed her forehead. "This plan will buy us a little time to think of how best to rescue Mariah. I'll not leave your daughter at their mercy. I made a promise to you, and I'll give my life to keep it."

Not sure what Rand had gotten in his head to do, Callie watched him lead the two horses from their stalls—the roan he called Blue and a dun by the name of Crow Bait. He slung Nate onto the dun and cut the rope binding his hands together. Taking a long piece of lariat, he pulled Nate's arms down on either side of the horse's neck and bound them as tightly as he could underneath the animal's powerful neck. In this position, Nate was lying forward on the dun with his face in the mane.

The outlaw squealed and grunted, trying to kick them.

"Oh, you don't like that, do you?" Rand said. "It's not that much fun when you're on the receiving end. I'll bet some of your victims would like to see you now."

Using more rope, Rand went over Nate's back and down around Crow Bait's belly several times. With Callie helping, it didn't take long. She couldn't wait to see what Rand was going to do with Blue.

"Callie, when I give the signal, I want you to run for the house as hard as you can. No matter what, don't look back. With any luck, they'll chase after Fleming and not you. When you get inside, bolt the door."

She nodded, laying a hand on his broad chest. His blue eyes staring into hers were determined. "Please be safe, Rand. Don't make me a widow."

"Don't worry." He gave a flicker of a grin. "If this works, I'll be sitting in the kitchen asking where the corn bread is before you even miss me."

Swallowing the lump sitting in her throat, she tilted her face for his kiss. His arms came around her as his mouth covered hers hungrily. There was no gentleness. It was demanding and raw like the one a man who had little hope of seeing the next sunset might give.

Unshed tears filled Callie's eyes. She felt so lost when Rand's arms dropped from around her.

"Remember. When you see us ride out those doors, you run. Don't look back. Keep your head down and race the wind." He put the Winchester in her hands.

"I will. Godspeed."

Rand grabbed handfuls of the roan's mane and leaped onto the bare back. He hadn't wasted precious time saddling the horse, but she wished he had. If Nate's brothers didn't get him, he could fall off and get trampled under the hooves.

Callie lifted her skirt with one hand, got a good grip on the rifle with the other, and readied.

When he gave several mighty yells and slapped Blue's flank with his hat, the two men exploded from the barn. As they cleared the entrance, Rand slid to the side of the roan, hanging only by the mane.

With a sharp cry, Callie's heart sprang to her throat. Though she knew him to be an excellent horseman and noted how clever he was to attempt to use Blue as a shield, terror gripped her.

She couldn't lose Rand. Nor could she lose Mariah again. Not when she'd just found her.

What had happened to the child? What were Nate's brothers doing to her?

It served no purpose to speculate. Shoving those thoughts to the back of her mind, she began to sprint between the barn and house, a distance of fifty yards. A sudden burst of gunfire erupted, kicking up the dirt around her feet.

Angry shouts echoed through the trees, sending shivers up Callie's spine.

One man screamed, "Don't hit Nate."

Pounding hooves beat the hard earth.

More gunfire.

A powerful urge to look back, to see where Rand was, swept over her. Ignoring it, she kept her eyes focused on the kitchen door.

Keep your head down and run, Rand had said.

About halfway, her breath came in gasping, shuddering gulps and her skirt tangled around her legs. She jerked the fabric clear and reached deep inside for the strength she needed.

Twenty-five yards to go.

She thought she heard a child's plaintive cry and stumbled, almost going down.

Quickly regaining her balance, she found her stride.

Then silence settled over the land. Only the sound of her heartbeat filled her ears.

Had they killed Rand?

If she turned around, would she find him lying in a pool of blood? And what about Mariah?

Please, dear God, don't let them be dead.

At last she reached the kitchen door, only to find that the knob refused to turn.

A jolt of memory, of telling Toby to lock it after she left, filled her head. "Toby, unlock the door. Let me in," she called. "*Hurry.*"

Callie huddled low, waiting, and took a moment to

glance behind her. No bodies were lying in pools of blood. There was no sign of Rand. Or her daughter. Or Nate.

When Toby finally unlatched and pulled the door open, Callie rushed over the threshold and slammed it shut behind her.

"I thought you was dead. Where's Papa?" Toby's voice quivered.

"I don't know, honey." She leaned down and drew him into her arms. His little body trembled against her. "I'm sure he's going to be fine. He's smart and knows how to take care of himself. I'm all right too. What we have to do now is make sure everything is locked. Can you help me bring down some furniture from upstairs so we can add an extra layer of security in front of the doors?"

Toby nodded. "My sister cried after you left, but I told her everything was gonna be okay. I told her she still had me an' I wasn't gonna let anyone get her."

"I'm sure she was real glad to hear that."

"Yep. She sucked her thumb and went to sleep."

Callie kissed his forehead. "I'm so very proud of you."

"Was my old papa out there?"

"Yes, honey."

Tears bubbled up in his eyes. "Please don't let him find me. Don't let him have me, even if tries to shoot us."

"Honey, I'm not ever going to turn you over to him. You belong to me and Rand. We're family. We'll fight with everything we have to keep him away from you." She tenderly wiped his eyes and kissed his cheek. "Let's get busy, and then I'm going to feed you. I'm sure you're hungry."

Toby nodded and attempted a feeble smile, though his bottom lip quivered. He was trying so hard to be brave. "My sister is too."

"Then we'll simply have to feed her."

Working as fast as possible, she pulled the table in front of the kitchen door and managed to get the tall chest in her and Rand's bedroom downstairs. Toby brought some smaller things and helped her drag the cowhide settee in front of the door that faced the road.

Callie blew away a strand of hair from her eyes and glanced around. Not the best, but it would have to do. She hurried to the kitchen to make Wren a bottle before she realized they'd never got to milk the cow that morning.

What was she going to feed the baby? She glanced out the window toward the barn but decided it was too risky. Then she remembered the cans of evaporated milk she'd bought at the mercantile. That would have to work, although the baby might balk at first.

She quickly punched a hole in the top of one of the cans and poured the milk into a bottle, adding some water and a little syrup to it. Wren began sucking immediately when Callie put the nipple into her mouth. When the taste hit her tongue though, her eyes grew wide and she tried to push it away.

"Here, sweet girl. This is all you have today. Please take it for your mama."

The baby seemed to understand the plea because she slowly started drinking, much to Callie's relief.

Once she'd fed Wren, she got out the fixings for

breakfast, though it neared midday. Every few minutes she glanced out the window in hopes of seeing Rand and the blue roan.

Those hopes were dashed. There was no sign of him.

Where was Mariah? Did Rand get her away from Nate and his brothers?

Please, God, make it so. Despite her prayers, she saw no movement of any kind. Not an animal, a branch on the live oak tree, or a bird stirred.

Her queasy stomach roiled. She wouldn't be able to force a bite of food down her throat.

Minutes later, she watched Toby eat in the deafening silence that played havoc on her nerves.

If only Wren would cry or something would make noise.

A sudden pounding on the door made her heart stampede like a herd of spooked cattle. She scrambled for the rifle.

Twenty-eight

"CALLIE, OPEN UP."

The sound of Rand's voice filled her with relief. She laid down the Winchester and pushed the table away from the door. With trembling hands, Callie let him in. The minute he stepped inside, she threw her arms around his neck.

"You made it. You're alive."

"Indeed I am, and you're a sight to behold." His lips brushed her cheek before they found her mouth.

"Papa, I missed you," Toby cried, burrowing between them.

Rand lifted him up. "I missed you too, son."

"I thought my old papa done killed you." Toby patted Rand's cheeks as though to assure himself that his new papa was alive.

"He's not going to kill me. I'm not going to let him. I have to make sure you and Wren grow up healthy and happy, because that's what papas do." Rand hugged him tightly, then put him down. Going to the cradle, he picked up Wren and held the child in his arms as gently as he would a priceless piece of china.

Callie's throat tightened. He adored his children and they him. If fate would be so benevolent as to deliver Mariah to her, she knew Rand would accept her daughter just as readily.

Letting her joy swallow her fears, she hurried to put coffee on. She knew the man she'd married, and he was kind and loving. "Rand, I know you're exhausted and hungry, but once you've eaten, I want to hear every detail of what happened after we parted."

Though everything in her yearned to ask about Mariah, she held her tongue. Toby didn't need to hear this. The boy was hanging on by a thread.

Troubled blue eyes met hers, and she knew Rand wouldn't have good news.

"Yes, we'll talk in a bit, darlin'." He pulled out a chair and sat down. "Right now I need to rest a bit and eat."

Her gaze warmed as she watched him. He stood Wren up on her wobbly little legs in his lap, and the three-month-old was trying her best to stick her chubby fingers into Rand's mouth. Toby crowded close, vying for his share of attention, all the while telling his new papa how he guarded the baby.

Earlier, Callie had seen the terror in Toby's eyes when she made it safely inside the house. It was no stretch to know that he'd thought he'd lost the people he loved most. He knew his father and realized better than anyone what Nate was capable of. Toby had witnessed the killings that Nate had never tried to hide and still lived with the horror.

A mist covered her vision. She stored up the sight of her family. Something told her she'd need it later to sustain her.

After Rand ate and gave his children his undivided attention until the baby fell asleep and Toby wandered off to his room to play, he took Callie's hand and led her upstairs to their sanctuary, their respite from the world.

Though it was only midday, they needed this privacy to talk. Rand closed the bedroom door and pulled her against his chest. Burying his face in her hair, he breathed her sweet fragrance. They stood locked in each other's embrace with only the ticking of the clock to remind him that time marched on.

Several long minutes passed before he moved. He simply wanted to hold her, to feel her heart beating wildly against his chest. Finally, he kissed her upturned face. When her lips parted slightly, he slipped his tongue inside.

She was truly his life, and he didn't know how he'd ever breathe again if he lost her.

"I couldn't wait to touch you," he murmured into her ear.

"Promise you'll always hold me," she whispered. "Even if you get angry and don't want to talk, hold me."

"Darlin', I find the idea of ever being mad at you utterly ridiculous. Nope, ain't gonna happen." He tucked a strand of hair behind her ear. "Not in this lifetime."

"Never say never." She stepped out of the circle of his arms. "Tell me what happened. Where is my daughter? Did you see her?"

Rand pulled her toward the bed and sat down beside her, taking her hand. "All hell broke loose when Nate and I rode from the barn. I slapped Crow Bait on the rump and the horse took off at a gallop. I rode for the cover of the trees. When Nate's brothers hightailed after him, I followed. They untied Nate in the nearest clearing, then continued on to Limestone Bluff, about two miles from here. The outlaws squeezed through a narrow opening between some rocks, and I couldn't follow without being noticed. Have a feeling that's where they're holed up."

Rand knew what she really wanted to know most of all. He'd have given anything on earth to put a smile on her face and regretted he couldn't do that yet. "I saw Mariah. Darlin', she looks just like you. Such a pretty little girl. I never had an opening to grab her without putting the child in grave danger."

Callie gave a strangled sob. "But they're not hurting her?"

"No. I don't think they've had her long. I was able to get pretty close to her once, and she appeared unhurt—just shivering from the cold."

He didn't share his fear that the child who carried Callie's blood in her veins would surely suffer the outlaws' wrath. No mother should have to hear that.

Callie sucked in a quick breath. "She's not wearing a coat?"

How like her to fret about Mariah being warm enough. "No, she wasn't. I'll go back after I'm sure you and the children are safe. I won't leave you unprotected. Though it's Sunday, Cooper probably rode into town to check on things this morning. We'll watch for him passing back by." He laid his hand along her jaw and leaned closer, focusing on the rosy lips that drew him like iron to a magnet.

Pounding on the bedroom door jarred them apart. "Papa, your horse is here. Crow Bait has come back."

Rand jumped to his feet and jerked the door open. "Thanks, Toby."

The boy's face had drained of color. He stood silently aside and allowed Rand to race downstairs ahead of him.

Sure enough, Crow Bait stood quivering by the barn. Lather covered the gelding's back. Rand drew his Colt, opened the kitchen door, and cautiously stepped out. He froze when he heard the whisper of Callie's skirts behind him.

"Go back inside, Callie," he said without turning around. "It could be a trap."

"All right, but if I hear shooting, I'm coming to help."

Satisfied at last that she, Toby, and the baby were out of harm's way, Rand proceeded toward the horse, ready to fire at the first sign of movement.

He zeroed in on the strip of brown fabric tied to Crow Bait's mane. No one had to tell him what the dark stains were. Blood spread over his fingers when he released it from the horsehair. Inside the rolled up fabric was a scrap of paper.

My son for the girl. Or she'll bleed more.

A muscle in Rand's jaw worked. How in God's name was he supposed to show this to Callie? Her worst nightmare had come true. They'd hurt her daughter.

With clenched fists, he stared toward the bluff

where Fleming and his brothers had disappeared and
yelled, "You better hide, you murdering piece of
scum. I'm coming for you."

Cruel laughter echoed from the trees.

Twenty-nine

LEANING AGAINST THE WINDOW, CALLIE CLAPPED HER hands over her ears to block out the evil laugh that sent chills through her bones.

Curled up in a tight ball over in a corner, Toby shook uncontrollably. He'd recognized the voice as well. "Honey, I know how frightened you are, and I wish I could hold you, but Papa Rand is out there unprotected and he needs me. He needs us. Try to be strong for me and for your papa. Can you go check on your baby sister for me?"

With no time to see if her words had made a difference, she snatched up the rifle. Opening the door a crack, she stuck the weapon out.

Just then, gunshots rang out.

Horror-stricken, she watched Rand climb onto Crow Bait's bare back and race toward her. Thank goodness he'd already shoved the table out of the way when he went out.

She readied to do whatever she needed to, praying the bullets would miss her husband, the love of her life. As he pulled to a stop by the steps and leaped

off the animal, she threw the door open wide and he
tumbled inside. Slamming it shut, she helped Rand
shove the table back into place.

"Are you all right, Rand? Did they hit you?" Her
eyes swept the length of him and settled on the bright
spot staining his shoulder. "You're bleeding!"

"Just a scratch. I'll live." Rand sat down on the
floor, breathing hard, his eyes fixed on their son. "Go
see to Toby."

Callie nodded and moved over to comfort the boy.

The second she knelt down beside the child, he
flung himself into her arms. "He's gonna kill us, ain't
he, Mama?"

"No, sweet boy. He might try, but he's not going
to succeed. Not ever." Callie smoothed Toby's black
hair, which was so much like his rotten father's, and
murmured soothing words.

Long minutes passed before his shaking stopped and
she could free herself from his grasp. "I've got to help
your papa, now," she said softly. "We won't leave you."

Though fear still glittered in Toby's eyes, he
nodded. Keeping low, she crawled over to where
Rand slumped.

Feeling Rand's back, she found the entrance
wound. Checking the hole in the front, she breathed
a sigh of relief. The bullet had gone through. She
carefully removed Rand's shirt, and when she did, the
scrap of brown fabric she'd seen him untying from
Crow Bait's mane fell out.

A piece of paper fluttered to the floor. When she
saw the words, fear squeezed her heart as though it
were caught in a vise.

My son for the girl. Or she'll bleed more.

She clutched the scrap of bloodstained cloth. Dear God, what had Nate done?

Seven years ago, she hadn't fought hard enough for her daughter. She raised her chin. Whatever befell her now, whatever she had to face, she was not going to abandon Mariah again. She had to find a way to save the child she loved more than her own life.

"Callie, I'm sorry." Rand's raspy words seemed to have gotten bruised when they squeezed through his throat. He covered her bloodstained hand with his. "We're going to get her. Hold fast to that."

"I'm trying," she whispered brokenly.

"Fleming won't kill her. That's his hold over us. He's a lot of things, but he's not stupid. We have something he wants, and the only way to get Toby is to keep Mariah alive."

She gave a quick nod, cleared her head, and rummaged around for the things she needed to tend to Rand's injury. When she raised her head a little too high, giving the shooter outside a target, a bullet shattered the kitchen window.

She'd managed to get the bucket of water and some clean rags, though. While she washed the wound, Toby scooted across the floor and laid his head on Rand's leg, just wanting to be near. Callie ached for the little boy and the innocence that Nate had stolen.

"I'm sorry you got hurt, Papa."

Rand laid one of his big hands on the boy's head. "Don't you worry. It's going to be all right."

Toby sniffled. "Yeah, but when? Why won't he leave us alone?"

"I wish I knew, son. Guess he can't give up."

"Who is Mariah?"

Callie's fingers stilled. Toby had overheard them. Now he'd feel responsible for something else he had no control over. She laid her hand on his head. "Mariah is an innocent, sweet little girl about your age, but you don't need to worry about her. That's our job."

With eyes wide in his pale face, Toby sat up. "My father's got her?"

"Yes," Rand answered, shrugging back into his shirt. "But not for long."

"We gotta go get her. Right now. Before…" Toby jumped to his feet, scrambling for the door.

Rand grabbed his arm before he got out of reach. "You're not going anywhere, son. I'll take care of it."

Tears ran down the boy's face as he tried to yank free. "Let me go. I hafta—"

"You'll stay here where it's safe," Rand said gently, holding Toby close. "I'll handle it, son."

Toby's torment splintered Callie's heart. "Toby, if we let you go out there, then he'd have both of you. It's not a solution, sweetheart."

"He wants me, an' once he has me, he'll let her go," Toby reasoned. "I can save her. I know how he is an' how to stay out of his way."

Though Toby spoke the truth, Callie knew he'd never seen this amount of rage and hate in Nate before. She doubted anyone had.

That her son was willing to put himself in such

danger for a girl he didn't know spoke of the immense depth of his heart. He was going to make quite a man. Unshed tears burned Callie's eyes. How could she make him understand that sacrificing himself would not free Mariah? Nate would destroy both children without a sliver of remorse.

"No, son, you can't fix this." Rand looked as miserable as Callie felt. "I know you think you're to blame for this situation, but you aren't. You can't make your father do what you want. Even if you could, I'm not going to let you."

The life drained from Toby and he went limp. "He'll kill 'er, then. I saw it before."

Chills raced through Callie. His solemn, simple statement held too much truth. Her reply was fierce. "No, he won't. We're going to fight with everything we have for Mariah. Besides, we have a few secret weapons."

A glimmer of hope replaced the dull despair in Toby's eyes. "We do?"

"Uncle Brett and Uncle Cooper and all their friends will come help," Callie said with much more confidence than she felt.

The boy's deep sigh filled the quiet. "I sure wish they'd hurry."

That made three of them. After cleaning and binding Rand's wound, Callie moved everything aside to put away later.

Rand drew his shirt back on. "I think the front of the house would be safer, and we can watch the road for Cooper. He should be passing by soon."

Careful of the window, Callie helped him stand.

They got the baby, and all four of them moved into the parlor.

With the ticking clock on the mantel loud in the room, she sat by the window with the Winchester propped on her lap. Rand occupied a chair nearby at the other window with another rifle and his Colt. Toby played quietly with Wren. When they spoke, they kept their voices low, as though Nate and his brothers might hear and charge into the house with guns blazing.

Two o'clock in the afternoon came and went.

No sign of anyone on the road.

No shooting outside.

No one dared to move. It was as if they hung suspended over a wide chasm and any sound or movement might send them plummeting over the edge.

Though Toby didn't complain, she knew the toll this took on him. Feeling responsible somehow for what his father did, he carried a huge weight on his young shoulders. What was worse, she didn't know anything she could say that would lift his burden.

Three o'clock.

After Callie changed the baby, she and Rand went to the kitchen. While he kept watch, she made another bottle using the canned milk. The remaining can on the shelf sent ripples of concern through Callie. What would the child do when they ran out? How would they stifle Wren's hungry cries? Callie said a quick prayer for help.

Once she had the bottle in hand, she and Rand returned to the parlor, where she fed the babe and put her down for a nap.

"Is anyone hungry? Rand, I could fix you something."

His blue eyes met hers. "Not hungry, darlin', but Toby probably is."

Toby looked up from the floor where he was staring at some carved wooden soldiers and his spinning top. He shook his head. "Do I hafta?"

"No," Callie assured him. "Just let me know when you want something."

Three thirty.

"I need to check your bandage. See if you're bleeding, Rand." Callie moved to the chair where he sat. Some blood had seeped through the wrappings. She gathered more clean cloths and rebound the wound.

Four o'clock and still no sign of anyone on the road. Callie's nerves couldn't take much more of this endless wait.

The sun would go down soon. When it did, Nate and his brothers would likely mount an assault. Would they be able to hold them off by themselves?

At five o'clock, with no glimpse of Cooper, Rand stood, strode for his coat, and put it on.

"Where are you going?" Callie's heart pounded with fear.

"Outside to take a look around."

"Rand, it's too dangerous. You're hurt and it's getting dark. You won't even be able to see what's lurking in the deep shadows."

He crossed to where she sat, pulled her to her feet, and tenderly kissed her. "Cooper isn't coming, darlin'. No one's coming, and I can't huddle inside this house like a jittery jackrabbit scared of my own shadow. It could be they've left. Wren needs milk. We're almost out of the canned stuff, and I need to get Crow Bait into the barn."

"I wish you weren't right, and I wish you weren't so god-awful stubborn."

"You're a fine one to talk, Mrs. Sinclair." He dropped another kiss on her lips. "I'll be careful. You take care of the children. If anyone gets inside the house—"

"I'll shoot and ask questions later," she finished.

"That's my girl." He moved the table back far enough to get to the door.

With fear squeezing her chest, Callie watched him slip into the gathering darkness, then hurried to slide the bolt back in place. She took the fact that no gunfire erupted as a very good sign. Maybe Rand was right. Maybe Nate and his brothers had left.

Or were they only preoccupied?

Her thoughts shifted to Mariah as they had so often during the day. Were they feeding her? Was she warm? Were they taking pleasure in hurting her?

Nate Fleming had no soul—he'd proven it again and again. The bloody piece of brown fabric swam across her vision, twisting her stomach into a knot.

Callie knew what she had to do. It was the only choice they'd given her, even if it cost her life.

Thirty

THE EERIE QUIET RAISED THE HAIR ON RAND'S NECK. Where had Fleming and his brothers gone?

The Colt was in Rand's hand the minute he left the kitchen. He took a zigzag path to the barn. He darted to the large live oak tree, then to the woodpile. From there, he moved to the tepee that Toby hadn't gotten to play in of late.

A quick glance inside told him no one hid in there.

Crow Bait raised his head from the winter grass he was grazing on next to the barn. Rand sprinted toward the building, collecting the animal as he went. When Rand opened the barn door, the horse trotted inside and went directly to his stall. Rand carefully drew the door closed and groped about in the inky darkness.

Though light made things more dangerous, Rand couldn't do what he must in the pitch black. He lit the lantern, keeping it away from the door and praying that it wouldn't attract trouble.

With his gun within easy reach, Rand fed the horses while listening for any sound outside. He worked quickly and as silently as he was able. He didn't aim to leave Callie and the children unprotected any longer than necessary.

The cow mooed low, giving thanks, Rand supposed, for easing her swollen udders. At last, the pail brimmed with fresh milk.

He blew out the lantern and rubbed his hands together to warm them, preparing to return to the house. With a firm grip on the pail, he slipped out the barn door into the shadows. Pressing against the side, he stilled, scanning the tree line for movement.

Other than a bird taking flight, nothing moved.

The bent, naked limbs of a nearby elm tree stuck out like bony witch's fingers. And beyond that, the dark house sat as though silently weeping.

Icy foreboding clawed up his spine.

Hiding in the deep shadows, Rand ignored the jagged pain in his shoulder and drew a ragged breath into his lungs. After several minutes, he began to move, darting from shadow to shadow. He finally reached the tepee. Though some of the milk had sloshed from the pail, it still appeared three-fourths full.

A short distance to the tree and he'd be home free.

Rand took a deep breath and sprinted for the live oak tree. Midway, a shot rang out, spraying the dirt at his feet.

So, the varmints were still there.

Taking refuge behind the tree, he readied for the last leg, praying Callie would have the door unbolted.

The sudden rifle shots coming from inside the house caught him by surprise. Callie was providing cover. He slid the Colt into his holster to free his hand and took off, making himself as small a target as possible.

His boot slipped on the porch step as he reached for the knob, and milk splattered the wooden stoop. He didn't have time to bemoan the fact, praying it wasn't too much. Thankfully, the knob turned, and when the door swung open, he hurried inside.

He'd made it.

Except for a sliver of pale winter moonlight shining through the broken window at the kitchen counter, the room was dark. Rand leaned against the door frame in an effort to catch his breath. Then Callie took the pail of milk and helped him push the table back into place.

"I guess that answers our questions," Callie murmured shakily.

"Yep. They're still there." Rand put his arm around her. His wife was one brave woman. Whatever needed done—be it taking up arms, putting a wheel back on the wagon, or rocking Wren to sleep—she rolled up her sleeves and jumped in. "I'm so proud of you, Callie."

She touched his cheek. "I haven't done anything that anyone else wouldn't do, so don't be making more of it than it is."

"No, ma'am. Wouldn't hear of it."

Two more shots rang out and the window in the door shattered into a million fragments. Rand jerked Callie to the floor and shielded her with his body. Toby screamed from the front of the house. Wren lent her shrieking cries to the bedlam.

"You go to the children," Rand yelled. "I'll make sure Fleming and his brothers don't get inside."

Callie pressed the Winchester into his hands and ran to calm Toby and Wren.

Lifting a box of cartridges from a shelf, Rand laid them on the kitchen counter and took a position at the window. "It's you and me, Fleming," he muttered. "You'll have a hell of a time getting *my* son. If this is what you want, you've got it."

As though in answer to Rand's challenge, a volley of shots peppered the small kitchen. He took cover until the firing stopped.

When it did, he rose and looked out into the blackness. A tall figure crept toward the back door, perhaps emboldened by the lack of return fire.

"Your mistake, mister," Rand said through gritted teeth a second before he pulled the trigger.

The man went down. "I'm hit, Nate," he cried.

Someone ran from the side of the tepee, firing as he went, and dragged the wounded man to safety.

One down and two to go. Make that one to go, since Callie had shot Nate Fleming in the arm when they'd been inside the barn.

Rand had no doubt he could hold them off until morning. Once daylight came, help was sure to come. He flexed his shoulder to rid some of the pain gripping him and inserted another cartridge into the rifle. Best to keep it fully loaded.

Glancing out again, he saw a dark-clothed form running from tree to tree. Calmly, he took aim. The minute he caught the man without cover, he squeezed the trigger.

The bullet crossed the space between Rand and the outlaw. It must've slammed into the man's leg because he grabbed for his thigh before the darkness swallowed him up.

After a period of several hours with no more bursts of gunfire, Rand breathed a deep sigh.

He'd repelled the attack, it seemed. By now, the outlaw brothers were probably somewhere licking their wounds. A comforting thought made it easier to breathe—at least with them nursing injuries, they would leave Mariah alone.

A noise from behind alerted him to Callie. "How are the children?"

"Sleeping. How are you holding up?"

"Shoulder hurts like the dickens, but I'll be fine." He opened up an arm and she walked into his embrace, laying her head on his chest. "I haven't heard or seen anything out there for a while. I think they've retreated for now."

"Why don't you try to get a little sleep, Rand? I can stand guard for a bit. Rest your shoulder, if nothing else."

He cursed the fact that they had no light, because he'd have loved to crawl into Callie's warm amber gaze and stay awhile. "I think I might, but only if you're sure you're not afraid to keep watch. I'll go check on the children and rest a bit."

Before he headed to the parlor, Rand took one more minute to savor the feel of Callie against him. Confident that he could find her mouth even if he were blind, he had no trouble in the dim shadows.

Callie's upturned face, her mouth, drew him like a thirsty man to water.

Hunger for her consumed him as he slanted a kiss across her lips. Her soft breath mingled with his in this fleeting moment of quiet uncertainty.

Then, releasing her, he turned toward the front of the house. When he got to the doorway, he turned for one last glimpse to store up just in case they didn't make it to sunrise.

⁓

As Callie watched Rand disappear into the gloom, she covered her mouth to keep the sob from spilling forth.

The kiss had almost undone her. She wished she could've kissed him with every single bit of the love inside her, but he knew her so well and would've known she was saying good-bye.

She knew what she had to do, yet the wreckage of her broken heart lay scattered and twisted. If only there were some other way. Even as she made the wish, she knew fate had stolen the other choices, leaving only one.

An agonizing eternity passed while she waited to make sure Rand wouldn't stop her.

When all was quiet, she crept upstairs to their bedroom, freezing at each deafening creak and groan of the old house. Once she reached their sanctuary without detection, she took the treasure box from a drawer and removed the priceless jewelry, putting the pieces into her pocket along with the little derringer Rand had given her after they married.

Then, finding paper and pencil, she hurriedly wrote a note in the darkness.

With the note in hand, she retraced her steps to the bottom floor and peeked into the parlor for one last glance at Rand and the children.

Most folks would say that she'd gone around

picking up strays, but that wasn't the case. *She* was the stray. They'd opened their hearts to her and given her more than she could ever repay. Guilt at leaving this way tore at her. She prayed Rand would understand and eventually forgive her. Even so, she knew she was betraying his trust. She was walking out on him like he'd feared from the start.

"I love you, my darling," she whispered.

The pain was so great, she could scarcely breathe. She knew when she walked out the door, she'd never see them again.

Even if by chance Nate didn't end her life, her betrayal of Rand would be complete. He'd never take her back.

Dashing away the tears that streamed down her face, she moved into the kitchen, placing the note on the table in clear view. Giving one last look around, she slipped silently out the door and into the night.

Everything was quiet. Nothing moved but the slight breeze that ruffled her hair. She pulled her coat tighter and set out.

Though she had only a vague idea of where Limestone Bluff was, she didn't worry. Nate Fleming would pounce on her before she got close.

She bypassed the barn, deciding that Crow Bait had been overstressed of late. Nor did she think about taking Blue. Rand would need the gelding. Besides, she only had to go two miles. She could walk.

The sudden hoot of an owl made her jump, but she picked her way forward. In the darkness, a thorny bush reached out and grabbed her dress. She jerked free and continued.

About a mile from the house, on the banks of a small stream, she sat down to rest. The sky had lightened to an ash gray.

As they so often did, her thoughts turned to Rand. She wondered what he'd think when he woke to find her gone. Would he hate her for walking out in the night while he rested?

She recalled his plea from another time when she'd thought leaving was her only option.

Please…for God's sake, don't let me wake up one morning and find no sign of you anywhere, he'd pleaded.

She had changed her mind back then and stayed. Only this time was different. She did this not for herself, but to save Mariah. Her daughter couldn't wait for Cooper or Brett to show up. Rand would argue that it was his place to save her. Yet she didn't see it that way. He was wounded. She was healthy. Besides, her body had nurtured her daughter for nine months. She was the mother, and mothers did what they had to do to ensure their children's safety.

Especially when she'd failed so miserably before. She had to find redemption and get Mariah back.

"This is the only way," she murmured. The trickling stream seemed to agree.

Callie rose and trudged on. In the blush of dawn, she could see the craggy landscape of Limestone Bluff in the distance.

Her breath fogged in the chilly air. A voice inside her head seemed to say, *Hurry, hurry.*

A rabbit skittered suddenly from the brush, catching her attention. When she glanced up, a man blocked her path. He held a deadly pistol pointed at her heart.

"Well, lookee here," Nate said. "I 'spect that long walk done tuckered you out. Ain't that right? Been waitin'. Knew you'd come."

Thirty-one

FEAR SAT LIKE A SCALDING LUMP IN THE BACK OF Callie's throat. Now that she was face-to-face with the devil, she rummaged for the courage that seemed to have fled. After a long moment, she straightened her spine.

She would do what she came for. Somehow or another.

"Hello, Nate. It's time you and I settled a score."

"Found me all right. Reckon it's time for the little party I planned for you." Though his lazy grin could make some women's hearts all aflutter, Callie only saw the evil lurking behind the curved lips and flashing eyes.

She found satisfaction in the bloody bandana tied around his upper arm. She wished she'd shot him dead.

Nate cruelly grabbed her and yanked her face close to his. She bit her lower lip to keep from crying out. She would not give him that power over her. Power and control was what the outlaw thrived on.

"We need to talk," Callie said. "I have something you want."

"Don't think so. Don't see my son anywhere." He shoved her up the trail.

"You may change your mind after you hear me out," she threw over her shoulder.

Nate Fleming grunted and pushed her forward.

Limestone Bluff was bare of vegetation, and that gave Nate and his brothers the advantage. They could see anyone coming long before they reached the hiding place. A few hundred yards farther and they arrived at the narrow place in the rocks that Rand had described. She squeezed through and found herself beneath a large outcropping. Two men sat near a campfire, nursing wounds. Nate's brothers, she assumed.

Mariah was nowhere to be seen. Her heart thudded painfully against her chest. Was she too late?

"Virgil, look what I found," Nate said.

"Reckon you done found us some entertainment, brother," Virgil said, getting to his feet. He wore a long duster and a thin smile that was even more sinister than Nate's. A brushy, black mustache added to the coiled danger radiating from the man. "Me an' Emmett was about to get bored. We got a powerful need for female companionship."

With a quick glance, Callie sized up Emmett. If her plan didn't work, he'd be the one she'd appeal to for help. His gentle eyes held a measure of compassion.

Nate threw her to the ground. "Later. Me an' her have unsettled business, don't we, girl?"

Callie sat up, ignoring the stinging pain from the places where the rocks had scraped the hide from her legs and hands. "I came to offer you a deal. It's the only one you're going to get, so you might want to give it some thought."

She prayed they wouldn't search her and find the

derringer and jewelry. Again, she scanned the area for signs of Mariah and at last spied what appeared to be a bundle of rags lying near a limestone boulder. The rags moved and she knew she'd found her daughter.

Nate narrowed his eyes and returned his gun to his holster. "You thinkin' to trick ol' Nate? I told you I want my son. That's the only deal I'll buy into."

"Toby would rather be dead than be with you."

The outlaw jerked her up by the hair and slapped her hard, snapping her head to the side. "I'm his father an' no one else. I'm sick of that man of yours tryin' to take my place." He delivered another stinging blow. "You've turned my boy against me, an' I'll make you pay dearly."

Callie wiped the blood from her lip and glared. "Just listen to what I have to say."

"I reckon I'm a reasonable man. Wouldn't you say so, Emmett?"

"Yep, you sure are a reasonable man, Nate," Emmett replied. "Guess that's why Mama always liked you best."

Nate ran a finger slowly down the row of buttons on her dress. "I wonder just how much alike sisters are."

Desperate to bring the attention back to her reason for coming, Callie lowered her voice so only Nate could hear. "I have something that'll get your attention, but you might not want to share it with your brothers."

Nate turned and said, "You boys get some coffee made. Me an' sweet Miss Callie are gonna get reacquainted." He gripped her arm. "This had better be good, or I'll cut out your gizzard an' feed it to your daughter."

"One stipulation…Mariah has to come with us."

"Nope. She'll stay here with the boys."

Callie shrugged as though it meant nothing to her. It took everything she had to keep her face passive. Nate pushed her through the opening with such force she lost her footing and met the ground with a bone-jarring thud.

"I want to make a deal," she said, struggling to breathe. With great effort, she rose to her feet. "My daughter and Toby in exchange for something that's worth a small fortune."

"No favors for you, sister-in-law?" He lifted a tendril of hair. "Maybe I'll keep you alive longer if you prove to be good at pleasuring me."

She twisted away from him. "I've accepted my fate. I only want to buy my daughter's and Toby's freedom. Nothing more."

"Where is this fortune?"

"Somewhere close. Are you willing to bargain?"

Nate's eyes glittered and he rubbed his chin. Greed had always ruled him. "Depends. Gotta see it first."

Hope rose that her plan would still work. She turned her back to him and removed her legacy from her pocket, along with the derringer. Swinging back around, she held out the ring and brooch, holding them so that the sunlight caught the stones. As she imagined, his black eyes shimmered with lust for the priceless treasures.

The minute he snatched them from her, she leveled the little pistol on him. "Give me my daughter. Send her out or you're dead," she ordered, her voice hard.

"Don't think so. I reckon I'll keep these trinkets an' the girl. You always trusted too easily."

As cocky as ever. Not much had changed there.

"I'm the one holding this derringer."

"But I have your daughter. One word from me and she's dead," he said silkily, leaning closer to her.

Wary, Callie took a step back. She knew Nate was right, but if she could kill him before he gave that one word...

With black eyes that glistened like the eyes of a serpent, he watched her every move.

She renewed her grip around the derringer. She backed up again but was met with the rock wall. She'd gone as far as she could go.

Just as she fired, he lunged and grabbed her wrist, yanking her arm skyward. The bullet went into the brush.

A second blurred movement of his hand produced his Colt from the holster. He pressed it to her forehead. "I should put a bullet in you right now."

Despair swept over Callie. She'd played her last card and come up short. He would kill Mariah first and make her watch. He took great pleasure from watching people suffer. Nate Fleming delighted in toying with them.

Dear God, how would she bear the horror of seeing him snuff out her daughter's life?

The knot that had been in her stomach since yesterday tightened until she could barely breathe. The need to retch rose up. "But you won't shoot me." She flashed him an icy stare. "It's too quick. You enjoy killing too much. You like watching the light go out of your victims' eyes. You killed Claire very slowly."

"She deserved everything she got." Nate stuck the ring and brooch into his pocket. "Never wanted to be a wife to me, an' she turned my son into a namby-pamby. Something I aim to rectify."

"I've wondered how you made Claire so ill. Poison?"

A grin flashed. "I was pretty proud I thought of it. Stole some purple nightshade from an old Chinaman. Just gave her a little at first to make her sick, then kept adding more and more until her poor faithless heart gave out."

Callie remembered the violent retching, headaches, confusion, and inability to walk. Claire suffered an agonizing death. Hate for this man ate at her like a canker sore. Yet she held her tongue. Maybe by some miracle she could still rescue Mariah. It would do no good to rile him worse.

He motioned her back through the opening, back-handing her to hurry her along. "Get me some rope, Virgil. Gotta tie up this hellcat. She tried to shoot me."

"You're losing your touch, brother," Emmett said, throwing a piece of wood onto the fire. "Never trust a woman."

Though blood filled Callie's mouth, her attention was on the young girl who crawled toward her.

Her daughter. Her Mariah.

Tears brimmed in Callie's eyes. At last she could see the child they'd stolen from her. Silent sobs rose. Before she could touch the girl to make sure she wasn't a dream, Nate yanked her hands behind her back and tied them with a piece of rope.

"Come say hello to your mama, gal," Nate hollered, then burst into mad laughter. "Too bad she can't save your sorry hide."

Mariah must've been a very pretty little girl before

Nate got his hands on her. The brown hair curling around her face gave her the appearance of an angel. But it was the luminous dark eyes that drew Callie's attention. They seemed to peer deep inside her soul, finding the things she'd hidden.

The little girl's lips were blue from the cold. Mariah's thin dress, torn and dirty, provided no protection from the elements. Dried blood and grime covered one side of her face.

Mariah's quiet voice trembled. "Is it true? Are you my mama?"

"Yes, sweetheart."

"What took you so long? I waited and waited all these years, but you didn't come."

The words cut Callie to the quick. She struggled with the ropes binding her hands. If only she could draw Mariah to her and shelter her from all the evil in the world.

"I didn't know where you were, honey. I searched for you. I'm sorry I wasn't there to help. I can see you're cold. Do you have a coat?"

The girl whimpered and shook her head.

Guilt wracked Callie for the warm coat she wore. She strained at her ropes and got them to loosen a tiny bit. Or maybe she imagined it. Her glance found Nate holding his hands to the fire. Would he untie her so she could get her coat off? It seemed about as unlikely as becoming a bird and flying out of this desolate place.

"I'm scared," the girl whispered.

"I know, sweetheart. If you'll get in my lap, you can snuggle into my coat and find some warmth.

Can you do that?" It was all Callie could offer at the moment, and she prayed it would be enough.

A second later, her daughter pressed against her and drew the coat around her thin body. For a moment, Callie could pretend that everything was all right.

She closed her eyes, savoring her angel baby's slight weight, the feel of the small heart beating next to hers.

"I'm going to take care of you now," she promised as her heart slowly shattered.

∽

Sometime in the early dawn, Toby shook Rand. "Mama's gone. Cain't find her anyplace."

Rand jolted awake. Rubbing sleep from his eyes, he sat up. "Maybe she's upstairs."

"Nope. I looked. I think she wrote you a letter." Toby handed him a scrap of paper.

My dearest Rand,

> *Please forgive me for running out on you. I have to save my daughter or I can't live with myself. I know you'll take care of the children. Thank you for giving me so much happiness. I'll love you until my heart stops beating. Your name will be the last word on my lips.*

>   *Callie*

The note slipped from Rand's fingers, and he sagged against the back of the sofa. Shards of pain sliced through his chest, making it impossible to breathe. He wouldn't have been in as much agony if someone had reached in and ripped his beating heart out.

This was far worse because it *hadn't* killed him.

This was a living death to be endured with no relief. His worst fear was realized. Callie had left him like all the others had.

She was gone and he knew she wouldn't come back.

His tortured lungs screamed with the need for air. She hadn't trusted him to get Mariah back and save their family.

She had no faith in him.

All the love, all the times he'd poured out his heart to her, all his promises had meant nothing. She'd left like all the others. Walked out in the dead of night.

And maybe that's what hurt worse than anything— that she didn't have the courage to look him in the eye and tell him that she didn't love him enough to stay.

When Toby crowded next to him and laid his head on his chest, Rand pulled him close, burying his face in the boy's hair. How could she have left their children who loved her so? How? He'd seen her love for them, at least. She may have hidden her true feeling for him. But not for them. Wren and Toby meant everything to her.

"Don't cry, Papa. It makes me sad. When is my mama coming home?"

"I don't know, son." He hadn't the heart to tell him the truth.

"Will she go away like my real mama and never come back?"

How could he tell the boy…

I'll love you until my heart stops beating. Your name will be the last word on my lips.

No. He couldn't believe it was all a lie.

With hope in his heart, he lifted the note and read it once more. Bit by bit his brain took in the meaning of her words. He suddenly realized he was wrong. She did trust him. She'd made her choice, not because she thought him incapable, but because she felt she didn't fight hard enough for her baby seven years ago. In her mind, she had to do it now. And in addition to her daughter, she was looking for redemption for herself. His pain eased just a little as pride took over.

She'd known the likelihood that Fleming would kill her was almost guaranteed, and yet she'd faced down her fears and gone anyway.

For Mariah, the child she'd lost.

The depth of a mother's love knew no bounds.

Rand got to his feet. He had to find Callie. He truly understood the depth of her love, and she was about to understand the depth of his.

He would not let this end this way. Fleming did not get to decide who lived and who died.

It didn't take long to feed Wren and change her. While he did that, Toby threw some of her things into a bag and got himself a hunk of bread to nibble on.

Then Rand loaded them into the wagon and raced down the road to Cooper's ranch. He felt sure Delta would watch after the children until this was over.

Hell hath no fury like a man about to lose his one true love. He would find Callie and get her and Mariah back...and then he'd kill Nate Fleming.

Only one question remained: Would he let the

buzzards peck out the outlaw's eyes and feast on his dead body?

∽

The sun was just coming up on the Long Odds Ranch when Rand kissed Wren and Toby and entrusted their care to Delta. He was outside waiting beside Blue for the others to saddle up and a rider to get back with Brett when Tom Mason galloped toward him and dismounted.

"I know you and I have a bone to pick with each other," Mason said, "but I really need to find your brother. It's very important."

"Don't have time to deal with this right now. I have to save my wife from outlaws."

"I see. Looks like you can use an extra hand, then. Mind if I ride along?"

Brett galloped up just then in a cloud of dust.

Rand stared at Mason. Might be best to keep the man where they could see him. "Suit yourself, but stay out of my way."

Fifteen of Cooper's men with Rand, Cooper, and Brett leading the way rode hell-for-leather toward Limestone Bluff.

Though Rand's shoulder felt as though someone had placed a hot brand to it, he pushed the pain aside. His wound was not going to prevent him from doing what he needed to. Thoughts whirled in his head. Would he get there in time?

He wouldn't want to be Fleming if they didn't. It would end on this day on this piece of Texas land that so many valiant men had fought and died to protect.

At the Alamo during the fight against Santa Anna's

men, Colonel William Travis had drawn a line in the sand. The ones who were with him in the cause stepped across. Rand's gaze lit on the determination on each of the riders' faces and knew they all stood with him.

This was his Alamo.

Like Travis and his followers, he'd lay down his life for justice.

He didn't intend to lose. Not to this murdering desperado.

The rocky cliffs of Limestone Bluff loomed in the early-morning light. A short while later, they reined up and dismounted in the shadows of the butte that he'd watched Fleming and his brothers disappear into the previous day. Rand slid his Colt from the holster. All was quiet. Maybe they'd caught Fleming off guard.

The expected gunshots never rent the air. As shot up as the men were, maybe they still slept, he reasoned. Maybe one or two had died. He had no way of knowing. It took all his self-control to keep from rushing ahead.

At last they reached the narrow opening between the rocks. Still no shots came.

Brett looked the obstacle over. "There's only one way to see what lies beyond the opening—from above. I'll scale the side and look. Then we'll know what we're dealing with."

"Be careful, brother," Rand felt compelled to say, although he knew Brett would.

"I will be silent. They won't hear me."

Rand watched him begin the long climb, praying that Brett wouldn't dislodge a single pebble.

Grim-faced, Cooper stood beside him with a hand on his shoulder. "He knows what he's doing. We're going to get Callie back."

"Fleming doesn't only have Callie." Keeping his voice low, Rand told him about her daughter, Mariah, and Fleming's threat to kill her. "That's why Callie ended up here. She came to save Mariah."

"We'll get both of them back. You know we don't let evil win. It's not in us."

Time dragged while they waited for Brett. It seemed to take forever before he dropped to the ground beside them.

"I saw no one. Not a thing moved on the other side of these rocks."

Without waiting to hear more, Rand rushed forward, squeezing through the opening. He couldn't believe his eyes.

The small enclosure was empty.

Everyone was gone.

Callie had vanished.

Thirty-two

Numbness washed over Rand. He was too late. He'd failed.

At least he saw no bodies and that heartened him a little. It had to mean Callie was alive. Didn't it?

What had Fleming done with her?

Cooper picked up an empty can of beans while Brett knelt to feel the embers of the campfire.

"I'd say we missed them by ten minutes." Brett stood, then climbed up the white cliff to a ledge and stood staring into the distance. "I see riders. I'd say that's Fleming. They're heading north toward Brushy Lake."

"It has to be them," Rand said. "Let's ride."

He was halfway to his horse by the time the rest seemed to realize it. Rand couldn't wait. They would have to catch up. He sprang into Blue's saddle and spurred the roan forward.

"Come on, boy. We've got to save our girls," he muttered into the breeze. He ignored the pain shooting from his shoulder and bent into the wind, focusing solely on his task.

Pounding hooves from behind told him the others

had lost no time in catching up. Rand put his head down and rode, willing the horse to eat up the ground.

Cooper pulled alongside and yelled, "We need a plan."

"Find the no-good varmints and kill 'em," Rand hollered back. That was the only plan he needed.

"If they make it to the lake, there'll be hundreds of places for them to hide. Be harder to flush them out."

"We have plenty of men. We'll get the job done."

Cooper nodded and fell back, letting Rand resume the lead.

Rand touched Blue's right flank and raced toward the ragtag group ahead. Thank goodness they hadn't seen him and his small army yet. Brush tore at his clothes and whipped his face, at times nearly unseating him. It didn't matter, though. Nothing did, except for finding and bringing Callie and her daughter home.

With fierce determination pounding in his chest, onward he thundered. When Rand got within a hundred yards of the last rider, the man turned to look back. He yelled something to the others and they spurred their horses.

Callie sat in front of Fleming on his mount. Mariah rode with one of the brothers. Both were probably bound.

Up ahead, sunlight sparkled on Brushy Lake, turning the blue water into thousands of glistening diamonds. If only Rand could sprout wings and fly so he could beat them to the landmark. But he couldn't. His powers lay in his dogged determination.

By the time he reached the landmark, the men and their captives had dismounted and hidden in the trees.

With his Colt in his hand, Rand reined up and leaped from the saddle.

A hail of bullets whizzed around him.

Diving into the thick brush, he looked around at the heavy vegetation. It would take everything they had to flush the outlaws out. This was not going to be an easy or quick fight.

Cooper skittered into the brush with him.

"Tell your men not to fire blindly," Rand said. "They might hit Callie or the girl."

"Already have. You just focus on your wife and child."

"Let's round up these bastards."

A shot whistled above Rand's head and slammed into the bark of a tree behind him, splintering it. He rose for a quick look. Just then, one of the outlaws sprang from his hiding place and raced for the wide girth of the trunk of a cottonwood tree.

Rand took aim and squeezed the trigger. Blood spurted from the man's chest as he went down. Rand wasted no time in finding another target when a raised head poked from a thicket. Nate Fleming. Rand drew a bead dead center between the man's eyes.

He missed when the man ducked into the brush.

Damn!

Brett crawled from his cover to join Rand and Cooper. "What do you think?"

"Gotta fan out. Trap 'em in a circle. I'll tell my men," Cooper said. "You and Rand keep the heat on the outlaws from here."

As Cooper crawled toward his men, Rand watched as one by one they slowly moved in a wide arc, giving

Nate and his other brother nowhere to go. Ten minutes later, all escape routes were cut off.

Where was Callie? Terror ran up Rand's spine. Fleming was ruthless enough to put a bullet in her head when he saw he had no hope of making it.

Please, God, don't let that happen.

Desperate to keep that from becoming reality, Rand began running from tree to tree, getting closer to the spot where he'd last glimpsed Nate Fleming. His lungs hurt with the need to take in air. But he doubted he'd draw in a deep breath until he had Callie safe in his arms.

A hunger to kiss her and tell her how beautiful she was swept over him. She was everything he wanted and needed.

Callie Quinn Sinclair had become his sole reason for living. And he would fight for her until he had no more blood left to spill.

A few more feet got him close enough to reach Fleming. When the outlaw raised his gun, Rand made a flying tackle.

∾

Gagged and bound, Callie listened to the snapping twigs, the crash of colliding bodies, and men's grunts. She had to get her and Mariah free. Rand needed her.

A strong sense that this was a time of reckoning filled her.

She strained against her ropes, willing them to loosen. The rough hemp cut into her wrists, bringing stinging pain. Three feet away, Mariah began to sob.

Nate had also gagged her and tied her to a small tree. Callie yearned to comfort her daughter.

Rustling movement caught her attention and she saw Emmett Fleming crawling toward her with a knife in his hand.

Her eyes widened as new fear rose

Dear God, please don't let him kill Mariah or do anything to hurt Rand.

Shaking her head, she shrank as far away as she could and readied to use her feet—the only weapon she had.

How could she have been so wrong about him? Mariah had told her how he'd sneaked food to her and tried to keep Nate away. Callie had witnessed Emmett's attempts to direct his brothers' cruelty onto himself when they sought to inflict more punishment on her and Mariah. Nate and Virgil had beat him senseless when he'd confessed to things he hadn't done.

Despite his small bits of kindness, though, she knew that in the end blood was thicker than water and his loyalty would always lie with his brothers.

She was about to kick Emmett as hard as she could when he spoke low, "For God's sake, be still so I can cut your ropes. I don't know how much time I have. Help your girl to one of the horses and ride."

"Why are you doing this? They'll kill you."

A far look came into Emmett's eyes. "I once had a wife and daughter. Nate stole them from me. He has this warped thinking that everything and everyone belongs to him. They died while in his hands, and I can honestly say that I hate my brother with a vengeance."

When the ropes fell from Callie's wrists, she laid a hand on Emmett's arm. "I won't forget this. Thank you."

He nodded and moved to free Mariah, then turned to Callie. "Go and don't look back."

∽

As Rand launched himself at Nate, they went tumbling. The jarring landing knocked Rand's Colt from his hand and sent mind-numbing pain through his bandaged shoulder. He gritted his teeth and slammed his fist into Nate's jaw. The resounding crack was satisfying. Several more blows connected with the outlaw's face.

Nate reached for a handful of dirt and threw it into Rand's eyes. Though temporarily blinded, Rand didn't loosen his hold. His fingers dug into Nate's shoulder and held on with every bit of strength he had.

The deadly battle in which they were locked took another turn when the outlaw threw him onto the ground and crawled on his chest. Nate Fleming's hands went around Rand's throat and tightened, squeezing his windpipe.

Unable to breathe and seeing the black edges of consciousness closing around him, he felt along the ground for a weapon of some sort. Reaching fingers located a good-sized rock.

He swung it, connecting with the back of Fleming's head, breaking his hold.

But when he jerked the man to his feet, he felt the hard tip of Fleming's gun pressed to his chest.

Fleming grinned. "Never bet against me. You lose, Sinclair."

The murdering scum had him. One second more and Rand's life would be over. He closed his eyes and pictured Callie's beautiful face. If he was going to die, he wanted his last thought to be of her.

"Drop the gun, Nate," Callie ordered harshly.

Rand opened his eyes to see Callie holding a pistol to Nate's head. Rope dangled from her wrists.

"I don't think so," Nate answered. "I like my chances. Bet I can put a bullet in this husband of yours before you can fire."

"You might want to reconsider," Callie replied. "You're surrounded and your brother Emmett has already given up. He doesn't have the stomach for killing like you do."

Keeping his gun on Rand, Nate spoke slowly. "I won't hang."

"Your choice." Callie's voice was hard and tight.

Fleming's black eyes met Rand's, and in that instant, he knew the outlaw was going to pull the trigger.

With no time to spare, Rand grabbed the gun and swung it away the moment the cartridge shot from the end. The deadly piece of metal went harmlessly into the trees while the gun that had nearly made Callie a widow fell to the dirt.

Fleming turned and bolted into the woods. Rand quickly gave chase. He wasn't going to lose Fleming this time. He followed the racket of snapping branches and crushed vegetation until he could see the tall, black-clothed figure ahead.

Higher and higher they climbed along the bluff that overlooked one side of the lake.

At last Rand emerged on a ledge. Caught without

his weapon, Fleming's eyes widened as he licked his dry mouth. Rand had cornered the animal at last. "There's only one thing to do—give yourself up."

"No." Nate glanced over the side of the ledge to the water below.

"It's a long way down."

"If I go down, I'll take you with me, Sinclair."

Sizing up the outlaw, Rand moved closer, ready for this fight. His gut told him only one would walk away. He shoved all his chips to the center of the table.

Few had ever beaten him when he was in a betting mood.

Rand rushed him. They hit the narrow ledge hard. His harsh breath came in gasping heaves as he attempted to pin Nate to the rocky ledge. Blood from Rand's shoulder, torn open during the fight, had soaked his shirt, but he had no time to worry about it. Praying for a little more strength, he managed to throw his legs around Nate's body. He couldn't hold him. Nate rolled, and suddenly Rand found himself beneath him.

The outlaw's hands closed around Rand's throat like a vise, squeezing tighter and tighter. His lungs screamed with the need to inhale. With blackness closing around him, Rand jabbed his fingers into Nate's eyes, breaking the hold.

Struggling for air, Rand pushed away and quickly got up. But he couldn't do more than cling to the limestone wall.

Nate seemed done for also as he stumbled to his feet. Unable to see, he had his hands out, groping. He stood right on the edge of the rock shelf. One step backward and the man would fall to his death.

Rand stood frozen. "Don't move, Fleming. There's nothing but air behind you. It's over."

Though he was blinded, Nate smiled. "You don't have me yet, sodbuster." He lunged for Rand and jerked him toward the edge.

Breathing hard and fighting the pain in his shoulder, Rand felt his strength ebbing. This day had taken everything he had. He'd given his all, but it hadn't been enough. His feet were on the lip of the precipice, with his heels extending over the edge. Cold sweat broke out on his forehead. Despair filled him because he knew he'd reached the end. He wouldn't see Callie again. Mind-numbing pain shot through his chest as his grip on Nate slipped.

His adversary must've sensed his waning strength. With one last punishing blow, Fleming sent him over the side.

Desperately fighting for purchase, Rand's feet scraped the rock wall as he managed to grab a protruding rock at the last second. Hanging suspended, Rand didn't know how long he'd have before his jerking arms gave out. He glanced down. It was a long way to the bottom. He wouldn't survive the fall.

Glancing up, he saw Fleming standing, peering over the edge. The man's gloating grin, his hard eyes, gave Rand the strength he needed. He couldn't let the man win. He wouldn't let him walk away after all he'd done to Callie and the children. He'd made a promise.

In a last ditch effort, Rand transferred his body weight to one hand, reached for the man's boot, and with a loud grunt, yanked.

Nate Fleming, who had brought so much pain to

so many people, plunged over the side to the jagged rocks below.

Deafening silence followed as Rand pulled himself back onto the rock shelf and collapsed in a quivering mass of muscle and bone.

It was over.

Time drifted as Rand learned to breathe again. Then Cooper and Brett were lifting him to his feet. Wiping the blood from his mouth, he went to the edge and looked down. Fleming lay twisted and broken on the sharp limestone.

The man had died as violently as he'd lived. Yet Rand took no joy from the death. Immense sadness filled him for the man who'd always made the wrong choices.

Brett laid a hand on his back. "Let's go home."

His brothers helped him down to where Callie waited. Rand swept her up into his arms when she ran to meet him and told her Nate Fleming had met his end. The man couldn't harm her or Toby or Mariah ever again.

"I love you, Rand. We're finally free of him. You saved me and Mariah. There were times I didn't know if we'd make it to the next moment."

He winced as she gently kissed his bruised mouth. "I didn't know either, darlin'. But we made it."

"Are you angry with me for leaving you and the children?"

"Nope. I understand the reasons why you left. How is Mariah? Is she all right?"

A shadow crossed Callie's eyes. "She will be over time."

"That's all we can ask. We'll shower her with love,

and the memories will fade." He set her on her feet. "I have a feeling Toby will help a lot. I'm sure he'll have her playing in his tepee in nothing flat and telling her they have to take care of Wren."

She sighed and leaned against him. "I feel as if a huge fire has passed through and left charred remains everywhere. But underneath the soot and ash is good, strong land that the fire couldn't touch. We have so much to be grateful for, Rand. Nothing can destroy what we have."

His heart couldn't contain the joy that burst from it. She was right. They had everything they needed, and nothing could take it. Ignoring the pain, he pressed his lips to hers in a kiss that made the heat pool low in his belly.

"I can't wait to get you home, Mrs. Sinclair."

Thirty-three

SURROUNDED BY THE BEAUTIFUL WATER OF BRUSHY Lake, Callie felt Mariah pressing against her, clutching her dress. She put her arms around her daughter's thin shoulders. "I want you to meet someone who's very, very special. Rand, this is my daughter, my Mariah."

Rand started to shake her hand, but when she moved in for a hug, his arms encircled her. "Young lady, I'm extremely happy to meet you. Our home is yours."

The girl's forehead wrinkled as she studied him. The timid smile that curved her mouth reflected her approval. "What do I call you?"

"Whatever you want. How about starting with Papa Rand?"

She twisted the hold she had on Callie's dress. "I'd like that. I never had a papa before. I never had anyone who wanted me, except maybe old Nellie Solomon. But she didn't have a choice."

"Whoever Nellie is, we owe her for taking care of you. And make no mistake, your mama and I want you very badly." He kissed her bruised and bloody cheek. Taking off his coat, he wrapped it around her. "This'll warm you right up."

Callie no longer had a shred of a doubt about Rand's acceptance. He'd already taken her lost Mariah into his heart and planted her right next to Toby and Wren in the garden of family he'd tilled and cultivated.

"Thank you, Rand," Callie said, putting her arm through his. "The size of your heart never ceases to amaze me."

"Gotta take care of my girls." He winked. "And my son. Ready to go home?"

"I mean to tend to your shoulder and see what new damage you did to it. You're bleeding something awful."

Her gaze lit on Emmett, who stood next to the horses with his hands bound. He stared sadly at Virgil's body, which lay at his feet, yet he seemed relieved. She owed Emmett Fleming. Out of all his brothers, he was the only one with a conscience. Without his help, things would've been a lot worse.

"Give me just a minute." She stepped toward the man who'd shown the size of his heart and hugged him. "Thank you for all you did. I owe you a great debt. When you go to trial, I'll ask the judge to grant leniency."

Emmett glanced down. "It's more than I deserve. I'm glad I could help right a few of the wrongs Nate did. Take care of that little girl. And my nephew."

"I will." Callie glanced toward Mariah. Her daughter's hand was clutching Rand's, and though her smile was slight, it was there. "You can be assured of that."

The sun was high in the sky by the time Callie washed Rand's wounded shoulder with lake water and rebandaged it. Some of Cooper's men had retrieved Nate's body and were tying it to a horse.

Brett was standing with Rand and her when Tom Mason came over. Callie and Rand moved closer, and when Cooper joined them, they created a circle around Brett.

"You're a difficult man to find," Mason said, offering his hand. "I'm—"

"Tom Mason. I know." Brett stared at the gesture of friendship a long moment before he briefly touched the man's hand. "Why are you looking for me? I've never laid eyes on you."

Mason's nervous gaze swept the protective shield around Brett. "Though I used to be a Pinkerton, I now locate things people have lost. I was hired to find you."

"By who?" Rand ordered.

"His sister. She hired me to locate her brother."

"You've mistaken me for someone else," Brett said in a tight voice. "I have no sister, no kin, no one except my brothers."

Watching the tall, proud Indian struggle against the hope that Mason might be right made Callie's chest ache. He couldn't allow himself to believe, because it was easier than facing the devastating pain if the news turned out to be untrue. She'd seen Rand face a similar dilemma. Her heart broke for these brothers who had made their own family when they had none. But despite all the odds stacked against them, they'd grown into big, strong men.

Cooper spoke up. "He'll need to see proof. I trust you have some."

"I do." Mason pulled an envelope from inside his vest. "Her name is Sarah. She wrote a letter in addition to sending the record of your birth."

"For your sake, you better hope this is true," Rand said, putting a hand on Brett's shoulder as he took the envelope.

Tom Mason smiled. "I'm very good at what I do. I assure you there has been no mistake. Sarah Woodbridge is his sister, and she is anxious to come and meet him."

Callie touched Brett's arm. "Sarah could be a lovely woman, and I'm sure you wouldn't want to miss the answers she may provide. Your life is about to change."

When Brett lifted his eyes to hers, she saw a glimmer of tears, and her heart broke.

He folded the envelope and tucked it into his shirt. "I'll look at this in my own time."

"Let's go home," Cooper said in his deep voice. "We're burning daylight. Rand, can I have a word?"

The two brothers moved away, and Callie saw Cooper hand Rand something.

Then everyone turned to their horses. Callie accepted a hand up onto Blue. She looked forward to the slow ride back to the ranch, sitting in front of her husband. She never wanted to be away from him again. He was her rock, the one who grounded her, the one who slayed demons. Nothing held meaning without him beside her.

The leather creaked as he threw his long leg over

the roan's back and settled into the saddle. When his hand slid around her waist, she leaned against the solid wall of his chest and breathed the scent of the wild Texas land that was their home.

"Mama, I love you. Thank you for coming for me," Mariah called from where she sat with Brett on his beautiful mustang.

Hearing her daughter call her Mama for the first time brought a lump to her throat, making it difficult to speak. Swallowing hard, she called back, "I love you too, sweetheart."

Her life wasn't in the gloaming any longer. She walked in golden sunshine, and when the night shadows came and the wind shook the trees, she would have no fear.

They'd gone about a mile when she saw a rider ahead, coming fast. When he drew up beside them, she recognized the man as one of Cooper's ranch hands.

"Gotta find Boss. Hope you can tell me where he is."

"What's wrong?" Rand asked. Callie could feel the tension in his body. Even tired and injured, he was ready to help.

"Miss Delta is having the babies. I was told to find Boss."

"That's great news." Rand told the cowboy that Cooper was at Brushy Lake, and the ranch hand galloped off without wasting any more time on conversation.

"Coop's going to be a father," Rand said, grinning.

Callie sighed and kissed him. "I'm so happy for them. Looks like our families are growing by leaps and bounds."

"I'm such a fool. I spent all these years convincing myself that I was happy being a bachelor, that it was the only way to keep everything locked inside. Thank goodness you found a key that could open my heart."

Happiness washed over her like waves on a seashore. "You found one for mine too. Maybe that's what loving someone is about. Finding and keeping keys for each other. We make a good team, sweetheart."

A flurry of activity began when they rode up to the house a little while later. While Callie gave Mariah a bath and found her something clean to wear, Rand collected Toby and little Wren. His family was finally all together and safe. And as families who loved each other did, everyone helped him pick up the wreckage from the kitchen and nail boards over the broken windows.

Then, as the purple shadows settled over the land, they sat around the table eating the best meal Rand had ever had. Maybe it was because of all the thankfulness in his heart. He made sure to give each child a measure of loving attention as they ate.

He had a special kind of attention planned for his wife after the house grew still and the little ones were in dreamland.

After he helped Callie make quick work of the kitchen, he relaxed in the parlor, surrounded by his beautiful family. Watching three of the best children he could ask for and a wife who stirred a fire inside, he knew without a doubt he was the richest man on earth.

The terror of the morning seemed far away.

Mariah and Toby played with the baby on a quilt

on the floor. From the minute Toby asked Mariah if she'd like to see his tepee, they'd been as thick as thieves. The girl fit in as though she'd always been there, even helping her mother with the supper dishes.

Questions about where she'd been all this time swarmed in his head like pesky flies. Shortly after they'd gotten back, Callie had taken Mariah aside for a talk. He assumed Callie had learned some things. He couldn't wait to find out.

The gentle squeak of the rocking chair drew Rand's attention. His eyes met the smoldering passion in Callie's gaze. His shy wife winked at him and he had no trouble reading her mind. Thank goodness it was about bedtime. He didn't know how much more torture he could take.

Finally, they put the baby in her crib upstairs, and Callie tucked Mariah and Toby into bed. He came to join her after finishing up a surprise he had planned for his beautiful wife.

They stood in the doorway for a moment, drinking in the sight. Peace rippled along Rand's tall frame. Curling his fingers around Callie's, he led her across the hall to their place of refuge. Lighting the lamp, he pulled her into his arms. "I'm going to kiss you senseless, darlin'. You might as well get ready."

"I was born ready, Mr. Sinclair." She melted against him and parted her lips slightly for his kiss.

Making good on his promise sparked the smoldering embers that were always just beneath the surface, but Rand wasn't ready for the pleasurable task of putting out the blaze. Not yet. He had lots more planned first. He swept her into his arms and carried her to the kitchen for the little surprise he'd prepared.

A warm fire in the stove.

A tub full of hot water.

A half-dozen candles providing soft light.

Callie gave a little squeal of delight. "When did you do this?"

"That, my darling, is a secret." He set her on her feet, closed the door, and propped a chair under the knob to keep out nosy children who might disturb them. Then he set to work stripping off his wife's clothes and kissing each raw scrape, especially the deep cuts the ropes had made into her wrists.

Then he lowered her into the warm water and hurriedly removed his clothes and the bandage covering his wounded shoulder.

Seconds later, he slipped into the water and pulled her against him. "I never get tired of looking at you and thinking how lucky I am." He picked up a washcloth and began washing away every hurt and fear and disappointment she'd suffered. He meant to shower her with so much love, she wouldn't have time to give the past one thought.

Callie swiveled and her brilliant smile sent his blood racing. Lifting his hand to her heart, she left a kiss on his lips that spoke of burning hunger and desire.

"I beg to differ. I am the lucky one. Out of all the places in the world to choose to hide in, I came here. To you."

Lifting her hair, Rand nuzzled the slender column of her neck.

"Before we get carried away, my wife, I have to

know where Mariah has been these seven years. Does anyone have a claim to her?"

"No, no one will fight us for her. An old woman by the name of Nellie Solomon took her in. It seems that Edmund brought Mariah to her as a babe and threatened to harm her if she didn't keep quiet about where the child came from. Mariah told me the folks in Tobacco Root, Kansas, called her Wild Nellie and claimed she was a witch. Edmund made her take Mariah because he said my baby was the devil's spawn. I know it's wrong to hate a man who's dead, but I do. I can't help it."

A muscle worked in Rand's jaw as stillness came over him. "Was Nellie mean to our daughter?"

"Relax, dear." Callie wiggled until there was not one iota of space between their bodies. Rand gave a small groan. She began to draw tiny circles on his arm. "Nellie treated her with kindness. She must be a little touched in the head, though, because Mariah said the woman sometimes forgot to feed her. From what I can gather, Mariah pretty much took care of the old woman. You'll never guess what our sweet girl asked."

Rand nibbled on her earlobe. "What?"

"If we'd take her back to check on Nellie. She's worried about the old woman, afraid that Nate might've killed her."

"Of course we will. It's little enough to ask." He caressed the enticing curve of her back and shoulder and waist. Following the outline of her luscious body, he found the contour of her breast. His breathing became ragged.

They were not going to get a wink of sleep this night, and neither cared.

≈∾

By the time they'd washed and kissed and caressed every inch of each other's bath-slickened skin, the water had grown cold.

Still, Callie's body craved more. Now that her fear was gone, she had to have the pleasure that Rand's lovemaking brought. Her aroused body was demanding release that only Rand could give her.

She stood while he wrapped her in a towel and carried her upstairs.

The second he laid her on the bed, she reached for him, pulling him on top of her. This coupling demanded immediate fulfillment. They would go slow later but not now; the need was too great.

With his ragged breath matching her heaving gasps, he entered her hard and fast.

Her cry of pleasure echoed in the room as moonlight streamed through the window, bathing her in liquid silver.

This act of passion was raw, primal, heightened. And it made her feel so alive.

The turbulent air swirled around them like a wild lightning storm, and each time he plunged into her, she felt the power and strength of their love. Her desire for him overrode everything in this mad, hurtling rush toward the point of no return.

Groaning, he ground his mouth to hers.

His bruising kisses took even as they gave back.

Callie found herself in the grip of a frenzied passion that was demanding and unrelenting.

She needed. Wanted. Hungered.

Her hands were touching, kneading, searing, then

pulling him deeper inside her in a quest for the shuddering moment of ecstasy.

On soaring waves of mind-numbing pleasure she climbed, reaching for that moment when she became one mind, heart, and soul with Rand.

Arching her back, she rose up to meet him.

As he exploded inside her, tremors of release rippled the length of her body. She gripped him tightly and rode the blissful high peaks.

Seconds later, as she lay gasping for air, he rose on an elbow to gently kiss the soft curve of her stomach. Callie smiled, threading her fingers in his silky hair, curling her body around his. Warm contentment spread over her.

God, how she loved this man.

∽

As dawn peeked into their window, the bed protested the shift of weight as Callie moved from Rand's side and got up. He grinned. Though he had yet to drift to sleep, he felt energized. He reached for her, but she evaded his grasp.

"No you don't, mister," she scolded. "We have lots to do today, and I think I hear the children stirring."

His darling wife was right, of course. He went over the things in his head. One visit to the lawyer about the adoptions to add Mariah to the list, and scrounging up another bed for his new daughter. But first would come the chores.

Suddenly he remembered something. He threw back the covers and picked up his trousers. Rummaging in the pockets, he drew out a small kerchief bundle and stood before Callie. "I meant to give these back to you yesterday, but I forgot."

He laid the emerald ring and the jewel-encrusted brooch into her palm. "Cooper retrieved these from Fleming's body."

Callie stared at them a minute. "I was willing to do anything to try to save Mariah. I thought these were my legacy, but they're not. Wren, Toby, and Mariah are my legacy. They're a million times more valuable than these pretty baubles."

"You're a wise woman, my darling." He gently kissed her and helped her into a clean dress.

"I suppose so, but I'm very damaged. I'll never be the same."

He held her face between his hands and stared into eyes that had seen so much sorrow. "I'll take you any way I can get you. About a year ago, a man came into my saloon. He'd been all around the world. He said in some Asian countries, they fill the cracks of favorite broken dishes with gold, believing that when something has suffered damage, it only becomes more beautiful. That is you, Callie. I'll take your cracks and broken pieces and fill them with gold. We'll celebrate each one."

"What a wonderful custom. Have I told you I love you?"

Rand took her hand and knelt down on one knee. "Callie, would you marry me?"

"We're already married."

"Marry me again. I want to do things right and proper this time. I want you to have your church, with plenty of guests and the children looking on at their mama and papa. Will you?"

He saw a quick rush of tears in her eyes. Lifting his hand to her heart as she tugged him to his feet, she kissed him. "Yes, I'll marry you twice, fifty, or a hundred times. I want to raise our children and grow old with you."

Rand gazed into her whiskey-colored eyes as he lifted her hand to his lips. "You, my darling, are the greatest love I'll ever know. There will never be another."

Two weeks later, Rand stood in front of the preacher, holding Callie's hand. He eyed Toby sitting beside Mariah, who bounced Wren in her lap. They perched in the first row of the church, looking spit shined and grinning from ear to ear.

Each child legally belonged to him now. He winked and they giggled. The preacher cleared his throat in disapproval.

Rand took Callie's hand and vowed once again to love and cherish this beautiful woman who'd taken refuge on his ranch, which he'd renamed. No longer was it the Last Hope. His land was the New Hope Ranch now.

He glanced at Callie and into the deep amber depths of her eyes. Love for her poured from his heart.

How did he ever survive before her?

She wore the new rose-colored dress he'd bought during the winter festival celebration, remembering how they'd danced and how he'd known that, despite the secret she kept that might tear them apart, he had no regrets about marrying her.

The minute the preacher ended the ceremony, Rand

swept Callie up. "We are good and properly hitched now, Mrs. Sinclair. You can't wiggle out of it."

Callie traced his jawline with a finger. "Not many women can say they're twice a Texas bride, and both times to the same man."

"We are unique. Just don't get any ideas about marrying anyone else," he growled.

"Don't you know by now you're my one and only love?"

Rand grinned. He lowered his head and slanted a sizzling kiss across her lips—one that sealed their love for all eternity.

Forever His Texas Bride,

From the author…

It's given me great pleasure to introduce you to my Bachelors of Battle Creek series. In it, I've shown how three ragged boys came together in the orphanage to form an unbreakable bond as brothers that forges their journey into adulthood. Tears still come into my eyes when I think of how they were so desperate for family that they created their own. Each of the two previous books was special and came from the deepest part of my heart, but I've saved the best for last with *Forever His Texas Bride*.

Brett Liberty's story goes to the very core of who I am, maybe who we all are, and what I stand for. Being a half-breed was the worst thing for a man in the 1800s because it meant he straddled two worlds with neither claiming him. In this story, Brett faces pure hatred to the point that others want him dead. He's never been with a woman, never known the softness of a woman's touch or the feel of her lips on his. But when he meets pickpocket Rayna Harper in the jail cell next to his, he finds a kindred spirit. The brush of her hand is almost unbearable in its tenderness, and when she curls up beside him on the narrow bunk, she curls up inside his heart as well.

This is a story of never giving up hope and reaching for a forbidden love that others are bent on denying. It's about how through compassion you *can* change. Brett and Rayna's deep love binds them together like a strip of the toughest rawhide and won't let them go.

Now, I'd like to share an excerpt of *Forever His Texas Bride*...

One

North Central Texas
Spring 1879

A PLAN? DEFINITELY *NOT DYING*. BEYOND THAT, HE didn't have one.

High on a hill, Brett Liberty lay in the short, blood-stained grass, watching the farm below. With each breath, pain shot through him like the jagged edge of a hot knife.

The bullet had slammed into his back, near the shoulder blade from the feel of it.

If a plan was coming, it had better hurry. The Texas springtime morning was heating up, and the men chasing him drew ever closer. Every second spent in indecision could cost him. He had two choices: try to seek help from the family in the little valley, or run as though chased by a vicious devil dog.

The blood loss had weakened him though. He wouldn't get far on foot. About a half mile back, Brett's pursuers had shot his horse, a faithful mustang he'd loved more than his own life. Rage rippled through his chest and throbbed in his head. They could hurt him all they wanted, but messing with his beloved horses would buy them a spot in hell.

He forced his thoughts back to his current predicament.

Through a narrowed gaze, Brett surveyed the scene below. The farmer who was chopping wood had a rifle within easy reach. The man's wife hung freshly washed clothes up on a line to dry under the golden sunshine while a couple of small children played at her feet. It was a tranquil day as far as appearances went.

Appearances deceived.

Help was so near yet so far away.

Brett *couldn't* seek their aid. The farmer would have that rifle in his hand before he made it halfway down the hill. The fact that Indian blood flowed through Brett's veins and colored his features definitely complicated things. With the Indian uprisings a few years ago fresh in everyone's minds, it would mean certain death.

Why a posse dogged his trail, Brett couldn't say. He'd done nothing except take a remuda of the horses he raised to Fort Concho to sell. He could probably clear things up in two minutes if they'd just give him the opportunity. Yet the group, led by a man wearing a sheriff's star, seemed to adhere to the motto *shoot first and ask questions of the corpse*.

He was in a hell of a mess and wished he had his brothers, Cooper Thorne and Rand Sinclair, to stand with him.

Inside his head, he heard the ticking of a clock. Whatever he did, he'd better get to it.

The family below was his only chance. Brett straightened his bloodstained shirt as best he could and removed the long feather from his black hat. Except for his knee-high moccasins, the rest of his clothing was what any man on the frontier would wear.

At last he gathered his strength and struggled to his feet. He removed a bandanna, a red one, from around his neck. On wobbly legs, he picked his way down the hill.

When the farmer saw him and started for his rifle, Brett waved the bandanna over his head. "Help! I need help. Please don't shoot. I'm unarmed."

With the rifle firmly in hand, the farmer ordered his wife and children into the house, then cautiously advanced. Brett dropped to his knees in an effort to show he posed no threat.

The man's shadow fell across Brett. "Who are you and what do you want?" the farmer asked.

"I'm shot. Name's Brett Liberty. I have a horse ranch seventy miles east of here." When he started to stand, the farmer jabbed the end of the rifle into his chest. Brett saw the wisdom in staying put.

"Who shot you?"

"Don't know. Never saw them before."

"How do I know you didn't hightail it off the reservation? Or maybe you're an outlaw. I've heard of Indian outlaws."

Brett sighed in frustration. "I've never seen a reservation, and I assure you, I don't step outside the law. I'm respected in Battle Creek. My brother is the sheriff. If I took up outlawing ways, he'd be the first to arrest me."

His dry mouth couldn't even form spit. Maybe the man wouldn't deny him a drink, and with a witness to the posse's actions, the sheriff might let him live. It was his only shot.

The ticking clock in Brett's head was getting louder, blocking out the buzz of the persistent bee. His pursuers would be here in a minute. "Please, mister, could you at least give me some water?"

Silently, the farmer backed up a step and motioned Brett toward the well with his rifle barrel.

"Thank you." Brett got to his feet and stumbled toward the water. He lowered the bucket and pulled it up, then filled a metal cup that hung nearby and guzzled it down. He was about to refill it when horses galloped into the yard and encircled him.

"Put up your hands or I'll shoot," a man barked.

Brett glanced up at the speaker, who wore a tin star on his leather vest. "Your warning comes a little late, Sheriff. I would've appreciated it much earlier. Would you be so kind as to tell me what I did to warrant this arrest?"

The bearded sheriff dismounted. Hate glittered in his dark eyes, reminding Brett of others who harbored resentment for his kind. Jerking his hands behind his back, the middle-aged lawman secured them with rope. "You'll know soon enough."

Ignoring the sharp pain piercing his back, Brett tried to reason. "I can clear up this misunderstanding if you'll only tell me what you think I did wrong."

No one spoke.

Brett turned to the farmer. "I'll give you five of my best horses if you'll let my brothers know where I am.

You can find them in Battle Creek. Cooper Thorne and Rand Sinclair."

The farmer stared straight ahead without even a flicker to indicate he'd heard. While the sheriff thanked the sodbuster for catching Brett, two of the other riders threw him onto a horse. With everyone mounted a few minutes later, the group made tracks toward Steele's Hollow.

The combination of blood loss and the hot sun made Brett see double. It was all he could do to stay in the saddle.

By the time they rode into the small town an hour later, Brett was doubled over and clinging to the horse's mane. The group halted in front of the jail and jerked him off the animal.

"Please, I need a doctor," Brett murmured as they rifled through his pockets.

After taking the bank draft from the sale of the horses and his knife, they unlocked a door that led down a dark walkway. The smell of the earthen walls and the dim light told him the builder had dug into a hill. They unlocked a cell and threw him inside.

"A doctor," Brett repeated weakly as he huddled on the floor.

"Not sure he treats breeds." The sheriff slammed the iron door shut and locked it. "See what I can do, though. Reckon we don't want you to die before we hang you."

"That's awful considerate." Brett struggled to his feet and clung to the metal bars to keep from falling. "Once and for all, tell me...what did I do? What am I guilty of?"

"You were born," the sheriff snapped. Without more, he turned and walked to the front of the jail.

❦

Panic pounded in Brett's temples like a herd of stampeding mustangs long after the slamming of the two iron doors separating him from freedom. This proved that the sheriff had targeted him solely because of his Indian heritage; he had no crime to charge him with.

His crime, it seemed, simply was just being born.

Dizzy, Brett collapsed onto the bunk as his hat fell to the crude wooden floor.

Movement in the next cell caught his attention. Willing the room to keep from spinning, Brett turned his head. He could make out a woman's form in the dimness. Surely his pain had conjured her up. They didn't put women in jail.

He couldn't tell what she looked like because she had two faces blurring together, distorting her features.

"You're in pitiful shape, mister."

Since his bunk butted up to the bars of her cell, she could easily reach through. He felt her cautiously touch one of his moccasins.

"Checking to see if I'm dead?" he murmured.

"Nope. Do you mind if I have your shoes after they hang you?"

Brett raised up on an elbow, then immediately regretted it when the cell whirled. He laid back down. "That's not a nice thing to ask a man."

"Well, you won't be needing them. I might as well get some good out of them."

"They aren't going to hang me."

"That's not what Sheriff Oldham said."

"He can't hang me because I didn't do anything wrong." It was best to keep believing that. Maybe he could convince someone, even if only himself. "I think he was joking."

"Humor and Sheriff Oldham parted company long ago. He's serious all the time. And mean. You don't want to get on his bad side."

"Wish I'd known this sooner. You sure know how to make a man feel better," Brett said dryly, draping his arm across his eyes and willing his stomach to quit churning. "What is your name?"

"Rayna."

"Who stuck that on you? I've never heard it before."

"It's a made-up name. My father is Raymond and my mother is Elna. My mama stuck 'em together and came up with Rayna. I've always hated it."

"Got a last name, or did they use it all on the first one?"

"Harper. Rayna Harper."

"Forgive me if I don't get up to shake hands, but I'm a little indisposed. I'm Brett Liberty."

Blessed silence filled the space, leaving him to fight waves of dizziness and a rebelling stomach. Keeping down the contents seemed all he could manage at present.

Rayna appeared to have other ideas. "Where did you get those Indian shoes, Brett? I'd sure like to have them."

"My brother." His words came out sounding shorter than he intended.

"Sorry. I've been in here for a while by myself, and

I guess I just have a lot of words stored up. Sometimes I feel they're just going to explode out the top of my head if I don't let some out. What are you in here for? I couldn't hear too well."

"For being born, I'm told." Brett was still trying to digest that.

"Me too." Rayna sounded astonished. "Isn't that amazing?"

Brett had a feeling that no matter what he'd said, she would say the same thing. He wished he could see her better so he could put a face to the voice. Even though the conversation taxed him, it was nice to know he wasn't alone. Maybe she'd even hold his hand if he died.

That is, if she wasn't too busy trying to get his moccasins off instead.

"Why do you think it's amazing?"

"Because it makes perfect sense. I figure if I hadn't been born, I wouldn't be in here for picking old Mr. Vickery's pockets."

"So you're a pickpocket?" Surprise rippled through him.

"Nope. I'm a spreader of good. I don't ever keep any of it. I take from those who have and give to the have-nots. Makes everyone happy. Except me when I get thrown in the calaboose."

"You're a Robin Hood." Brett had seen a copy of the book about the legendary figure at Fort Concho. He'd learned it so he could share the tale with Toby, Rand's adopted son. Brett had taken the six-year-old into his heart and loved spending time with the boy.

"I'm a what?"

"A person who goes around doing good things for the poor."

"Oh. I guess I am. It makes me so sad that some people have to do without things they need and no one helps them. This past winter, my friend Davy froze to death because the only place he had to sleep was under a porch. He was just a kid with no one except me to care."

Rayna's big heart touched Brett. She seemed to speak from a good bit of experience. "Do you have a place to sleep whenever you're not in here?"

"I get along. Don't need you to fret about me. Worrying about them putting a rope around your neck is all you can handle. Do you reckon it hurts a lot, Brett?"

"I wouldn't know." Hopefully he wouldn't find out.

"I'll say a prayer for you."

"Appreciate that, Miss Rayna Harper."

Pressure on the bottom of his foot made him jump. He raised his head and saw that she'd stuck one bare foot through the bars and was measuring it to his.

"Stop that," he said, drawing his legs up. "The doctor'll be along soon. I'm not going to be dead enough for you to get them."

The next sound to reach his ears was sawing and her soft, "Oh dear."

"Why did you say that? What's wrong?"

"The sawbones had best hurry or you won't be needing him. They've started building the gallows."

That ticking clock in his head had taken on the sound of tolling bells.

Two

BRETT MUST'VE LOST CONSCIOUSNESS. PANIC GRIPPED him when he came to. For a moment, he couldn't remember where he was or why he was behind bars.

When it came flooding back, he called, "Rayna, are you still here?"

"Oh dear Lord, I thought you were dead. You haven't made a sound for hours."

"Not dead yet, so don't get your hopes up," he joked weakly.

The iron door separating the cells from the sheriff's office rattled. Footsteps sounded, then a key grated in the lock to his cell. He turned his head to see a slight, spry man carrying a black medical bag.

"Doc?" Brett murmured.

The doctor hurried to the bunk and felt Brett's forehead. "Sheriff, he has a raging fever. This bullet has got to come out. I want him transported to my office right away."

Brett heard the sheriff's gravelly voice. "Nope. Ain't leaving here."

"Get me some light then," the doctor snapped.

"Lanterns. Three of them plus a pail of clean water and some cloths. And quick."

"A lot of fuss for a stinking half-breed," the sheriff grumbled.

Doc turned Brett onto his belly and pain shot like a thunderbolt through him. He bit down on his lip until he tasted blood to keep from crying out. He couldn't suppress a moan though.

"It's all right, son. Not everyone in this town shares the sheriff's views. I'm going to take care of you."

Brett relaxed for the first time since this nightmare began. His mind drifted like a lazy cloud on a summer's day. His ranch and beloved horses filled his mind. The smell of lush, sweet grass surrounded him, and the vivid blue sky stretched overhead as far as the eye could see.

Please help me get back to the Wild Horse. The thought of not seeing his beloved ranch again brought the sting of tears. The Wild Horse was the one place where he'd ever been happy and safe.

"Will I die, Doc?"

"Not if I can help it, son." The doctor sounded reassuring at least.

By the time the sawbones finished examining the wound, the sheriff was back with lanterns. Once the doctor could see, he set right to work, first producing a bottle of whiskey from his bag and holding it to Brett's lips.

When Brett tried to refuse, the kindly man pressed, "You'll need something for the pain when I remove the slug. Don't try to be a hero."

Finally, Brett accepted a drink but instantly regretted

it. The liquor left a burning trail down his throat to his belly and released a fit of coughing. "No more. I'll deal with the pain. Just get on with it."

"As you wish."

A few seconds later, Brett regretted his decision. The pain was far worse than anything he'd experienced, even in the orphanage when Mr. Simon took off his belt and whipped him as he curled into a ball on the floor.

He heard screams and realized they came from him. And then everything went black as he slipped beneath murky, swirling water.

❦

In the next cell, Rayna plugged her ears with her fingers to block out the noises. A drop of water fell onto her dress and she realized she was crying.

The Indian was in such agony. And she couldn't help.

His plight told her he was one of the have-nots, like her. Though she'd only just met him, it would kill a part of her if he died. He reminded her of a wounded animal—like the hawk she'd secretly cared for years ago after a storm snapped its wing in two.

Her father had raised a ruckus when he discovered she'd hidden the hawk in the wagon amongst the pile of bones. He'd cursed her, then yelled that bone-pickers had no business trying to be softhearted. Their only job was to collect the bleached buffalo skulls and fragments left behind after the hunters had passed through. The pickers received eight dollars a ton when they delivered them to be shipped back East where factories used them to make bone china and ground them into fertilizer. That eight dollars barely kept them fed.

Raymond Harper had made her dump the hawk out beside the trail, saying that nature would take care of things.

Rayna shut her eyes against the memory of how it squawked and hopped around, desperately trying to fly. Her father calmly took out his gun and shot it, then turned to her. "Now quit your sniveling."

Six months ago, after he went to sleep, she finally ran away.

The lonely expanse of prairie was better than staying with him. Anything was better than being a bone-picker's daughter. Bone-pickers had no soul. But *she* did. She did her best to make sure of that.

The doctor was muttering to himself in Brett's cell, sounding very frustrated. She guessed he was having a hard time finding the bullet fragment.

"Can I help, Doc?" she asked softly.

He whirled. "Rayna child, I didn't know he'd thrown you in jail again. Yes, I wish I had your good eyes. I can't see as well as I used to." Doc Perkins left Brett's cell and returned a moment later with Sheriff Oldham.

"I'll open her cell, but she better not try to escape. I hold you responsible for her," Oldham muttered.

"For God's sake, Sheriff, you have the door separating the cells from your office bolted. They don't even have a window."

"Can't be too careful."

The minute the key turned in the lock, Rayna

rushed out and into Brett's cell. "Tell me what you want."

"The bullet fragment, child. There's so much blood. Take these forceps and see if you can get it."

Rayna took the pointed metal instrument from the doctor. He held a lantern up high. She stared at the open wound and again thought of that hawk. She couldn't save that bird, but maybe she could save Brett Liberty.

With a trembling hand, she moved the torn, raw flesh aside, trying not to gag. So much blood. She took a deep breath and blocked out everything except her task. Repeated tries found no success however.

Tears of frustration trickled down her cheeks. She wasn't a failure. She *wasn't*. And she wasn't going to give up.

Minutes ticked by and Brett's breathing became more and more shallow. She had to do this, not only for him, but for herself.

Finally, the light glinted off a piece of metal. Grabbing onto the spent bullet with the forceps, she pulled it out and dropped it into a tin pan beside the bed before she could lose it inside him again.

"You did it, child. He may well owe his life to you."

"Do you think Brett will live?"

"He has a lot better chance now." He took the stained forceps from her and dropped them into the pan with the fragment. "I'll wash the wound and you can help me apply a bandage. Did you know you make a fine nurse?"

It was news to her that she made a fine anything.

She was nothing but a picker. Of bones, of pockets, and now of bullet wounds.

"I'm glad I could help. He seems nice."

Doc Perkins dipped a cloth into the water and began cleaning away the blood from Brett's shoulder. "I agree. He's not a monster to be locked up like some wild animal."

"I don't know why the sheriff wants to hang him."

"Hate. Pure hate. His entire family was massacred by the Comanche when he was a boy. Oldham never got over it."

Rayna rolled Brett onto his side so the doctor could get to the blood that had run down to the thin mattress beneath. Minutes later, she helped wrap the wound with gauze overlaid with strips of muslin that they tied together.

Doc stood back. "We've done all we can for him. The rest is up to the good Lord."

"Thank you, Doc. I'll sit with him as long as Sheriff Oldham will let me."

"I'll tell him I've ordered you to." He laid a hand on her shoulder. "I'm guessing your life has always been between hay and grass, but you have a big heart. That's plain to see."

"I do care, and that's a fact."

The room felt empty after he left. She sat on the edge of the bunk and touched Brett's dark hair. It was soft just as the hawk's feathers had been.

She sensed a wound much deeper than that left by the bullet. One that had scarred his soul. Her brother had once told her that kisses held magic, healing. They never had for her, but maybe they would for Brett.

Rayna lightly traced his lips with her fingertips. She could steal a kiss and he'd never know. It was too tempting. She'd never kissed anyone before without being forced. Just one time, she wanted to know how it felt because *she* wanted to. Bending her head, she gently placed her mouth on his.

It felt nice. Real nice.

So much that she tried it again.

∼

Brett forced his eyes open, then promptly shut them against the glare of the lanterns. Why were there lanterns there? Where was he?

Someone moved beside him and a cool hand touched his forehead.

"Who?" he murmured.

"Rayna. Don't you remember?"

Images of his flight from the posse, the bullet slamming into his back, and the jail in Steele's Hollow came flooding back. "Is this a wake? Am I dead?"

"No, silly."

"What are you doing in my cell?" He tried to joke. "Did you escape so you could steal my moccasins?"

"I thought about it. I do believe they're the right size if I stuff the toe with newspaper."

"Don't get any ideas," he muttered, but his lips curved a little against his will.

The light finally allowed him to see her clearly. He couldn't say she was especially pretty—not traditionally so, in any case—but her cloud of auburn curls reminded him of the flames of a campfire on a cold night. Her eyes danced with mischief.

Their color was as difficult to nail down as she was. One minute they were blue, the next green. They changed with each movement. *They*, he decided, were beautiful.

As he pondered that, sleep overtook him again.

The next time he woke to find a hand in his trousers. His head jerked around as he flared back into full consciousness. "Trying to pick my pockets now? I'm afraid you'll be sadly disappointed. I'm one of the have-nots."

Color flooded Rayna's cheeks. "I was only giving you something."

Brett threw his long legs over the side of the bunk and, with great effort, struggled to a sitting position. "Giving me something? Now that's a new wrinkle."

"It's true." She sat down beside him.

"Then I suppose I need to see what you left in my pocket. Does it bite?"

"Good Lord, what kind of a person do you think I am?"

"God only knows." He allowed a smile as he stuck his hand in his trouser pocket and found a small object. He pulled it out. It was a smooth piece of wood that someone had carved into the shape of a heart. He stared into her blue-green eyes and raised a brow.

"You need it more than I do," she said. "My grandfather carved it a long time ago. It's always brought me good luck."

Brett fought the impulse to laugh and, except for a quirk of his lips, managed to keep a straight face. His gaze swept the iron bars, the plank floor, and the grim windowless space. "Yes, I can certainly see that this brought you all manner of good fortune."

Rayna twisted a piece of her dirty, threadbare dress. "Well, it did before I got here to Steele's Hollow."

He caught the quick glisten of tears before she looked down. He took her small hand in his. "Thank you," he said softly. "It's the best present anyone ever gave me."

"So you'll keep the heart? It would mean a lot."

"In that case, I can't refuse."

He tucked the small heart into his pocket. "You never told me why you're in my cell."

Her hand curled inside his. "I was helping Doc. He can't see well and had trouble locating the bullet fragment, so he got the sheriff to let me try."

"Then I owe you a debt of thanks." He squeezed her fingers impulsively.

He took in the woman who'd saved his life. Both delicacy and strength showed in her face. It seemed apparent that she'd had her share of disappointments. Still, it hadn't beaten her down. She had plenty of spunk and then some.

"I think I'll lie back down if you don't mind."

She rose and stood beside the bunk, then hesitated. "I wonder… Do you think I could stay? Just for a while? Maybe watch you sleep? Just in case you start feeling poorly again and need…something."

Brett studied her face and noticed that, though she'd blinked away the shimmer of tears, worry and fear darkened her eyes. Through the haze of his pain, he saw that Rayna hungered for human contact. He couldn't deny her that. He turned on his side to make more room. "Lie down beside me. We'll watch each other sleep."

"Do you snore?"

"I never stayed awake to find out."

"I'll take that as a no." She curled up next to him and laid her head on his arm. "Good night, Brett."

"Good night." He hesitated a long minute, impulse warring with reserve...then slowly laid his other arm protectively across her stomach.

A sense of peace flooded over him. This slight woman who seemed to have no one had awakened a part of him that he'd long buried. He impulsively kissed the top of her head, silently vowing to protect her for however long he had left.

Outlaw Hearts

BY ROSANNE BITTNER

From the author…

Outlaw Hearts is the story of wanted man Jake Harkner, who became an outlaw because of a traumatic childhood that led him to think there was no other way to live…until he met a woman who completely changed his life…and his hardened heart. Together they struggle through a life on the run while raising a family, until the law finally finds Jake. This story is about the power of love, a love that is strong enough to see through an outlaw's heart into the goodness that lies deep inside, a love that rises above all obstacles to hold two people together against all odds. This book was so dear to me that when I finished it, I knew I had to write a sequel. Recently I did just that, and along with the reissue of *Outlaw Hearts* in 2015, the sequel, *Do Not Forsake Me*, will also be published, continuing the beautiful love story of Jake and Randy Harkner, and bringing the readers into the lives of their grown children, who possess the same qualities of strength and enduring love as their parents. I'd like to share with you an excerpt from *Outlaw Hearts*.

In Chapter One, Miranda Hayes witnesses outlaw Jake Harkner shoot a man inside the Kansas City mercantile where Miranda is shopping. Startled and frightened, she pulls a small handgun from her purse and shoots Jake, thinking he might kill her, too. To her surprise, the dangerous-looking man just stares at her, seemingly dumbfounded, then stumbles out of the store and flees. Everyone in town praises Miranda's bravery in fending off a notorious wanted man, but secretly Miranda can't help wondering if the man is perhaps not as bad as his reputation would dictate. He could have shot her, but he didn't, and now she feels guilty that the man has ridden off somewhere, wounded and in pain because of her.

In Chapter Two, Miranda, a widow living alone, goes home to her farm, where she finds a surprise waiting for her...

Two

SHE OPENED THE SHED DOOR, THEN GASPED WHEN SHE saw a strange horse inside the shed, nibbling away at fresh oats. The animal was still saddled, a rifle and a shotgun resting in boots on either side of the saddle.

Fear gripped Miranda in the form of real pain in her chest. Whose horse was this? She noticed a dark green slicker tossed over the side of the stall. It looked familiar. Hadn't Jake Harkner been wearing a slicker like that when she saw him in the store?

Every nerve end came alert as her gaze quickly darted around the shed, but she saw no sign of human life. She put her hand to the strange horse's flank and could feel that the animal was cool. Apparently it had been here for several hours. If so, where was the man who had ridden it?

She moved closer to study the animal, noticing dried blood on the saddle and stuck to the left side of the horse's coat. Whoever had ridden it was bleeding, which made it even more likely it was Jake Harkner! But why here? The man couldn't possibly know where she lived! And where was he? Waiting for her? Hiding somewhere, ready to shoot her down in revenge?

She put a hand to her head, which suddenly ached fiercely. Her heart pounded so hard she could feel it in her chest. She felt like a fool for not checking everything more thoroughly before Sheriff McCleave left. Now he was too far away to even hear a gunshot.

She moved past the draft horses to the wagon and reached under the seat to take out her father's Winchester that she always kept there. She cocked the rifle and looked around, holding the gun in a ready position.

"Wherever you are, come out now!" she said sternly, trying to sound unafraid. Her only reply was the soft quiet of the early evening. She checked around the shed once more, then walked back outside, her eyes glancing in every direction, her ears alert. She checked behind the shed, scanned the open land all around the cabin.

She slowly approached her tiny log home, walking completely around it, seeing nothing. She approached the root cellar at the north wall of the building, swallowing back her fear as she reached down and flung open the door, then pointed her rifle into the cellar. "Come on out if you're in there!" she demanded. "Just get out and ride away and no one has to be hurt!"

Again her reply was only silence. She moved around to fling open the other heavy metal door, wishing it was brighter outside so she could see better down into the small dugout. "Did you hear me? Come out of there!" She reached down and picked up a couple of medium-sized rocks, flinging them into the dark hole, but all she heard were thuds as they hit the dirt floor. She knew from the size of the cellar and the small space in the middle of the surrounding shelves that if someone was down there, she could hardly have missed him with the rocks.

She backed away then, watching the cellar a moment longer, before turning and heading for the cabin's front door, her heart pounding even more wildly. Unless the owner of the horse had just wandered off, the cabin was the only place left where he could be. She looked down and saw a couple of spots of what could be blood on her porch. Why hadn't she or the sheriff noticed it before?

She cautiously pushed open the door with the barrel of her rifle, then stepped inside. Raising the rifle to a ready position then, she headed for her curtained-off bedroom, hoping she wasn't so worked up with fright that she would pass out if confronted. She moved to the wall and pressed her back against it, then peered around just far enough to peek through a crack between the edge of the curtain and the door frame.

At that moment Miranda Hayes thought perhaps her heart would stop beating altogether, and she found it impossible to stifle a gasp. "My God!" she whispered. There on her own bed lay Jake Harkner, apparently unconscious, one of his infamous revolvers lying on his belly. How had he ended up here, in her own house? Did he know she lived here? Had he come to kill her but been overcome by his own wound?

She stepped inside the room, quickly raising her rifle again when he moaned. She studied him a moment, noticing that his forehead and the skin around his eyes looked sickly pale. Blood stained the cotton blankets beneath him, and his forehead and hair were bathed in sweat as well as more blood from where Luke Putnam had slammed his rifle across Jake's head. She had worked enough with her father to know this was not a man ready to rise up and shoot her. He looked more like a dying man.

She moved a little closer, her rifle still in her right hand as she reached out with her left hand to cautiously take hold of the revolver resting on his stomach. He made no move to stop her. She turned and laid the gun on a chair and, mustering more courage, she reached across him and pulled the second revolver from its holster. When he still made no move to stop her, she set her rifle in a corner and then took the two revolvers hurriedly into the main room, placing them into a potato basket under a curtained-off counter. If he did come around, she didn't want him to be able to find his guns right away.

She hurried back to the bedroom, wondering what she should do. If she went to town for help, he could die before she got back, and she was not sure she wanted to be responsible for that. Besides that, it was getting dark, and she couldn't be traveling to town at night. There was nothing to do for the moment but try to help him.

"Mr. Harkner? Jake Harkner?" she spoke up, leaning closer.

Her only reply was a moan. She breathed deeply for courage and began removing his clothing—first his boots, then his gun belt and his jacket. It was a burdensome project. The man was a good six feet tall and built rock-hard. On top of that, in his present state he was dead weight. With a good deal of physical maneuvering she pulled off his pants and shirt and managed to move his legs up farther up onto the bed and straighten out his body. She hurriedly gathered some towels and stuffed them underneath him as best she could, then unbuttoned and pulled open the shirt of his long johns so she could see the wound, a tiny hole just below his left ribs.

She knew from working with her father and from his medical books that most vital organs were on the right side of a person's body, and she also knew that the small caliber of her pistol could mean no terribly dangerous damage had been done. The biggest problem was that the man had bled considerably, which was probably the reason he had passed out; or she supposed it could be from the vicious blow he had taken to the head. He could have a fractured skull.

She felt underneath him, pressing her hand at his back at the inside of his long johns, trying to see if perhaps the bullet had passed through him, but she already knew that for the size gun she had used, that was unlikely. She felt no wound at his back, and the sick feeling returned to her stomach. The bullet was still inside him and should come out, and there was no one but her to do it.

She knew that the first thing she had to do was to get him to drink some water to replace the body fluids he had lost from blood and perspiration. She worked quickly then, going to get a ladleful of water from the drinking bucket in the main room and bringing it back into the bedroom. She raised Jake's head and tried speaking to him again, asking him to drink the water. All she got was another groan. She managed to pour some of the water into his mouth, and she watched him swallow. More ran out of his mouth and down to the pillow. From the looks of her bed and the man in it, she knew both needed considerable cleaning up; but for the moment her biggest concern was getting out the bullet.

She went into the main room to get her father's doctor bag. "Why are you doing this, Miranda?" she muttered to herself. "Just let him die." Wouldn't society be better off? That was what Sheriff McCleave had said. Still, her Christian upbringing had taught her that every man had value, and she reasoned there had to be a reason why this man had led the life he led. Why had he killed his own father, if indeed that was true? She could not forget the strange sadness in his voice when he had told the clerk this morning that it took more than a war to make a man lead a lawless life.

She set the doctor bag on the table and quickly built a fire in the stone fireplace at the kitchen end of the cabin. She hung a kettle of water on the pothook to heat, then grabbed more towels and the doctor bag and went back into the bedroom. She watched Jake Harkner while the water heated. Had God led him here deliberately? Was she supposed to help him? To her it seemed a kind of sign, that for some strange reason he was supposed to be a part of her life, that there was some purpose for his being here.

She took a bottle of laudanum from the bag and uncorked it, again leaning over Jake and raising his head slightly. "Try to drink some of this," she said. "It will help kill the pain. I've got to try to get out the bullet, Mr. Harkner. I doubt that it went very deep. It was a small gun I used, and the bullet had to go through your woolen jacket first."

"San...tana," he muttered. "I tried...sorry... Pa. Pa!"

The word "Pa" was spoken with a hint of utter despair. Miranda found herself feeling a little sorry for him, then chastised herself for such feelings. *If the man wasn't in such a state, you'd probably be dead by now*, she told herself. Again she felt like a fool for wanting to help him, yet could not bring herself to let him just lie there in pain. She shoved the slim neck of the bottle into his mouth and poured. Jake swallowed, coughed and sputtered. "No, Pa," he murmured. "Stay...away. Don't...make me drink it!" His eyes squinted up and he pressed his lips tight when Miranda took the bottle away. He let out a whimper then that sounded more like a child than a man.

Miranda stepped back in astonishment. His whole body shuddered, then he suddenly lay quiet again. He had mentioned his father twice, the first time with such utter pain, this time with an almost pitiful, childlike pleading. The laudanum would take affect quickly. She went back into the main room and rummaged through a supply cabinet until she found some rope. She went back into the bedroom and used the rope to tie Jake's wrists and ankles to the sturdy log bedposts, afraid that when she started cutting into him he would thrash around and make her hurt him more—or perhaps he would come awake and try to grab her.

"As soon as this is over and I see you don't have a fever I'll give you a bath and a shave," she said as she fastened the ropes tightly. "You'll feel a lot better then. I don't mean you any more harm, Mr. Harkner." She had no idea if he heard her. She only knew she had to keep talking to keep up her own courage. She had seen her father remove bullets a couple of times, but she had no real experience of her own. All she knew to do was to dig with a knife, or perhaps she would have to reach inside the wound with her fingers to find the bullet. Somehow it had to come out.

She went back to the fireplace to find the water was finally hot. She poured some into a pan and brought it back into the bedroom, setting it on a small table beside the bed. She then retrieved a bottle of whiskey from her pantry, something her father always kept around for medicinal purposes only, for he had not been a drinking man himself.

She doused Jake's wound with the whiskey. His body jerked, but his eyes did not open. She poured more whiskey over her own hands and her father's surgical knife. She drew a deep breath then and said a quick prayer. "Heavenly Father, if you meant for me to do this, then help me do it right."

Fighting to keep her hands steady, she began digging. Jake's body stiffened and a pitiful groan exited his lips but he did not thrash about. Miranda fought tears as she dug deeper and more sickening groans welled up from what seemed the very depths of the man. She swallowed, then reached inside the wound with her fingers, feeling around until she touched what she thought must be the bullet.

"Please let it be," she whispered. She got hold of the object between two fingers and pulled, breathing a sigh of relief when she retrieved the bullet and held it up to look at it. She smiled with great delight, an almost victorious feeling coming over her then as she dropped the bullet onto the small table beside the bed.

She wet a cloth with the hot water and began washing around the wound to get rid of as much fresh and dried blood as possible. She poured more whiskey over it, then threaded some catgut into her father's stitching needle. She soaked some gauze with whiskey and ran it over the catgut, then doused the wound again with the same whiskey before beginning to stitch up the hole.

She hoped she had done the right thing, then untied Jake's wrists and ankles and managed to get his arms out of his long johns so she could pull the top of them down under his hips. Then she wrapped the wound, reaching under his hard, heavy body over and over to bring the gauze around and then tie it. She decided then that all his clothes needed washing and realized the man could have another kind of accident while lying there unconscious. She pulled the long johns all the way off him and tossed them to the floor then wrapped a towel around his privates and between his legs, feeling a little embarrassed, but knowing it had to be done. Any nurse in a hospital would have done the same. When it came to medicine, there was no room for modesty.

"I'll give you a good bath when I'm sure you're all right otherwise," she told him. There came no response. She removed her prize quilt from the bed, glad to see he had gotten no blood on it. She replaced it with an older blanket and covered him, but his legs were so long that his feet hung over the end of the bed. As she drew the blanket up to his neck, she noticed another scar at his left shoulder, a sign of stitches at his right ribs, and as she drew the covers to his neck, a strange, wide scar at the right side of his neck.

She dipped some gauze into the hot water then and began washing the wound at the side of Jake's head, noting that the blow of Luke Putnam's rifle had left a deep gash from just in front of Jake's left ear across his left cheekbone. An ugly blue swelling surrounded the cut. She cleaned it as best she could and dabbed at it with more whiskey. "I'm afraid you're going to have another scar here," she said.

She jumped back when Jake's eyes suddenly flew open. He stared at her a moment his dark eyes looking glassy and blank. "Santana?" he muttered. His eyes closed again. Miranda put a hand to her chest and breathed deeply to stop her sudden shaking. Was she crazy to do what she had just done? She clenched her fists, forcing herself to stay calm. The man certainly couldn't do her any harm tonight and he didn't even know where his guns were.

She longed to just lie down now, but she remembered the poor draft horses were still in harness. She lit one lantern and set it on the table, then lit another and carried it outside.

It was dark out now, which made everything seem more frightening. She hung the lantern in the shed and began the arduous task of removing the harness from the horses, a job difficult for most me and doubly difficult for her small arms, especially tonight, when her whole body screamed from a day of emotional upheaval and a tenseness that brought physical pain. Suddenly she realized that in her concern for the horses, she had left her own rifle inside the house. She quickly took down the lantern and closed the shed door, then hurried back to the cabin to find everything the same. She went into the bedroom to check on Jake once more, only to find he had not moved. His breathing was deep and rhythmic, and she thought his forehead already felt a little cooler.

She picked up his clothes and carried them into the main room, where she took down a wooden laundry tab and set it near the fire. She threw his clothes into a tub, poured hot water over them and added some lye soap. She would scrub them and hang them out in the morning. At least that would leave the man even more helpless for the time being—not only would he not have his guns, but he wouldn't even have any clothes to put on!

She closed her eyes and tried to make herself sleep, realizing the much-needed rest was not going to come easily. It had been a long day. It was going to be an even longer night.

About the Author

Linda Broday resides in the Panhandle of Texas on the Llano Estacado. At a young age, she discovered a love for storytelling, history, and anything pertaining to the Old West. There's something about Stetsons, boots, and tall rugged cowboys that get her fired up! A *New York Times* and *USA Today* bestselling author, Linda has won many awards, including the prestigious National Readers' Choice Award and the Texas Gold Award. Visit her at www.LindaBroday.com.